DALE BROWN'S DREAMLAND

End Game

WRITTEN BY DALE BROWN AND JIM DEFELICE

HARPER

Harper
An imprint of HarperCollins*Publishers*
77–85 Fulham Palace Road,
Hammersmith, London W6 8JB

www.harpercollins.co.uk

This paperback edition 2006
1

First published in the USA by
HarperCollins 2006

ISBN-13: 978 0 00 718253 4
ISBN-10: 0 00 718253 8

Typeset in Times by Palimpsest Book Production Limited,
Grangemouth, Stirlingshire

Printed and bound in Great Britain by
Clays Ltd, St Ives plc

Dreamland
Duty Roster

LIEUTENANT COLONEL TECUMSEH 'DOG' BASTIAN
Dreamland's commander has been mellowed by the demands of his new command – but he's still got the meanest bark in the West, and his bite is even worse.

MAJOR JEFFREY 'ZEN' STOCKARD
A top fighter pilot until a crash at Dreamland left him a paraplegic, Zen has volunteered for a medical program that may let him use his legs again. Can Dreamland survive with a key member away?

CAPTAIN BREANNA 'RAP' STOCKARD
Zen's wife has seen him through his injury and rehabilitation. But can she balance her love for her husband with the demands of her career . . . and ambitions?

MAJOR MACK 'THE KNIFE' SMITH
Mack Smith is the best pilot in the world – and he'll tell you so himself. But filling in for Zen on the Flighthawk program may be more than even he can handle.

CAPTAIN DANNY FREAH
Danny commands Whiplash – the ground attack team that works with the cutting-edge Dreamland aircraft and high-tech gear.

JED BARCLAY
The young deputy to the National Security Advisor is Dreamland's link to the President. Barely old enough to

shave, the former science whiz kid now struggles to master the intricacies of world politics.

LIEUTENANT KIRK 'STARSHIP' ANDREWS
A top Flighthawk pilot, Starship is tasked to help on the Werewolf project, flying robot helicopters that are on the cutting edge of air combat. Adjusting to the aircraft is easy, but can he live with the Navy people who are in charge of it?

CAPTAIN HAROLD 'STORM' GALE, USN
As a young midshipman at Annapolis, Gale got Army's goat – literally: he stole the West Point mascot just before the annual Army-Navy game. Now he's applying the same brashness to his role as commander of the *Abner Read*. An accomplished sailor, the only thing he hates worse than the enemy is the Air Force.

Dreamland
Weapons Systems

MEGAFORTRESS

Refurbished B-52s, complete with new skin, new wings and tail section, new engines and new sensor systems. Besides generic versions, Dreamland flies EB-52s that carry AWACS and ground-surveillance radar, and others that carry electronic warfare and snooping equipment.

FLIGHTHAWK

Unmanned fighter aircraft typically flown from the lower weapons bay of the Megafortress. Depending on its configuration, a Megafortress will carry two or four of the robot aircraft.

WEREWOLF

Robot helicopters capable of being controlled from long-range through Dreamland's dedicated satellite system. The versatile Werewolves look like miniaturized versions of the Russian Kamov Ka-50 Hokum helicopter gunship.

PIRANHA

A joint Navy/Air Force unmanned underwater probe, typically launched from a Megafortress on an ocean surveillance mission. Difficult to detect, the Piranha is often used to shadow enemy submarines.

DESTROYER – LITTORAL DD(L)

The Navy's experimental destroyer, designed for warfare near coastlines. Considerably shorter than a conventional destroyer, the ship lies low in the water, its hull and superstructure angled to deflect radar waves. DD(L)s carry a lethal combination of Harpoon and Standard missiles, along with torpedoes and a sophisticated canon.

SHARKBOAT

The modern version of the classic PT boat, designed to operate with littoral warships such as the DD(L) 01 *Abner Read*.

Prelude:

Dreams

Allegro, Nevada (outside Las Vegas)
5 January 1998
0310 (all times local)

He'd had the dream so many times it was more something he remembered than something he invented. Tiny bits of reality blurred into a jumbled progression that began and ended the same way. The beginning: running up Meadowview Street back to his condo, pursued by the sun. This was not a normal sun – he felt its stretching fingers grope his body, burning holes in his arms, neck, and face.

The end: the black wing of a redtail hawk sailing suddenly across and through the windscreen of his aircraft.

Neither of those things had an exact parallel in real life, even when the grotesque distortions were stripped away. Zen had gotten back to the house from his run well before the sun rose, and the robot plane that caused the air accident struck well behind the cockpit, snapping off his tailplane. But the logic of the dream crowded out history, sometimes even when he was awake.

The middle of the dream was always different. It usually involved bits and pieces of recent events, sometimes from sorties he'd flown for Dreamland, but more often just things that happened during the day. Often his wife Breanna was in the dream, talking to him or flirting or even making love. Today she was cooking him breakfast and complaining about the people who owned the condo downstairs. Their baby was screaming at the top of its lungs, keeping them awake.

'How can you let a baby cry like that?' she asked. 'Let's have a barbecue.'

The scene changed from their kitchen to a friend's backyard patio. Instead of working the stove, Breanna was working the grill. When she turned away from it, Zen saw that it was piled high with wood.

'Too smoky,' he said, sitting in the cockpit of his F-15 rather than his wheelchair.

It's too soon for the dream to end, he thought. But he coughed, and he was awake.

He still smelled smoke. Real smoke, from burning wood. The baby was still crying.

A baby the people downstairs didn't have.

Not a baby, the smoke alarm.

'Bree!' he yelled, jerking up.

She wasn't beside him.

'Bree! *Breanna!*'

Zen started to get out of bed. His dazed brain forgot he was paralyzed, as if that fact belonged only to the dream. He tumbled to the floor.

Just as well – thick smoke curled above his head. He coughed, nearly choking.

Someone else coughed in the bathroom down the hall.

Breanna, his wife. 'Help me!' she cried.

Flames shot up from the floor ahead, illuminating the pitch-black condo. Zen pushed forward despite the heat and flames jumping in front of his face.

Part of his mind was still back in the dream. Was he dreaming? What was dream, and what was real?

He remembered getting into the airplane on the last day he walked, whacking his shin on the side of the cockpit as he got in, thinking the bruise was going to hurt for weeks.

'Help me!' cried Breanna.

He pushed his head next to the carpet and kept going. The bathroom door was closed.

'Open the door, open the door!' he yelled.

He heard a sob, but the door remained closed. Pitching himself to the right, he reached up with his left hand and pulled down on the handle. Smoke flooded into the room. It smelled like metal being incinerated. Zen started to cough and couldn't stop.

'Breanna!' he yelled. 'Where are you? Bree? Bree? Bree?'

He lay on his back as the flames climbed over him. He felt himself falling as the room collapsed.

Zen woke with a shudder so violent the bed rattled. It had been a dream, a new variation of the familiar nightmare.

He reached instinctively for his wife, but she wasn't there. He remembered now: She was in Chicago with relatives; she'd intended on flying back last night but had been snowed in, her flight canceled.

5

Just as well, Zen thought, squirming to get himself upright in the bed. He was still shaking from the dream. He wouldn't have wanted her to see him like this.

But she'd seen him worse, much worse. He wished she were here, to touch.

To save.

If there had been a real fire, she would have been the one saving him, a notoriously deep sleeper.

And a cripple. A fact that didn't vanish when he opened his eyes.

That would change. He'd walk again. He was starting his treatments today, experimental treatments, but they would give him his legs back.

Maybe that was what the dream meant, why the ending had changed. He needed his legs back to save his wife, to be with her for real.

Zen ran his fingers over his scalp and glanced at the clock at the side of the bed. It was only a few minutes past three. But there was no way he was going back to sleep now. If Breanna were beside him, he might have managed it, might have hugged her warmth and shaken off the memory of the nightmare, but without her, the only thing to do was get out of bed and get some coffee, check the overnight sports scores and get a jump on the day.

I

Test Run

Gulf of Aden,
off the coast of Somalia
5 January 1998
1914

The darkness had erased the line between heaven and earth, and even with his infrared glasses Captain Val Muhammad Ben Sattari had trouble finding the quartet of small aircraft as they approached the oil tanker. Built as civilian pleasure craft by a Russian company, the two-engined Sparrows were relatively quiet, their twin piston engines producing a soft hum rather than the loud drone generally associated with military aircraft. By the time the Iranian captain finally found them, the lead airplane was less than three hundred meters away, its hull planing through the water. The other three amphibious aircraft were in line behind it, ugly ducklings heading toward their rendezvous.

Four or five years ago Sattari might have looked on the tiny airplanes with amusement or even disdain. He was a fighter pilot by training and inclination, one of Iran's best – when it still had an air force, before the black robes had run it into the ground. But with his new perspective and responsibilities, he saw the value of small, simple aircraft.

Sattari tucked the glasses into their waterproof pouch inside his tac vest and pulled the brim of his campaign cap down. Much depended on the night's mission. It would test all of the components of the force he had built, putting them all in action to test their strengths, but also their weaknesses. For among the many hard lessons Captain Sattari had learned was that there were always weaknesses. Success required finding them before the enemy could.

Success also required the respect and unquestioning trust of the men who followed him. Both of which he would earn tonight.

Or die trying.

'We're ready to go, Captain,' said Sergeant Ahmed Ibn, holding the captain's AK-47 out to him. The ranking noncommissioned officer of the commando unit, Ibn's skeptical sneer was as obvious and comfortable as his wet suit; with every glance he implied that at thirty-nine, the ex-fighter pilot was both too old and too soft to lead a team of young commandos.

Sattari checked the gun and slung it over his shoulder. 'Let's go then.'

Aboard DD(L) 01 *Abner Read,*
off the coast of Somalia
1921

Lieutenant Kirk 'Starship' Andrews stared at the green-hued shadow near the lip of the Gulf of Aden. The shadow

10

belonged to a boat seven miles away. It measured no more than thirty feet, with a low cabin toward the bow and a flat, probably open stern. Under other circumstances Starship might have thought it was a small fishing vessel or a pleasure boat. But no one sailed the Gulf of Aden for pleasure these days, and it was a rare fisherman who went out this late at night, let alone plied these waters near the tanker routes from the Persian Gulf.

Which meant the shadow was either a smuggler or a pirate.

Starship thought the former much more likely. He knew from experience that pirates tended to move in packs, with at least three and often as many as a dozen small boats.

'*Werewolf One* to Tac Command, I have the subject in sight.'

'Tac. Clear to proceed.'

'Roger that.'

Starship leaned toward the screen as he pushed his hand against the Werewolf's throttle bar. The procedure for checking out suspicious ships was straightforward: a high-speed run at low altitude, stem to stern (or vice versa), allowing the sensors aboard the Werewolf to get a good look at the target. After the first flyover the images were analyzed by specialists in Tac – officially, the Tactical Warfare Center, the nerve center of the *Abner Read* – who passed the information on to the tactical commander and the ship's captain, who would then tell Starship what to do next. The *Abner Read* was about twenty-five miles to the southeast. Depending on what Starship saw, the ship's captain would decide whether it was worth bothering to pursue.

The Werewolf was a UAV, or unmanned aerial vehicle, which Starship flew from a station in a corner of the Tac Center. Combining the agility and vertical maneuvering capability of a helicopter with some of the speed of a conventional plane, it looked something like a downsized Kamov Ka-50. It had diminutive wing-mounted jet engines and a tail to go with the two counterrotating rotors at the top. Its top speed, which Starship himself had never reached, was around 400 knots, more than a hundred knots faster than most helicopters.

The Werewolf was not a Navy aircraft, nor was Starship a sailor. Both the robot and Starship had been shanghaied from Dreamland two months before, following attacks by pirates in the Gulf of Aden. Easy to fly and versatile, the Werewolf had been pressed into service as a replacement for a Navy UAV that was at least a year behind schedule. The Dreamland craft had done such a good job that everyone from the ship's captain to the Navy secretary sang its praises.

The same could not be said for Starship. He'd gotten this gig by being the right man in the wrong place. Already an accomplished Flighthawk pilot, he had made the mistake of cross-training in the Werewolf program so he could help out as a relief pilot during the testing program, which used mostly civilian jocks. When the Werewolves were rushed into duty with Xray Pop, Starship suddenly found himself the only military officer both qualified to teach others how to fly the craft and available for temporary duty aboard the *Abner Read*. Originally scheduled to last two weeks, the assignment was nearly six weeks old and showed no sign of ending soon. The Navy people rode him unmercifully, then turned around and claimed he was indispensable.

As the only Air Force officer aboard the *Abner Read*, he would have felt out of place in any event. But he particularly disliked the ship's captain, whom in his more charitable moments he thought of as a blowhard. The tactical commander and ship's executive officer, Lt Commander Jack 'Eyes' Eisenberg, was nearly as bad.

The *Abner Read* was a cutting-edge ship, a next-generation 'littoral combat vessel,' officially called a DD(L) for littoral destroyer. About the size of a corvette, it had the firepower of a destroyer but only a third of the complement. Supposedly, the officers and crew had been chosen as the most forward-thinking people in the service. Having come from Dreamland, Starship had a different perspective. And used to the much more easy-going and fluid procedures of Dreamland, he chafed at the 'fussy' discipline and stringent shipboard rules.

Starship had trained two sailors to fly the robot helicopter, but the ship's captain insisted that he be at the stick during 'prime time' – the hours between dusk and dawn when the pirates were most likely to strike. That meant duty from 1600 to 0700 – or whatever stinking bells the Navy used to confuse landlubbers like himself. That might not have been so bad if he didn't have to oversee the maintenance and ordnance people assigned to the aircraft during the day. It wasn't their fault that

13

they were unfamiliar with the systems – but it wasn't his fault, either, though the captain seemed to think it was.

The image in the main screen in front of Starship sharpened. There were two large crates toward the stern; this was almost certainly a smuggler, bringing anything from canned goods to weapons into the northern coast of Somalia, despite UN strictures.

'Coming up on him,' Starship said. 'Two crates. Uh, got, um, maybe a deckhand, only one person I see – smile for the camera, scuzzball.'

'We can do without the color commentary,' snapped Eyes.

Man, I am working with a bunch of old farts, Starship thought.

The Werewolf's flight station, adapted from a control unit designed to be used by soldiers near the battlefield, had one large display screen and two smaller ones, all touchscreen panels. While they could be configured in a number of ways, Starship typically left the large screen as his main view screen, displaying either infrared or daylight video from the Werewolf's nose. He usually put the system's engineering panel in the top left-hand screen, toggling it with the weapons screen when appropriate. Below that he always put a God's-eye-view map, generally referred to as a 'sitrep,' or situation report, map showing where he was and what was around him. The area the Werewolf flew over was rendered as a wire model, with green and red lines delineating the topography. The Werewolf was a stubby yellow double cross that, if you squinted just right, looked a little like the aircraft itself.

'Tac, we have a tanker out here,' said Starship, spotting a much larger vessel ten miles beyond the suspected smuggler. 'Want me to check it out?'

'Negative, Werewolf. We have him on the sonar array. One problem at a time.'

Starship reached for his cup of the crankcase oil the sailors claimed was coffee. As he did, the Werewolf's flight control computer buzzed with a warning – the radar had caught sight of an aircraft approaching from the north. Before the pilot could react, the screen flashed a proximity warning – the airplane was heading at a high rate of speed on a direct vector toward him; he had thirty seconds to evade.

Starship pushed the Werewolf stick to the left, starting an easy circle away from the airplane's flight path. The computer had been programmed to be overanxious so that the Navy newbies he was training didn't fly into anything; he wasn't really in any danger of a collision. But it was curious that the other plane was flying so low. As he banked parallel to its flight path, the radar caught sight of three other airplanes, all at very low altitude and obviously following the leader.

'Tac, I have something unusual here. Four aircraft very low to the water, no running lights, no radar – can I follow them and find out what's going on?'

'Hold tight, Werewolf.'

Old farts.

Captain Harold 'Storm' Gale stared at the holographic display on the bridge of the *Abner Read*. The three-dimensional projection rose from a table behind the helmsman's station and could be used for a variety of purposes. In this case, it was taking various sensor data to render a map of the area they were patrolling. The *Abner Read*, in green, sat at the right-hand corner. The smuggler the Werewolf had spotted – yellow – was toward the center, with the tanker another yellow block beyond it. There were no aircraft.

'I don't see any airplanes,' Storm told Eyes. 'You're sure Airforce got it right?'

'He has them on his radar,' said Eyes.

Storm reached to the communication control on his belt, flipping into the Werewolf circuit. The wireless communications system allowed him to talk to all of the ship's departments directly.

'Airforce, what are we looking at here?'

'Four unidentified aircraft, flying low and fast.'

'What types are they?'

'Not sure. I haven't seen –'

'Get closer.'

'Tac just told me –'

'Get closer!'

Storm flipped back to Eyes. 'Have *Airforce* find out what the aircraft are.'

'What about the boat, Captain?'

'A single smuggler, no weapons visible?'

'Affirmative, Captain. He's twenty minutes away, at our present course and speed.'

'Threat to the oil tanker?'

'Doesn't appear so.'

'Have the Werewolf pursue the airplanes. We'll set a course for the smuggler in the meantime.'

'Aye aye, Captain.'

The computer estimated the aircraft were moving at 280 knots. The computer calculated the lead aircraft's likely course based on the past observations – a straight line toward the eastern tip of Somalia.

'Werewolf, please close on the bandits and identify,' said Eyes.

Gee, no kidding, thought Starship.

'Tac, be advised these aircraft are now out of my sensor range. It'd be helpful if you turned on your radar and gave me a hand.'

'Negative. We're staying dark.'

'Do we have an Orion above?' asked Starship. As the words came out of his mouth, he realized the answer was going to be negative – the radar planes had been pulled off the gulf duty two days before, sent to Europe to help in the Kosovo mess.

'We're on our own.'

'Yeah, roger that. OK, I'm maneuvering to follow.'

Starship arced behind the planes and revved his engines to max power.

More smugglers, probably, though the fact that there were four of them was curious. He could guess that they weren't combatants; the planes were too small and slow.

Five minutes later, with the aircraft still out of sight, Starship asked the computer to recompute his targets' course and probable location. The computer declared that they should be five miles dead ahead. They weren't, and when five more minutes passed and he didn't fly through them, Starship told Tac the obvious.

'Looks like we lost them. They probably put the pedal to the metal as soon as they picked me up on radar.'

'Repeat?'

'I believe they accelerated away. My screen is clear.'

'You're sure they're gone?'

'Either that or I just flew through them.'

'Stand by, Werewolf,' said Eyes, his voice dripping with venom.

'It wasn't *my* fault I lost them, Commander. They had a head start. If you'd allowed me to chase them when I wanted to –'

'Stand by,' snapped the other man.

Starship continued southward; he was about sixty miles from Tohen, a tiny village on the northeastern tip of Somalia. Port Somalia – an oil terminal port built by the Indians and not yet fully operational – was another ten miles to the southeast.

'Airforce – what's your story?' barked Storm, coming onto the communications line.

'Lost them, Captain.'

'Where are you?'

The captain knew *precisely* where he was. It wasn't a question but an accusation: Why didn't you do what I wanted you to do? Starship read off the GPS coordinates, then translated them into a rough position off Somalia.

'According to the computer, the aircraft are about a half hour from Somalia. Among the possible targets –'

'Somalia's not my problem,' answered Storm. 'Go back north and find that smuggler.'

'Your call.'

'Excuse me?'

'Aye aye, Captain. Werewolf turning north.'

Las Vegas University of Medicine,
Las Vegas, Nevada
5 January 1998
0825

'You're early!'

Zen shrugged as he wheeled his way across the thick rug of Dr Michael Vasin's office. 'Yeah, figured I'd get it over with.'

'Tea?'

'Coffee if you have it, sure.'

Vasin picked up the phone on his desk and asked his assistant to bring them some. Then he got up and walked to the nearby couch, shifting around as Zen maneuvered his wheelchair catty-corner to him. Indian by birth, the doctor spoke with a pronounced accent, even though he had been in America since college.

'And everything square with work?'

'Squared away,' Zen told him. The doctor did not know the specifics of what Zen did, officially anyway. But he was friends with one of Dreamland's most important scientific researchers, Dr Martha Geraldo, who had referred Zen to him for the experimental program. So he probably knew a little, though neither man tested the specifics of that knowledge.

Vasin's assistant came in with a tray of herbal tea, coffee, and two small cups. She was a petite, older woman, efficient at handling minutiae and thoughtful enough to ask after Zen's wife, whom she had never met. When she left, Zen found Vasin staring out the large windows behind his desk. The Vegas Strip lay in the distance.

'The desert is not a good place for gamblers,' said the doctor absently.

Unsure how to respond, Zen said nothing.

'Jeff, I want you to understand, there are no guarantees with this. It may have absolutely no effect on you. Absolutely no effect. Even if regenerating nerve cells in the spine is possible, it might not work in your case for a million different reasons.'

'I understand.'

Vasin had already told him this many times.

'And, as we've discussed, there is always the possibility there will be side effects that we don't know about,' continued the doctor.

'I read everything you gave me.'

'I'm repeating myself.' Vasin turned around, smiling self-deprecatingly. 'I want you to understand it emotionally. There's always a possibility – unforeseen – that things could be worse.'

Zen had already sat through two long lectures from Vasin and another by one of the researchers on his team outlining the potential pitfalls and dangers of the technique. He had also signed a stack of release forms.

'I'm about as aware of the dangers as I can be.'

'Yes.' Vasin rose. 'Ready to get the ball rolling?'

'I thought you'd never ask.'

Air Force High Technology Advanced Weapons Center (Dreamland)
1100

Lieutenant Colonel Tecumseh 'Dog' Bastian checked his altitude and location, then radioed to the event controller, who was sitting inside a highly modified Boeing RC-135, circling above at forty thousand feet.

'*Dreamland Raptor* to Event Command – Jerry, are we firing this missile today?'

'Event Command to *Dreamland Raptor*, we're still hanging on *Dreamland Levitow*,' answered the controller, referring to the EB-52 that was to fire the target missile. 'Colonel, you sound like you're anxious to get back to your paperwork.'

Not at all, thought Dog, who greatly preferred his present office – the cockpit of Dreamland's experimental long-range attack version of the F-22 Raptor – to the one with his cherrywood desk twenty thousand feet below. Flying cutting-edge aircraft was undoubtedly the best part of Dreamland.

The F-22 bore only a passing resemblance to the 'stock' model. Its wings had been made into long deltas; in the

21

place of a tailfin it had a faceted quadrangle of triangles over the elongated tailpipe. The plane was twenty feet longer than the original, allowing it to accommodate an internal bomb bay that could be filled with a variety of weapons, including the one Dog was waiting to launch. The length also allowed the plane to carry considerably more fuel than a regular F-22.

'All right, *Dreamland Raptor*, we're proceeding,' said the event controller. '*Dreamland Levitow* is on course. They are firing test missile one. . . . Test missile has been launched. We are proceeding with our event.'

Test missile one was an AGM-86C whose explosive warhead had been replaced with a set of instruments and a broadcasting device. Also known as an Air Launched Cruise Missile, or ALCM, the AGM-86C was the conventional version of the frontline nuclear-tipped cruise missile developed during the 1980s and placed into storage with the reorganization of the nuclear force in the early 1990s. In this case, the missile was playing the role of a nuclear weapon.

The missile in Dog's bomb bay was designed to render such weapons obsolete. The EEMWB – the letters stood for Enhanced ElectroMagnetic Warfare Bomb, but were generally pronounced together as 'em-web' – created an electronic pulse that disrupted electric devices within a wide radius. Unlike the devices that had been used against power grids in Iraq during the 1992 Gulf War, the EEMWB used terahertz radiation – known as T-Rays or T Waves – to do its damage. Conventional electronic shielding did not protect against them, since until now there had been no need to. Occupying the bandwidth between infrared and microwave radiation, T-Rays were potentially devastating, yet extremely difficult to control and direct. While their potential had long been recognized, their use remained only the wishful daydream of weapons scientists and armchair generals.

Until now. The Dreamland weapons people had found a way to use carefully fabricated metal shards as antennas as the pulse was generated. Computer simulations showed they could design weapons that would fry circuitry at five hundred miles.

There were two likely applications. One was as a weapon to paralyze an enemy's electronics, a kind of super E bomb that would affect everything from power grids to wristwatches. The other was a defense against nuclear weapons such as the one the AGM-86C simulated. The EEMWB's pulse went through the shielding in conventional nuclear weapons that protected them from 'conventional' electromagnetic shocks. By wiping out the nanoswitches and all other control gear in the weapons, the EEMWB prevented the weapon from going off.

It was possible to shield devices against the T-Rays – both *Dreamland Raptor* and *Dreamland Levitow* were proof. But the process was painstaking, especially for anything in the air.

Dog's EEMWB had a fifty-mile radius. If successful, tests would begin in the South Pacific two weeks from now on the larger, five-hundred-mile-radius designs.

'*Dreamland Raptor*, prepare to fire EEMWB,' said the event controller.

'*Dreamland Raptor* acknowledges.' The EEMWB's propulsion and guidance units came from AGM-86Cs, and it was fired more like a bomb than an antiair weapon, with the extra step of designating an altitude for an explosion.

'Launch at will,' said the event coordinator.

'Launching.'

Jan Stewart glanced at the screen at the left side of the control panel on her EB-52, checking the sitrep screen for her position and the location of the Dreamland landing area, now about fifteen miles away and due south. If the shielding failed when the EEMWB exploded, she would have to fly Dreamland Levitow back to base by dead reckoning on manual control – not a prospect she relished.

Actually, Captain Stewart didn't relish flying the *Levitow*, or any Megafortress, much at all. She'd been a B-1 jock and had come to Dreamland to work in a project designed to test the B-1 for conversion similar to the EB-52 Megafortress. A week after she arrived, the project's funding was cut and she was pressed into the Megafortress program as a copilot. She outranked a lot of the other copilots and even pilots in the program, but because she was a low-timer in the aircraft, she'd been relegated to second seat by the program's temporary head, Captain Breanna Stockard. Worse, Breanna had made Stewart *her* copilot.

Bad enough to fly what was still essentially a B-52 after the hotter-than-fire B-1B. Worse – much, much worse – to be second officer after running the show.

Today, though, Stewart was boss. Her nemesis had been scrubbed at the last minute due to a snowstorm in Chicago.

'EEMWB detonation in twenty seconds,' said Lieutenant Sergio 'Jazz' Jackson, who was serving as her copilot.

'Yup.'

A tone sounded in her headphones, indicating that the weapon had detonated. Stewart hot-keyed her communications unit to tell the event commander, but got no response.

She pulled back on the stick slightly, but the airplane failed to move.

Had the shielding failed?

Only partially – her configurable control panel was still lit.

She'd go to manual control right away.

Interphone working?

'Prepare for manual control,' she said.

'Manual?' said Jazz.

Immediately, Stewart realized what had happened – she'd turned the aircraft over to the flight control computer for the missile launch as part of the test protocol, and neglected to take it back.

It was a boneheaded mistake that would cost her at least two rounds of beers. Thank God the Iron Bitch hadn't been here to see it.

'I mean, taking over control from the computer,' Stewart told Jazz lamely.

'That's what I thought,' said the copilot.

'*Dreamland Levitow*,' said the event controller. 'Please repeat your transmission. I'm sorry – we were caught up in something here.'

I'll bet, thought Stewart, not entirely convinced that Breanna hadn't somehow conspired with them to make her look bad.

Dr Ray Rubeo, Dreamland's head scientist, was waiting for Colonel Bastian as he unfolded himself from the *Raptor*'s cockpit.

'So how'd we do, Doc?' Dog asked, coming down the ladder. Techies were already swarming over the *Raptor*, preparing it for a complete overhaul. Besides thoroughly analyzing the shielding and systems for signs of damage from the T-Rays, the engineering team was planning a number of improvements to the plane, including a new wing structure that would lower its unfueled weight by five percent.

'It's premature to speculate,' said Rubeo.

'Do it anyway.'

Rubeo frowned. 'I'm sure that when the results are analyzed, the models predicting the impact of the weapon will be shown to be quite correct. All of the test instruments reported full hits. And,' he paused dramatically, 'one of the ground technicians forgot to remove his watch, and now finds that it no longer functions.'

Dog laughed. The scientist touched his earring – a habit, the colonel knew, that meant he was planning to say something he considered unpleasant. Dog decided to head him off at the pass.

'Ray, if the full-sized weapons won't be ready for testing –'

'Bah. They're sitting in the bunker, all eight of them. Though the tests are unnecessary.'

Then obviously I'm about to get harangued for more money, thought Dog, starting toward the Jimmy SUV waiting to take him over to the hangar area where he could change. Sure enough, Rubeo fell in alongside him and made the pitch.

'If you are going to proceed with the project, Colonel, I need several more technicians to assist while the team is away.'

'Can't do it, Ray. You've seen the budget.'

'Colonel, we are past squeezing water from a stone. We need more people.'

Dog stopped to watch *Dreamland Levitow* practicing touch and goes on the nearby runway. As part of a new policy at Dreamland, the EB-52 Megafortress had been named for Sergeant John L. Levitow, an Air Force Medal of Honor winner. A crewman in an AC-47 gunship during the Vietnam War, Sergeant Levitow had thrown himself on a live flare inside the hold of his damaged aircraft following a mortar hit. Despite numerous wounds, he managed to toss the flare outside of the aircraft before it ignited, saving the entire plane.

Rubeo renewed his pitch as the plane passed overhead. 'Colonel – we need more people.'

'If the EEMWB project gets funding, we'll have more slots.'

'Only if it's approved as part of the Anti-Ballistic Missile Program, which it shouldn't be.'

Rubeo had made this point before: The EEMWB was not a good ABM weapon, since the lead in technology would last, by his estimate, no longer than five years.

And it was not selective – everything in the area was disabled, not just the target. Dog didn't disagree, but he didn't see that as an argument against proceeding with the weapon, which would provide a decent solution until other technologies matured. And he especially thought this was a good idea since it would help him get the people Rubeo needed.

'We have to be practical,' said Dog.

'Colonel, I'm the most practical scientist I know.'

'That isn't saying much, Ray,' Dog told him, climbing into the truck.

Near Port Somalia
5 January 1998
2304

Captain Sattari felt the slight burn at the top of his shoulders as he paddled in unison with the others, propelling the small boat toward their target. The wind came at them from the west, trying to push them off course. They compensated for it as they stroked, but the boat still drew a jagged line forward.

Sattari allowed himself a glance to the other three craft, gauging his performance; it seemed to him that their boat was doing better than two of the others, and not much worse than Sergeant Ibn's, which was in the lead.

The raft lurched with a sudden swell. Sattari gripped his oar firmly and dug at the water, stroking hard and smooth. His instructor had claimed propelling a boat was a matter of finesse, not strength, but the man had rowed every day of his life for years, and surely took strength for granted. Sattari's chest rose and fell with the roll of his shoulders, as if he were part of a large machine. He heard the hard, short breaths of the men around him, and tried to match them.

A light blinked ahead. Ibn's boat had stopped a few meters away. They changed their paddling and surged next to the other raft with a well-practiced flare. First test passed, thought Sattari. He reached for his night glasses and scanned around them as the other boats drew up.

Sergeant Ibn moved in the other raft until he was alongside his commander.

'No sign of the Indian warship,' said Ibn.

'No. Nor the helicopter.'

A helicopter had nearly run into one of the airplanes roughly seventy miles from shore. Captain Sattari was not sure where it had come from. It seemed too far from Port Somalia to belong to the small Indian force there, nor had the spies reported one. The Somalian air force had no aircraft this far north, and it seemed unlikely that it had come from Yemen.

'The helicopter most likely belonged to a smuggler,' said Ibn.

'Perhaps,' said Captain Sattari. 'In any event, let us proceed.'

'God is great.'

Sattari put his glasses back in their pouch and began helping the four men on his boat who would descend to the pipes below them to plant their explosive charges. The charges they carried were slightly bigger than a large suitcase, and each team had to place two on the thick pipes below.

Sattari positioned his knee against the side of the raft, but cautioned himself against hoping it would brace him; he'd already seen in their drills that the raft would easily capsize. The trick was to use only one hand to help the others balance their loads; this was a heavy strain, but the team he was assisting managed to slip into the water without a splash or upsetting the raft.

The men on the raft on the other side of him did not. The little boat capsized.

Sattari picked up his paddle, as did the other man on his raft. They turned forty-five degrees, positioning themselves to help if necessary. But the two men on the other boat recovered quickly; within seconds they had their vessel righted and were back aboard.

'Good work,' Sattari told them.

He turned back toward Ibn's raft. The sergeant had gone below with the others, but one of the two men still aboard had a radio scanner, which he was using to monitor local broadcasts. As Sattari picked up his oar to get closer, the coxswain did the same. They pushed over silently.

'Anything, Corporal?' Sattari asked the radioman.

'All quiet, Captain.'

'There was nothing from the Indian warship?'

'No, sir. Not a peep.'

Sattari scanned the artificial island, roughly two miles away. Aside from a few dim warning lights on the seaward side, it was completely in shadow. It slumbered, unsuspecting.

'We will proceed,' Sattari said. 'God is great.'

Aboard the *Abner Read*,
off the coast of Somalia
2340

Storm took Admiral Johnson's communication in his cabin. The admiral's blotchy face was rendered even redder by the LCD screen. Johnson was aboard his flagship, the *Nimitz*, sailing in the waters north of Taiwan.

'What's going on out there, Storm?'

'Good evening, Admiral. I'm about to send a boarding party over to a boat I suspect is a smuggler.'

'That's what you called me about?'

'No,' said Storm. 'About an hour ago we spotted four aircraft flying very low and fast toward northeastern Somalia. We were not able to identify the aircraft. Given the size of the force, they may have been terrorists going ashore to a camp we don't know about. Since they were flying in the direction of Port Somalia, I tried to contact the Indian force there, but could not. I wanted to send –'

'Port Somalia? The Indian tanker station? What is your exact location?'

'We're about eighty nautical miles –'

'*Exact* location.'

Storm looked over to the small computer screen near the video display, then read off the GPS coordinates.

'What are you doing so close to that end of the gulf?' said Johnson. 'You're supposed to be chasing pirates.'

'With all due respect, Admiral, that's what I'm doing. I have a smuggler in sight, and we're preparing to board her. I called to alert you to these aircraft, so a message

31

could be sent through the normal channels. I don't know whether their radio –'

'You know as well as I do that you're a good deal east of the area we discussed two days ago. A good deal east.'

'I'm within the parameters of my patrol area. I'm not in coastal waters.'

When Johnson was displeased – as he was just about every time Storm talked to him – his cheeks puffed slightly and his eyes narrowed at the corners, so that he looked like the mask of an Asian sea devil. When he became really angry – which happened often – his forehead grew red and he had difficulty speaking. Storm saw the space above his eyebrows tint, and decided it was time to return the conversation to its point.

'Should I attempt to contact the Pentagon to alert the Indians at Port Somalia?' he asked.

'No, you should not.' Johnson scowled. 'We'll handle that here.'

The screen blanked before Storm could respond.

Off the coast of Somalia
2345

Captain Sattari felt his gloved hand slipping from the rope. Swinging his left arm forward, he managed to grab hold of the cross-hatched metal fencing at the side of the support pillar. For a moment he hung in midair five meters over the water and rocks, his fate suspended.

If I slip, he thought, the man behind me will fall as

well. He will be killed, and even if I survive, I will never be able to draw a breath as a man again.

He'd practiced this climb for months. He could do it. He *had* to do it.

With a ferocious heave, Sattari pulled himself to the pillar. Hanging by three fingers, he hunted for a better handhold. His left arm seemed to pull out of its socket before his right hand found a grip.

Up, he told himself, forcing open the fingers on his left hand. Sattari jerked his arm upward, throwing it against the fencing. His right arm had always been stronger than his left; he found a good hold and rested for a moment, then attacked the fence again, trying but failing to get a toehold so he could climb rather than pull. Again and again he forced his fingers to unclench; again and again he felt his shoulders wrenching. Even his right began to give way before he reached the top.

The first man up stood by the rail, waiting. Sattari took the rope he had carried up, tied it to the rail, then tossed it down. The captain helped the man who had started up behind over the rail, then went ahead.

Their target was a pipe assembly and tank housing fuel for the boats that docked here. Besides the large tanks containing ship fuel, there were two tanks that held the lighter – and more flammable – marine fuel used by small vessels. The tanks and some of the associated machinery sat behind a Cyclone fence topped with barbed wire. The point man began cutting a hole through the fence with a set of large wire cutters; Sattari went around the decking to the corner to act as a lookout while the others prepared to set explosives on the tanks.

A pair of metal staircases led down to the lower docking area just beyond the turn where he took his position. A small boat was tied to the fiberglass planks, and he could hear it slapping against the side with the current.

Sattari could also hear his heart, pounding in his chest. Never had he been this nervous, not even on his first solo flight.

The Indians had roughly two dozen men permanently on the island; another three or four dozen workers came out during the day when ships were docked or to finish up the many small items that still had to be perfected before the official opening in a few weeks. At night, a force of no more than eight men were on duty, manning lookouts on the northern and eastern sides of the large complex.

A local spy had reported that the watchmen varied their patrols admirably, making it impossible to time their rounds. However, this area was consistently neglected; like many security forces, the guards concentrated their efforts on what they thought the biggest prize was.

Sattari heard a noise behind him. He turned; the man who had cut the hole in the fence raised his hand in the air. The charges had been set.

They retreated to the ropes. Remembering the trouble he'd had climbing with the gloves, Sattari pulled them off. Better to burn his hands, he thought, than to lose his grip. He slung his gun over his shoulder and took hold of the rope, waiting for the point man before starting.

Sattari was about a third of the way down when his

companion said something. The words were garbled in the wind; as Sattari glanced toward him to ask what he'd said, a gun barked from above.

Without consciously thinking about what he was doing, Sattari hooked his foot taut against the rope and swung up his gun. A muzzle flashed above him; he pushed the AK-47 toward the burst of light and fired. His bullets rattled sharply against the steel superstructure. Thrown off-kilter by the kick of the gun, the captain swung to his right and bounced against the fence. Before he could grab on and stabilize himself, he saw two shadows moving above and fired again. This time one went down, though whether because he was ducking or had been hit was impossible to say. The other shadow returned fire. Sattari squeezed the trigger of the AK-47 once, twice, several times, until its magazine was empty.

He let the rifle drop against its strap and skidded down the rope. The captain hit the water and bounced backward, rolling against a rock, half in, half out of the sea. Pushing forward, he willed himself in the direction of a boat floating nearby. Gunfire erupted from above. As he was about to dive into the water, he saw a shadow behind him on the rocks; it had to be one of his men. He twisted back, half hopping, half crawling, aiming to grab the man and drag him into the sea and safety. Bullets danced around him, but Sattari focused only on the black shadow that lay in front of him. He grabbed the man and pulled, growling as he did, a threatened bear cornered in an ambush. Pulling the soldier over his shoulder, he went back to the water, growling the whole time.

The steamy hiss of a rocket-launched grenade creased the air; a long, deep rattle followed. The water surged around him, pushing him down, but Sattari kept moving until hands reached out and grabbed him. The commando was lifted from his back, and Sattari was pulled into the raft. He pushed himself upright, looking around. They were the last boat to get away.

'Detonate the charges,' he told the coxswain when he saw his face.

'Now, Captain?'

'Now.'

Aboard the *Abner Read*,
off the coast of Somalia
2345

Starship steadied the Werewolf a mile in front of the small boat's bow. The *Abner Read* was now less than two miles away, but the warship sat so low in the water that even if the smugglers had infrared glasses they probably didn't know it was there.

'Werewolf, we're about to radio them to stop,' said Eyes. 'Go ahead and turn on the searchlight.'

'Roger that,' said Starship.

The halogen beam under the Werewolf's nose caught the bow of the little boat dead on. Starship looked at the image from the Werewolf's video feed; he saw shadows in the cabin but couldn't make out much else.

A warning was broadcast in English, Arabic, and French

on all of the maritime radio channels. Starship came over the craft and fired a 'log' – an LUU-2 illumination flare – which lit up the boat and the sea around it. At the same time, a boarding party pushed off the *Abner Read* in a rigid-hulled inflatable boat.

Called a SITT, or shipboard integrated tactical team, the specially trained team of sailors was heavily armed and well-versed in dealing with smugglers. Starship's job was to get a good look at the boat so the boarding party would know what to expect. He would train his weapons on the smuggler's craft. The boat was so small it was likely the Hellfire missiles or even his 30mm cannon could sink it within seconds if he fired.

So could the *Abner Read* – its forward deck gun was already zeroed in.

'I have nobody on the forward deck,' Starship reported. 'Uh-oh, here we go – two guys coming out to the stern. Going to the boxes.'

'Are those weapons?'

'Negative – looks like they're trying to cut the crates loose. Want me to strafe them?'

'Unidentified ship has failed to acknowledge,' said Eyes, whose remarks were being recorded as evidence of the encounter. '*Abner Read* SITT team is en route. Werewolf, see if you can stop the smugglers from throwing the contraband overboard.'

'Roger that,' said Starship. He selected the aircraft's 7.62 machine gun and sent a string of bullets into the rail of the small boat. He saw the people on the boat ducking as he flew past; wheeling the helicopter around, he steadied the nose to spray the stern again, using his weapon to keep them away from the back of the vessel.

A man emerged from the cabin. A second later the Werewolf's flight control computer sounded a tone in his ear – the smuggler had fired a rocket-launched grenade at the small aircraft.

Starship jammed his throttle, ducking the grenade. Then he reached to the weapons panel, dialing up the Hellfire missiles.

'I have hostile fire,' he told Tac. 'Permission to launch Hellfires?'

'Negative, negative,' said Eyes. 'Don't sink him.'

'I'm under fire,' Starship repeated. The men at the rear had gone back to the large crates.

'Do not sink that boat. We want the cargo intact.'

Stifling a curse, Starship keyed back to the light machine gun. As he nudged his stick forward, the man near the cabin picked up an automatic rifle and began firing. The tracers gave Starship something to zero in on as he pressed his own trigger. With the second burst, the man crumpled to the deck of the boat, sliding toward the low rail as it rocked in the water.

Starship returned his attention to the rear deck, where the two crewmen had succeeded in pulling one of the crates from its tie-downs and were shoving it over the side. As it went over, the entire boat began to tip as if it were going to capsize. Starship continued northward and banked back around, dropping the small helicopter to ten feet over the waves. The men continued working on the crate. If he wanted the cargo, he would have to shoot them; warning shots would no longer do.

He got close enough to see the worried scowl on one of the men's faces before he fired; the man fell limp on the deck as he passed over. Still, the other crewman refused to give up. He struggled with the chain that held the crate down as Starship zeroed in, finger dancing against the trigger. When the bullets caught him, they spun him in a macabre death dance, a large part of his skull flying off as if it had been a hat. The man danced off the side of the boat and disappeared.

'Defenses have been neutralized,' Starship said, taking the Werewolf back over the boat slowly. 'I think the crew's all dead. They got one of the crates over the side but I saved the other.'

'SITT is en route,' said Eyes.

A spray of water hit Storm as he stepped out onto the flying bridge. The smuggler's boat was two hundred yards away, off his starboard side; the SITT crew was aboard inspecting her. Storm's communications gear could connect him instantly with the team as well as everyone on his own ship, and he had the crew's frequency tuned in; he listened to the boarding party as it went about its work. The Werewolf hovered just over the bow of the little boat, its nose slowly moving back and forth as its pilot trained its weapons on the vessel.

'Captain Gale to SITT – Terry, you there?'

'Here, Captain.'

'What do you have?'

'RPGs. Crate's filled with grenades and launchers. Have some heavy machine guns in the hold.'

'Get it all on video. Make sure we have a good record. Then get back here and we'll sink it.'

'Aye aye, Captain.'

Storm went back inside. He was just about to see if he could hunt down a cup of coffee when Eyes's excited voice erupted in his ear.

'Port Somalia has just been attacked!' shouted Eyes. 'There's a fire on the artificial island, and the sonar array picked up the sound of a large explosion.'

Storm's mind jumped from shock to reaction mode, sorting the information, formulating a response. The airplanes they'd seen before – they had to have been involved.

What would Admiral Johnson say now?

'Get Airforce down there right away,' said Storm. 'Bring the SITT crew back, then sink the smuggler's vessel, cargo and all. Prepare a course for Port Somalia,' he added, speaking to the navigational officer. 'I'll be in my quarters, updating Admiral Johnson.'

Off the coast of Somalia
6 January 1998
0023

The commando Sattari rescued had broken his leg falling from the decking to the rocks, but had not been shot. He slumped against the captain as the men paddled against the current. They attacked the waves like madmen, pushing against the spray, which seemed to increase with every stroke.

Sattari could hear the explosions behind them and saw the yellow shadows cast by a fire, but dared not take the time or strength to look back.

'Another kilometer,' yelled the coxswain. He was referring not to the rendezvous point but to the GPS position where the boat would turn to the north; the pickup would be roughly four kilometers beyond that.

Still, Sattari repeated the words aloud as a mantra as he worked his paddle: 'Another kilometer to go. One more kilometer to success.'

Aboard the *Abner Read*, off the coast of Somalia
0023

The smoke from Port Somalia rose like an overgrown cauliflower from the ocean, furling upward and outward. It was so thick Starship couldn't see Port Somalia itself.

If the aircraft they'd seen earlier had deposited saboteurs – not a proven fact, but a very good guess – it was likely that the planes would be returning to pick up the men. The *Abner Read* had activated its radar to look for them.

Starship's job was twofold. First, scout the water and see if he could find any trace of the saboteurs. Second, check the nearby shore, which was the second most likely escape route. And he'd have to do all that in about ten minutes, or he'd risk running out of fuel before getting back to the ship.

He saw the Indian corvette to his right as he approached the outer edge of the smoke. The ship looked like an upsized cabin cruiser, with a globelike radar dome at the top. Designed for a Russian Bandstand surface targeting radar, the large dome held a less potent Indian design. But it was the small dish radar behind the dome that got Starship's attention – the Korund anti-aircraft unit extended its sticky fingers toward the Werewolf, marking a big red X on it for the ship's SS-4 antiaircraft missiles.

'*Werewolf One* being targeted by Indian vessel,' Starship reported to Tac. He hit the fuzz buster and tucked the little helicopter toward the waves, weaving quickly to shake the radar's grip. 'Hey, tell these guys I'm on their side.'

'We're working on it, *Werewolf One*. They're having a little trouble identifying targets.'

'Duh. Tell them I'm not a target.'

'We're working it out. Stay out of their range.'

'It's ten kilometers,' protested Starship.

'Head toward the shore and look for the raiding party. We'll let the Indians look at the water.'

'Yeah, roger that,' he said, jamming his throttle to max power.

Off the coast of Somalia
0028

The light looked like the barest pinprick in a black curtain, yet everyone aboard the raft saw it instantly.

'There!' said the coxswain. He lifted a small signal light and began signaling.

'Go,' said Sattari, pushing his oar. 'Stroke!'

The little raft heaved itself forward as the men pushed at the oar. Sattari felt the commando he had rescued stirring next to him.

'Rest,' he told the man. 'We're almost there.'

'Ship!' said the coxswain.

Sattari swept his head back, though he continued to row. The low silhouette of the Indian patrol boat had appeared to the northeast; it was perhaps three kilometers away.

'Stroke,' insisted Sattari. The pinprick had grown to the size of a mayfly.

Sattari had personally told the commander of each of the four midget submarines to leave if threatened – even if that meant stranding the team he was assigned to retrieve. He did not regret the order, nor did he curse the Indian ship as it continued to move in the direction of the light. He only urged his men to row harder.

His own arms felt as if they were going to fall off. His head seemed to have tripled in weight, and his eyes ached.

'Two hundred meters!' called the coxswain.

A searchlight on the Indian ship, barely a kilometer away, swept the ocean.

'Stroke!' yelled Sattari. 'Stroke!'

And then they were there, clambering over the rail at the stern. The sleek conning toward the bow looked like the swept cabin of a speedboat, and the entire craft was not much longer than a runabout.

'Get aboard, get aboard,' said Sattari.

He pulled the raft close to him, then plunged his knife into its side. As it began to deflate, he saw the Indian patrol boat bearing down on them, its lights reaching out in the darkness.

One of the other commandos took the raft and began to pull it down into the hatch.

'No. Let it go. It will give them something to look at,' said Sattari. He tossed it off the side, then pulled himself down the hatchway. The submarine's crewman came down right behind him, securing the hatch.

'Commander, we are aboard. Dive,' Sattari said loudly, though the command was clearly unnecessary; he could feel the small vessel gliding forward, already sinking beneath the waves.

Aboard the *Abner Read*,
off the coast of Somalia
0032

'The Indians have spotted a commando boat about five kilometers from Port Somalia,' Eyes told Storm. 'Empty.'

'Submarine?'

'Unsure. They don't carry sonar. That's a Russian Project 1234 boat. I'm surprised it made it across the Arabian Sea. I don't envy their sailors.'

Storm studied the hologram. The *Abner Read* had a world-class passive sonar – the Littoral Towed Array System, or LITAS – which was carried on a submerged raft behind the ship. Built around a series of hydrophones, the system picked up and interpreted different sounds in the water. In theory, LITAS could hear anything within a twelve-mile radius of the ship, even in shallow waters where sounds were plentiful and easily altered by the sea floor. Very loud vessels – such as the Indian ship, which the system identified even though it was thirty-five miles off – could be heard much farther away.

The *Abner Read* also carried an active sonar developed by DARPA as part of a project known as Distant Thunder. The sonar was designed to find very quiet electric submarines in what the engineers called 'acoustically challenging' waters. The *Abner Read* had used it with great success to find a submarine operating on battery power in the canyonlike Somalian waters to the west. Like all active sonar, however, the device not only alerted the prey that it was being hunted, but told it where the hunter was, an important concession against a wily captain. Storm preferred to hold it in reserve if at all possible.

The northwestern tip of Somalia loomed about fifteen miles ahead. By altering course slightly, Storm could cut off the most likely escape route north and still be in a good position to chase a submarine if it headed west.

What to do when he caught it was a separate problem. Admiral Johnson had not answered his message, and Storm needed his permission before engaging.

Given that Port Somalia was an Indian installation, the submarine might be Pakistani. They had exactly six subs – four French Daphne-class boats well past their prime, and two Augustas, modern boats that could sprint to about 20.5 knots while submerged, and could be extremely hard to find in coastal waters – worthy adversaries for the *Abner Read*.

Of course, if it was a Pakistani boat, he wouldn't be allowed to attack at all; the Paks were in theory allies.

The Iranians had Kilos, even more potent submarines, though they hadn't moved from their ports in months.

'We'll move closer to shore, close down the distance with the submarine, if there is one,' Storm told Eyes. He glanced at the hologram to see where the Werewolf was. 'Have Airforce check the area where the raft was spotted, look for others.'

'He's low on fuel.'

'Well, tell him to get moving.'

Starship slid over the village five miles inland from Port Somalia, following the road as it wound back toward the coastline. Six small buildings stood next to each other, shouldering together between the road and a nearby cliff.

Nothing.

Nothing on the road either.

The computer gave him a warning tone. He was at 'bingo,' his fuel tanks just full enough to get him back to the *Abner Read*.

'Werewolf to Tac – I'm bingo, heading homeward.'

'Negative. We need you to scan the area near the Indian warship.'

Naturally.

'I can give you five minutes,' he told Eyes, planning

46

to cut into his reserves. 'Am I looking for something specific?'

'They found a raft. See if you can spot anything similar. We believe there may be a submarine in the area, but we haven't heard it yet.'

Ah, an admission of mortality from the all-powerful Navy, thought Starship as he whipped the Werewolf toward the Indian patrol boat. The ship's radar remained in scan mode; they saw him but were no longer targeting him.

'Couldn't the patrol boat pick him up on sonar?' Starship asked.

'A boat that class isn't always equipped with sonar. And this one is not.'

Starship took the Werewolf a mile and a half north, then turned to the west, sweeping along roughly parallel to the shore for nearly three miles before sweeping back. The flight control computer gave him another beep – he'd used half of his ten minute reserve.

'Not seeing anything, Tac.'

'How are you on fuel?'

'One more pass and then I absolutely have to come home,' said Starship.

'Acknowledged.'

Storm stared through the binoculars, watching the Werewolf as it came toward the ship. The helicopter had turned on its landing lights, and it looked like a sea anemone trailing its tentacles through the ocean.

It was a good little machine. It would be even better if it were equipped with a sonar system like the AQS-22

– a suggestion Storm had sent up to the chain of command weeks ago. The idea had yet to be acknowledged as received, let alone considered.

What he needed were a few short circuits up the chain of command, just like the Dreamland people had.

'We think we have something, Storm,' said Eyes. 'Very light contact, has to be a battery-powered propeller, six kilometers west of Port Somalia. At this range, with the Indian patrol boat so loud, it's hard to tell.'

'Let's head down there. I'll put in another call to Admiral Johnson. Maybe he'll answer me sometime this century.'

Off the coast of Somalia
0108

The helmsman controlled the midget submarine from a seat at the nose of the craft, working at a board that reminded Captain Sattari of the flight simulator for American F-4 Phantom jets he'd practiced on years before. The craft was steered with a large pistol-grip joystick; once submerged, it relied on an internal navigational system. The vessel was run by two men; the vessel's captain sat next to the helm, acting as navigator and watching the limited set of sensors.

The four submarines in Sattari's fleet had been designed by a European company as civilian vessels, intended for use in the shallow Caribbean and Pacific coastal waters. Converting them to military use had taken several months, but was not particularly difficult; the work primarily included measures to make the craft quieter. The acrylic bulbous nose and viewing portals had been replaced and the deck area topside stripped bare, but at heart the little boats were still the same submarines that appeared in the manufacturer's pricey four-color catalog. They could dive to three hundred meters and sail underwater for roughly twenty-eight hours. In an emergency, the subs could remain submerged for ninety-six hours. A small diesel engine propelled the boats on the surface, where the top speed was roughly ten knots, slower if the batteries were being charged. The midgets were strictly transport vessels, and it would be laughable to compare them to frontline submarines used by the American or Russian navies. But they were perfect as far as Sattari was concerned.

He called them Parvanehs: Butterflies.

The captain glanced back at the rest of the team, strapped into the boats. Among the interior items that had been retained as delivered were the deep-cushioned seats, which helped absorb and dampen interior sounds. Three of the men were making good use of them now, sleeping after their mission.

Sattari turned to the submarine commander.

'Another hour, Captain Sattari,' the man said without prompting. 'You can rest if you wish. I'll wake you when we're close.'

'Thank you. But I don't believe I could sleep. Are you sure we're not being followed?'

'We would hear the propellers of a nearby ship with the hydrophone. As I said, the Indian ship has very limited capabilities. We are in the clear.'

Sattari sat back against his seat. His father the general would be proud. More important, his men would respect him.

'Not bad for a broken-down fighter pilot, blacklisted and passed up for promotion,' he whispered to himself. 'Not bad, Captain Sattari. Thirty-nine is not old at all.'

Aboard the *Abner Read*,
off the coast of Somalia
0128

'What kind of submarine? A Pakistani submarine?'

'I'm not close enough to tell yet, Admiral,' Storm told Johnson over the secure video-communications network. 'We're still at least twenty miles north of it. There are two surface ships between us and the submarine, and another oil tanker beyond it. They may be masking the boat's sound somewhat. I'll know more about it in an hour.'

'You have evidence that it picked up the saboteurs?'

'No, I don't,' admitted Storm.

Johnson's face puckered. 'Pakistan, at least in theory, is our ally. India is not.'

Storm didn't answer.

'And there are no known submarines in this area?' said Johnson.

'We've checked with fleet twice,' said Storm, referring to the command charged with keeping track of submarine movements through the oceans.

'I find it hard to believe that a submarine could have slipped by them,' said Johnson.

'Which is why I found this submarine so interesting,' said Storm. While it was a rare boat that slipped by the forces – and sensors – assigned to watch them, it was not impossible. And Storm's intel officer had a candidate – a Pak sub reported about seven hundred miles due east in the Indian Ocean twenty-eight hours ago. It was an Augusta-class boat.

'All right, Storm. You have a point. See what you can determine. Do not – repeat, *do not* – fire on him.'

'Unless he fires on me.'

'See that he doesn't.'

Off the coast of Somalia
0158

Sattari leaned over and took the headset from the submarine captain, cupping his hands over his ears as he pushed them over his head. He heard a loud rushing sound, more like the steady static of a mistuned radio than the noise he would associate with a ship.

'This is the *Mitra*?' he asked.

'Yes, Captain. We're right on course, within two kilometers. You'll be able to see the lights at the bottom of the tanker in a few minutes. I believe we're the first in line.'

Sattari handed the headphones back, shifting to look over the helmsman's shoulder. A small video camera in the nose of the midget submarine showed the murky ocean ahead.

From the waterline up, the *Mitra* appeared to be a standard oil tanker. Old, slow, but freshly painted and with a willing crew, she was one of the vast army of blue-collar tankers the world relied on for its energy needs. Registered to a company based in Morocco, she regularly sailed these waters, delivering oil from Iranian wells to a number of African customers.

Or so her logbook declared.

Below the waterline, she was anything but standard. A large section of the hull almost exactly midship had been taken out and replaced with an underwater docking area for the four midget submarines. The vessels would sail under the tanker, then slowly rise, in effect driving into a garage. The submarines measured 8.4 meters, and the opening in the hull was just over twenty, leaving a decent amount of space for maneuvering.

The murky image on the forward-view screen suddenly glowed yellow. The camera aperture adjusted, sharpening the image. A set of large spotlights were arranged at the bottom of the hull; as the Parvaneh came closer, another group of colored lights would help guide the sub into the hold.

'Is the tanker moving?' Sattari asked.

'Three knots.'

The submarines could dock whether the mother ship was moving or not, and as long as it wasn't going more than four knots, most of the helmsmen felt it was easier to get aboard when the ship was under way. But in this case, the fact that the tanker was moving was a signal that there were other ships in the area. Sattari sat back in his seat, aware that not only was his mission not yet complete, but the success or failure of this final stage was out of his hands.

Aboard the *Abner Read*,
off the coast of Somalia
0208

'Tac, I'm clear of that freighter,' said Starship, flying the Werewolf south. 'Tanker is two miles off my nose, dead on. I'll be over it in a heartbeat.'

'Roger that.'

Starship whipped the little aircraft to the right of the poky tanker. He could see two silhouettes at the side of the superstructure near the bridge – crewmen looking at him.

His throat tightened a notch, and he waited for the launch warning – he had a premonition that one of the people aboard the ship was going to try shoving an SA-7 or even a Stinger up his backside. But his premonition was wrong; he cleared in front of the tanker and circled back, ramping down his speed to get a good look at the deck.

'Take another run,' said Tac as he passed the back end.

'Roger that. Ship's name is the *Mitra*,' added Starship. The name was written at the stern.

'Keep feeding us images.'

* * *

Storm had handpicked the crew for the ship, and the men who manned the sonar department were, if not *the* very best experts in the surface fleet, certainly among the top ten. So the fact that they now had *four* unknown underwater contacts eight miles away perplexed him considerably. As did their utter failure to match the sound profiles they had picked up with the extensive library in the ship's computer.

And now they seemed to be losing contact.

'Has to be some sort of bizarre glitch in the computer because of the shallow depth and the geometry of the sea bottom nearby,' insisted Eyes. 'Maybe it's an echo.'

'That's impossible,' said Storm.

'I know.'

Eyes recognized the tone. It meant – not everything works in the real world the way it's drawn up on the engineering charts, Captain.

Still, he was *convinced* his people were right.

So what did that mean?

That either he was looking at four submarines – four very quiet submarines – that no one else in the world had heard before, or that he was being suckered by some sort of camouflaging device.

Like an underwater robot trailing behind the submarine, throwing up a smoke screen.

The problem with that was that decoys normally made a lot more noise. These contacts were almost silent.

'We have mechanical noises in the water,' said Eyes. 'We're having some trouble picking up the sounds, though, because of that tanker.'

'Explosion?'

'Negative.'

'Torpedoes?'

'Negative. He may have some sort of problem. He may be using the tanker to turn around and check behind him, just as we theorized, Storm. He's done everything we thought he would, just slower.'

'We didn't think he'd split himself into four equal parts.'

'You *really* think we're chasing four submarines?'

Storm folded his arms in front of his chest. The truth was, they'd had all sorts of glitches with their equipment from the moment they'd left port. It was to be expected – the gear was brand new and the bugs had to be worked out.

'Airforce find anything on that tanker?' asked Storm.

'Negative. Tanker checks out. They do a run down to South Africa from Iran. Goes back and forth every couple of weeks.'

'Let's give the submariner a few more minutes to make a mistake,' said Storm. 'Then we'll turn on the active sonar. At least we'll find out how many of him we're chasing.'

'Aye aye, Captain.'

Off the coast of Somalia
0208

Captain Sattari was the next to last man out of the small submarine. The small interior smelled so horribly he nearly

55

retched as he grabbed hold of the rope guideline and jumped onto the narrow metal gangway at the side of the hull.

'Captain Sattari! Ship's commander needs to see you right away,' said the sailor leaning toward him at the end of the decking. 'He's on the bridge, sir. He asks you to hurry.'

Sattari glanced back as he entered the doorway at the side. Two other submarines had arrived; one was starting to unload and the other was just being secured.

The sailor ran ahead. Sattari did his best to keep up. Not familiar with the ship, he knocked his shin as he went through one of the compartments to the ladder that led to the bridge.

'We have an American warship behind us,' said the ship's captain when he reached the deck. 'He's sent a helicopter to circle us. He may be tracking the submarines with passive sonar.'

'Do we have all the subs?'

'The fourth still has not come inside. I believe he is within a half kilometer at this point, or perhaps closer. I thought it best not to use the sonar.'

'You're sure these are Americans?'

'Quite sure. The ship identified itself as the *Abner Read*. Devil's Tail.'

The American littoral destroyer had made quite a name for itself in the Gulf of Aden in the few months it had been there. But it rarely ventured to the eastern end of the gulf, and Sattari had not seen it during his earlier scouting missions.

Beside the point now. It was here.

Discovery by the Americans would be catastrophic. Even if the Americans left them alone for the moment – and really, why would they help the Indians? – they would be on the lookout for his midget submarines in the future. It was one thing to evade the Indians and even the Chinese; quite another to have to deal with an American dragnet.

Not that he did not relish the day he would face them in combat. He welcomed the chance to avenge the defeat they had dealt his father.

'Can you launch the decoy once *Boat Four* is aboard?' Sattari asked.

'With them this close, I would think it highly likely they would realize where it came from.'

'Turn on the sonar as the submarine comes into the ship,' said Sattari.

'The sonar?'

'For a brief moment. Then drop the decoy. Continue on as if nothing has happened.'

'As you wish, Captain.'

Aboard the *Abner Read*,
off the coast of Somalia
0215

'Shark Gill sonar! Dead ahead – he must be right under that oil tanker!' Eyes's voice was so loud Storm thought he would've heard him without the com set.

'Excellent,' said Storm, though in truth he felt disappointed. Shark Gill was the NATO code word for the sonar used in Russian Kilo-class submarines. Most likely he had been trailing a Russian boat that had managed to evade the fleet – *not* the commandos, since Russia and India were allies.

'See if the captain of the tanker would honor a request to move off to the west,' said Storm. 'Tell him that our helicopter has been tracking some mines in the area – get him scared and get him out of there.'

'The sub may follow.'

'I doubt he'll make it that easy for us, now that he knows we're here,' said Storm. 'Turn on our active sonar as well – let's make sure he knows precisely how close to him we are.'

Off the coast of Somalia
0216

Sergeant Ibn came up to the bridge to report to Sattari while the tanker captain was talking to the Americans.

'All our men are back. No losses. Mission accomplished,' said the sergeant, his face as grim as ever.

'The success of the mission is entirely yours,' Sattari told him. 'You trained everyone superbly – I for one benefited greatly from your drills.'

The sergeant turned beet red, then bent his head.

Had Sattari mistaken shyness for skepticism? No, he thought; Ibn – and most likely the others – were wary of an unproven commander whose experience was entirely in the cockpit. They must have felt, and with some justification, that he had only gotten his position because of his father, who still had some influence with the government. Or else they thought the entire scheme of equipping a special operations group with gear and machines any civilian – any *rich* civilian – could buy was preposterous.

They would not think so now.

Ibn remained at attention.

'Relax, Sergeant,' Sattari told him. 'See to the men.'

'Thank you, Captain.'

Was there more respect in his voice? Less doubt?

Perhaps. But more important, Sattari felt sure of himself. He had done it; he had succeeded. Tonight was only the start.

'The Americans want us to go west,' the tanker captain told him. 'They say they have spotted some mines.'

Had he not been so tired, Sattari would have burst out laughing.

'Comply. Make as much noise as you can.'

'The decoy will begin chattering any moment now.'

'That's fine,' said Sattari. 'They will think the submarine launched it. Combined with the sonar they heard – they won't be able to piece the different parts together.'

The ship's commander was a short, sinewy man who had somehow managed to keep his face clear of wrinkles despite having spent his life at sea. He looked at Sattari as if he didn't understand, and the commando leader felt compelled to explain further.

'You see,' Sattari said, 'these Americans are clever people. They love puzzles, and they love to piece them together. In this case, the fact that the pieces don't fit will confuse them. Their instincts will be to press ahead and attack. They will realize it's a decoy soon enough, then they will look for the submarine in earnest.'

'You speak of the Americans as if you know them very well,' said the ship's captain.

'I speak from unfortunate experience.'

Aboard the *Abner Read*,
off the coast of Somalia
0218

'Ship is turning to port. I wouldn't say they're burning up the ocean,' reported Starship.

'Take a run over them. Make sure they see you.'

'Have to be blind not to,' said Starship. But he did as he was told, moving the Werewolf down toward the tanker. Again he passed so close that he could see a man on the ladder of the superstructure. Again he felt a chill and a moment of premonition, sure he was going to be shot down.

I'm not even on the stinkin' helicopter, he reminded himself as he circled away, unfired on. Relax.

'We have a decoy in the water,' Eyes told Storm. 'Loud. Imposter.'

Imposter was a nickname for a Russian MG-74 decoy,

a versatile torpedo-tube-launched noisemaker that could employ a variety of techniques to confuse a tracking ship, including jamming sonar and simulating the sound of a large submarine.

'You have a contact with the sub that launched it?'

'Negative. We didn't hear the tube flood or launch, either. Tubes could have been open for a while. Not adding up, Captain. Now we don't have any contacts at all.'

'Nothing!'

'I know, I know,' said Eyes quickly. 'We're looking, Storm. I don't know why we can't find it.'

This was the point in the chase where a hunter had to be patient; sooner or later the prey would make a mistake and give himself away. No matter how clever – and the captain of the submarine had proven himself *quite* clever – he would eventually slip.

The problem was, Storm was not a patient man. He stared at the holographic display, trying to puzzle out where his adversary had gone.

'You're *sure* he's not trailing that tanker?'

'Negative.'

Oh my God, thought Storm, what if he managed to get underneath us?

Impossible.

But a logical explanation.

'Change course – hard to starboard,' he shouted to the helmsman behind him on the bridge. 'Eyes – make sure the SOB isn't hiding right beneath us or in our wake somehow.'

* * *

61

Starship skipped over the waves, staring at the infrared feed and trying not to let it burn through his eyes. There was nothing on the surface of the water – no periscope, no radio mast, no nothing.

Navy guys stared at the sea all the time, and claimed to love it. How sick was that?

The submarine wasn't under them. But neither was it anywhere in the five-mile grid they marked out in the ocean as its most likely location, nor in the wider circle that Storm had the ship patrol after the grid proved empty.

They'd been beaten. And the worst thing was, Storm didn't even know who had done it.

A hard-ass Russian submarine captain in a Kilo, who'd wandered close to Port Somalia by accident and then thought it best to get away before he got blamed?

Or the captain of a submarine who had in fact picked up the saboteurs and scooted clean away?

'All right,' he growled into his microphone. 'Eyes – we're going to have to call off the search. We can't stay here forever.'

'Aye aye, Captain.'

Storm's anger flashed as the command was passed and the crew began to move, tacitly accepting defeat. His right hand formed into a fist but he restrained himself from pounding the bulkhead.

He thought of that later, in his cabin, when he stared at the ceiling instead of sleeping. It was a measure of how much he had changed in the months since the fight with the Somalian pirates.

Whether it was a change for the better, he couldn't tell.

The day's worth of tests were mostly variations on ones Zen had already gone through before Christmas. He was injected with a series of dyes and then X-rayed and scanned, prodded and listened to. The technical staff took a stack of X-rays, MRIs, and ultrasounds. Then they hooked him up to a machine that measured nerve impulses. This involved inserting needles into various parts of his body. The doctors had done this several days before. Now they inserted more, and left them in for nearly two hours.

He didn't feel the ones in his legs, but he did get a prickly sensation in his neck when they were inserted along his upper back. It didn't hurt, exactly, but lying there was more difficult than he had imagined.

'Done,' said Dr Vasin finally. Two aides came over and helped Zen sit up.

'So I can walk now?'

'Jeff.'

'Hey, Doc, loosen up. Just a joke.' Zen pushed his arms back. His muscles had stiffened. 'Tomorrow I go under the knife, right?'

'Laser, and then the injections. Bright and early, but listen –'

'I know. No guarantees.'

'This is a really long process, Jeff. And I have to be honest, brutally honest –'

'Ten percent chance. I know.'

'Ten percent is very optimistic,' said Vasin.

'It's OK. I understand.'

'Operation one is tomorrow. The procedure itself is relatively simple, but of course it *is* a procedure. No food after seven P.M., just in case we have to put you out.'

'Beer's not food, right?'

'Not after seven. And for the duration of the test period, alcohol and coffee are forbidden.'

'Well, there goes the bender I was planning. Don't worry, Doc,' added Zen, 'I'm just joking.'

Needles and sensors removed, Zen got dressed and wheeled himself out into the hallway. He headed toward the lounge area, where he could call for a taxi before taking the elevator down. He was surprised to see Breanna waiting for him.

'Bree?'

'You called for a taxi?'

'What are you doing here?'

'Like I said – need a taxi?'

'I thought you were snowed in.'

'I shoveled the runway myself.'

She leaned over and kissed him. Zen grabbed her around the neck and hugged her, surprising himself at how much he missed her.

'Everything all right?'

'I feel like a pincushion. Other than that, I'm fine.' He thought of telling her about the dream but decided not to. It would fade, eventually.

'Operation still on for tomorrow?'

'Not much of an operation,' he told her. 'They just inject me with crap. Don't even knock me out.'

'Crap,' she said sarcastically.

'Let's go grab something to eat, OK? I'm fasting from seven P.M. After that, no food until tomorrow night. I want to have a beer. I can't have any during the two weeks of injections. No coffee, either.'

'No beer or coffee? You sure this is worth it?' Breanna laughed.

'Hope so.'

II

Impossible!

Navy Ministry Building,
New Delhi, India
6 January 1998
0900

Deputy Defense Minister Anil Memon stared at the table, trying to master his rage as India's Prime Minister continued to speak about the need for a 'measured response' to the latest provocation. The minister claimed that there was no obvious link between the attack at Port Somalia and the Pakistanis – an absurd claim in Memon's opinion. Memon knew that he should hold his tongue, but finally he could not.

'Who else would have launched the attack?' he said. 'Who else has connections to these pirates?'

'We have no proof of connections,' said the Prime Minister.

'They are Muslims. What other proof do you wish?' Memon ignored the disapproving stare from his boss, Defense Minister Pita Skandar. 'They will attack again and again. They will strike our ships. They do not wish to see us prosper. Anyone who does not realize that is a fool.'

'You haven't proven your case,' said the Prime Minister.

'How many of my sailors must die before you consider it proven?' said Memon.

'They are my sailors too, *Deputy* Minister,' said the Prime Minister, his anger finally rising. 'More mine than yours.'

'Then let us act. Mobilize. Send the new carrier to blockade the Pakistani ports.'

'My deputy speaks with passion,' said Minister Skandar softly. 'Take into account that he is young.'

'I assumed he spoke for you,' said the Prime Minister.

'He goes further than I. I would not block the Pakistani ports quite yet. But the *Shiva* should set out immediately. Its trials are complete. We must show that we are resolved.'

The Prime Minister nodded, then turned to the Chief of the Naval Staff for his opinion. The discussion continued for a few minutes more, but Skandar's recommendations had clearly set the course, and within a half hour the meeting concluded.

Memon, feeling defeated and frustrated, sat in his seat as the others began filing out. When he finally rose, Skandar touched his sleeve, signaling that he should stay. Cheeks flushing, Memon sat back down.

'You win no points by being too fiery in the cabinet room,' said Skandar.

'The Muslims must be behind this,' said Memon. 'They are the only ones who benefit. The intelligence services simply are inept in gathering evidence.'

'We must examine everything in context.'

A large man, with a shaved head and an emotionless smile, Skandar appeared almost godlike. But of late Memon had begun to wonder if the man generally referred to as the 'Admiral' was simply old. Not quite thirty years before, he had distinguished himself as a young officer in charge of a raiding party in the 1971 war with Pakistan. Promotions quickly followed. In time, Skandar became the head of the Naval Staff, the highest uniform post in the navy.

In 1994, Skandar retired to run for congress. Winning election easily, he had been asked to join the Prime Minister's government as the Defense minister. The old admiral at first demurred, but soon was persuaded that he could do much to help the services.

Memon had been among those who helped persuade him. The admiral's 'price' for agreeing was that Memon would join him as deputy minister. He'd done so, despite the fact that he had hoped for his own minister's portfolio. Like many other young Indians, he saw Skandar as the one man in the government with enough stature to bring India's military into the twenty-first century.

The admiral had done better than any one of them, Memon included, might have hoped, adding aircraft to the air force, tanks to the army, and above all ships to the navy. It thrilled Memon, who wished India to take her rightful place in the world. But of late Skandar had seemed only an old man, talking of abstractions rather than actions.

'Admiral, the context is before our eyes,' Memon told him. 'We are being attacked.'

'In the next century, who will be the superpowers of Asia? Russia is a shadow of herself. We pick over her bones to build our own forces. The United States? They are preoccupied with Europe, Taiwan, and Japan, spread so thin that they cannot afford to send more than a token force to the Gulf of Aden.'

'China is our ultimate enemy. I realize that,' said Memon. 'But you're worrying about fifty years from now. I'm worrying about today.'

'Our actions today will determine what happens in fifty years.' Skandar smiled. 'You're still young. Full of fire. That is admirable.'

At thirty-eight, Memon did not consider himself particularly young. But since he was half Skandar's age, the comment was not meant unkindly.

'What do you think of joining the *Shiva*?' added Skandar.

Memon had been instrumental in the conversion of the ship from the Russian, Tiazholyi Avianesushchiy Kreyser, or Heavy Aircraft-Carrying Cruiser, *Kiev*. To Memon, the *Shiva* epitomized India's new aggressiveness, and he would love to be aboard her. Its captain, Admiral Asad Kala, was an old acquaintance.

But why was Skandar suggesting it? To get him out of New Delhi?

'I would like nothing better than to join the *Shiva*,' said Memon warily. 'If you can spare me.'

'Good, then.' Skandar rose. 'You should make your plans immediately.'

'This isn't a B-1, Captain. You're not going to get up over that mountain unless you start pulling the stick back now.'

Jan Stewart clenched her teeth together but did as she was told, jerking the control yoke toward her. The EB-52 Megafortress lifted her nose upward, shrugging off a wave of turbulence as she rose over Glass Mountain at the northern edge of Dreamland's Test Range 4. As soon as she cleared the jagged peak, Stewart pressed the stick forward, aiming to stay as close to the mountain as possible. But it was no good – though a vast improvement over the B-52H she had been converted from, the Megafortress was still considerably more comfortable cruising in the stratosphere than hugging the earth. Her four P&W power plants strained as Stewart tried to force gravity, momentum, and lift into an equation that would get the plane across the ridge without being seen by the nearby radar sentry, a blimp hovering two miles to the west.

The computer buzzed a warning:

DETECTED. BEING TARGETED.

Stewart sensed her copilot's smirk. If only it had been Jazz, or *anyone* other than Breanna Stockard.

'Defense – evade – ah, shit,' Stewart said, temporarily flustered.

ENEMY LASER LOCKED.

73

'ECMs,' said Stewart, back in control. 'Evasive maneuvers. Hold on.'

'ECMs,' acknowledged Breanna.

Stewart banked hard and nailed the throttle to the last stop, trying to pirouette away from the laser targeting them. Her efforts were not in vain – the airborne antiaircraft laser fired and missed by about fifty yards. But the respite was brief. The EB-52 couldn't rebuild momentum quickly enough, and the laser recycled and sent a full blast at the cockpit. Several thousand joules of energy – simulated – struck the ship just aft of the pilots' station. The blast fused the satellite antenna and blew out the assorted electrical circuits, as well as punching a six-inch-wide hole across the top of the fuselage. The emergency panel in front of the pilots lit up like a Christmas tree, and alarms sounded throughout the aircraft. Ten seconds later a second salvo burned a hole through the metal covering the fuel bag immediately behind the wings. The temperature in the fuel delivery piping increased tenfold in an instant, and an explosion ripped across the plane's backbone.

'We're dead,' said Breanna.

Stewart leveled off silently, easing back on the thrust as Breanna called the test range coordinator to acknowledge that they'd been wiped out.

'Roger that,' said the coordinator. 'Got you on that second blast. Good work.'

'You want another run?'

'Negative. We've got plenty of data. Thank you very much.'

'Pleasure is ours,' said Breanna.

Stewart ground her back molars together, stifling a scream. She took the Megafortress up through eight thousand feet, circling at the eastern end of the range before contacting the control tower for permission to land.

'Tower to EB-52 Test Run, you're cleared to land. What's wrong? Didn't you have your Wheaties today?'

'Test Run,' snapped Stewart, acknowledging the clearance but not the sarcasm. The controller chortled as he gave her information about the wind, rubbing in the fact that she'd just had her clock cleaned by a pair of robots in a blimp and an ancient C-130.

'You're getting better,' said Breanna as Stewart rolled toward the hangar bunker.

'Don't give me that, Stockard. I really don't need a pep talk from you. I got toasted.'

'The purpose of the exercise was to get toasted. We're just guinea pigs.'

'I could have made it past the ridge if you hadn't made me pull up,' said Stewart angrily. 'I had plenty of clearance.'

'The computer would have taken over for you if you hadn't pulled back on the stick.'

'The safety protocols are too conservative.'

'Why are you so touchy? It's only a test. Nobody's keeping score. If we'd gotten through on that pass we would have had to take another run anyway.'

'I could have made it,' insisted Stewart, powering down at the signal from the crewman outside.

Breanna sighed, and pretended to busy herself with the

postflight checklist. She'd had Stewart fly as pilot to give her more experience behind the stick, not to show her up. Stewart had the qualifications to be a lead pilot, but so far she just wasn't hacking it. Hopefully it would come in time.

If her personality let it.

'Hey, Bree, Dog's looking for you,' said Danny Freah, sticking his head up at the rear of the cockpit area.

'What's up?'

'We're moving out. You'll never guess where.'

'Mars.'

'I wish. Going back to the Gulf of Aden. We're going to work with Xray Pop and the infamous Captain Storm. Hey, Stewart, you're invited too. Looks like your first Whiplash deployment is about to begin.'

'Great,' said Stewart, her tone suggesting the opposite.

'Newbies buy.'

'Screw yourself, Captain.'

'What's buggin' her?' said Danny after the pilot left the plane.

'Doesn't like to buy,' said Breanna.

By the time Breanna and Danny got to Conference Room 2 in the Taj Mahal, Colonel Bastian had started the briefing. A large map at the front of the room showed northeastern Africa, the Gulf of Aden, and part of the nearby Indian Ocean. Somalia sat like a large, misshapen 7 wrapped around the northern and eastern shores of the continent. During its last deployment, the Dreamland Whiplash team and the Megafortresses supporting it had seen action on land and above the sea at the north, where the Gulf of Aden separated Africa from the Saudi peninsula. Today, the eastern shore of the war-torn country was highlighted, with a large X near the town of Hando on the Indian Ocean.

'I'm going to start by giving you all some background on political situation here,' said the colonel. 'As many of you already know, pirates have been roaming the Gulf of Aden for nearly a year. They've been taking advantage of trouble elsewhere – specifically in the Balkans, in the Philippines, Japan, and Taiwan – to prey on oil tankers and other merchant ships traveling through the gulf.'

'While the cat's away, the mice do play,' said Major Mack Smith down in front. He turned around, smiling for everyone behind him, as if he were in junior high and had just made the most clever statement in the world.

'The Navy sent a small warship called the *Abner Read* into the gulf a few months ago,' continued Dog, ignoring Smith. 'Some of us supported them. We won a major victory against the strongest group of pirates two months ago. Things have been relatively calm since, with some sporadic attacks but nothing on the order of what we'd seen before. Yesterday, however, there was a major attack on Port Somalia, an oil terminal that has just been opened by the Indians. The Indians are blaming Pakistan and are threatening to retaliate. That's not sitting too well with the Pakistanis, who say they had nothing to do with this attack. Both countries have nuclear weapons. Our satellites have detected preparations at the major Indian ballistic missile launching area and at its Pakistani counterpart.'

'Saber rattling,' said Mack.

'Our immediate mission is to beef up Xray Pop, the task force that the *Abner Read* heads. We're going to help it figure out who's behind the attack. We're also going there to show both sides just how serious a matter this is.'

'Blessed are the peacemakers –' said Mack.

'Thank you, Major, but I can do without the running commentary,' said Dog. 'We will be under the operational command of Xray Pop's commander, Captain "Storm" Gale. A lovely fellow.'

Everyone who had been on the last deployment snickered.

Dog turned to the projection behind him, using a laser pointer to highlight an X on the eastern coast of Somalia at the north.

'This is Port Somalia. It's an oil terminal, the end point for a pipeline the Indians have paid to be built to deliver oil from northern Somalia and the Gulf of Aden. It's part of an ambitious network that they are constructing that will give them access to oil from the entire Horn of Africa, all the way back to the Sudan. A second port is planned to open farther south later this year.'

The colonel clicked the remote control he had in his left hand and a new map appeared on the screen behind him. India sat at the right, Somalia on the left. The Arabian Sea, an arm of the Indian Ocean, sat between them. Above Somalia was the Saudi peninsula, with Yemen at the coast. Iran and Pakistan were at the northern shores of the sea, separating India from the Middle East.

'To give you some idea of the distances involved here,' said Dog, 'it's roughly fifteen hundred miles from Port Somalia to Mumbai, also known as Bombay, on the coast of India, not quite halfway down the Indian subcontinent. Three hours flying time, give or take, for a Megafortress, a little less if Lightning Chu is at the controls.'

The pilots at the back laughed. Captain Tommy Chu had earned his new nickname during recent power-plant tests by averaging Mach 1.1 around the test course, defying the engineers' predictions that the EB-52 could not be flown faster than the speed of sound for a sustained period in level flight.

'Timewise, we are eleven hours behind. When it is noon here, it is 2300 hours in Port Somalia, same time as Mogadishu. Problem, Cantor?'

Lieutenant Evan Cantor, one of the new Flighthawk jocks recently cleared for active combat missions, jerked upright in the second row. 'Uh, no sir. Just figuring out days. They're a half day ahead. Just about.'

'Just about, Lieutenant. But don't do the math yet. We'll be based at Drigh Road, the Pakistani naval air base near Karachi. We'll use Karachi time for reference. That's thirteen hours ahead. A section of the base has already been cordoned off for us. Problem, Lieutenant Chu?'

'Just trying to figure out how many watches to wear,' said Chu.

'Why Karachi?' said Breanna.

'Mostly because they won't object, and they're relatively close,' said Dog. 'But we'll have to be very, very aware that we're in an Islamic country, and that our presence may be controversial to some.'

Controversial was putting it mildly. Stirred up by local radicals, civilians near the air base the Dreamland team had used in Saudi Arabia during their last deployment had come close to rioting before the Megafortresses relocated to Diego Garcia in the Indian Ocean.

'We'll have four Megafortresses: the *Wisconsin*, our old veteran; and three newcomers, the *Levitow*, the *Fisher*, and the *Bennett*.'

The choice of the planes was not haphazard; all were radar surveillance planes, with both air and sea capabilities. Information from the Megafortresses's radars would be supplied to the *Abner Read* via a link developed by Dreamland's computer scientists, giving the small littoral warrior a far-reaching picture of the air and oceans around it. Additionally, an underwater robot probe called Piranha could be controlled from one Flighthawk station on each plane, and special racks and other gear allowed the Megafortresses to drop and use sonar buoys.

'We'll rotate through twelve-hour shifts, with overlapping patrols, so there are always at least two aircraft on station at any one time,' continued Colonel Bastian. 'Lieutenant Chu has worked up some of the patrol details, and I'll let him go into the specifics. We're to be in the air as soon as possible; no later than 1600.'

The trip would have been long enough if they'd been able to fly in a straight line – somewhere over nine thousand miles. But political considerations forced them to skirt Iran and Russia, adding to the journey.

'I believe everyone knows everyone else on the deployment. The one exception may be Major Mack Smith, who's back with us after a working vacation in the Pacific. Mack has been pinch-hitting for Major Stockard while he's on medical leave for a few weeks, and he'll continue to head the Flighthawk squadron during the deployment.'

Mack, ever the showoff, turned and gave a wave to the pilots behind him.

Though he'd helped develop the Flighthawks, he had extremely little time flying them. That wasn't a serious deficiency handling the odd piece of paper-work at Dreamland, where Zen was only a phone call away; it remained to be seen what would happen in the field.

'One question, Colonel,' said Danny Freah, whose Whiplash team would provide security at the base. 'How long are we going to be there?'

Dog's mouth tightened at the corners – a sign, Breanna knew, that he was about to say something unpopular. 'As long as it takes.'

Las Vegas University of Medicine, Las Vegas, Nevada 1200

'I'll just say I can't go.'

'No way. You can't do that.'

'Sure I can do that. You're my husband.'

'Yeah, I do seem to remember a ceremony some-where.' Zen laughed. The two nurses at the other end of the room looked over and gave him embarrassed smiles.

'Jeff –'

'No, listen Bree, it's fine. Things are going great here. I still can't eat anything, but other than that, I'm in great shape. I may even go for a walk later.'

'Don't joke.'

'I'm not joking. It was a figure of speech.' Zen pulled his gown primly closer to his legs. When the phone call was finished, he'd go back facedown on the bed butt naked, but somehow it felt important to preserve what modesty he could.

'The operation was OK?'

'Bing-bing-bing. Didn't feel anything. Laser looked pretty cool. The nurse are great,' he added. 'I won't describe them or you'll get jealous.'

The women – neither of whom was under fifty – blushed.

'I love you, Jeff.'

'I love you too, Bree. Take care of yourself, all right?'

'You're *sure*?'

'Shit yeah.'

'I'll call.'

'Call when you can.'

'Jeff?'

'Yup?'

'I love you.'

'I love you too.'

Captain Sattari's knee, bruised in the recent action at Port Somalia, started to give way as he climbed from the back of the Mercedes. He grabbed hold of the door to steady himself, pretending to admire the splendor of the private villa three miles east of Chah Bahar on Iran's southern coast. Being thirty-nine meant the little tweaks and twists took longer to get over.

The villa *was* something to admire; its white marble pillars harked back to the greatness of the Persian past, and its proud, colorful red tower stood in marked contrast to the dullness that had descended over much of the land in the wake of the mullahs' extreme puritanism. Jaamsheed Pevars had bought the house before he became the country's oil minister. He was one of the new upper class, a man who had earned his money under the black robes and thus owed them some allegiance. A decade before the small company he owned had won a contract to inspect oil tankers for safety violations before they entered Iranian waters. Inspection was mandatory, as was the thousand dollar fee, only half of which went to the government.

'Captain?' asked Sergeant Ibn, getting out from the other side.

'Impressive view.'

Sattari shrugged off his knee's complaints, and the men walked up the stone-chipped path that led to the front door. A servant met them, bowing with the proper respect before leading them through the portico out into a garden where his host was waiting.

'Captain Sattari,' said Jaamsheed Pevars, rising as they entered. 'I greet you on your great success.'

As Sattari started to take his hand, he saw Pevars was not alone. The captain immediately stiffened; visitors generally meant trouble, usually from the imams who were constantly demanding more progress. But the man with his back to him was not one of the black robes. As he turned, Sattari was startled to see it was his father. Smiling broadly, General Mansour Sattari clasped the younger man to his chest.

'Congratulations on your success,' said the general.

'Thank you, sir. Thank you.'

'And Sergeant Ibn. How are you?'

'Fine, General. Happy to see you.'

'And I you. Are you watching over my son?'

'The captain needs no one to oversee him.'

The general beamed. A servant came with sparkling water, setting down a large glass for the visitors.

'A great success,' Pevars said. 'You have proven the concept. Now it is time to push the Indians further.'

'We are prepared.'

'Are you?' said the oil minister. 'There have been questions.'

'Questions?' said Sattari. He glanced at his father. Was that why he was here? Did the general doubt his own son?

'Some of the black robes are demanding a return on

the investment,' said Pevars. 'The price of oil has sunk so quickly lately that they are becoming concerned. The timetable –'

'We're completely ready.'

'The sooner you can press the attacks and instigate the conflict, the better,' added Pevars. 'The commodities market shrugged off the attack.'

'They will not be able to ignore the next one.'

'My son is wondering why I am here,' the general told Pevars. 'And I should explain to him. Some of the imams in the council want to make sure the Indians are punished. And they want the war between the Indians and Pakistan to show that the Chinese cannot be trusted.'

'I can't guarantee a war,' said Sattari. 'The idea was to affect oil prices, not start a war. I have only a small force, four small aircraft and one large one, all primarily transports. I have one old ship, a hulk that just today we have covered with new paint. My four midget submarines are useful as transports but carry no weapons besides what a man can hold. I have thirty-six commandos. All brave men, all ready to die for Allah and Iran. That is the sum of my force.'

'You were chased by the Americans,' said his father.

'Yes. They complicated our escape.'

The Americans were a great enemy of Sattari's father. A year before, a small force of commandos and aircraft had attacked one of the general's installations in the North, destroying a secret antiaircraft laser he had developed. The strike had lessened his influence in the government; naturally, he wanted revenge.

'There was a rumor that you ran from them,' said Pevars.

'Who said that?'

'One of the black robes,' said his father.

So that was what this was about. Sattari guessed that the imam had a spy aboard the *Mitra* who had radioed back a report of the action before they reached port.

To be called a coward after the success of his mission! That was typical of those fellows. It was a favorite tactic, to tear down everyone else.

But did his father think he was a coward? That was an entirely different matter.

'I did not run,' Sattari said. 'Exposing our force would have been idiocy. Worse than cowardice.'

'I'm sure,' said the general. 'Do not let lies depress you.'

'I won't.'

'Some sweets,' said the oil minister. He clapped his hands for the servant.

Aboard the *Abner Read*,
off the coast of Somalia
1538

'What do you have for me, Airforce?' asked Storm as Starship stepped onto the bridge.

'I was hoping I might have a word in private.'

'This is private enough,' said Storm, glancing around the bridge. There were only two other men on the bridge,

86

one manning the wheel and the other the bridge navigation system. But as far as Storm was concerned, the entire ship's company could be here. He expected everyone aboard to show discretion where it was appropriate, but otherwise there was no place for secrets. The *Abner Read* was a small vessel. Everyone eventually ended up knowing everyone's business anyway.

'Captain, I was going to ask, considering that we now have two other men trained to handle the Werewolf, and that the Dreamland people are going to be based at Karachi –'

'You angling to leave us, mister?'

'I was thinking I might be more useful working with the Whiplash ground team, providing security. They can't deploy the Werewolves there without another pilot because of commitments at the base.'

'Request denied. We need you out here, Airforce. You're the only pilot worth a shit on this ship.'

The young man's face shaded red.

'Don't thank me,' added Storm. 'Just do your job.'

'Yes, sir.'

Starship snapped off a quick, confused salute and left. Storm went back to studying the holographic display. They were two miles north of 'Abd Al-Kūrī, an island off the tip of Somalia. The submarine they had chased the other night had not reappeared. Nor, for that matter, had the guerrillas.

The intelligence people back in Washington had no idea who had launched the attack. The Indians were blaming the Pakistanis, but as far as anyone could tell, they had no evidence except for decades' worth of animosities. Storm – who also had no evidence beyond the faint submarine contact – thought the Chinese were behind it. They were rivals for dominance of Asia, and it was possible they wanted to tweak the Indians' noses while the world was preoccupied elsewhere.

'Eyes, what's the status of the Dreamland patrols?'

'Due to start at 1800 hours. Looks like your old friend Colonel Bastian is taking the first patrol himself.'

Storm gritted his teeth. Bastian had proven himself a decent pilot and a good commander, but he was also a jerk.

Better that than the other way around, though.

'Have them report to me as soon as possible,' Storm said.

'Aye, Skipper. The Indian destroyer *Calcutta* is about a hundred miles east of Port Somalia. They should reach it in three or four hours. I thought we might send the Werewolf down to greet them. Let them know we're here.'

'If the circumstances allow, be my guest.'

Aboard the *Wisconsin*, taking off from Drigh Road, Pakistani naval air base 1600

Colonel Bastian put his hand on the throttle glide and brought the engines up to full takeoff power. The Megafortress rolled forward, quickly gaining momentum. As the plane touched 200 knots, the flight computer gave

Dog a cue to rotate or pull the nose of the aircraft upward. He did so, pushing the plane up sharply to minimize the noise for the surrounding area, much the same way a 747 or similar jet would when taking off from an urban area.

Passing through three thousand feet, the colonel trimmed the aircraft and began flying her like a warplane rather than an airliner trying to be a good neighbor. His copilot, Lieutenant Sergio 'Jazz' Jackson, had already checked the systems; everything was in the green.

The ocean spread itself out before the aircraft as Dog banked the Megafortress westward. A cluster of small boats floated near the port; a pair of freighters chugged slowly away. A Pakistani gunboat sailed to the south, its course marked by a white curve cut into the blue paper of the sea.

Starting with his copilot, Dog checked with the crew members to make sure the computer's impressions of the aircraft jibed with their experience. Immediately behind the two pilots on the flight deck, two radar operators manned a series of panels against each side of the fuselage. The specialist on the right, Sergeant Peter 'Dish' Mallack, handled surface contacts; the operator on the left, Technical Sergeant Thomas 'T-Bone' Boone, watched aircraft.

The Megafortress's array of radars allowed it to 'see' aircraft hundreds of miles away. The actual distance depended on several factors, most of all the radar cross section of the targeted aircraft. Under the right conditions, an airliner might be seen four hundred nautical miles away; a stealthy F-22, shaped specifically to avoid radar, could generally get well inside one hundred before being spotted. MiG-29s and Su-27s, the Russian-made fighters common in the area, could reliably be detected at two hundred nautical miles.

The surface search was handled by a radar set developed from the Nordon APY-3 used in the JSTARS battlefield surveillance and control aircraft. Again, its range depended on conditions. An older destroyer could be spotted at roughly two hundred miles; very small boats and stealthy ships like the *Abner Read* were nearly invisible even at fifty miles under most circumstances. A radar designed for finding periscopes in rough seas had been added to the mission set; an extended periscope from a Kilo-class submarine could be seen at about twenty miles under the best conditions.

Downstairs from the flight deck, in the compartment where the navigator and bombardier would have sat in a traditional B-52, Cantor was preparing to launch the aircraft's two Flighthawk U/MF-3 robot aircraft. The unmanned aerial vehicles could stray roughly twenty miles from their mother ship, providing air cover as well as the ability to closely inspect and attack surface targets if necessary.

The Flighthawks were flown with the help of a sophisticated computer system known as C^3. The aircraft contained their own onboard units, which could execute a number of maneuvers on their own. In theory, a Flighthawk pilot could handle two aircraft at a time, though newer pilots generally had to prove themselves in combat with one first.

The Megafortress carried four Harpoon antiship missiles and four antiaircraft AMRAAM-plus Scorpion missiles on a rotating dispenser in the bomb bay. A four-pack of sonar buoys was installed on special racks at each wingtip.

'How are you doing, Cantor?' Dog asked.

'Just fine, Colonel.'

'How's your pupil?'

'Um, Major Smith is, um, learning, sir.'

'I'll bet,' said Dog.

'I'm good to go here, Colonel,' said Smith. 'Everything is rock solid.'

'That's good to hear, Mack. Don't give Cantor any problems.'

'Problems? Why would I do that?'

Dog was too busy laughing to answer.

Indian Ocean
2000

The torpedo was not a good fit. At 4.7 meters long – roughly fourteen feet – it just barely fit beneath the smooth round belly of the Sparrow. More importantly, at roughly seven hundred kilograms – a touch over fifteen hundred pounds – it represented nearly twice the aircraft's rated payload, making the plane too heavy to take off with full fuel tanks.

But the limitations of the small, Russian-made seaplane were almost assets. For the Sparrow could 'fly' across the waves at a hundred knots on a calm night like this, approaching its target at two or three times the speed of a conventional torpedo boat or small patrol boat, while being quite a bit harder to detect than a conventional aircraft. When in range, about ten kilometers, it could fire the weapon, and then, considerably lighter, take to the sky and get away.

Which was the plan.

'Target is now fifty kilometers away,' said the co-pilot. Their target, an oil tanker bound for India, was being tracked by the largest aircraft under Sattari's command, an ancient but serviceable A-40 Beriev seaplane sold as surplus by the Russians some years before. The aircraft had just passed overhead at eighteen thousand feet, flying a course generally taken by a transport to India from Greece.

'Begin turn to target in ten seconds.'

Captain Sattari grunted. He was still angry over the meeting with the oil minister and his father earlier – so mad, in fact, that he had bumped the pilot from the mission and taken it himself. Not because he felt he needed to prove his courage or ability, but to help him master his rage.

Flying had always helped him in this way. It had nothing to do with the romance of the wind lifting you into the sky. No, what settled Sattari was the need for concentration, the utter surrender of your mind and senses to the job at hand. Planning the mission, checking the plan, then flying it as precisely as possible – the process freed him, chasing the demons of anger and envy and frustration from his back, where they hovered.

'The A-40 reports that there is a warship south of the tanker,' reported the copilot. 'Heading northward – three miles south of him. An Indian destroyer.'

A destroyer?

'Are they sure it's Indian?'

'They've overheard transmissions.'

The tanker was a more important target, but if the black robes wanted to provoke a war, striking a destroyer would certainly make them angrier.

And no one could call him a coward then.

'Compute a new course,' said Sattari. 'See if it's possible to strike the destroyer if we use the tanker as a screen. We can always drop back to our original prey.'

Aboard the *Wisconsin*, over the Gulf of Aden 2010

'MiGs are scrambling off the new field at Al Ghayda,' T-Bone warned Colonel Bastian. 'Two aircraft, MiG-29s. Just about one hundred miles from us, Colonel.'

'Mack, Cantor, you hear that?'

'Roger that, Colonel. We'll meet them.'

Dog keyed in the Dreamland communications channel to alert the *Abner Read*.

'*Abner Read*, this is *Wisconsin*. We have two MiG-29s coming off an airfield in Yemen. We expect them to be heading in our direction.'

'Bastian, this is Storm. What are you doing?'

'Minding our p's and q's, Captain. As normal.'

The Navy commander snorted. 'Are you where you're supposed to be?'

Dog fought the urge to say something sarcastic, and instead answered that they were on the patrol route agreed to earlier. 'I would expect that you can see that on the radar plot we're providing,' he added. 'Is it working?'

'It's working,' snapped the Navy captain. 'What's with those airplanes?'

'I assume they're coming to check us out. The Yemenis gave us quite a bit of trouble when we were out here a few months back.'

'If they get in your way, shoot them down.'

'I may just do that,' said Dog. '*Wisconsin* out.'

'Sounded kind of cranky,' said Jazz.

'Most pleasant conversation I've ever had with him,' Dog told his copilot.

Cantor glanced at the sitrep panel in the lower left-hand corner of his screen, making sure the Flighthawks were positioned properly for the intercept.

'Fifty miles and closing,' Cantor told Mack. 'Weapons radar is off.'

'Yeah, I can see that,' said Mack. 'You're lagging behind me, cowboy.'

'We're going to do this like we rehearsed,' said Cantor. 'I'm going to swing out. You get in their face.'

'Flying wing isn't the most efficient strategy.'

'We're not flying F-15s, Major. This is the way Zen teaches it.'

'Oh, I'm sure it'll work against these bozos,' said Mack. 'I'm just pointing out, it's not the best strategy to shoot them down.'

'We're not supposed to fire at them.'

'Hey, don't bitch to me. Complain to Colonel Bastian.'

I will, thought Cantor. I definitely will.

Mack steadied his forearm on the narrow shelf in front of the control stick, listening as the *Wisconsin*'s copilot attempted to hail the MiGs. The bogeys were doing about 500 knots; with his Flighthawk clocking about 480, they were now about ninety seconds from an intercept.

If he'd been in an F-15 or even an F-16, the MiGs would be toast by now. An F-22 – *fuggetaboutit*. They'd be figments of Allah's imagination already.

Mack jangled his right leg up and down. Unlike a normal aircraft, the Flighthawk control system did not use pedals; all the inputs came from a single control stick and voice commands. This might be all right for someone like Zen, stuck in a wheelchair, or even Cantor, who'd probably been playing video games since he was born, but not for him. He loved to fly. He had it in his belly and his bones. Pushing buttons and wiggling your wrist just didn't do it.

'They're breaking,' said Cantor.

'*Hawk One.*'

The MiGs, which had been in a close trail, were getting into position to confront the Megafortress. Mack started to follow as *Bogey One* cut to the east, then realized the plane was closer to *Hawk Two*.

'I got him, Major,' said Cantor.

'Yeah, yeah, no sweat,' said Mack, swinging back to get his nose on the other airplane.

'If they go for their afterburners, they'll blow right by you,' warned Cantor.

'Hey, no shit, kid.'

The computer's tactics' screen suggested that he start his turn now, recommending that he swing the Flighthawk in front of the MiG to confront it.

'Wrong,' Mack told it. Doing that would take him across the MiG's path too soon, and he might even lose the chance to circle behind him. Instead, he waited until his MiG began to edge downward. Then it was too late – the Yemen pilot opened up the afterburners and spurted forward, past the Flighthawk, even as Mack started his turn.

'He's going to use all his fuel, the idiot,' muttered Mack, putting his finger to the throttle slide at the back of the Flighthawk stick. Even so, there was no way he could catch up with the MiG; it was already flying well over 600 knots.

'They know where we'll be, Major,' said Cantor. 'They can't see us yet but they learned from the encounters back in November.'

'Big deal,' said Mack under his breath.

Cantor pulled his Flighthawk back toward the Mega-fortress, aiming to stay roughly parallel to the other fighter's path. The MiG-29 Fulcrum was an excellent single-seat fighter, highly maneuverable and very dangerous when

96

equipped with modern avionics and weapons. But it did have some shortcomings. As a small aircraft, it could not carry that much fuel, and teasing the afterburners for speed now would limit what it could do later. And their limited avionics meant the Flighthawk was invisible to them except at very close range. Guessing where it was wasn't the same as knowing.

As soon as the Yemen jet turned to try and get behind the Megafortress at close range, Cantor made his move, trading his superior altitude for speed and surprise. He reminded himself not to get too cocky as it came on, staying precisely on course and resisting the temptation to increase his speed by pushing his nose down faster.

'Bogey at one mile; close intercept – proximity warning,' said C^3, the Flighthawk's computer guidance system.

'Acknowledged, Computer,' said Cantor. He gave the stick a bit of English as his target came on. The Flighthawk crossed in front of the MiG in a flash, its left wing twenty yards from the aircraft's nose. As he crossed, Cantor pushed his stick hard to the right, skidding through the air and lining up for a shot on the MiG's hindquarters.

He didn't quite get into position to take the shot, but that didn't matter. The MiG veered sharply to the west, tossing flares and chaff as decoys in an effort to get away.

'*Hawk Two* has completed intercept,' Cantor reported. '*Bogey One* is running for cover.'

Off the coast of Somalia
2010

Starship acknowledged the radio call from the approaching Indian destroyer, identifying himself as an aircraft from the *Abner Read*. He was ten miles northeast of the ship, the *Calcutta*, too far off for them to realize that the aircraft was too small to hold a pilot.

'*Werewolf One*, our commander wishes you to pass along a message to your commander,' said the radioman aboard the *Calcutta*.

'Sure,' said Starship.

'He salutes Captain Gale on his many victories. He hopes that he will have an opportunity to visit the *Abner Read* in the future.'

'I'll relay the message,' said Starship.

Starship circled over the Indian warship twice, then began heading back toward the *Abner Read*, close to 250 miles away. He double-checked the auxiliary screen showing the status of *Werewolf Two* – the computer was flying the aircraft in a routine patrol pattern around and ahead of the ship – then turned his full attention to the sea in front of him. An oil tanker was about a mile and a half northwest of him, low in the water with its full load.

Something else was there, too – a plane almost in the waves, moving at 100 knots, about five miles north of him.

'Werewolf to Tac,' said Starship. 'Hey, check this contact out!'

Indian Ocean
2012

Captain Sattari grinned as the torpedo fell off its rail. Freed of the weight, the Beriev rose abruptly. Sattari caught a glimpse of his well-lit target five miles off, just beyond the oil tanker. He banked and tucked back closer to the waves, trying to keep the plane no higher than fifty feet, where it should not be seen by the destroyer's Russian-made radar system.

It would take the torpedo less than three minutes to run to its target. The destroyer would undoubtedly detect the fish once it cleared the tanker, and take evasive maneuvers when the torpedo was detected. But he'd gotten close enough to narrow the odds of escape; the torpedo was designed to home in on its target, and if the crew aboard the destroyer was not swift, he would score a great victory.

Pointless to even think about it now, he told himself, finding his new course.

'Aircraft!' said his copilot, manning the passive infrared sensors. 'Helicopter!'

'Where?'

'Three miles to our southeast.'

'Pursuing us?'

'Uncertain. His radar is operating. He may see us.'

Sattari squeezed the throttle for more power.

'*MiG Two* continuing toward us at a high rate of speed,' Jazz told Dog.

'Open the bay doors.'

'He's not targeting us, Colonel.'

'Bay doors.'

'Bay.'

The rumble of the missile bay opening shook the aircraft. Dog double-checked his position, then reached to the communications panel.

'Yemen MiG-29, this is EB-52 *Wisconsin*. You can get as close as you like, but if you get in my way you're going to swim home.'

'Big words, yankee-man.'

Dog laughed. 'I guess he told me.'

'Ten miles, sir.'

'Relax, Jazz. He just wants to prove his manhood so the rest of squadron will buy him beers.'

'They're Muslim, Colonel. They don't drink alcohol.'

'That was a joke. Ease up.'

'I'm trying.'

Having blown the intercept, Mack tried desperately to think of some way to save face as he swung back toward the *Wisconsin*. He was pretty far out of the picture now, five miles behind the MiG, which was still picking up speed as it came at the Megafortress. If this had been more serious, the bogey would have launched its missiles by now.

Of course, if it *had* been more serious, the Megafortress would have launched its own antiaircraft missiles.

Game or not, he knew he'd had his fanny waxed, and he needed to get revenge. He watched as the MiG changed course, turning to the west away from the EB-52. The computer, drawing its probable course in the sitrep screen, momentarily showed it breaking off, but it quickly caught on – like its companion, the plane was angling for a high-speed run from behind, a good position to launch heat-seekers.

Mack was too far behind the MiG to follow and too far ahead of the Megafortress to follow Cantor's strategy and cut the MiG off behind the plane. So instead he began his own turn to the west – he'd make his intercept *after* the MiG passed the EB-52.

And, just to make the experience special, he'd toss a few flares in the MiG's face as he went by.

The Yemen aircraft came at the Megafortress at 550 knots, clearly not interested in riding alongside the American plane. This suited Mack perfectly, and he began climbing out ahead of the EB-52, ready to trade the height for speed when he wanted.

'*Hawk Two*, what the hell are you doing?' demanded Colonel Bastian.

'Just getting ready to say hello.'

'Stay out of my flight path. I have a job to do here.'

Grouch, thought Mack.

Aboard the *Abner Read*,
off the coast of Somalia
2015

'This looks a lot like those contacts we had the other night,' Starship told Eyes as he scrambled to follow the aircraft he'd just spotted. The slow-moving plane, about five miles north of Starship's Werewolf, was so low the sensors showed it on the surface of the water.

'Good, copy, we concur here. Track him.'

'Yeah, I'm on that.' Starship swung the Werewolf westward as the bandit continued to pick up speed. The image in the forward-looking infrared showed that the airplane had two engines set high behind the wing; it was small, almost surely a civilian aircraft. The threat file in the Werewolf's combat computer couldn't identify it.

Starship followed at about two miles, ratcheting his speed up as the strange aircraft continued to accelerate. Starship tucked his Werewolf downward, trying to get a better look at the underside of the craft. But the other plane was so low to the waves that he had a hard time; he kept jerking his hand involuntarily as the shadows changed on the screen. Finally he backed off his speed, dipping so close to the water that he nearly ditched.

'Definitely no weapons,' he told Tac. 'Looks like a civilian craft. Are you going to contact them?'

'Stand by,' said Eyes, his voice tense.

The distance between the two aircraft had widened to four miles. Starship began to climb and accelerate. As he did, the bandit veered to the east.

'He's climbing,' Starship told Tac.

'Werewolf, Indian destroyer *Calcutta* is reporting it's under fire. They've been torpedoed. Stand by to render assistance.'

'What do you want me to do with this aircraft?'

'He has no weapons?'

'Negative. Look, maybe he launched the torpedo.'

'Way too small for that. We'll hand him off to *Dreamland Wisconsin*. Get back over to the *Calcutta*. They need assistance.'

'Roger that,' said Starship, changing course.

Aboard the *Wisconsin*, over the Gulf of Aden 2015

Dog stayed on his course as the MiG-29 closed in behind him. If the plane showed any hostility – if it simply turned on the radar used to guide its missiles – he would shoot it down with the Stinger antiair mines in the *Wisconsin*'s tail. He'd do the same if the aircraft flew as if it would crash into him. But the pilot gave him a half-mile buffer, flying below and off his right wing, close enough to win some sort of bragging rights back home but not quite enough to justify an aggressive reaction.

Dog saw Mack adjusting course to make a pass at the MiG just as it cleared from the Megafortress. Mack cut things considerably closer than the MiG driver did, not only twisting the Flighthawk to within a hundred feet of the Yemen plane, but shooting flares as he did. His timing was a little off, but the other pilot, either confused or panicked, jerked hard to the north and dove a few seconds after the encounter.

Part of Dog thought the Yemen idiot had gotten what he deserved: most likely, a pair of speed pants that needed some serious laundering.

Another part of him was angry as hell at Mack for acting like a two-year-old.

'*Hawk Two*, get your nose back into formation.'

'Oh, roger that, Colonel,' said Mack, just about chortling. 'Did you see him?'

Luckily for Mack, the commo panel buzzed with an incoming transmission from the *Abner Read* on the encrypted Dreamland communications channel. As soon as Dog keyed in the communication, the face of Lt Commander Jack 'Eyes' Eisenberg appeared on the screen.

'Bastian, we have a possible submarine approximately two hundred miles south of us. It just launched an attack on an Indian destroyer. We'd like you to help locate it with your Piranha unit.'

'We're not carrying Piranha,' Dog told him. The undersea robot had not been ready when they took off, and it hadn't made sense to delay the patrol – facts that Dog had already explained. 'Piranha will be aboard the next plane out. We have sonar buoys – we can drop those.'

'Affirmative, good. Also, Werewolf has been following an aircraft just north of there. Airplane appears to be civilian but hasn't answered any hails. May be a smuggler. We'd like to find out what it's up to. Send one of your Flighthawks to pursue the aircraft.'

'Bit of a problem there, *Abner Read*,' responded Dog, doing his best to ignore the sailor's haughty tone. 'The Flighthawk has to stay within twenty miles of us. We can't be in both places at the same time.'

'I don't understand. How come the Werewolf can be so far from us?'

'The control and communications systems are different,' said Dog. 'Basically, the Flighthawks are considerably more difficult to fly and require a greater bandwidth than the Werewolf.'

They also represented an older generation of technology – much had changed in the three years since they began flying.

'All right. Stand by.' The line snapped clear.

'Dish, how close do we have to get to detect a periscope?' Dog asked the radar operator.

'Going to depend on too many factors to give you a guarantee,' Captain Peter Mallack answered. 'Specs say we should be able to nail him at fifteen miles, though. Of course, if he's on the surface –'

'What if he isn't using his periscope?'

'We won't find him without sonar buoys, or until Piranha's operating.'

'Thanks.'

'Bastian, what's your problem?' snarled Storm, appearing in the communications panel.

'Physics. I can't be in two places at one time,' said

Dog. 'I can look for the sub or inspect your unknown aircraft, but not both.'

'That's ridiculous – send one of your aircraft after this flight, and then get your butt down south and find this submarine. Drop your buoys. Jee-zus, Bastian. Since when do I have to tell you your job?'

Same old Storm, thought Dog, looking at the captain's red face.

'The Flighthawks were designed to stay close to the Megafortress,' said Dog, keeping his voice neutral. 'I don't like those limits myself, but we're stuck with them at the moment. Do you want me to follow the plane or to look for the submarine?'

Storm, apparently interrupted, glanced at someone else on the bridge.

'We can continue to track him with our radar,' added Dog. 'Out to about three hundred miles or so, maybe more depending on his altitude.'

Storm turned back to the screen and raised his hand. 'Hold on Bastian, hold on.'

'Hey, Colonel, I have the aircraft on the viewscreen,' said T-Bone over *Wisconsin*'s interphone. 'Computer can't ID it, but it's about the size of a Cessna. Two engines.'

'You think there's a possibility that plane launched a torpedo?'

'Doesn't look big enough. Hard to tell from here, but guessing from the size of the engines and given his speed, I doubt he could have taken off with it. You might have a better idea.'

'Doesn't look likely,' said Jazz, who'd brought up some of the data on his screen. 'If it's a smuggler, he might have been working with that tanker. Might be a seaplane.'

'I'm not positive it's a seaplane,' said T-Bone.

'Thanks. Stand by.'

He glanced at the video screen at the lower left of his control panel. Storm was still busy, so Dog used the circuit to talk to Starship. '*Wisconsin* to *Werewolf One*. Starship, this is Colonel Bastian. How are you?'

'Busy, Colonel; just coming up to the Indian destroyer now. But OK, sir.'

'Can you give us anything else on that aircraft? Was he aboard that tanker? Next to him? Had he been in the air and en route south?'

'Don't know on any of that, Colonel. I'm sorry.'

Starship broke to answer a communication from the destroyer; Dog heard him being directed to the starboard side of the ship, where the destroyer had several men in the water.

'All right, *Werewolf One*,' said Dog. 'Contact us when you get a chance.'

'Werewolf,' said Starship quickly.

'Bastian?'

'Yes, Storm. Go ahead.'

'Concentrate on the submarine. Where's the Piranha?'

'The aircraft carrying it will be taking off in about an hour.'

'Hurry it up. Get it over there ASAP.'

'Roger that.' Dog switched over to the interphone.

'T-Bone, continue to track that aircraft Werewolf was after. Update me every few minutes.'

Aboard the *Abner Read*,
off the coast of Somalia
2018

Starship could see the Indian destroyer listing heavily to its starboard side as he approached. The torpedo had exploded close to the hull, but either by deft maneuvering or good luck, the Indian warship had sustained only a glancing blow. That was still enough to do heavy damage, however, and the crew was working feverishly to block off sections of the ship that were being flooded.

The Werewolf's searchlights made small circles on the foaming waves near the crippled ship. A small boat had disembarked from the destroyer and was approaching the area. Starship dropped the robot aircraft into a hover, concentrating on illuminating the area near the boat.

The Indian ship radioed to ask that he move toward the bow of the destroyer. It took a few seconds for Starship to understand what the radioman was saying through his accent.

'Roger that. Moving toward bow.'

Large bits of debris floated near the ship. The Werewolf's search lamps caught a twisted pipe sticking out from the side of the ship, an obscene gesture directed back at whoever had attacked it.

Something bobbed at the far right of his screen, just

outside the area he was illuminating. He nudged the stick, moving the robot helo toward it and zooming his optical video feed to full magnification.

A head bobbed in his screen.

'*Calcutta*, I have something,' he told the destroyer. 'Have the boat follow my beam.'

He waited anxiously, lights trained on the seaman. The boat reacted in slow motion. Starship lost sight of the man for a second and started shouting. 'Get over there, damn it! Get over there! Get him before he drowns! Come on! *Come on!*'

As the prow of the rescue boat came into view, the head bobbed back up. Starship saw someone in the boat reaching with a pole, but the man in the water didn't take it. The boat got closer; one of the sailors leaned out toward the stricken man. Starship kept the Werewolf steady, trying to stay close enough to give them plenty of light but not wipe them out with the wash of the rotors.

The man in the boat grabbed the stricken sailor by the back of the shoulders. He hauled him into the boat.

Starship's eyes were glued to the screen. He saw the head coming out of the water, and then the arms and the top of the man's back – and nothing else.

The man had been severed in two by the explosion.

Bile ran up Starship's throat. He threw his hand over his mouth but it was too late; some of the acid spurted out over his shirt. Eyes tearing, he tried choking it back down, struggling with his other hand to control the Werewolf.

* * *

109

Storm paced the bridge, anxious to get his ship south. The *Abner Read* was built for stealth, not speed; still, she could touch forty knots, a good speed for a small craft.

Right now she was doing 38 knots. Even if they held that speed, it would take roughly five hours to reach the destroyer.

'I'm going out for some air,' he told the others. Then he walked out onto the flying bridge at the side.

No more than a platform that could be folded into the superstructure, the design of the flying bridge had been carefully calculated to have minimal impact on the *Abner Read*'s radar signature. Not only was it the highest point on the low-slung ship, but it was one of the few dry and flat surfaces outside. The main deck sloped down and was often lapped with waves.

The salty breeze bit Storm's cheeks. The wind was coming up and he felt a chill. But it was a good chill, the sort of wind that reminded him why he'd wanted to join the Navy in the first place.

The aircraft the Werewolf had seen near the oil tanker bothered him. It seemed similar to the ones they'd spotted the night Port Somalia was struck. If it had been a little bigger, he supposed, it might have launched the torpedo itself.

Maybe it was working with the submarine that made the actual attack. Or maybe the tanker.

There'd been a tanker nearby when he lost the other submarine as well. This was a different ship, but the parallels had to be more than a coincidence.

Didn't they?

The submarine might be the same vessel he had chased the other night, able to hide along the coast because its clever captain knew the waters so well. A Chinese Kilo, maybe.

But then what was the aircraft doing? Was it Chinese as well?

Storm decided the submarine was the key to the mystery. He would find it and then – since he couldn't attack – he'd give the exact location to the captain of the Indian destroyer, who no doubt would be anxious for revenge.

Assuming his ship didn't sink before then.

Storm allowed himself one more deep, luxurious breath of air, then went back inside.

**Aboard the *Wisconsin*,
over the Gulf of Aden
2045**

Dog nudged the Megafortress into position to launch the first sonar buoy twenty miles north of the stricken destroyer. The Megafortress would set a large underwater fence around the area, waiting for the sub to make its move.

'What's the destroyer's situation?' Dog asked Jazz.

'Nothing new,' said the copilot. 'Still fighting the damage. They've had a couple of sonar contacts but they seem to have been false alarms.'

As Dog and Jazz launched the buoys, Dish searched

for the submarine's periscope. A half hour later they had covered every inch of the target area without finding anything.

'Best bet, he's sitting down about three hundred meters, just about as low as he can go, holding his breath and waiting for the destroyer to limp away,' said Jazz.

'He'll be waiting a long time.'

'He won't get by the buoys without us knowing.'

Dog wasn't so sure about that. In theory, the hunters had all the advantages – the buoys could find anything in the water down to about 550 meters or so, and an extended periscope or snorkel could be easily detected at this range.

But the reality of warfare was never quite as simple as the theory, especially when it involved a submarine. Dog had worked with the Navy on sub hunts before, and they were always complicated and tricky affairs. In NATO exercises, submarines routinely outfoxed their hunters.

'Just a waiting game now, Colonel,' said the copilot. 'We'll get him eventually. We just have to be patient.'

'For some reason, Jazz, being patient has always seemed the hardest thing to do,' Dog said.

Approaching Oman on the Saudi Peninsula
2145

Captain Sattari felt the sweat rolling down his arms and neck. His clothes were so damp it seemed he'd been out in the rain. He was cold, and in truth was afraid, sure that he was being tracked by a powerful American surveillance radar, positive that some unseen fighters were scrambling along behind him to take him down. Every bit of turbulence, every vague eddy of air, sent a new shiver down his spine. He had the engines at maximum power; the airspeed indicator claimed he was doing 389 knots, which if true was at least thirty miles an hour faster than the engineers who made the plane had said was possible. But it was not nearly fast enough.

'We're at the way point,' said his copilot.

'Yes,' said Sattari, and he moved his aircraft to the new course. Oman loomed fifteen miles ahead.

If I can make it to the twelve-mile limit, he told himself, *then I will be OK*. In the worst case, if the Americans pressured the emir, they could blend in with the civilian government and escape.

Sattari scolded himself for thinking like a defeatist, like a refugee. He tightened his grip on the plane's wheel, flying. The surveillance plane must be far away, or surely it would have tried to contact him by now.

Unless it was vectoring fighters to intercept him. Or planning to alert the authorities on shore.

Oman was not as friendly toward the Americans as it once had been, and was unlikely to cooperate. Still . . .

'Two minutes to the landing, Captain,' said his co-pilot finally.

The radar warning receiver switched off. They were

no longer being watched – or was it a trick to make him think that?

Even when he saw that the landing area was empty, Sattari was not convinced he wasn't being followed. He taxied to the dock, then turned the plane around to make it easier for his copilot to get out and handle the refueling.

'Hurry,' he told the copilot as he feathered his propellers. 'I wish to take off as soon as possible.'

'Is that wise? Shouldn't we wait a day or two?'

'No. If we are no longer being followed, it is best to leave right away. And if we are being followed, there is no sense delaying the inevitable.'

Aboard the *Abner Read*,
off the coast of Somalia
9 January 1998
0111

Storm studied the Indian destroyer with his night glasses, examining the damaged ship from about a quarter of a mile away. The *Calcutta* listed six degrees to starboard – a serious lean, as Airforce put it when he described the situation earlier. But the damage had been contained. The Indian ship no longer appeared in danger of going to the bottom. More than twenty of her men had been killed or were still missing, another thirty or so injured.

With a crew of forty officers and 320 enlisted, the

114

Calcutta displaced 5,400 tons, a good 1,200 less than a member of the U.S. Navy's Arleigh Burke Block I class, a rough contemporary. The Indian ship was a member of the Delhi class, a guided missile destroyer that used both Russian and western components and weapons system. A 100-millimeter gun sat on her forward deck just about where the torpedo had exploded. The anti-submarine torpedo battery aft of the gun had caught fire immediately after the strike and now sat charred and mangled at the side, a cat's claw of burnt metal. Storm guessed that the Indians' own weapons had caused many of the causalities.

'Corpsmen are ready to disembark,' said the crewman in the *Abner Read*'s fantail 'garage.'

'Proceed,' said Storm.

A panel in the well of the ship's forked tail opened and a rigid-hulled inflatable boat sailed out and sped toward the stricken destroyer, carrying medicine and two corpsmen to help the Indians. Once the men were safely aboard, the *Abner Read* would head eastward after the Pakistani oil tanker, which was now about fifty miles away.

Unless he could spot the submarine first.

'Eyes, what's the status of our treasure hunt?'

'Nothing, Storm. Submarine is nowhere to be found.'

'What about Piranha?'

'It's been in the water two hours now without a contact.'

Impossible, thought Storm. *Impossible!*

He thought of punching the bulkhead in frustration. Then, realizing he was only thinking about it, he smiled at himself. He had changed in the past few months.

'Keep on with the search,' he told Eyes. 'Tell the Dreamland aircraft controlling Piranha that we'll be heading for that oil tanker within a few minutes.'

Las Vegas University of Medicine,
Las Vegas, Nevada
1530

Zen rolled himself off the elevator into the lobby and saw his taxi waiting outside. He was glad: Despite the fact that he'd spent the day doing almost absolutely nothing, he felt exhausted.

The needles were already routine, as were the monitors, scans, and tepid herbal tea offered up by Dr Vasin's interns in place of their overheated coffee. The light exercises they gave him to do with dumbbells were a bare shadow of his normal daily routine. So why was he so tired?

Partly because he wasn't sleeping. He missed Breanna, and found it difficult to sleep without her.

And he continued to have the dream. It distracted and annoyed him, kept him guessing what it was really about. Better that, though, than worrying about whether the experiments were actually going to do anything. So far, he felt exactly the same.

'I'll get the door for you, sir,' said a young man, trotting ahead as he came down the hall.

Zen stopped. The kid was just being polite, but his goofy smile irked him. Zen forced a gruff 'Thank you' as he rolled past.

Aboard the *Islam Oil Princess*,
in the Arabian Sea
0350

A light spray of seawater wet Storm's face as the rigid-hulled inflatable drew close to the Pakistani oil tanker. The first boat had already deposited most of the shipboard integrated tactical team, and the SITT members were fanning out above.

The tanker's crew and its captain were cooperating, but Storm wasn't taking any chances. The Werewolf, with Starship at the controls, hovered overhead. The aircraft's floodlights made it look like one of the riders of the Apocalypse, the gun at its nose a black sword as it circled menacingly around the forecastle.

Storm had decided he would go aboard personally, partly as a gesture of respect to the other captain, and partly to show him how seriously they were taking the matter.

'Secure, sir,' said the ensign in charge of the landing team, speaking over their short-range communications system.

'Very good,' said Storm. He'd exchanged his shipboard headset for a tactical unit, which had an earset and a mike clipped to his collar. He didn't bother with the helmet most of the boarding party wore, though he did have a flak vest on. 'I'll be aboard shortly.'

Storm checked back with Eyes as he waited for the boat to draw alongside the tanker.

'No sign of the submarine at all,' Eyes said. 'Piranha

has gone to silent mode, just waiting. If it's nearby, she'll hear it when it moves out.'

'Keep me informed. Storm out.'

The petty officer who headed the boarding team in Storm's boat leapt at the chain ladder on the side of the tanker as they drew near. He pulled himself up two rungs at a time, leading his team to the deck.

This is the way my crew operates, Storm thought, following. A seaman from the *Abner Read* met him at the rail and helped him over, then led him up to the tanker's captain, waiting with Storm's ensign on the bridge.

At nearly seven feet tall, the captain towered over Storm. A rail of a man, he gripped Storm's hand firmly when they were introduced.

'You were near the Indian destroyer when it was struck by a torpedo,' said Storm, dispensing with the preliminaries. 'Why didn't you stop?'

'They did not ask for our assistance.' The Pakistani's English was good, his accent thin and readily understandable.

'You saw the submarine?' asked Storm.

'No. We did not understand what happened. It was only your man here who told me that the ship had been fired on. From our viewpoint, we thought they were simply testing their weapons. The explosion was in the water.'

'Perhaps we could speak in private, Captain,' suggested Storm.

'As you wish.'

The tanker captain led him off the bridge, down a short flight of stairs to a small cabin nearby. A desk sat opposite a bunk at least a foot too short for its owner; the space in between was barely enough for two chairs.

'Drink?' asked the Pakistani. He produced a bottle of scotch from the drawer of the desk

'No, thank you,' said Storm.

'Then I won't either,' said the other captain. He smiled and put the bottle back.

'The Indian destroyer was hit by a torpedo. I'm sure it made quite an explosion.'

'We were a few miles away.' The captain spoke softly, and it was not possible to tell if he was lying or not. It seemed unlikely to Storm that he didn't realize what had happened, though if he had no experience with warfare, he might have been confused at first. 'The Indians do not generally regard ships flying the Pakistani flag as friends,' added the man. 'They did not ask us for assistance.'

'Would you have stopped if they did?'

'Absolutely.' The captain leaned back in his chair. 'Who fired the torpedo?'

'Possibly a submarine. Though it would have been possible for you to fire it as well.'

The captain jerked upright. 'Impossible.'

'Not necessarily.'

'Search my ship.'

'I intend to.'

The Pakistani captain frowned. 'The Indians no doubt

119

accused us. Probably they invented the submarine, and the torpedo. A hoax to cover their own incompetence. I would not be surprised if they blew up themselves by accident.'

'There was an aircraft in the area,' said Storm. 'It was spotted after the attack. Did you see it?'

'I don't recall.'

'What was he smuggling?'

'I don't know what you mean.'

'Come on, Captain. Don't make me order my men to tear your ship apart piece by piece. Was the airplane picking up medicine? Or was it delivering something?'

The Pakistani wore a pained expression.

'I know that many ship captains are poorly paid,' said Storm. 'In this region, one earns what one can.'

'I am not a smuggler, Captain.'

'Fine. We will search your ship.'

'You have the guns. Do as you will.'

Storm, frustrated but determined, got up. He paused at the doorway. 'Information about the submarine would be very helpful.'

'If I had any to give, I would.'

'Search the ship,' Storm told his ensign on the bridge.

'We've already gone over the deck, Captain. We haven't found any sign that they fired a torpedo, no launch tube, no sign of bolts or anything where it could have been mounted.'

'All right. Keep looking. Find out what they smuggle. They must do more than run oil over to Pakistan. I want a full inventory, down to the last toothpick.'

Dog undid his restraints and squeezed out from behind the stick of the Megafortress, taking a moment to stretch his legs before they began the trek back to their base. It had been a frustrating sortie. Not only had they failed to locate the submarine, but Major Smith proved himself an extremely annoying Flighthawk pilot, refusing to let the computer handle the robot during refuelings. The procedure was notoriously difficult; the Megafortress's large and irregular shape left a great deal of turbulence immediately behind and below it, and even Zen occasionally had trouble making the connection. For that reason, the routine had been hard-wired into both the Megafortress's flight control computer and C³, which directed the U/MFs. But Mack insisted on trying it himself – even though it took no less than five approaches for him to get in. Dog found himself becoming so short-tempered that he nearly let Jazz take the stick.

Mack and Storm. Between them, he was going to end up in an insane asylum.

Dog walked to the end of the flight deck, where a small galley complete with a refrigerator and a microwave had been installed. He ducked down to the fridge and found a small milk container, then reached into a nearby cabinet for a pack of oatmeal cookies. The techies complained about the crumbs, but there was something comforting about the old-fashioned snack, especially when you were having it aboard one of the most advanced warplanes in the world.

'Captain Gale for you, Colonel,' said Jazz.

Dog sighed and flipped on the communications unit at the auxiliary station next to one of the radars where Dish was working.

'Bastian here.'

'You have anything new?'

'Negative, Storm. I'd surely have told you if I did.'

'We just finished turning that tanker inside out. Nothing.' Storm squinted toward the camera. 'I think it has to be some sort of Chinese sub.'

'Why Chinese?'

'They hate the Indians. I'm going to return to the Indian destroyer. They have the damage under control. They're heading back east at sunrise. There's an Indian task group supposedly setting sail. I assume they'll meet up.'

'All right.'

'Tell your people – this task force is headed by a small battle carrier. It's a combination aircraft carrier and missile ship. It used to belong to the Russians. The Indians have fixed it up considerably. We'll have a full briefing for you. They have an air arm aboard – a dozen Su-33 Sukhois.'

'We can handle them.'

'Don't shoot them down,' said Storm quickly. 'I know you people are light on the trigger.'

'Anything else?'

'That's it.'

'We're going off station in a few minutes. *Levitow* will continue controlling Piranha.'

'Good,' said Storm, his sharp tone suggesting the opposite as the communication screen blanked.

Dog straightened. He glanced over Dish's shoulder. The sergeant was busy fine-tuning the large screen in front of him, which showed that there were two ships, a cargo container carrier and a garbage scow, sailing twenty miles to their south.

On the other side of the aisle, T-Bone was tracking a pair of civilian airliners heading toward India, and a cargo craft flying south along the African coast. Except for their Flighthawks and the *Levitow*, the sky in their immediate vicinity was clear.

'Say, T-Bone, can you give me more information about that civilian plane we tracked?' Dog asked. 'The one that was near the oil tanker.'

'Don't have that much to give you, Colonel.' T-Bone reached to a set of switches at the right of his console, fingers tapping quickly over the elongated keyboard. A radar plot appeared on the auxiliary screen to the right of T-Bone's station.

'This is the first solid long-distance contact we had.' T-Bone's fingers danced again. A new image appeared, showing Dog an enhanced radar view. T-Bone did a double tap on the lower keyboard at his right. A window opened on the screen.

'This is the spec screen where the computer – and me – tried to figure out what the hell it was,' explained the sergeant. The computer used the radar return to analyze the aircraft's structure, identifying its type and capabilities. Depending on the range, it could also identify weapons the plane carried, which could also be done by analyzing the radars emanating from the plane. Knowing an enemy plane's type and capabilities before engaging it was an enormous advantage, and much of the work that went into perfecting the Dreamland radar system had been aimed at doing that. The onboard computer library had data on nearly everything that had ever flown, right back to the Army's Wright Model A.

'No hit in the library, see?' said T-Bone, pointing to the screen. 'Light aircraft, civilian type, two engines far back on the fuselage. Looks like a small seaplane, with the engines up there to stay out of the spray. Hull is boat-shaped.'

'Definitely makes sense,' said Dog. 'Why wouldn't we have seen him earlier?'

'Two possibilities. One, he was outside our range, flying in from the east. Two, he was on the surface of the water, probably at that oil tanker. If he's a smuggler –'

'Far south for that.'

'Maybe they're changing tactics because the *Abner Read* has done such a good job farther north.'

'Maybe.'

It wasn't that he didn't think Storm was doing a good job; clearly they were missing something.

'Get Dreamland Control. Send this information back. I want Dr Rubeo to get some of his people on this. I want to know what type of aircraft this is, what's it's capable of. Dish . . .'

'Yes, sir,' said the sergeant, turning around.

'Get as much data as you can on the torpedo that

damaged the Indian ship. Size, that sort of thing. Give that to Dreamland Command as well. I think this little aircraft is more of a problem than we know.'

III

Be Boarded, or Be Sunk

Aboard the *Shiva*,
in the Indian Ocean
10 January 1998
0800

Anil Memon zipped his windbreaker as he stepped out onto the observation deck of the *Shiva*. India's deputy defense minister immediately grabbed for the railing, thrown off balance not by the rolling of the ship but the roar of one of her Su-33s charging off the ramped runway below. The warplane lurched into the sky, her left wing bucking down for a brief moment before the thrust from her two massive engines muscled her upward.

'An impressive site, Mr Memon, is it not?' said the commander of the *Shiva,* Admiral Kala. A short, slight man, he did not weigh much more than 120 pounds, but he was one of the most respected commanders in the navy. 'When we have five more ships like this, no one will challenge India's greatness, not even the Americans.'

Memon smiled. To get five more ships such as the *Shiva* would not be easy.

He turned his attention back to the sea, scanning the

surface for the wounded destroyer *Calcutta*. One of the lookouts had said it was just visible on the horizon, but even with his powerful binoculars he couldn't see it.

'It's to port, ten degrees,' said the admiral, guessing what he was looking for.

Memon adjusted his view and saw the mast.

'I was aboard the *Calcutta* last year,' Memon said. 'I can't imagine she was struck by a torpedo from a submarine. She would have heard the vessel before the attack.'

'We will know the answer soon.'

A sailor appeared behind them, his uniform so crisp that a scent of starch filled the air.

'Admiral Kala, communication with the American ship has been established.'

'Very good. Deputy Minister Memon, will you join me?'

Memon followed the admiral back into the superstructure of the ship. Allowing for the metal walls and the pipes, the interior of the *Shiva* seemed more like the inside of a large office complex than that of a ship. The halls still smelled of fresh paint, and even the decking had a glow to it.

The ship had three different secure communications suites. The one the sailor led Admiral Kala and Memon to looked like a television studio, and had a special copper-enclosed booth at the side where top-secret conferences could be held without fear of anyone aboard eavesdropping.

Admiral Kala pointed to a phonelike handset below one of the screens at the left side of the space, then picked up the one next to it.

'This is Admiral Kala, the commander of the Indian aircraft carrier *Shiva*. To whom am I speaking?'

'Captain Gale, of the USS *Abner Read*. What can I do for you, Admiral?'

'We thank you and your crew for rendering assistance to the *Calcutta*,' said Kala. 'Her captain told me personally of your aid.'

'Right.'

'I have been given to understand that you tracked and stopped a Pakistani vessel that had been in the vicinity.'

'Damn straight. My people searched it stem to stern. We found nothing. Anything else I can do for you?'

'This is the deputy defense minister,' Memon said into his headset. 'It has not escaped my notice that the United States not only had a warship in the area, but an aircraft as well.'

'The *Abner Read* was nearly two hundred miles away. What's your point?'

'You had a helicopter close enough to launch the torpedo,' said Admiral Kala.

'You know what, Admiral? I'm a little busy right now. Maybe you should take your inquiries through diplomatic channels.'

'Captain –'

'Frankly, sir, I don't know you from Adam. And I'm not going to listen to slander.'

The line went dead.

Memon felt his cheeks burning. But the insult did not appear to have registered on the admiral's face.

'We should inspect the tanker ourselves,' suggested

Memon. 'It would not be impossible to mount a torpedo tube on its deck, camouflaging it in some way. Or perhaps arranging so it could be fired from below the waterline. I don't trust the Americans.'

The admiral walked silently to the carrier's combat control center, a level below the bridge at the center of the island superstructure. Memon followed, still seething – the American should have been put in his place. It was true that the *Calcutta* did not believe the Americans had been involved in the attack, but his question had been a natural one.

The *Shiva*'s position as well as that of its aircraft and the different vessels around them were tracked on a large plexiglass display at one side of the combat center. The admiral consulted the display and then the charts on the nearby map table as Captain Adri, the ship's navigation officer, and Captain Bhaskar, the executive officer, looked on.

'The tanker is sailing toward Karachi,' said Admiral Kala, tracing its course. 'We can intercept it fifty miles from Pakistani coastal waters, if we change course within the hour.'

'That will mean leaving the *Calcutta* to wait for the oceangoing tug,' said Adri, glancing at his charts. 'It will be another twenty-four hours at least.'

'We should search them ourselves,' said Memon, folding his arms.

'Captain, in my opinion we should not,' said the executive officer. 'The Americans have already done so.'

'Change course, Mr Adri,' said Admiral Kala. 'I will inform the *Calcutta*.'

Cantor steadied the pool cue against his fingers, pulling it back and forth as he lined up the shot at the far end of the table. He had to hit the cue ball straight and hard.

Not a problem. He'd just think of it as Major Mack Smith's head.

'Eight ball in the corner,' he told Jan Stewart, watching from the nearby couch.

'Never.'

Thwack! The ball flew down the table. The eight ball jammed hard against the cushion at the side of the hole and dropped straight down. The cue ball rebounded off the nearby rail and sailed back to him.

'You've been practicing,' said Stewart, getting up.

'Just found the proper motivation.'

'Yeah. I've been thinking the cue ball is Captain Stockard, but it doesn't seem to help. Another game?'

Cantor glanced at the clock on the wall of the large room.

'Yeah, OK. Rack 'em up. Then I'm going to have to check with the maintainers and make sure the Flighthawks are all ready to rock. I have to preflight in an hour or so.'

'Chief Parsons will make sure the planes are ready.'

'Yeah, but if I don't let him growl at me, he'll be in a bad mood the rest of the day,' said Cantor, applying some chalk to the tip of his cue.

'Isn't that Mack's job?'

133

'The chief said that if Mack bothers him one more time, he'll hold me personally responsible.'

' 'Nuff said.'

The Dreamland contingent had been given a pair of buildings once used by a Pakistani fighter wing at the far end of the sprawling complex. The aircraft they flew might have been old – the wall opposite the clock had a logo for the Shenyang F-6, which had all but been phased out of active service years before – but their facilities were top-rate, including the rec room that the Dreamland team had adapted as an informal squadron ready room, office, and general hangout. Besides the pool table, there were two foosball tables and a Ping-Pong setup. Beyond the briefing area sat a full kitchen with electric appliances, including two large refrigerators.

'Who's bothering who, Cantor?' said Mack, striding into the ready room. His timing was perfect: He distracted Stewart so badly that she sent the white ball curling off to the side; she barely missed scratching and hardly dented the triangle of pool balls.

'Nobody, Major.' Cantor eyed the table. The break was so poor it hadn't left him any shots. 'Fourteen, I guess, corner pocket.'

'You're up in two hours,' said Mack.

Cantor narrowed his eyes until he saw only the cue ball. He rapped the ball so hard it flew at the fourteen, which fell into the pocket with a resounding thud. As an extra bonus, his cue ball bounced the twelve into the opposite corner.

'Nice shot, junior,' said Mack.

'You got something you need me to do, Major?'

'No, I'm just making sure you're ready to go.'

'I read the schedule.' Cantor called the eleven in the side. This time he hit it so hard it rebounded off the pocket – and sank into the opposite pocket.

'Which side did you call?' Stewart asked.

'No, your shot.'

'Guts is sick, so I'm going in *Levitow*,' added Mack. 'I'm going to tell Breanna to load two Flighthawks on the plane.'

Cantor knew he should keep his mouth shut. After all, not having Major Mack Smith sitting next to him for eight or ten hours was more than he could wish for. But he couldn't help himself.

'I don't think you can take two planes, Major. In all honesty, one – I mean, no disrespect but –'

'What are trying to say, junior?' Mack slammed the refrigerator door.

'I just think you could use a little more practice.'

'Listen, kid, I've been flying since you were in grammar school.'

'But not the Flighthawk.'

Mack threw one of the desk chairs out his way and stormed across the room. Cantor was sure for a moment that the other pilot was going to hit him. It wouldn't be a fair fight – Mack had nearly a foot on him and possibly fifty pounds – but he was so angry at the other pilot that he actually started to relish hitting him.

'You telling me I don't know how to handle them?' demanded Mack.

'You can't do two. No.'

'You better go check on your aircraft, kid. I got stuff I have to do.'

Cantor bit down on the inside of his cheek. He wanted to punch him – he really did.

It wasn't the size advantage that held him back. Mack was a major, and he was a lieutenant. Throwing the first punch would pretty much guarantee he was gone from Dreamland.

Throwing the second punch would be a different story.

They stared at each other. Then Mack snorted in contempt and walked out of the room.

'Whoa,' said Stewart on the other side of the table.

'Yeah,' said Cantor. 'I wish he'd taken a swing.'

Colonel Bastian shifted in his seat in front of the secure video screen, listening as Ray Rubeo described what the Dreamland scientists had done with the radar intercepts of the aircraft.

'The design appears similar to a number of studies conducted by the Beriev company in Russia,' continued Rubeo, Dreamland's head scientist. 'Approximately thirty-five feet long with a wingspan of forty-two feet. Notice the wing shape – here in this slide we superimpose the print from the Beriev design documents onto the image generated from the intercept. And, of course, the engines are in the same location.'

'But this was just a study,' said Dog. 'No planes were built.'

'No planes were sold or registered anywhere that we could find through simple checks. But that doesn't mean no planes were built.'

'How can we find out if there were any? Can we call the CIA?'

Deep dimples appeared in Rubeo's cheeks.

'Yes,' he said. 'I asked Major Catsman to try that. They say they're researching it. In the meantime, I took the liberty of having one of our technicians who speaks Russian contact the company.'

'And?'

'I can give you a very good deal on one, Colonel. Less than half a million dollars.'

'Could it carry a torpedo?'

'The problem is not so much whether it *could* carry one, for certainly it could.' Rubeo sighed, as if he were a college professor working a particularly dull class through a complicated calculus solution at the end of a long day. 'Assume a Russian surface torpedo at 7.2 meters – a bit over twenty-one feet. It will sit awkwardly below the fuselage but nonetheless may be carriaged there. A smaller torpedo – the French-built L5, for example, at roughly fourteen feet – still awkward but doable. In terms of balance, the longer Russian design is actually easier to accommodate –'

'But the problem is weight,' said Dog. 'With those engines, that small a plane won't be able to fly with the extra weight? Or at least not take off.'

'Precisely.'

'How far could the plane go on the surface?'

Something foreign creaked into the corner of Rubeo's mouth – a smile.

'Very far, Colonel. Several hundred miles.'

'So he's the culprit.'

'No, I didn't say that, Colonel. Scientifically –'

'That's all right, Ray, we're not trying to prove the Theory of Relativity here. We need to get a list of where these planes have been sold.'

'I put the question to Jed Barclay at the NSC. He said that he would have to work with the State Department, but would provide us with information before the end of the day.'

'You know, Ray, you're almost becoming human.'

'I take it that was a joke, Colonel?'

'Along those lines,' said Dog. 'Keep me updated.'

He was alone in the Dreamland Security trailer, which was parked between the two buildings they were using at the base and the parking area for the Megafortresses and Flighthawks. His legs felt a little stiff – he hadn't had a chance to take his customary morning run, and in fact hadn't in several days now. He glanced at his watch, considering whether he had enough time to do a circuit around the buildings before preflighting his next sortie. He decided he did, but before he could head into the small room at the back of the trailer and grab his sweats, there was a sharp rap at the door.

'Come!' he yelled.

Lieutenant Cantor burst through the door as if he were running from a mob.

'What's up, Cantor?' Dog asked him.

'Colonel, I gotta talk to you. I really gotta talk to you.'

'Seat.' Dog pointed. 'Sit.'

Cantor pulled out a chair. 'Colonel – it's Major Smith.'

'I know he's pain in the ass,' said Dog. 'But his post is only temporary. When we get back –'

'That's not it, Colonel. I just don't think he's ready to fly the Flighthawks on his own. Not two.'

'Listen, Cantor, Mack has worked with the program before. He's just rusty.'

'He hasn't flown in combat. He can't handle two planes. He'll get his ass kicked. Not that I wouldn't,' added Cantor.

'Lieutenant, I don't particularly like Mack Smith. But he was shooting down MiGs before you joined the Air Force.'

'In planes. That's the problem, Colonel. He's flying the Flighthawk as if he were flying an F-15 Eagle, or maybe an F-16.'

'Mack's a cowboy, I'll give you that,' Dog told the lieutenant. 'Most days I wonder how he manages to fit his head into a helmet. But . . .'

Dog paused. He realized that he was reacting defensively, partly in reaction to a decision he had made – putting Mack in temporary charge of the Flighthawk program – and partly to a much lower ranking officer questioning the competence of a superior officer. But Cantor was not being disrespectful or insubordinate. His only offense was the fact that he wore a lieutenant's single bar.

And that Cantor took his policy of inviting 'open discussion on any topic whatsoever' seriously.

'I understand your concerns,' said Dog. 'I think they're serious, and I think you've presented them in the proper manner. They're now my concerns. OK?'

'Yes, sir.'

'Fair enough. We ready to fly?'

'We will be, Colonel.'

'Good.'

Cantor nodded, then got up and left. Watching him, Dog worried that he'd come off as too patronizing. He'd meant everything he said, but now that it was out of his mouth, it seemed a little phony-baloney.

For the first time since they deployed, he wished Zen were there.

Las Vegas University of Medicine,
Las Vegas, Nevada
1700

The dream was exactly the same. The only difference was that Zen started shouting as soon as he smelled the smoke.

When he finally managed to escape from semiconsciousness, Zen found himself surrounded by doctors and nurses on the table used to measure the nerve impulses. He looked up at a sea of anxious faces.

'Hello,' he said bashfully. 'I guess I was dreaming.'

'Jeffrey, are you all right?' asked Dr Vasin.

'Oh, yeah. I'm fine.'

Vasin looked skeptical, but merely nodded, then left the room. The others began poking and prodding. When they were done, a male aide came and helped Zen dress.

'Dr Vasin wants to talk to you in his office,' said the aide as he helped Zen slide into his wheelchair.

Zen wheeled himself down the hall to the doctor's office.

'Come in, come in,' said Vasin, still wearing his concerned grimace. 'How are you feeling?'

'Bored, actually.'

'Bored?'

'Yeah. I'm not used to lying around all day. I'm sorry I fell asleep.'

'It is good that you were so relaxed.' Vasin raised his head, but kept his eyes fixed on Zen, as if he were looking at him through the bottom half of a pair of bifocals. 'Can you tell me about your nightmare?'

'Ah, it was nothing.'

'Please.'

Reluctantly, Zen gave him a quick summary, adding that the dream recurred often.

'Like this?' asked Vasin.

'The part with my wife and the fire is different. A little. It started a few days ago.'

'You're worrying about your wife?'

'Not really.'

He realized it was a lie as the words left his mouth. Breanna wasn't the sort of woman you worried about.

And she'd certainly proven that she could take care of herself. So why was he worried?

'Yeah, maybe I am. A little.'

'Are you concerned about walking?' asked Vasin.

'Sure.'

The answer seemed to mollify the doctor – but only for a moment.

'Have you spoken to Dr Hamm?' asked Vasin.

'The shrink? Just during the evaluations last week.'

Vasin grimaced at the word 'shrink.' Hamm was a psychologist with a wall of certificates. They'd talked about the obvious: whether Zen wanted to walk again or not.

Duh.

'If you feel the need to discuss things, sometimes a specialist will assist you in placing things into context,' said Vasin.

'OK, thanks,' said Zen. He backed away half a turn of the wheels, then stopped. 'Any reprieve on coffee and beer?'

'No caffeine or alcohol. You feel the need?'

'Just checking,' said Zen turning to go.

Drigh Road
2200

'No, Mack, my point is *not* that I don't want you to fly. Nor am I relieving you of your assignment.' Dog jabbed his finger in the air as he spoke, underlining each point. 'My point is, only two people have been able to handle two Flighthawks at a time in combat – Zen and Starship. In both cases they flew the aircraft in combat for considerable time before handling two.'

'There's always a first time.'

Dog could practically see the steam coming off Mack's head. 'I don't want you launching two planes.'

'So what the hell are we supposed to do? Leave one home? That's bullshit, Colonel. What if one goes down?'

'You bring both. You keep one in reserve. Got it?'

'Yes, sir.' His tone would have made a drill sergeant proud.

'Good,' said Dog, matching it.

Somehow it seemed easier to deal with people when they were being unreasonable, Dog decided as he walked over to his aircraft.

An hour later Dog contacted Storm, tested his theory and found it wanting. Explaining to the captain what he thought had happened was more frustrating than talking to a wall.

'It's that airplane, and the others that you saw like it, that we have to look for,' said Dog. 'They're the key to this. Not a submarine. The submarine doesn't exist.'

'Just because you didn't see it doesn't mean it doesn't exist, Bastian.'

'I didn't see it, the Indian destroyer didn't see it, and most importantly, you didn't see it. You're telling me the *Abner Read* would have lost a Kilo. I just can't believe it.'

The backhanded compliment mollified Storm slightly. His tone softened infinitesimally as he continued.

'I could see those aircraft unloading guerrillas for the attack on Port Somalia,' Storm told Dog. 'But not carrying a torpedo for hundreds of miles. We don't even know where they flew from.'

'Yemen. Iran. Iraq. Somalia. We reposition the Mega-fortress patrol areas to watch those coastlines. They'll show up again.'

'And in the meantime, I don't have any air cover, and I can't use Piranha. Because you can't be in two places at the same time,' added Storm, sarcastically referring to the mission the other night.

'You have the Werewolves. And my pilot.'

'What about Piranha? We can't run that from the ship.'

Not only did they not have the control unit, but Piranha had to be within fifty miles of one of its control buoys to feed data, so that even if the *Abner Read* did have one, the robot would be of limited value.

'We'll put the probe into autonomous sleep mode until we need her again,' suggested Dog. 'We'll park her out there.'

'We still need her now. We need to find that submarine.'

'Storm, you're obsessing about a submarine that's not there.'

'You don't understand submarine warfare, Bastian. This is what happens when you deal with a good sub and crew. You're never really sure they even exist.'

'You have to agree the plane is suspicious.'

144

'Find it, then – but keep Piranha in operation on the search grids my people direct.'

Dog killed the link before he said something he would regret.

Aboard the Shiva,
in the northern Arabian Sea
11 January 1998
0400

The Pakistani tanker was twenty miles away, too far to be seen with even the best pair of binoculars. But in the *Shiva*'s combat control center, the tanker could be viewed from every conceivable angle, thanks to the two Sukhoi fighters and a helicopter flying near the tanker. The helicopter sent back live infrared video, which was displayed on a large television at the front of the combat control center.

To Memon, the combat center looked overwhelmingly chaotic and sounded even worse, with officers and enlisted personnel nearly shouting in an undecipherable patois. But he realized the tumult was actually highly organized, and that the singing voices were a sign that things were going well. The sound one did not want to hear as action approached, the admiral said, was silence.

'When will we attack?' Memon asked Captain Bhaskar, the ship's executive officer.

'I'm afraid I don't have time for your questions, Mr Memon. I have work here.'

He turned and walked toward the radar section, Memon's eyes burning a hole in his back.

'The marines will take off in twenty minutes,' said a lieutenant who was standing nearby. He was tasked to maintain communications with the ship boarding team; Memon could not remember his first name but resolved to find a way to help him in the future. 'Two Sea King helicopters. We'll see their positions on this screen here. They will be accompanied by a Mk42B with Sea Eagle missiles.'

The Mk42B was a special version of the Sea King helicopter equipped with antiship missiles and special search radar. All of the Sea Kings were variants of the Sikorsky SH-3 built by Westland; in America, the originals were known as Sea Kings, with an Air Force version called the Jolly Green Giant.

'When the aircraft are airborne,' continued the lieutenant, 'the admiral will give the tanker the order to stop and be boarded. The marines will secure the ship and the search will begin. The divers will arrive in a second wave, once the tanker is secured. No inch of the tanker will be left unexamined.'

'And if they launch a torpedo at us in the meantime?'

'We will be at safe distance and detect it instantly. The decoys will be launched to detonate it a mile from the ship. The hull of this ship is considerably better protected than the *Calcutta,* and even if we were to be struck, we would survive. And the tanker will be dealt with mercilessly. The jaws of hell will receive it.'

'Yes,' said Memon. 'That would be most appropriate.'

Mack felt the Megafortress lift up abruptly beneath him as it came off the runway. Somehow being a passenger made him feel out of sorts. It wasn't just that there was no way to anticipate the tugs and pulls of flight properly. It was the fact that you were just along for the ride, like you were a passenger in a bus. And who wanted to be in a bus?

He was still sore at Bastian for demanding that he fly only one plane at a time. That seemed ridiculously cautious. The argument that only Starship and Zen had handled two in combat was ridiculous; the same could have been said about them before they did it. He'd done fine on his last sortie.

However, he would follow his master's orders. No sense going against the old graybeard, especially with his daughter at the helm of the plane. She'd be tattling in no time.

Mack shared the Flighthawk control compartment with Ensign Gloria English, who would be taking over as Piranha pilot once they reached their station. The ensign was a Navy girl; he didn't hold that against her, but unfortunately her face could sink a thousand ships. Even though she had literally nothing to do for the next two hours, English was busy at her station, examining previous mission tapes.

'*Levitow* to Flighthawk leader. Mack, we're climbing

through ten thousand feet,' said Breanna a short time later. 'You're going to want to start getting ready.'

'You don't have to tell me my job, Captain,' snapped Mack. 'I have it under control.'

'I don't doubt that. Flight plan calls for a launch in ten minutes. We'll be over international waters –'

'Yeah, yeah, yeah. I know the drill.'

Same old Mack, Breanna thought as she prepared the Megafortress for the Flighthawk launch. He'd seemed a little more mature over the past few months, but bad cream always curdled in the end.

'Captain, we have two Sukhoi Su-33s orbiting directly to the west, fifty miles,' reported Stewart. 'Flying at twelve thousand feet. One helicopter as well. Additional aircraft from the south – three helicopters. All aircraft are Indian.'

'Where are they coming from?'

'Believe the Indian warship to the south,' said Stewart, tapping the configurable display in front of her. Data from the surface and airborne radars were forwarded to her station when they were operating, giving her a much longer-range view than normal.

'Ship on the surface,' added Stewart. 'Oil tanker.'

'Flighthawk leader, be advised we have a pair of Indian Sukhois ahead,' Breanna told Mack.

'Yeah, I see them on the sitrep.'

'Let's go ahead and launch,' said Breanna. 'Get *Hawk Three* off the wing before we get too close.'

'Yeah, roger. Let 'er rip.'

Aboard the *Shiva*,
northern Arabian Sea
0430

Memon watched the oil tanker on the screen in the combat center. The image was blurred and shadowy, but one thing was clear – the tanker was not stopping. The helicopter with the antiship missiles and its two companions with the marine boarding party were now less than two miles away.

Memon had donned a headset that allowed him to switch into the different radio channels being used during the mission. He listened now as the admiral repeated his warning.

'You are ordered to halt your ship. If you do not stop and allow yourself to be boarded, you will be sunk. Those are your alternatives.'

There was a flurry of activity to Memon's right. An airplane coming from the vicinity of Pakistan had been picked up on radar about fifty miles away. Two of their planes were going to meet it.

The voices spiked with excitement – something had flared from below the plane.

A missile launch!

Memon's stomach tightened. The treacherous Pakistanis had lured them into a trap.

The voices calmed – the plane was identified as an American Megafortress, bound for the Indian Ocean near Africa. It had launched a small robot aircraft, not a missile.

'You look disappointed,' said Captain Bhaskar.

Memon pulled off his headset. 'How's that?'

'You want a battle, don't you?'

'I don't run from conflict. We must not be intimidated.'

As Bhaskar frowned, one of the officers behind him announced that Admiral Kala had just given the order to stop the tanker.

Aboard the *Levitow*,
over the northern Arabian Sea
0432

'Tanker being targeted!' said Stewart, practically shouting. 'The helicopter is going to fire – Sea Eagle antiship missile, active radar.'

'Jam it,' Breanna told her copilot.

'Captain –'

'Jam the guidance radar, now. Full ECM suite,' said Breanna. She put her hand on the throttle glide, urging more speed from the Megafortress. '*Hawk Three* – be advised Indian helicopters are firing on the oil tanker.'

'Roger that. I see it. What do you want me to do?'

'Just stay close.'

'I'm hugging you,' said Mack.

Breanna reached to the communications panel. But before she could tell Colonel Bastian what was going on, Stewart reported that the ECMs were on.

'They're firing anyway,' added the copilot. 'We're not optimized for weapons like that.'

Breanna hit the preset on the communications panel

so she could broadcast on the UHF frequency universally used for emergencies.

'This is *Dreamland Levitow* to Indian helicopters. Why are you firing on an unarmed civilian vessel?'

'First missile missed,' said Stewart. 'They're going to try again.'

'Where are the Sukhois?'

'A mile and a half south. Aircraft carrier – bear with me,' said Stewart, struggling to sort out the alerts and icons that were flashing on her screen. 'Ship-to-ship – they have a targeting system for SS-N-12 Sandbox anti-ship missile. Surface-to-air. Short-range – um, SA-N-4 Gecko. Guns.'

The SA-N-4 was a Russian-built short-range anti-aircraft missile. Guided by radar, it was not a threat to the Megafortress as long as she stayed above sixteen thousand feet. The guns – they would be 30mm antiaircraft cannon – were likewise not a threat.

'SS-11 – Grisons,' added Stewart. 'That's it.'

'Also short-range. All right. Concentrate on the Su-33s,' Breanna told her copilot.

Also known to NATO as CADS-1, Dagger and Chestnut Tree, the SS-11 Grisson was a close-in weapons system and was not a problem at present. The Sukhois were the real threat, though Breanna was confident she could handle them.

'*Wisconsin*, this is *Levitow*,' said Breanna, clicking into the Dreamland Command communications channel.

'More missiles!' warned Stewart.

'Continue ECMs,' said Breanna. Even if the electronic countermeasures confused the targeting radar, eventually

151

whoever was piloting the helicopter would simply get close enough to hit the tanker without guidance. It was a pretty big target and it would be hard to miss.

'Breanna?' said Colonel Bastian, coming on the screen.

'We have a situation here – Indian helicopter firing missiles at an oil tanker. There are Sukhois – other helicopters. I can't let them kill civilians.'

'Stand by.'

'Sukhois are changing course,' warned Stewart.

'*Hawk Three* – Mack, we have their attention.'

'Good.'

Aboard the *Abner Read*,
off the coast of Somalia
0435

Bastian's voice boomed in Storm's ear as he switched into the channel.

'Indian aircraft are attacking a Pakistani oil tanker,' said Dog. 'One of our aircraft is in the vicinity.'

Typical Dreamland, thought Storm. Always getting their bull necks into the middle of a firefight.

'Explain it to me simply, Bastian.'

'I just did. The aircraft is *Dreamland Levitow,* an EB-52 with Captain Stockard in command. You can speak to her directly on the Dreamland Command line.'

Captain Stockard – aka Breanna *Bastian* Stockard. A chip off the old renegade, trouble-seeking block.

'I'll take care of it,' he said. He had one of his radio

152

operators make the hookup. In seconds he had the pilot on the line. 'This is Captain Gale. What's going on?'

'A helicopter gunship launched two radar-guided missiles at a civilian oil tanker. We've blocked them with our ECMs but they're maneuvering for another shot. Two Sukhoi jets changing course to intercept us.'

'Indians?'

'Roger that.'

Storm knew the aircraft must be from the *Shiva*, India's new, so-called superweapon.

'Don't interfere,' said Storm. He could just imagine what Admiral Johnson would do to him if he got into a pissing match with the Indians.

Not that he wouldn't mind taking the *Shiva* down a few notches.

'Stand down, Captain,' he told Breanna. 'We're not at war with the Indians.'

'This is a civilian ship —'

'What part of "stand down" do you not understand?'

'Can I defend myself?'

'Get your butt out of there.'

'Yes, sir,' she snapped, and the connection died.

Aboard the *Levitow*,
over the northern Arabian Sea
0435

Mack changed course, bringing the Flighthawk ten miles ahead of the Megafortress, on a direct line with the mother ship's nose. The two Sukhoi Flankers were forty-five miles ahead, flying abreast of each other, one on his left wing and one on his right. They were climbing at a good pace, but both Mack and the Megafortress were more than ten thousand feet above them.

'Weapons ID'd on Sukhois,' said Stewart, passing along information that had been gleaned from the Megafortress sensors. 'Air-to-surface missiles, long- and short-range. Only air defense weapons are Archer heat seekers; four apiece.'

The Archers were short-range weapons, similar – some said superior – to the American Sidewinder.

C^3's tactics section offered up a suggestion – fly north, tackle the bogey there, then hit number two.

'Yeah, like number two is going to be stupid enough to suck his thumb while I'm zeroing out his buddy,' Mack told the computer mockingly.

'*Dreamland Levitow* to Flighthawk leader – Mack, we're going to cut north.'

'*Levitow,* tell you what – I'm going to take *Bogey One*,' said Mack, using the ID on the screen. 'Suggest you pound *Two* with a Scorpion missile.'

'Negative, negative, Flighthawk – we're ordered to disengage.'

'What do you mean? Run away!'

'Yeah, well, those are my orders. Stay with me. Do not attack.'

Mack jerked the control stick to the right so hard the aircraft took almost eight g's, skidding through the sky as it tried to follow his instructions.

* * *

Breanna continued to stew as she held the Megafortress on the course north, tracking toward the Pakistani coast. To allow a civilian ship to be fired on was unconscionable.

But so was disobeying a lawful order from a superior.

Zen would say screw it. Zen would say you do what you gotta do, and deal with fallout later.

And her father?

He wouldn't have handed her off to Storm if he didn't think she should do what he said. They were under Captain Gale's command.

'We're going back south,' she told her copilot. 'Open the bay doors. Maybe we can bluff them.'

'But –'

'We're not firing,' added Breanna. She punched up the weapons panel, activating the AMRAAM-plus Scorpion missiles' radar herself. 'I have the weapons screen on my station. *Hawk Three* – we're changing course. Keep an eye on those Sukhois.'

'Now you're talking, Breanna.'

'Hang on,' she said, pulling the Megafortress south.

The Sukhois had turned back west when the Megafortress went north, and were slow to react as it swung back. By the time they turned to meet the Megafortress, Mack already had *Hawk Three* on a dead run at the leader's nose.

As he closed to within a mile, the Sukhoi's radar finally found him. But that was far too late. The Indian pilot threw flares and electronic chaff in the air, probably mistaking the radar indication or the blur speeding toward him for a missile. He also inexplicably jerked his plane in Mack's direction, perhaps panicking in his sudden haste to get away. The move would have been fatal had Mack been allowed to fire his cannon; the Sukhoi presented a fat target, and even a quick burst would have riddled the fuselage with bullets.

Instead, Mack went after the second Sukhoi, five thousand feet below and a mile southwest of his leader. Jamming his stick in that direction, he managed to skid through a turn and point the U/MF's nose at the bogey. Here was one advantage of flying a robot plane: The aircraft took somewhere over nine g's in the maneuver, which would have scrambled the brain of anyone sitting inside, even Mack's. C^3 used the entire airfoil as a brake, pitching the airplane's tail up and then spinning onto the course like a knuckleball floating toward the plate.

And here was one disadvantage of flying a robot plane: Mack got a disconnect warning from the computer. He was eighteen miles away from the Megafortress, and would disconnect in five seconds if he didn't get closer.

'Twenty, twenty, I'm supposed to have twenty miles,' he grumbled. Hoping the computer was just being conservative, he stayed on his course toward the Indian aircraft.

'Disconnect in three seconds,' said the computer.

Cursing, Mack pushed the stick in the direction of the Megafortress to the east, but it was too late; the main screen went white and black letters appeared at the center: CONNECTION LOST.

To Jan Stewart, it seemed as if someone had hit the fast-forward switch on the world. Icons on her configurable screens popped up in rapid succession. She no sooner interpreted one and began to act on it when two more flashed on the other side of the dashboard. The radar operators were jabbering in her ears, and she was also trying to listen to the radio channel used by the Indian pilots as well.

'Flighthawk is no longer under direct control,' she told Breanna. 'Uh – on course to return.'

'Roger that.'

'You want to launch the second one?' asked Stewart.

'No time. It'll be back inside a minute anyway if we're still on this course. Hail the Indians again and tell them not to attack.'

'I've tried. They're not acknowledging us at all.'

'Where are the helos?'

Stewart looked at the sitrep screen but couldn't find them. She started to change the zoom but her brain froze; she couldn't remember how to do it, even though it was something she did maybe ten times an hour on a normal flight.

'Shit!' said Breanna.

'Don't yell at me,' snapped Stewart, but as she raised her eyes from the screens to the windscreen, she realized Breanna hadn't been cursing at her at all – a black-rimmed fireball rose from the oil tanker ahead.

They were too late.

Aboard the *Shiva*,
northern Arabian Sea
0436

When Memon reached the bridge, he found Admiral Kala receiving a report from the air commander. Two of the jets patrolling above the tanker they were stopping had encountered an American aircraft, probably a B-52. They believed they had been fired upon without warning.

Memon was shocked by the report. While the United States was not technically a military ally, the two countries had many economic and diplomatic ties. This was a betrayal of the worst sort.

'The aircraft is now flying back in the direction of our helicopters,' added the air commander. 'It is acting in a hostile manner.'

'What happened to the plane that was fired on?'

'The missile flew close to one of our aircraft but he was able to avoid it. There were no radar guidance indications – the situation is unclear to me.'

'Shoot them down,' said Memon. 'They've provoked it.'

The air commander turned to him. 'Shoot down an American plane?'

'We were fired at first, Admiral,' he said, making his plea directly to Kala. 'We have a right defend ourselves.'

'Warn them to leave,' said the admiral. 'If they do not, shoot them down. They are a danger to the *Shiva,* as well as the boarding force.'

Aboard the *Levitow*,
over the northern Arabian Sea
0436

Mack smacked the button to change the screen configuration. The view from the Megafortress's forward television camera snapped onto his main screen. A red tongue of fire filled the lower left-hand corner.

'They hit the oil tanker,' said Ensign English next to him.

'Looks like it.'

'The Flighthawk disconnected?'

Mack turned to her, ready to tell her to mind her own business. But the puzzled look on her face stopped him.

'Yeah, the intercept took me too far away after the Megafortress changed course.'

'Sucks.'

'Yeah.'

'It'll come back, though, right? It's programmed to fall back into trail?'

'Yuppers.' The Megafortress's latest maneuvers had increased the distance between it and the Flighthawk; C^3 predicted it would be another four minutes before it could catch up if the EB-52 stayed on its present course and speed.

'The Indian aircraft carrier is preparing to launch more aircraft,' English added. 'I'll bet they're going to launch another set of fighters and send the ones providing air cover over the ship to intercept us. The ones you chased away were equipped for surface combat, not air-to-air. They only had two short-range missiles.'

'How do you know they're going to launch?' asked Mack.

'They're maneuvering to get into the wind. They don't know what they're doing yet,' added English. 'Their procedures are awkward. The ship is still brand new and they're learning. They also may not be as well-equipped as we are. Things we take for granted, they're working through.'

'Yeah, I can understand that,' said Mack, tapping his fingers against the still useless control stick.

Breanna banked into a turn to the west, angry with herself for flying north and then taking so long to change her mind. She'd accomplished absolutely nothing.

The tanker was on fire and the crew was abandoning ship. The Sukhois that had chased them earlier were about thirty-five miles to the northeast, at the border of Pakistani territory. One of the two planes patrolling over the Indian carrier was moving northward in their direction.

'ID weapons on that Su-33 coming for us,' she told Stewart.

'Uh –'

'Heat-seekers only or AMRAAMskis?'

'No weapons radar for –'

'Go to weapon query mode,' said Breanna. 'The W3 button at the left side of the screen. Box the target, then tap the button.'

'Heat-seekers,' said Stewart. 'Four AA-11s. That's it.'

'*Levitow,* this is Flighthawk leader. Bree, we have to launch the second Flighthawk.'

'Negative, Mack. Colonel Bastian said you're only supposed to fly one at a time.'

'*Hawk Three* is not under my control. It'll be four minutes before it'll catch up to us. The Indian aircraft carrier is getting ready to launch more planes; I say we launch *Hawk Four*.'

'If we launch it now, it'll stay up for the entire flight.'

'We need to launch,' insisted Mack. 'I'll let the computer fly it,' he added in a calmer voice. 'Come on.'

'Stand by.'

Breanna looked at the sitrep plot. At their present course and speed, *Hawk Three* would catch up with them three and a half minutes from now; by then the Sukhoi would be all over them. Any maneuvering she did would delay the Flighthawk even longer, unless she went back in the direction of the other Indian airplanes.

No brainer.

'Jan, we're going to launch the second Flighthawk,' she told her copilot. 'Emergency launch.'

'OK,' said Stewart. 'Single aircraft taking off from the Indian carrier.'

Mack let the computer run through the abbreviated takeoff checklist, watching the screens flash by. The Megafortress tilted and swung upward, the Flighthawk powering away.

A single Flanker was accelerating from the southeast, pedal to the metal. What Mack wanted to do was swing back and intercept him before he launched his missiles. If everyone else had been standing still this would be a difficult task, but with all three planes moving well over 500 knots, the calculus was tortuous. And Mack didn't want to chance losing another aircraft.

The tactics section of C^3 studied its library of similar situations and suggested a basic intercept scheme. With no time to argue, Mack tapped the screen, accepting the computer's suggestion as a template for his plan.

'Flighthawk leader to *Levitow* – Bree, I'm going to shoot this sucker down.'

'Orders are still *no*.'

'Bullshit. He'll fire those heat-seekers as soon as he's in range.'

'Mack –'

'I don't feel like walking home.'

'We'll take him with the Stinger air mines.'

'He can fire from five miles out, long before the Stinger can target him.'

Breanna hesitated.

'If he doesn't break off in sixty seconds, take him,' she said abruptly. 'As you attack, we'll cut north.'

'Roger that.'

Aboard the *Wisconsin*,
near Somalia
0436

The *Wisconsin* was more than a thousand miles away from the *Levitow,* so there was no possibility of seeing it, even with the powerful array of radars in the aircraft. But Dog sensed things weren't going well – Breanna hadn't checked back with him since their earlier communication.

'*Dreamland Wisconsin* to *Dreamland Levitow*,' he said, using the Dreamland communications channel. 'Breanna, what's your situation?'

'We're being pursued by a hostile Indian aircraft,' she said. Her helmeted face appeared on the com screen. 'We're going to shoot him down if he doesn't break off.'

'I thought you were ordered to get out of there.'

'We're trying, Daddy. But at this point I don't think we have any other options.'

The word *Daddy* caught him off guard; he felt a flash of emotion he couldn't afford in a combat situation.

'Do what you think best,' Dog told her.

'I am.'

Her image lingered on the screen. Dog stared at it for a moment, then hit one of the presets to contact Storm.

Aboard the *Levitow*,
over the northern Arabian Sea
0440

Stewart tried the hail again, this time simultaneously broadcasting on all radio frequencies the Indians were known to use.

'*Dreamland Levitow* to Indian flight pursuing us. We will consider you hostile if you continue on your present course. This is your last warning.'

She waited for thirty seconds. Something blipped on the right screen – a fresh radar contact.

'Nothing, Captain,' she told Breanna. 'Another aircraft is taking off from the carrier.'

Mack dipped his wing at the exact moment he got the cue from the computer. The Flighthawk peeled down and away from the Megafortress, arcing back toward the approaching Sukhoi. The Indian was seven miles away, technically within range to fire the Russian-made air-to-air missiles; the closer he got, the better his odds of a hit. Mack activated the weapon screen; a gray bar across the center of his main view told him he had no shot.

'Flighthawk leader, this is *Levitow*,' said Breanna.

'Don't try and talk me out of this, Bree. You know I'm right.'

'Flighthawk leader, you are ordered to engage the plane pursuing us and take it down. It has refused to answer hails. It poses an imminent threat to my plane and crew.'

About time you got religion, Mack thought.

'Flighthawk leader, please acknowledge for the record,' she added.

'Trying to get me off the hook later on, huh?'

'Please acknowledge for the record.'

'We're all in this together, hon. Now watch me write my name in this asshole's front end.'

Mack pushed his stick forward. The targeting bar began blinking yellow, even though the enemy aircraft was not yet in sight. The triangular aim cue at the center of the bar began blinking red, and Mack pressed the trigger. As he did, the Sukhoi flew in from the right side of the screen. His first few shots missed, but the next dozen or so blew through the nose and then the cobraesque cowl that led to the forward edge of the wing.

In an instant Mack was beyond the Sukhoi. He turned back to the west, trying to find both the Megafortress and the aircraft he'd just shot at.

He saw the Sukhoi first, its outline synthesized at the left of his screen. It was moving away, but still moving – he hadn't taken it down.

How the hell could that be?

The Megafortress, which was supposed to have turned north after he made his attack so he could sweep in behind her, was still moving west. Before he could ask her about it, Stewart gave him a direction to cut to a western course. Breanna followed with an explanation.

'*Hawk Four*, the plane that took off from the aircraft carrier has activated radar indicating AA-12 AMRAAMskis. We want to get as much air between us as we can. Catch up to me.'

'All right, yeah,' said Mack, pushing the throttle slide to max.

The Flanker that had taken off from the carrier had at least two Russian-made Vympell R-77 air-to-air missiles, better known in the West as the AA-12 Adder, or, more collo-quially, an 'AMRAAMski.' The weapon was the best non-American-made air-to-air missile in the world at medium range. Very similar to the American AMRAAM for which it had been nicknamed, it could strike another airplane at about forty nautical miles in a head-on confrontation; from the rear its effective range was roughly a third of that, depending on the speed and ability of the plane it was chasing.

Breanna had about forty nautical miles between her and the aircraft, but her advantage was quickly diminishing. And she had to worry not only about the Su-33 that Mack had just tangled with – the plane was moving southwest, its status unclear – but the two jets that had gone north earlier. They'd changed course again and were now headed in her direction.

'Broadcast another warning to the Indians,' Breanna told her copilot. 'Tell them that if they take any more aggressive action, we will shoot them down.'

'Working on it.'

Breanna glanced at the sitrep. 'Mack, you have to catch up to me.'

'I'm at max power.'

'*Bogey Four* is forty miles and gaining,' said Stewart. 'That's the one with the AMRAAMskis.'

'ECMs.'

'Countermeasures,' said Stewart, confirming that she had begun filling the air with fuzz and fake signals. Though state of the art, the electronic countermeasures employed by the Megafortress did not make it invulnerable to radar-guided missiles, which had a number of techniques of their own to see through the haze. Breanna's basic strategy at the moment was to make it more difficult for the Indian aircraft to lock onto her and fire, essentially playing for time. In the best-case scenario, her pursuer would give up or receive orders from the aircraft carrier to return.

It didn't look like that was going to happen.

Bogey Four was closing the gap at roughly five miles a minute; Breanna decided her best defense was an aggressive offense.

'Mack, I'm going to swing south and try for a nose-to-nose attack.'

'You're going to take on the fighter?'

'I'm going to get into a position to fire the Scorpions. You cut east as I make the turn and catch those two bozos coming down from the north.'

Mack didn't answer right away. Breanna guessed that he was having trouble translating what she wanted to do into a plan; the Flighthawk's twenty-mile tether complicated everything.

'Yeah, roger. I got it,' he said finally.

'*Hawk Three* will come under your control about the time I'm going to fire the AMRAAMs. Stay with *Hawk Four* – the computer will bring her close to me and we'll be all right.'

'Yeah, yeah, OK.'

'No, Mack – do as I'm telling you.'

'Jeez, relax, will you? I got it.'

'Stewart, you got that?' said Breanna, turning to her copilot.

'It's "In Your Face,"' said the copilot, using the slang for a simulation exercise that followed the same attack pattern on a long-range pursuer.

'Yeah, that's it exactly. Two missiles. Wait for a lock.'

'Roger that.'

'Everybody, hang on,' said Breanna, powering the Megafortress into a turn.

Mack had never truly appreciated the difficulty of flying the Flighthawk in air-to-air combat before. It was like trying to hit a home run when the baseball was tied to an elastic band.

As for Breanna's tactics – well, they were aggressive. But if he'd been the jock in the Su-33, he'd be salivating right now: The Megafortress made herself a huge target less than forty miles in front of him.

Apparently the Indian jock thought the same thing – he fired two radar missiles almost immediately.

Mack tried to zone out the blare of the crew's conversation and the bucking of the Megafortress around him as the others responded. The Flanker continued toward the Megafortress. If its radar missiles somehow missed the big plane, he'd use his heat-seekers or cannon to down what he thought was a fat target.

Mack turned his attention to the two airplanes he'd encountered earlier. They were flying at warp speed toward him, closing to within twenty miles. He began a turn, easing up on his throttle as he made sure he was parallel to the path the Megafortress was going to take. He needed to anticipate Breanna's next move as well as his targets'; when they saw her moving, they would slide farther west. He wanted to come at them over their wings, lacing them as he flew north and then with luck getting in behind them if they escaped and drove toward the Megafortress.

'Fire Fox One!' said Stewart, warning that the Mega-fortress had just fired a radar missile.

The Megafortress jerked hard to the left, taking evasive maneuvers to avoid the enemy missiles. Disoriented, Mack caught himself as he started to move the Flighthawk stick as if to correct.

The Sukhois didn't realize where the Megafortress was going, and instead kept on their earlier course. Ironically, this took them closer to Mack quicker, and the targeting bar began blinking yellow.

Then the computer flashed a warning:

DISCONNECT IN THREE SECONDS.

'Son of a bitch!' yelled Mack. The screen went red and he fired, figuring it was too late to worry about where he was.

'First AA-12 off the screen – into the water. We're clear. Second is tracking,' said Stewart. She punched the button to eject more chaff. Everyone else in the airplane seemed to be yelling at her, telling her what to do. Her stomach leapt toward her mouth, and her heart felt like a thorough-bred racing up and down her chest.

'Closing, AA-12 is closing,' she warned. She felt like her head was about to explode.

An American AMRAAM would have been fatal at forty miles head-on, but Breanna had escaped AMRAAMski shots at ten. Still, the one homing in on her now seemed particularly tenacious, doggedly sniffing her out despite her maneuvers and the countermeasures. Breanna wanted to stay close to the Flighthawk and yet not make herself an easy target for either the missile or the two Flankers closing from the north. That was at least one too many goals, and as the AA-12 continued to close, she had to concentrate on the missile. She jerked hard left, pushing the Megafortress down on its left wing and ejecting chaff as she went. It was roughly two miles away.

It's either going to hit us or sail by in two seconds, she thought.

She was too busy holding the aircraft out of a spin to count.

Mack saw his first bullets hit the target dead-on.

Then the screen blanked. He'd lost the Flighthawk connection again.

As the air-to-air missile closed in, Stewart did something she had never done in all her days as a pilot in a cockpit: She closed her eyes and prayed.

When she opened them, she saw something red trailing through the sky about two miles away; it looked like a ribbon flying in the wind.

'Get me a location on the two Flankers out of the north,' Breanna said.

'*Bogey Four* –'

'We shot *Bogey Four* down,' said Breanna. 'His missiles missed. The other planes are our priority now.'

Mack pounded the side of his console in frustration. Then he remembered *Hawk Three*.

The Flighthawk's on-board computer had brought the aircraft back to the mother ship while he was tangling with the Sukhoi. Mack reconnected by voice command; the main screen blinked, and he was back in command. He had to stare at the sitrep for a moment before he could figure out exactly where everyone was. The Megafortress was eighteen miles southwest, flying west. The Indian Flanker he had just attacked had broken from its pursuit and was heading southeast. The other was several miles behind him. *Hawk Four* was to the north, turning back in the direction of the Megafortress.

'*Levitow,* this is Flighthawk leader. I have *Hawk Three*. *Bogey Two* is three miles behind me. Come up north and I'll slice and dice him as he turns.'

'Yeah, roger that, Mack.'

The Megafortress icon began pointing to the right. Mack slid his finger against the throttle, slowing to let his opponent catch up. The Indian aircraft couldn't see him, thanks to the Flighthawk's diminutive size and radar-evading shape; as long as Mack could correctly predict his course, he'd soon have the plane in the sweet spot of his targeting pipper.

The other aircraft lost some speed turning to intercept the Megafortress, but within a few seconds it was steaming over Mack's left wing. Mack slammed his throttle as it came close, then pointed his nose down to get a shot. The red band told him he was dead-on; he squeezed the trigger. His first three or four bullets caught the center fuselage behind the cockpit; the next dozen riddled through the engine.

The enemy aircraft tucked off to the left, damaged. Mack struggled to stay with it; if he'd been wheeling an F-15 across the sky he'd have overshot by several miles. But the Flighthawk forgave him, shoving its stubby little airframe into a tighter turn than Mack could have hoped. The rear end of the Sukhoi sailed back and forth in front of him; Mack started to fire, then lost the shot.

'Come west, Mack,' said Breanna.

'I have to finish this guy off first.'

'West.'

The targeting bar went red. Mack nailed the finger on the trigger. The Flanker dove straight down; Mack got a warning that he was almost out of range. This time he leveled off and headed for the mother ship.

Breanna blew a slow breath into her face mask, forcing her lungs to completely empty themselves before taking another breath. They were finally clear.

'*Bogey Four* is down – hit by our Scorpion,' said Stewart. '*Bogey Three* is circling back in its vicinity. *Bogey Two*, unknown damage.'

'Was there a parachute?' Breanna asked.

The airborne radar operator answered that he hadn't detected one.

'Helicopters launching from the carrier,' he added.

They would be search and air rescue aircraft. Even though he'd been trying to shoot her down, Breanna hoped they'd find the pilot.

She glanced at the communications panel. She had to tell Storm what had happened. He wasn't going to like it.

'All right. Everybody take a deep breath,' she told her crew. 'Flighthawk leader, we can refuel if you want.'

'Roger that. *Three*'s getting thirsty. What was my score there? I get one or two?'

'I hate to be the one to break this to you, Major, but all of your aircraft are still in the air.'

'You're kidding.'

'Check the long-range plot on the sitrep.'

'They didn't ditch on the way back to the carrier?'

'Apparently not.'

Mack cursed.

'I'm sure you did decent damage to them,' Breanna said. 'The important thing is, you kept them from getting us.'

'Yeah,' said Mack, clearly deflated. 'Roger that. Lining up for a tank.'

Aboard the *Shiva*,
in the northern Arabian Sea
0500

Memon felt tears brimming in his eyes as the executive officer and the flight operations commander reported to the admiral. One of their Sukhois had been shot down; its pilot was missing. The three other Flankers had been severely damaged. None would be available for the rest of the cruise.

The decision to challenge the American aircraft had been a foolish one. But what was the alternative?

The Americans had just proven where they stood. It

was very possible that they were behind the strike on the *Calcutta,* despite all of their claims and supposedly peaceful gestures.

So be it. They would pay for this.

'I will make the report to the Chief of Naval Operations,' said Memon. 'Coming from me –'

The admiral shook his head. 'No. It's my job. The decision was mine. The consequences are mine. I will talk to the admiral myself.'

'The crew of the tanker will be taken aboard shortly. Their ship has been abandoned,' said Captain Bhaskar, the executive officer. 'The boarding party saw no sign of torpedo launching stations or targeting equipment. It has not been an auspicious day.'

'Tomorrow will be a better one,' said Memon defiantly.

IV

Monkeys in the Middle

Washington, D.C.
1920, 10 January 1998
(0520, 11 January, Karachi)

Jed Barclay took the steps two at a time, running up to his boss's office in the West Wing of the White House. He made the landing and charged through the hall, barely managing to put on the brakes as he came to Philip Freeman's door.

The National Security Advisor's secretary looked up from her desk in the outer office. 'Jed, this isn't high school.'

'I have to talk to Mr Freeman.'

'Catch your breath first.'

Jed nodded, but walked immediately to the door to Freeman's inner office. He knocked, then went inside.

'An Indian airplane was shot down,' he told Freeman, huffing. 'By one of our Megafortresses. Others were damaged.'

'You ran all the way up here from the situation room downstairs?' said the National Security Advisor.

'You said to bring you the details immediately and in person,' said Jed, still catching his breath.

Freeman motioned with his hand. 'I didn't mean you had to run. Sit down, Jed. Fill me in.'

Jed began recounting what Colonel Bastian had told him about the encounter, then added the information he had gleaned from the Pentagon report and the intercepts the NSA had provided at his request.

'It happened less than twenty minutes ago,' said Jed. 'There's some information on the DoD network.'

'Yes, I was just looking at the Defense Department report,' said Freeman. He reached to the phone behind his desk.

Five minutes later Jed and his boss were shown into the Oval Office. President Kevin Martindale stood in front of his desk, phone in hand. He motioned for Freeman and Jed to take seats at the side, then continued his conversation, walking back and forth as he spoke. He quickly wrapped up the conversation, telling his caller – clearly a congressman – that he would talk to him before the State of the Union address later that month.

'Good evening, Philip, young Jed.' Martindale replaced the phone on its cradle and sat on the edge of the desk. 'So what's going on in the Arabian Sea?'

'The Indians' new aircraft carrier just destroyed an unarmed Pakistani oil tanker,' the National Security Advisor said. 'One of our Dreamland aircraft was in the area and warned them not to fire. Four Indian aircraft attacked our plane. We shot one down. The others may have been damaged.'

'We're sure the oil tanker was unarmed?'

Freeman turned to Jed. 'It's the same tanker the *Abner*

Read stopped the other day,' he said. 'They searched it pretty thoroughly.'

There was a knock at the door. Secretary of State Jeffrey Hartman was ushered into the room by one of the President's aides. As he took his seat, he gave Jed the sort of glare one gave a new puppy who'd messed on a rug. Jed and the Secretary had had a serious run-in a few weeks back over information given to the UN; if it had been up to Hartman, Jed would be down in the Antarctic conducting penguin surveys. Fortunately, Jed's boss couldn't stand Hartman, and the incident had actually helped Jed rather than hurt him.

'Dreamland, again,' said Hartman after the President summarized what had happened. 'And this clown Gale. Where's Chastain?'

He was referring to Secretary of Defense Arthur Chastain.

'He left the Pentagon a short while ago and should be here shortly,' said the President. 'The question I have for you, Mr Secretary, is what will Pakistan do about the tanker?'

'Immediate mobilization,' predicted Hartman. 'And India will step up its mobilization as well. The Chinese will use that to justify their own saber rattling. Where's their new aircraft carrier?'

'The *Deng Xiaoping* and its escorts are already in the Gulf of Aden,' said Jed.

Hartman scowled in his general direction, then turned to the President. 'Did the Indians at least have a reason for the attack?'

'I think they, um, they thought the tanker was connected to the attack on the *Calcutta*. They wanted to inspect it.'

'With what? Deep sea divers?' said the President, snorting in derision. Martindale didn't make many jokes, but when he did they tended to be acerbic.

'Who was involved in the *Calcutta* attack?' said the Secretary of State.

'Possibly a submarine,' said Freeman. 'The *Abner Read* has been chasing one.'

'Um, Colonel Bastian has a theory that the Indian destroyer that was hit by a torpedo the other night was attacked by a small aircraft,' said Jed. 'We've been trying to track it down. We think it may have come from Iran.'

'Iran? Why would they attack India?' said Hartman.

'Oil m-m-money, maybe,' said Jed, his tongue tripping over itself. He struggled to get past the stutter, forcing himself to complete his thought. 'Th-The Indians have been setting up new deals with African nations to have enough supply. That's what Port Somalia was all about.'

'Bastian has proof of this?' asked Hartman.

'Just a theory,' said Jed.

'It would be just like the Ayatollah and his black robes to stir the pot,' said President Martindale. 'They'd love to see the Indians and Chinese go at it. They don't particularly like the Pakistanis either, since they didn't support their Greater Islam Alliance. But does the colonel have proof?'

Jed shook his head.

'Talk to the Indians. Find out why they fired on the tanker – and on us,' Martindale told the Secretary of State.

'What should I say about their plane?' asked Hartman.

'I'm tempted to say we're launching a full investigation

into why we only shot down one out of four,' said the President.

'You have a helluva lot of explaining to do this time, Captain Stockard. A *helluvalot*.'

Storm looked at the pilot's image in the video screen. She had her helmet and crash shield on – typical Dreamland arrogance.

'I did what I thought was best under the circumstances,' Breanna told him. 'Or would you have preferred that my aircraft be shot down?'

'I would have *preferred* that you kept your nose clean. You went back toward that tanker deliberately, even though you were ordered away. That's insubordination, mister. At the very least.'

The pilot didn't answer. Belatedly, Storm remembered he was talking to a ma'am, not a mister. But he wasn't about to apologize or change the subject.

'Resume your normal patrol,' he told her.

'I have.'

'Good.' He killed the transmission. His headset buzzed, indicating that Lieutenant Commander 'Eyes' Eisenberg wanted to talk with him.

'Aircraft from the Chinese carrier *Deng Xiaoping* are

181

approaching, Storm,' the tactical commander told him when he switched into the circuit. 'The carrier is fifty miles north of us, just exiting the Gulf of Aden.'

Storm had hoped to get a look at the new Chinese carrier, if only to find out what all the fuss was about. But he'd never get that far north fast enough.

The Werewolf could, though. If the Chinese could fly over him, he could fly over them.

Hell, he could do better than that.

'Very well,' said Storm. 'Where's the Werewolf?'

'Routine patrol overhead, Captain,' said Eyes.

'Get Airforce on the line. I want him to go tell our Chinese friends we think the world of them.'

The first ship Starship saw as he flew Werewolf Two toward the Chinese flotilla was a destroyer of the Jingwei class, whose forward deck was dominated by a twin 100mm gun. More important to Starship was the battery of HQ-7 surface-to-air missiles. The HQ-7 was a Chinese version of the French Crotale Modulaire, an excellent short-range antiair system with a range of roughly six miles. Starship had flown the Werewolf against Crotales in field exercises and done very poorly; in fact, it was the only system he'd consistently failed to get past. Though ostensibly in the same class as the Russian SA-8B Gecko, Starship had found the Crotale's guidance system harder to fool and the missile more maneuverable and persistent.

'Ship in sight,' he told Eyes. 'Hull number 525 – frigate.'

'Good. Copy. Be advised, aircraft are approaching you.'

Starship could see two black streaks in the dim sky to his right. The threat identifier gave them captions: J-13s.

'Aircraft approaching – flying over,' said Starship. The J-13 was a Chinese-made two-seat fighter based on the Russian Sukhoi Su-27, but at least two generations more advanced. Capable of carrying a wide array of missiles and equipped with the latest Russian avionics and radar, the plane was considered on a par with the F-18 Super Hornet – and might even be superior in some respects. These seagoing versions were still being studied by the West; they had not yet seen combat.

Starship frowned at them as they rolled through inverts while rocketing past. Pointy-nose zippersuits were all alike – always showing off.

Not that he wouldn't have done the same thing if he were flying an F-15.

Another warship loomed to his right, three miles ahead. From the distance it looked as if it were the size of a battleship, and in many respects it was as powerful as a World War II battlewagon. But the ship was actually a destroyer – the *Fu Zhou,* which carried four-packs of cruise missiles on each side. The cruise missiles were 3M-80 Moskits – SS-N-22 'Sunburns' in NATO parlance, supersonic antiship missiles with a larger warhead and greater range than the American Harpoon. With a top speed of Mach 2.5, the missile was extremely difficult to defend against, even for a state-of-the-art warship like the *Abner Read.*

Updated by the Chinese, the vessel had been laid down as a Russian Sovremennyy destroyer. As they often did, the Chinese had built on Russian technology, adding improvements and funding weapons purchases the cash-strapped Russians could only dream of. The result was a ship that was not quite state-of-the-art, but was nonetheless an awesome power.

A half mile beyond the destroyer was a vessel that was state-of-the-art, as advanced as anything on the water, including the *Abner Read*: the People's Liberation Army Navy's pride and joy, the aircraft carrier *Deng Xiaoping*.

The nickname 'flattop' fit *Deng Xiaoping* perfectly. Unlike nearly every other aircraft carrier in the world since the CV-1 Langley, the *Deng Xiaoping* did not have an island. Her surface and antiair radars were located at the sides of the craft, adjacent to but not on the flight-deck surface.

The *Deng Xiaoping*'s flat deck was shaped like a fat V, with elevated ramps placed at each head. The arrangement allowed the carrier to launch two J-13s almost simultaneously, and still have space to land planes behind them. Besides thirty-six J-13 fighters, *Deng* carried four KA-27 Helix helicopters for antisubmarine warfare and six Z-8 helicopters, which were Chinese versions of the French Super Frelon, equipped with uprated engines and avionics systems. Four Z-8s had large radar units that hung off the side of the aircraft like a large water pail; when airborne, they provided radar coverage for the carrier. The other two were used for search and rescue operations.

'American helicopter, this is the People's Liberation Army Navy Aircraft Carrier *Deng Xiaoping*. Identify yourself.'

'Dreamland *Werewolf Two* from the Littoral Warship *Abner Read*,' said Starship. 'Captain Gale extends his compliments to the captain of the vessel, and wishes to present a token of his admiration. Requesting permission to land.'

'Dreamland?' said the carrier radioman, his voice losing its businesslike snap.

'Affirmative. This aircraft is currently assigned to the *Abner Read*.'

'You know Colonel Dog Bastian?'

'He's my commander.'

'American helicopter, you will change course,' said the controller. He directed the Werewolf to proceed west for a mile, then to fall into a landing pattern approaching from the ship's stern.

'I believe they've given me permission to land,' Starship told Eyes.

'Good. What was that business about Dreamland?'

'Got me.'

Starship followed the controller's directions, angling toward the carrier as if he were one of its aircraft. The approach gave him – and the *Abner Read*'s crew – a good look at the side of the ship, which was faceted to lower its radar profile. It was somewhat lower to the water than an American carrier would have been, though it still towered over the *Abner Read*, whose deck was always awash with the sea.

'There's a J-13 on deck, ready to launch,' he told Eyes. 'I'll get good video of it.'

'Keep the cameras rolling.'

After operating off the *Abner Read* for the last several

weeks, the *Deng Xiaoping*'s deck looked like the entire state of Kansas spread out in front of him. As Starship skipped in over the stern, he saw a dozen sailors race from the port side, parallel to the landing area. Unsure what was going on, he slowed down, barely moving forward.

'I got a dozen guys with guns running onto the deck,' Starship told Eyes. 'You think they don't understand I'm a robot and they're trying to kidnap the crew or something?'

'Be ready to get out of there.'

Starship reached the third white circle on the deck, where he'd been directed to stop. As he settled onto the flattop he finally realized what the sailors were doing – they were an honor guard.

'The People's Liberation Army Navy Aircraft Carrier *Deng Xiaoping* welcomes Dreamland,' said the controller. 'It is an honor and a pleasure to host you.'

'Same to you,' said Starship. 'There . . . um, when the rotors stop, remove the case from the area between the skids. Just cut the ropes.'

There was a bottle of scotch in the case. Starship watched as two sailors – not part of the honor guard – approached. Even though the rotors had stopped spinning, they crawled toward the aircraft on their hands and knees, cut away the case, and took Storm's present away.

'Dreamland Werewolf, you are cleared to take off. Our compliments to your commander, Captain Gale. And please remember us to the colonel, Dog Bastian.'

'Roger that, *Deng*. Pleasure's all mine,' said Starship, revving the Werewolf for takeoff.

Aboard the *Deng Xiaoping*,
the Arabian Sea
0630

The master of the *Deng Xiaoping*, Captain Yaun Hongwu, smiled when he saw the bottle. Americans were fond of such gestures. He would have to think of something appropriate in return.

Hongwu knew of Captain Gale's ship, the *Abner Read*. Like his own, it belonged more to the twenty-first century than the twentieth. Though it was the size of a coastal corvette, he would not like to have to take it on.

The aircraft had been something new all together. It looked like a miniaturized version of the Russian Hokum; undoubtedly it would be several times as powerful, coming from Dreamland.

All China knew of Dreamland. Barely a year before, the brave crew of a Dreamland Megafortress had saved Beijing from certain annihilation by intercepting a rogue nuclear missile a few miles from the city, dodging Chinese warplanes and missiles to do so. The man who had commanded the flight, Lieutenant Colonel Tecumseh 'Dog' Bastian, was a hero to Hongwu personally – his actions had saved Hongwu's mother and father, his younger sister, and countless aunts, uncles, and cousins.

Perhaps in the future he would have a chance to thank the colonel personally.

Allegro, Nevada
1800

The time differences could drive you nuts. When it was six p.m., or 1800 in Nevada, it was seven a.m. in Karachi – tomorrow. Today was already yesterday there.

Six P.M. was also time for Zen to talk to Breanna, the best part of his day.

And the worst. He missed her incredibly. Separation was a fact of life in the military, but the truth was, they'd never been separated on a deployment since their marriage. If one was in danger, the other was. He'd never even thought about it before.

'Dreamland Command,' answered Danny Freah when Zen dialed the special 800 number that connected with the Dreamland Command trailer. The line allowed family members to stay in contact during missions.

'Hey, Danny. Bree around?'

'No, uh, tied up.'

The line was not secure, and both men had to be careful what they said.

'Running late?' asked Zen.

'Late and hairy.'

Zen felt as if he'd been punched in the gut.

'Hairy?'

'She's OK,' said Danny quickly.

'What's going on?'

'Jeff, I can't get into details here. I'm sorry. I'll have her call you, OK?'

No, it wasn't OK. Not at all.

He should be there. Rather than getting himself stuck in the back with needles that weren't doing anything and wouldn't do anything.

'Yeah, sure. Have her call me when she gets a chance.'

'I wouldn't wait by the phone, if you get my drift. Could be hours,' asked Danny.

'I'm easy,' lied Zen.

Drigh Road
1200

'You were under orders to get out of that area, Breanna. Why didn't you follow them?'

Breanna looked at her father. She'd worked with him now for more than a year and a half, and yet she still felt awkward.

'Innocent people were being attacked,' said Breanna. 'I couldn't turn away.'

Some commanders might have told her that her first duty was to her own crew and country; others might have reminded her that lawful orders were to obeyed. But the colonel only frowned and said nothing.

'My mistake was not acting right away,' Breanna told him. 'If I'd acted right away, then maybe I could have prevented the attack. I second-guessed myself, and I don't know why.'

'You honestly think that's the problem?'

She nodded.

'Breanna, the situation here is extremely volatile. The

189

Indians are pressing for a formal investigation. If that happens, you're not going to be on very firm ground. You were given an order, started to comply, then changed your mind for no good reason that I can see.'

'I'll deal with that if I have to,' she said.

'If I had more Megafortress pilots, I'd put you on furlough. I really would.'

'Why?'

'Why do you think?'

'Daddy, you would have done the same thing.'

His face blanched as soon as she said *Daddy*.

'I did what I thought was right. I'm willing to deal with the consequences if I have to.'

'I wonder if you really are,' said the colonel. 'Dismissed.'

The words wounded her more deeply than any criticism of the mission. Walking back to her room, Breanna felt hot tears slipping from her eyes.

Dog had finally managed to make his way to his temporary quarters and was just taking off his clothes to catch a nap when a sharp rap at the door interrupted him.

'Go away, Danny,' he said, recognizing the knock instantly.

'Colonel, I will if you want me to, but Storm is looking for you on the Dreamland channel and claims it's urgent.'

'I'll be right there,' grumbled Bastian.

He tucked his shirt back in, rubbed his eyes and opened the door. Captain Danny Freah stood in the hallway, shifting his weight from one foot to another, looking a little sheepish.

'I'm sorry,' said Danny.

'Not your fault,' said Dog.

'Haven't had much sleep, huh?' asked Danny, following as Dog walked toward the door.

'No rest for the wicked.'

'You ought to get another pilot to sit in for you,' suggested Danny.

'I look that tired?'

'You do.'

Dog laughed. 'I respect your honesty, Captain.'

'Just telling it like it is.'

'How's security?'

'Pakistanis have been cooperative. They have close to three companies on our perimeter, along with two armored vehicles. Politicians are protesting, but the people here are OK. Hasn't been stirring in town about us, and of course everybody's been keeping a low profile. I thought I ought to mention – the *Levitow*'s encounter with the Indian carrier aircraft has gotten back to the base commander. He wants to host the crew for lunch.'

'Just what we need,' said Dog.

The bright noonday sun hit him in the face as they went outside the building and crossed to the Dreamland trailer. Sergeant Kurt 'Jonesy' Jones snapped to attention outside the trailer; inside, Sergeant Ben 'Boston' Rockland got up from the console as the colonel and Freah came in.

'At ease, Boston,' Dog told the sergeant. 'How are things?'

'All quiet, Colonel.'

Dog slipped in behind the communications console. He put on the headset, then authorized the encrypted communication. Storm's face immediately appeared in the screen.

'I hope you're happy, Bastian,' said the Navy captain. 'Now we're peacekeepers.'

'I'm not sure I follow.'

'The President wants Xray Pop to sail east into the Arabian Sea. We're supposed to help encourage the Indians and the Pakistanis to make peace.'

'All right.'

'You talked to the NSC about that loony theory that a plane dropped the torpedo that attacked the Indian destroyer?'

'It's not a loony theory, Storm. It's the only explanation for what happened.'

'So where'd the plane go?'

'I don't know for sure. My guess, though, is somewhere in Iran.'

'We'll need to set up new patrol grids. Eyes will contact you with the information when we have the plan worked out.'

'What exactly are we supposed to do?'

'Damned if I know. Maybe Washington thinks the Indians and Pakistanis will run away if we show our faces,' said Storm. 'We're to patrol in the Arabian Sea. I need around-the-clock air cover as well as radar surveillance, airborne and on the surface. Not only are the Indians there, but the Chinese aircraft carrier *Deng*

Xiaoping is on a course due east. It'll be in the Arabian Sea no later than twenty-four hours from now. The Chinese don't like the Indians.'

'What about whoever it is who's attacking the Indians?'

'We watch for them. But – and let me make this as absolutely crystal clear as I possibly can – under no circumstance, absolutely no circumstance, are you to engage anyone without a specific order from me personally. Do I make myself clear?'

'Crystal.'

'Make sure all your people get the word. And knock some sense through your daughter's thick skull before she ends up being court-martialed – if it isn't already too late for that.'

The screen blanked.

Breanna wanted to talk to Zen, but she didn't want to go back to the Dreamland Command trailer. So she hiked over to the Pakistani side of the base, found a pay phone, and used her international phone card to make the call.

It was a bit past eleven P.M. back in Nevada, and she wasn't sure that Zen would still be up, but her husband grabbed the phone before the first ring ended.

'Yeah,' he snapped.

'Jeff?'

'Bree, God, are you OK?'

'Sure. Why?'

'I was worried.'

'I'm fine.' Breanna ran her finger down the metal

wire connecting the handpiece to the phone. 'How did everything go today?'

'Same old, same old. Boring.'

'Are you doing well?'

'Doc says so. I don't feel bupkus. And still no beer.' He laughed, but she could tell his heart wasn't in it. 'Are you OK?'

'I'm fine. You shouldn't worry.'

'Hey, I'm not worried.'

Among the many things she loved about her husband was the fact that he was a terrible liar. But she let this one go, and matched it with her own.

'We're doing fine out here. I'm doing great. Piece of cake,' she told him. 'I want you to get better. OK?'

'Getting better every day. You're OK?'

'Yes.' Breanna glanced to the side and saw two other people waiting to use the phone. 'I do have to go, though. Take care, OK?'

'Roger that.'

'I love you.'

'Me too, babe.'

Mack walked sullenly to the Dreamland Command trailer, where Dog had just convened a meeting with all of the flight crews and officers. He'd spent the last hour reviewing the tapes of his encounters. He'd severely damaged at least one of the planes, and managed to get lead into everything he tangoed with. But he hadn't shot anybody down, and as far as he was concerned, that was as bad as missing completely.

'Hey, Major, heard you had some fun,' shouted Cantor, trotting up behind him.

'Yeah,' muttered Mack.

'Got pieces of three of them?'

'Don't rub it in,' snapped Mack, pushing through the small crowd at the door of the trailer.

A five-handed poker game made the command trailer seem crowded. With nearly two dozen people crammed inside, it felt like the mosh pit of a rock concert. The air conditioner couldn't keep up with the load, and the place smelled sweaty. Mack managed to squeeze to the far side of table at the center of the room, standing behind Stewart, who'd gotten there early enough to snag a seat.

'All right, I think we're all here,' said Colonel Bastian, standing near a large map of the Arabian Sea. 'Thanks for coming over. I know some of you were sleeping. If it's any consolation, so was I. Or I should say, I was about to.'

Mack listened as Dog laid out the change in orders and their mission.

'More peacekeeping crap,' Mack groused.

'That'll do, Major,' said Dog.

'Aw, come on, Colonel. You know this is garbage. They're sending the *Abner Read* to stand between two aircraft carriers? That's like sending a canoe to tow the *Titanic* into port.'

Everyone laughed, or at least snickered – except for Bastian.

'Then start thinking of yourself as an iceberg, Mack,' said the colonel. 'And shut up.'

Mack clamped his teeth together as Dog laid out the change in patrol areas and schedules. They would continue to have two Megafortresses in the air at all times. One would orbit in the eastern Arabian Sea. The other would patrol to the west – first near the coast of Iran, then eastward, following the *Abner Read* as it made its way to the northern Arabian Sea.

'I want to still look for that airplane,' said Dog. 'The one we believe fired the torpedo.'

'Waste of time,' said Mack under his breath – or so he thought.

'Excuse me, Major?'

'Nothing.'

'Out with it, Mack.'

'I looked at those images and the intercepts. I have to tell you, Colonel, no disrespect to the eggheads and Dr Ray, but there's just no way, *no way*, that little plane carried a torpedo, let alone fired it.'

'Then who did?'

'Either the oil tanker or a submarine. My money's on a Chinese sub, probably doing some advance scouting for the *Deng Xiaoping*. He saw his shot, knew he could get away with it. The Indians couldn't find a lit Christmas tree in a bathtub at night. And the *Abner Read* – well, no offense to our Navy friends, but they're in the Navy for a reason, if you know what I mean.'

'Fortunately for you Mack, I don't. Dismissed. Everybody go get some sleep. A few of us are so sleep deprived we're starting to become delusional.'

Dreamland
0100 (1400, Karachi)

The guard snapped to attention, recognizing Zen as soon as he got off the elevator.

Then again, how many people on the base were in wheelchairs?

'Major Catsman inside?' he asked.

'Yes, sir.'

Zen locked his wheelchair and raised himself up to look into the retina scan. The doors to the Dreamland Command Center flew open, and Zen wheeled himself into the arena-style situation room that helped coordinate Whiplash missions.

'Zen, what are you doing here?' Catsman's eyes were even more droopy than normal.

'Couldn't sleep. Thought I'd find out what's going on over there.'

'Officially, you should be back home in bed.'

'I am. Off the record, tell me what you can.'

Catsman gave him an abbreviated version of the day's events.

'It's only going to get worse,' she added, with uncharacteristic pessimism. 'Now we're just monkeys in the middle out there.'

Zen knew he should be there. He could feel it, a magnetic force pulling him. The hell with the experiments – the hell with everything but Breanna.

Maybe the dreams were omens. He couldn't lose her, not for anything.

'I wouldn't worry about her.'

'Huh? About Bree? I'm not worried,' said Zen.

'She's a hell of a pilot.'

'Damn straight. Only pilot I trust.' Zen forced himself to smile. 'I just wanted to know, you know, what was up. Thanks for telling me.'

He was a bit too nervous for her, wasn't he? It wasn't that he didn't think she knew what she was doing, or that she couldn't take care of herself.

Maybe it was time to go back home, get some rest. Clear his head.

'How are the treatments going?' Catsman asked.

'They're going,' Zen said, wheeling himself back up the ramp.

Iran
12 January 1998
1900

Captain Sattari eyed the big aircraft on the nearby ramp, waiting for the last gear to be loaded aboard. Already, two of his submarines had been loaded into its belly through a bay originally intended to hold search and rescue boats. Their crewmen and ten of Sattari's guerrillas waited inside.

At nearly 150 feet long, the A-40 Albatross was one of the biggest flying boats ever made, and the only jet-powered one to enter regular service. This particular aircraft had been sold by the Russians as surplus, and according to all the official records had been scrapped a year ago.

'We're ready, Captain,' said Sergeant Ibn. 'The pilot would like to take off as soon as possible.'

Their destination was a point exactly thirteen miles south of Omara, a small city on the western Pakistani coast. The submarines would disembark and proceed to another point thirty miles away, rendezvousing with the other two subs, which had been deposited the day before. Together, they would proceed to their next target – an oil terminal in the port of Karachi.

'Yes, we should go,' said Sattari, but he didn't move. He wasn't afraid of the Indians, let alone the Pakistanis. But the Americans – the Americans were waiting for him. He'd cheated them the other night, hadn't he? Now they would want revenge.

They had undone his father, stripping him of the weapon that would have made him the most powerful man in Iran. Now he was a mere toady of the black robes.

That was unfair. He hadn't been their messenger the other day – more like a father shielding his son. And in truth, the imams had not done wrong by Sattari personally – their slanderous lies behind his back excepted.

'Let us go,' said Sattari, shouldering his rifle. 'Fate awaits us.'

Aboard the *Shiva*,
in the northern Arabian Sea
13 January 1998
0130

Memon woke to a series of loud raps at the cabin door. Disoriented, he could not interpret the sound or even remember where he was. Then a voice from behind the door called his name.

'Deputy Minister Memon? Sir, are you awake?'

'Yes,' said Memon.

'The admiral had me call for you.'

Memon pushed himself upright. 'I'm awake,' he said.

'Aircraft from the Chinese carrier *Deng Xiaoping* have been spotted,' said the man. 'The admiral wanted you to know. He's on the bridge.'

'I'm coming,' said Memon.

Aboard the *Wisconsin*,
over the northern Arabian Sea
0130

The sitrep screen made the situation below look almost placid. That was the strength and weakness of sensors, Colonel Bastian thought as he surveyed the scene; they couldn't quite account for the spitting and hissing.

The *Deng Xiaoping* had sailed day and night at top speed; it was now within fifty miles of the Indian carrier *Shiva*. Dish, working the surface radar, added that the ships were both turned into the wind, making it easier for them to launch and recover aircraft.

'Thanks, Dish,' said Dog. 'T-Bone, we have all their aircraft?'

'Roger that, Colonel. Four J-13s from the *Deng,* split into two orbits, one roughly five miles and the other fifteen from the carrier in the direction of the *Shiva*. There's another two-ship of J-13s over the carrier as an air patrol, and a helicopter with airborne radar. Indians have two Su-33s riding out to meet them. They have two other aircraft over their carrier. The two Pakistani F-16s I told you about earlier are well to the east now; they should be running home soon to refuel. Haven't spotted their replacements yet.'

'Cantor, you see those Indian Flankers?' Dog asked.

'Just coming into range now, Colonel.'

'Keep your distance, but don't let them get between you and the *Wisconsin*.'

'Copy that, *Wisconsin*.'

Dog checked the sitrep. They were to the west of both carriers and their aircraft. He tapped the Dreamland Command channel and updated Eyes. The *Abner Read*'s executive officer once more reminded him that he was not to interfere with the other ships 'no matter what.'

'I get the message,' said Dog.

Cantor watched the Su-33 grow in his view screen, waiting until the aircraft was exactly three miles away to start his turn. By watching Mack's mission tapes as well as those from his own encounters, he'd determined that was the sweet spot – far enough away so the Sukhoi pilot couldn't detect him, but close enough so that no last second maneuver could get him free. The Flighthawk swung through a tight arc, crossing behind the Sukhoi. The separation at the end of the turn was about a mile – close enough for a sustained burst from the Flighthawk cannon.

And it had to be sustained. Mack had gotten bullets into all of the fighters he'd faced, but taken none of them down. The Russian-made craft were even tougher than advertised.

But the Sukhoi pilot had no idea the Flighthawk was tagging along right behind it. It had a dead spot behind its tail, and unless his wingman flew very close, the Flighthawk was almost impossible to detect. Mack figured he could stay there all night.

'American aircraft, you are ordered to remove yourself from our vicinity,' said the Indian carrier, broadcasting over all frequencies. The transmission was directed at the *Wisconsin*, not *Hawk One*, which couldn't be seen by the carrier from this distance, a little over fifty miles away. Cantor heard Jazz tell the carrier blandly that they were in international waters and were on a routine patrol. He drew out his words matter-of-factly; Cantor thought he could be telling his wife that he'd bring home a bottle of milk.

Cantor nudged his throttle, easing toward the Su-33 as he continued to probe its weaknesses. By relying solely on the Megafortress's radar, he was depriving the Indians of any indication that he was there.

The problem wasn't shooting one of the Flankers down – he could do that easily. The difficulty was taking two. The Su-33 could easily outaccelerate the Flighthawk because of its larger engines. So the trick would be to get ridiculously close before starting the first attack.

And to fire without using the radar. Because once he turned the weapons radar on, they would know something was there.

The Flighthawk cannon could fire in a pure bore-sight mode – basically, point the nose and shoot – though in a three-dimensional knife fight it made little sense to give up the advantage of having the computer help aim the shots. But get this close – under a hundred yards – he couldn't miss, especially if he took the aircraft from below. Counterintuitive – it meant he had to climb against an aircraft that could easily outclimb him. But doable maybe, if he got off at least two long bursts before jabbing his radar on and gunning for the other plane, which would be over to his right. By the time the second plane caught on, it would be flying right into his aiming cue.

Cantor glanced at the sitrep and saw that the Mega-fortress was nearing the end of its patrol orbit. He tilted his wing down and slid away, still undetected by Indian radar or eyeballs.

'Until we meet again,' he told the Flankers as they rumbled on.

Las Vegas University of Medicine,
Las Vegas, Nevada
1200

The blood sample was the last straw.

They'd spent all morning taking scans whose results Zen could tell from the faces of the technicians were disappointing. Vasin appeared briefly, asked for some blood samples, then went off to a meeting.

The nurse tasked to get the sample kept muttering that she couldn't find the vein, then jabbing him and apologizing as she came up empty.

'It's right there,' Zen told her.

'I'm trying,' she said, jabbing him again. 'I'm sorry.'

What the hell was he doing here when Breanna needed him on the other side of the world?

The nurse finally managed to get the needle in correctly and filled up three test tubes. Zen made up his mind as he watched the third tube fill up. The nurse pulled out the needle, taped a gauze in place, then apologized for having had so many problems.

'It's OK.' Zen waited for her to leave, then began changing from the gown to his civilian clothes.

'Jeff, what are you doing?' asked Dr Vasin.

'Getting dressed. I thought you were at a meeting.'

'It was just postponed. Why are you getting dressed?'

'I'm not sure this is working –'

'You're doing fine.'

'Yeah, but –' Zen stopped himself. He couldn't tell

Vasin why he was worried about his wife; the mission was classified. 'I'm just getting bored.'

'At this stage in the process – a very difficult time,' said Vasin. 'But you don't want to stop now.'

'Why?'

'As I explained, once the process begins –'

'Nothing's happened.'

'Of course not.'

'The tests aren't going well. I could tell from everyone's reactions.'

'We must give it time. Once the process begins, stopping in the middle – it is worse than rolling the clock back. Come – let's go have a little lunch, you and I. A little change of pace. They're having chicken pilaf in the cafeteria. A very good dish.'

'All right,' agreed Zen finally. 'All right.'

Off the coast of Pakistan, near Karachi
0135

Captain Sattari unfolded himself from his seat and made his way to the rear of the midget submarine, trying to stretch out the cramps in his leg.

His men had been remarkably quiet for the past twenty-four hours. It seemed to him that traveling in the midget submarine was by far the hardest task they had. The rest would be simplicity itself compared to this.

He tapped each man's shoulder as he walked, nodding.

They were professionals, these men; he couldn't see their anticipation in the dim light, much less their fears or apprehensions. The faces they showed to their commander – to the world, if it looked – were of hard stone. Warriors' faces.

As was his.

'We have to surface to check our position,' said the submarine commander when he returned to his seat at the front of the small sub. 'There are no ships nearby. I suggest we do so now.'

'Yes,' said Sattari. He sat in his seat as the midget submarine's bow began nosing gently upward. Originally designed as a pleasure boat for sightseeing trips, the Parvaneh could make no abrupt moves. But this helped her in her mission. Rapid movement in the sea translated into sound, and the louder a vessel, the more vulnerable it was to detection.

The helmsman leveled the boat off three meters below the surface. The periscope went up slowly. The screen at the control station showed an image so dark that at first the captain thought there was something wrong with the tiny video camera mounted on the telescoping rod.

'Nothing,' said the captain to Sattari. 'Just blackness.'

Sattari nodded. Next the submarine captain raised a radio mast. Three triangular antennas were mounted on the wand. Two were used to pick up GPS, global positioning signals, from satellites. The third scanned for nearby radio signals, a warning device that would let them know if a ship or aircraft was nearby.

'We are three miles from Karachi,' announced the submarine commander. 'We're ahead of schedule.'

'Very good,' said Sattari.

'There are no ships near us. Would you like to surface?'

A short respite on the surface would be welcome. To breathe fresh air, if only for a moment – Sattari was tempted to say yes, and felt the eyes of the others staring at him, hoping.

But it would increase the risk of being spotted. They were too close now, too close.

'No. We will have fresh air soon enough. Push on,' Sattari said.

Aboard the *Levitow*, over the northern Arabian Sea 0243

Breanna ignored the challenge from the Chinese aircraft, staying on course in Pakistani coastal waters. She had to drop a buoy soon or risk losing the inputs from the Piranha, which was trailing the submarine following the Chinese aircraft carrier. But she didn't want to drop the buoy while the J-13s were nearby; it might tip off the Chinese to the fact that the submarine was being followed.

'*Levitow,* this is Piranha,' said Ensign English. 'Bree, I can't stay with the submarine much longer. I'm slowing the Piranha down, but the submarine will sail out of range within a half hour.'

'All right, I have an idea,' Breanna told her. 'Flighthawk

leader, can you run *Hawk Three* south about eighteen miles and pickle a flare?'

'Repeat?' said Mack.

'I want to get the J-13s off my back. They'll shoot over to check out the flares, don't you think?'

'Yeah, I guess.'

'Throw some chaff, too, so their radars know something's there. Let's do it quick – we don't have much time.'

'I'm going, Captain. Keep your blouse on.'

Breanna shook her head, then glanced at her copilot. Stewart was doing a little better than she had the other day, keeping track of the Chinese patrols as well as a flight of Pakistani F-16s that were roughly twenty minutes flying time to their north. But Stewart still had a way to go. The copilot in the EB-52 had a great deal to do; in some respects her job was actually harder than the pilot's. In a B-52 four crewmen worked the navigational and weapons systems. Computers aboard the EB-52 might have taken over a great deal of their work, but someone still had to supervise the computers.

'How you doing, Jan?'

'I'm with you.'

'I'm going to have Mack toss some flares south of us. Hopefully the J-13s will go in that direction and we can drop a buoy.'

'Uh-huh.'

'I'm going to take us down through three thousand feet so we're ready to drop the buoy. When I give you the signal, I want you to hit the ECMs – I'm going to make it look like we're reacting to the flares that Mack lights, as if we're worried about being under attack. Then you launch. All right?'

'Yeah, yeah.'

'Are you all right, Captain?'

'I'm *all right!*'

Breanna turned her attention back to the sky in front of her, lining up for the buoy drop.

Mack pointed his nose toward the sky and rode the Flighthawk south. Neither of the Chinese J-13s dogging the Megafortress followed. The Chinese navy had encountered Flighthawks before, and referred to them as 'Lei Gong' – the name of an ancient Chinese thunder god, which Mack supposed was a compliment. But it wasn't clear from the J-13s' actions whether they knew he was there.

Mack continued to climb, meanwhile plotting out what he would do. The Chinese aircraft carrier was thirty-two miles away, off his right wing as he flew south. Karachi was ten miles almost directly opposite his left wing. The Indian aircraft carrier was about fifty miles south from the Chinese carrier. An assortment of small escorts were scattered between them, including the Chinese submarine, which was submerged south of Karachi in Pakistani waters.

'All right, Bree, light show begins in ten seconds,' he said, reaching his mark. 'Get ready.'

'Make it a good one.'

* * *

'Sukhois – I mean, J-13s, the Chinese planes – they're biting for it. They're going south,' said Stewart, eyes pasted to the radar plot.

'Buoys!' said Breanna.

Stewart tapped the panel to ready a control buoy for the Piranha. She missed the box and had to tap it again.

Why was everything so hard on this deployment? Back at Dreamland she'd done this sort of thing with her eyes closed. She'd driven B-1s through sandstorms and everything else without a single problem. But she was all thumbs now.

Maybe it was Captain Stockard, breathing down her neck. Breanna just didn't like her for some reason. Maybe she resented working for another woman.

'Buoy!'

Stewart put her forefinger on the release button and pushed. A control buoy spun out of the rear fuselage, deploying from a special compartment behind the bomb bay, added to the planes after the Piranha had become part of the Dreamland tool set.

'ECMs,' said Breanna. 'I'll take the chaff.'

Stewart realized she'd forgotten the stinking ECMs. They should have already been fuzzing the airwaves.

'I'm trying, I'm trying,' she said, hands fumbling against the controls.

Mack jerked the little Flighthawk to the west, leaving a trail of fire and tinsel behind him. He tucked the plane into a roll and then put its nose down, flying it so hard that the tail threatened to pull over on him in a cartwheel. The Flighthawk didn't peep about it, merely trying to keep up with the dictates of the control stick.

The J-13s were racing toward him, wondering what was going on.

If he pushed the nose of the fighter down right now, and slammed the aircraft exactly ninety degrees due east, slammed max power and went for broke, he could take a shot at one of the Chinese planes. If he timed it properly – and if C^3 worked out the angle right – he would slash the fighter across its wings.

This was not the sort of attack you'd make in an F-15. For one thing, you'd never get close enough to use your guns. For another, the g forces as you changed direction to bring the attack would slam you so hard you'd have to struggle to keep your head clear. And . . .

Mack remembered something Cantor had told him during their sortie over the Gulf of Aden: *You're not flying an F-15.* He felt a twinge of anger, and then, far worse, embarrassment.

The punk kid was right. If he really wanted to fly the stinking Flighthawk, he would have to forget everything he knew about flying F-15s or anything other than the Flighthawk. He was going to have to live with its limits – and take advantage of its assets.

And, umpteen kills to his credit or not, he was going to have to face the fact that he had a lot to learn. He was a newbie when it came to the Flighthawk.

'No more F-15s,' he told the plane. 'Just U/MF-3s.'

'Repeat command,' answered the flight computer.

'It's you and me, babe. Just you and me.'

Breanna jerked the Megafortress back and forth across the water, shimmying and shaking as if she thought she was being followed by an SA-6 antiair missile. Finally she eased up, putting the plane into a banking climb and heading back to the west.

'English, how are we looking?' she said to the ensign.

'Buoy is good. I have control.'

'Great.'

'But . . .'

'But?'

'I have a contact at long range, submerged, unknown source. There's another sub out there,' explained English. 'Except that the sound profile doesn't match anything I know. Which is almost impossible.'

'Did the Chinese sub launch a decoy?'

'We would have caught that. It's not a known Pakistani sub either. I'd like to follow it, but I can't watch the Chinese submarine and this at the same time.'

'Stand by,' Breanna told her. 'I'll talk to Captain Gale.'

Aboard the *Abner Read*,
in the northern Arabian Sea
0301

Storm studied the hologram. The Chinese aircraft carrier *Deng Xiaoping* and the Indian carrier *Shiva* were pointing their bows at each other, boxers jutting out their chins and daring their opponent to start something. The Indian carrier had eight planes in the air, along with two ASW; antisubmarine helicopters. The Chinese had twelve planes up, plus two helicopters supplying long-range radar and three on ASW duty.

Two destroyers and one frigate accompanied the Chinese vessel, along with a submarine being tracked by Dreamland's Piranha. The Indians had one destroyer, an old frigate, and two coastal corvettes, which were a little smaller than frigates but were packed with ship-to-ship missiles. The edge went to the Chinese, whose gear was newer and, though largely untested, probably more potent. But at a range of fifty miles, where both task forces could rely on antiship missiles as well as their aircraft, the battle would be ferocious.

And if both navies were to turn on him, rather than each other?

The problem would not be hitting them – he was thirty-five miles to the west of the two carriers, well within range of his Harpoon ship-to-ship missiles; the ship-to-air SM-2 missiles, packed in a Vertical Launching System at the forward deck, could take down an airplane at roughly ninety miles and hit a ship at the same distance. The problem was that there were simply too many targets – the *Abner Read* had only sixteen vertical launch tubes on her forward deck, and while they could be loaded with torpedoes, antiair or antiship missiles, the weapons mix had to be preselected before battle. Reloading was a laborious undertaking and could not be done during a fight.

Storm had eight Harpoons and eight antiaircraft missiles loaded.

Precisely how many missiles it would take to sink either of the carriers was a matter of immense debate and countless computer simulations. According to the intel experts back at the Pentagon, precise hits by four Harpoons should be enough to disable the Indian carrier; the Chinese ship could be crippled with three. In neither case would the ships be sunk – the Indian vessel was known to have been up-armored at the waterline – but the hits would disable enough of their systems to take them out of a battle and leave them highly vulnerable to a second round of attacks to take them to the bottom.

None of the so-called experts had been in battle, however; Storm had, and he suspected their estimates were optimistic. Two months ago it had taken four Harpoons to sink an old Russian amphibious warfare ship that had light defenses and no appreciable armor. Storm and his officers had concluded that it would take at least six very well-placed missile hits to permanently disable either one of the vessels. The real question was how many missiles it would take to get six hits. The answer depended not only on the proficiency of the people firing the missiles and the defenses they faced, but sheer luck. The intel officer threw around some fancy mathematics he called regression analysis and claimed that seven launches would yield six hits, but Storm knew he was just guessing like everyone else.

Missiles were not the *Abner Read*'s only weapon. Storm could use his below-waterline tubes to fire torpedoes at a submarine, and his 155mm gun to hit a surface ship that came within twenty-two miles. His accompanying Sharkboat had four Harpoons and a much more limited 25mm gun. And then there were the Megafortresses . . .

'Tac to bridge – Storm, *Dreamland Levitow* needs to talk to you right away. Piranha's picked up another submarine contact.'

Storm hit the switch on his belt and opened the com channel. 'Talk to me, Dreamland.'

'The Piranha operator has an unknown contact near Karachi,' said Breanna Stockard. 'I'm going to let her fill you in.'

'Do it.'

Another voice came on the line – Ensign Gloria English, who'd been assigned to wipe the Dreamland team's noses.

'Captain Gale, we have an unknown contact near the Karachi port, two miles south of the oil terminal. It appears to be headed toward shore. I can't follow it and the Chinese submarine at the same time.'

'It's going toward shore?'

'Affirmative. I'm going to punch in the coordinates through the shared-information system. They should be there – now.'

Storm looked at the holographic table. A small yellow dot appeared near the coast, roughly twenty miles from the Chinese submarine. Given the direction it was heading, he knew it might be a Pakistani vessel.

Or an Indian boat preparing an attack?

It seemed too far for that.

'Ensign English – what sort of submarine is it?' asked Storm.

'Sir, I can only tell you what it isn't. It's not a Kilo boat, it's not anything the Pakistanis have, at least that we know of. Same with the Indians.'

'You're *sure* it's not Indian?'

'I tried matching against German Type 209s, Kilos, and Foxtrots,' she said, naming the three types of submarines in the Indian fleet. 'No match. I even tried comparing the profile to the Italian CE-f/X1000s. Nada.'

'Help me out here, Ensign. What are those Italian boats?'

'Two-man special forces craft, submersibles. They only have a range of twenty-five miles, but I thought I better be sure. I checked comparable Russian craft as well.'

Was this the boat that had launched the torpedo at the Indian destroyer and taken the special forces teams in and out of Port Somalia?

If so, it was a Pakistani vessel, returning to port.

Not port, exactly. Storm looked at the hologram. There was no submarine docking area anywhere near Karachi.

That he knew about. Which made the sub worth following.

But if Piranha turned off, he'd lose track of the Chinese submarine. That might put his own ship in danger; it was out of range of his sonar array.

It had to be a Pakistani sub. In the end, English would be wasting her time following it – he couldn't do anything about the Paks.

'Stay with the Chinese Kilo. That has to be your priority,' Storm told her. 'Get as much data on this as you can. We'll want to look into it.'

'Aye aye, sir.'

Storm hit the switch on his com unit, tapping the small buttons to contact Colonel Bastian.

'Bastian, this is Storm,' he said when the colonel's face appeared on the bridge communications screen. 'Piranha has an unidentified contact near Karachi. It can't stay with it. But I'd like to figure out just what the hell it is.'

'What'd you have in mind?'

'Since your Megafortress can't be in two places at the same time, I want you to get another one out there. The sub will have to surface soon, and you can catch it on your radar.'

'Can't do that, Storm. We're on a very tight rotation as it is. If you want coverage –'

'Damn it, Bastian. Find a way to make it happen.' He killed the connection with an angry slap at the control unit.

Karachi oil terminal
0305

Captain Sattari looped the wire from the explosive pack around the terminals, then strung it across the metal girder to the base of the stanchion below the massive tank. The explosives were rigged to ignite the collector unit at the Karachi oil terminal complex. Designed to capture fumes from the storage tanks and prevent them from leaking into the environment, the system was the terminal's weak link – blow it up, and the resulting backforce would rip through the pipes and cause fires and explosions in the storage tanks themselves.

Or at least the engineer who had analyzed the terminal believed that to be the case.

Sattari climbed over the long concrete barrier, letting the wire roll out of its spool as he went. He could feel the sweat pouring down his back and the sides of his body. He welcomed it – the poison was running from his body, the poison of fear.

The terminal consisted of several different tank farms, connected by a vast network of piping. Three different docks were used by ships loading and unloading. The gas collection system was at the extreme eastern end, located on a man-made pennisula with a rock jetty that extended to the sea.

The team's demolition expert waited near the rocks. Sattari was glad to find he was not the last man to bring back the wire; two more men had yet to report back. He held up the wire for the man's cutters.

'Thank you, Captain,' said the man, quickly stripping the strands and attaching them to his unit.

There were backup timers on each of the explosives, all set for the same time, but to do maximum damage to the tanks the explosives all had to go off at once, and the best way to guarantee that was by igniting them together. The signal would be received here by short-range radio, then instantly transmitted to the units.

Sergeant Ibn climbed up over the nearby rocks. 'The next to last boat is leaving,' he told the captain. 'You should go.'

'No,' said Sattari. 'Two more men.'

'Captain.' The rocks were covered in shadow, but even in the dim light Sattari knew that his captain was looking at him reproachfully. 'You should be back aboard the submarine, sir. I will wait for them.'

'Thank you, but I will not leave my men,' said Sattari. 'We will come when we have ignited the tanks.'

'Very good, Captain. Very good.'

Ibn put his hand to his head and snapped off a salute. How much had changed in just a few short days; the aches and bruises, the sweat, even the fear, they were all worth it.

Sattari returned the salute, then turned back to look for the others.

Aboard the *Shiva*,
northern Arabian Sea
0310

Memon felt his chest catch as he read the message:

WITHDRAW TO 24° 00' 00'. DO NOT PROVOKE THE CHINESE.

— ADM. SKANDAR

He handed the message to Captain Adri, who smirked but said nothing before giving the paper back to Admiral Kala.

'We will recover the aircraft,' the admiral said in a tone that suggested he was talking to himself rather than giving orders. 'Then we will sail south, and farther out to sea.'

'We've been cheated,' said Memon as the others went silently to their tasks.

Drigh Road
0312

'Hey, Colonel, what can we do for you?' said Danny Freah, rubbing his eyes as he sat down in front of the communications console in the Dreamland Command trailer. Sergeant Rockland, known as Boston, was on duty as the communications specialist. He walked to the other end of the trailer and began making some fresh coffee.

'Sorry to wake you up, Danny,' said Dog, talking from the *Wisconsin*. 'But Piranha has an odd submarine contact near the Karachi port. Storm thinks it may be his mysterious submarine and he wants to see where it surfaces. If it surfaces.'

'You want me to take *Whiplash Osprey* up and reconnoiter?'

'That's exactly what I want you to do.'

'Question – do I tell the Pakistanis what I'm up to?'

'No. He thinks this is their submarine, the same one that attacked the *Calcutta*. Run it as a training mission.'

'Will do.' Danny got up from the console. 'Yo, Boston – go wake up Pretty Boy.'

'Action, Cap?'

'Not really. Just a midnight joy ride. But it'll have to do for now. Roust the Osprey crew on your way.'

* * *

Fifteen minutes later, Danny, Boston, and Sergeant Jack 'Pretty Boy' Floyd peered from the side windows of Dreamland's MV-22 Osprey, using their Mk1 eyeballs to augment the craft's search and air rescue radar and infrared sensors. They were less than fifty feet above the churning gray waves, heading south toward the spot where the Piranha had lost contact with the vessel.

'Gotta be an underwater cave, Cap,' said Boston. 'I say we dive in and find the sucker.'

'Go for it,' said Pretty Boy. 'That water's a stinking sewer.'

'You comin' with me, dude,' joshed Boston. 'You my swimmin' buddy.'

Danny peered out the window, using the night-vision gear embedded in his smart helmet to look at the shoreline. There was a small marina just ahead; pleasure boats bobbed at their moorings. Beyond them a channel led to a set of docks used by container ships. A little farther south sat a large oil terminal, where tankers unloaded their cargo.

It seemed to him this would be a particularly bad place to hide a submarine base. While an enemy might not look for it here, there were so many small boats and commercial vessels that someone was bound to stumble across you sooner or later.

'Whiplash leader to *Levitow*. Bree, can you spare me some attention?'

'What do you need?'

'Punch me through to Ensign English, would you? I want to pick her brain for a second.'

'Stand by.'

'English here.'

'Ensign, this is Danny Freah. Help me out here – why do we think this submarine is Pakistani?'

'We're not really sure. The only thing we know is that it's not similar to known submarines operating in any fleet nearby, nor a Russian or American, for that matter. It could be anyone's.'

'How about a special operations craft?'

'Possible, Captain. I wouldn't rule anything out. It may even be a noisemaker.'

Before Danny could thank her, the aircraft was buffeted by a shock wave.

'Holy shit!' yelled Boston. 'Something just blew up half of Karachi!'

V

Fires of Hell

Northern Arabian Sea,
offshore of the Karachi oil terminal
13 January 1998
0312

The explosion was so immense that it blew one of the men into Captain Sattari, and they tumbled backward into the water. Sattari found himself on his back under the waves, surrounded by darkness. He tried to push himself upright but was paralyzed.

I'm going to die, he thought.

Rather than panic, the idea filled him with a kind of peace. He felt his arms and legs relax; he thought of his triumph now, another mission executed with complete precision.

Then he felt himself being pulled upward. One of his men had grabbed him and was hauling him out of the water.

The man who had fallen on top of him struggled to his knees as Sattari coughed the water from his lungs.

'The boat, Captain,' said his man. 'Into the boat.'

Sattari pushed himself in the direction of the raft.

He found one of the gunwales with his hand and flopped forward, landing in the bottom like a seal flipping itself out of the water. He got upright as the others entered the craft. In a moment they were heading out to sea.

A mountain of fire had erupted from the collection system, setting off a tank of light fuel about fifty yards away. The heat was so warm he could feel it here, more than a quarter mile away. There were rumbles, more explosions – the entire terminal would burn, and burn for hours.

The Pakistanis would have no choice now but to attack. The Indians would retaliate. The Chinese would come to Pakistan's aid. The Indians would be destroyed, and with luck, the Chinese would be severely bloodied as well. Iran would be free of her two rivals – and the price of oil would soar.

Sattari picked up his oar and began helping the others, each stroke pushing them farther out to sea.

There was an aircraft nearby; he heard the loud drone, something like a helicopter, or two perhaps, very close.

'The sub is there, she's there,' said one of the men, spotting a blinking light in the distance.

'Strong strokes!' said Sattari. 'We are almost home, men.'

It was a wildly optimistic lie – they had another thirty-six hours of submerged sailing to do before reaching their next rendezvous – but the men responded with a flurry of strokes.

Aboard the *Shiva*,
northern Arabian Sea
0314

'A huge fireball – I can see it from here. Someone must have set the entire oil terminal on fire.'

Memon watched the admiral as the pilot's report continued over the loudspeaker.

'The Pakistanis have set their oil tanks on fire as an excuse to attack us,' Memon told the admiral when the report ended. 'We should strike before the Chinese can.'

'Our orders say to do nothing to provoke the Chinese,' said Captain Bhaskar. 'Admiral Skandar himself directed us to withdraw.'

'The hell with Skandar – he's not here.'

'You're supposed to be representing him, aren't you?' said Adri.

Memon pressed his lips together. Captain Adri was nothing but a coward. 'The circumstances have changed. If Admiral Skandar were here, he would order the attack himself.'

'Aircraft from the *Deng Xiaoping* have changed course and are heading in our direction,' reported the radar officer.

'Will we wait until their missiles hit us to fire back?' Memon asked.

'Prepare for missile launch,' said the admiral. 'Air commander – shoot those fighters down.'

Danny grabbed hold of one of the restraining straps at the side of the Osprey as the aircraft wheeled around to head toward the terminal. The pilots had flipped on the Osprey's searchlights, but the towering flames from the explosion were more than enough to illuminate the facility and surrounding water. The force of the explosion probably meant that at least one of the two liquefied natural gas tanks at the terminal had been detonated. Geysers of flame shot up, as if competing with each other for brilliance.

Danny reached to the back of his smart helmet and hit the circuit to tie into the Dreamland Command channel.

'Danny Freah for Colonel Bastian. Colonel?'

The software smart agent that controlled the communications channels buzzed the colonel, whose voice soon boomed in Danny's ear.

'What's going on?'

'An attack on the Karachi port oil terminal. Big attack – has to be sabotage. My bet is that submarine we were looking for wasn't Pakistani at all.'

'Stand by, Danny.'

The Osprey drew parallel to the conflagration, then veered away, the fire and secondary explosions so intense that the pilot feared for his aircraft.

'Danny, we're going to swing *Levitow* over that way to use its radar to search for periscopes,' said Dog. 'In the meantime, search the immediate area for small boats, anything that might be used by a spec-op team to get away. You know the drill. And if you see any survivors who need help –'

'Yeah, we're on that, Colonel,' Danny told him, moving forward to confer with the pilots.

Aboard the *Levitow*,
over the northern Arabian Sea
0317

'Coming to new course,' Breanna told Stewart. 'We should be within visual range of the terminal in less than five minutes.'

'Roger that,' said Stewart.

Breanna heard a tremble in her copilot's voice. There wasn't much she could do about it now, so she ignored it, quickly checking the panels on the configurable 'dashboard' in front of her.

'Piranha to *Levitow*,' said Ensign English over the interphone. 'Captain, I've put the Piranha into a circle pattern around our last buoy. The Chinese submarine is twenty miles from the buoy. At most, we have an hour before we'll lose contact.'

'Roger that, Piranha. Thanks, Gloria. That vessel did not launch or have any contact with the one we've been trailing?'

'Affirmative. We would have heard it. These are two unrelated boats.'

The radar warning receiver began buzzing. Without waiting for her copilot, Breanna hit a preset to display the threat panel at her station. One of the Chinese escort vessels had activated the targeting radar for its antiaircraft batteries. They were outside its effective range, though of course that might not keep them from firing.

'Jan – ECMS,' said Breanna, deciding not to take any chances.

'ECMS, yes. Communication on the guard frequency,' added the copilot. 'All aircraft are being warned to stay away from the Chinese fleet or be shot down.'

'How far away?'

'Not specific. Pakistanis are declaring an emergency – they're saying the same thing.'

'To us?'

'Um, not specifically.'

'J-13s heading our way,' broke in the airborne radar operator.

'All right, everyone, let's take this step by step,' Breanna told her crew. 'We're proceeding on course to look for a possible submarine. Be prepared for evasive maneuvers. We will defend ourselves if necessary.'

'Indian aircraft are approaching Chinese task force at a high rate of speed!' said the radar operator, shouting now. 'Two J-13s going to meet them. They're gunning for each other, Bree.'

The radar warning receiver lit up with a new threat – a Pakistani antiaircraft battery northeast of Karachi was trying to get a fix on them. The missiles associated with the radar were American Hawks, early generation antiaircraft weapons still potent against low and medium altitude aircraft out to about twenty-five miles.

The weapons' aim could be disrupted with a specific ECM program stored in the Megafortress's computer; they represented a low threat. Even so, the sky was starting to get a bit crowded.

'Jan, see if you can get word to the PAF that we're a friendly. Broadcast an alert – see if you can make contact with one of their patrols.'

'F-16s scrambling in our direction,' answered Stewart.

Crowded indeed. 'Surface radar – Smitty, you have any periscopes yet?'

'Looking, Captain.'

'J-13s are goosing their jets,' said Stewart. 'They'll be within range to fire their missiles in zero-one minutes.'

**Aboard the *Wisconsin*,
over the western Arabian Sea
0317**

'Indian and Chinese planes are mixing it up, Colonel,' said T-Bone. 'This is going to get ugly fast.'

Dog hit the preset to connect with the *Abner Read*. 'Eyes, this is Bastian. The Indian and Chinese aircraft are firing at each other. There may be an attack under way against that Chinese carrier.'

Storm came on the line. 'Get your aircraft out of there,' he told Dog. 'Stay just close enough to get radar pictures of what's going on if you can. But if there's any doubt –'

'The contact we had earlier must have been some sort of special operations craft that dropped off commandos,' Dog continued. 'If you want us to look for it –'

'Pull back, Bastian. For your own good. I don't want any casualties. They're not worth it.'

'Roger that,' Dog told him.

Aboard the *Levitow*,
over the western Arabian Sea
0318

Mack continued to climb, pulling the Flighthawk five thousand feet over the Megafortress's tail. The Flighthawk's threat panel showed that the two J-13s were armed with Chinese versions of the radar-guided AMRAAMski. He'd make his attack as the first plane closed to nineteen miles; if he played it right, he would be able to jerk back and take a quick shot at the other, which was riding about a quarter mile behind and to the east. And if he played it wrong, Breanna would still have some space to take evasive action.

Played it wrong?

He had to admit it was a possibility.

'*Hawk Three*, we're under orders to break contact with the Chinese and Indian forces,' said Breanna. 'We're breaking off the search.'

'Repeat?'

'I'm changing course and going north, Mack. Stay with me.'

'Don't worry about these guys,' Mack told her. 'I'll dust them.'

'Negative, Mack,' said Breanna. 'Stay with me!'

Aboard the *Abner Read*, in the northern Arabian Sea 0318

'Can we send one of those Flighthawks close enough to the Chinese fleet to get infrared images?' asked Eyes. 'This is an intelligence bonanza. If these idiots are stupid enough to fight each other, we might as well benefit.'

Storm thought that was an excellent idea – except that as Bastian was fond of pointing out, the Flighthawks had to stay close to the Megafortresses, and they had to stay a good distance away from the Chinese or risk getting shot down.

But he had an asset that could get as close as he wanted it to. Best of all, he didn't have to deal with Bastian's people to get it done.

Or maybe more accurately, the person who he had to talk to no longer belonged to Bastian.

'Eyes, get the second Werewolf airborne. I'm going to talk to Airforce personally,' Storm added, flipping into the communications channel. 'Starship? You hear me?'

'Yes, Captain.'

'Listen carefully, Airforce. Take *Werewolf One* and

head toward the Indian task force. I want pictures of that carrier and everything it does. Get *Two* airborne and hustle it over toward the Chinese. Same thing there.'

'That's going to leave us naked.'

'Do I have to explain every single detail of what I'm thinking to you, son?'

'Yes, sir. I mean no. *Werewolf One* en route.'

Aboard *Whiplash Osprey*, near the Karachi oil terminal 0320

'Hey, Cap, is that a wake down there? Some sort of wave?' said Boston, pointing out the window.

Danny went to the left side of the aircraft and peered out at the water about twelve feet below.

'I'm not sure what you're looking at, Boston.'

'Let's get lower. Can we get lower?'

Before Danny could hit the interphone line on the communications system to talk to the pilots, the Osprey veered sharply to his right.

'Chinese aircraft is challenging us, and trying to lock with weapons radar,' said the pilot. 'I have to get out of here.'

'Go ahead, go!' Danny told him. And before the word was out of his mouth, the Osprey had settled her tiltrotors and jerked back toward shore.

Aboard the *Levitow*,
over the northern Arabian Sea
0321

Breanna acknowledged the Karachi tower's instructions, telling the Pakistani flight controller that they were clearing out of its airspace. The transmission was overrun by a radio call from another group of aircraft.

'*Dreamland Levitow*, this is Whiplash leader,' said Danny on the Dreamland channel.

'*Levitow.*'

'Bree, we're being targeted by some Chinese aircraft.'

Breanna glanced at the sitrep. The *Levitow* was thirty miles due west of Karachi, over Pakistan. *Whiplash Osprey* was three miles south of the city, close to the oil terminal. Apparently the J-13s that had been following them had broken off once the Megafortress changed course. They were now approaching the Osprey.

'Hang on, Danny,' she said, jerking the control stick to turn the big aircraft around. 'Cavalry's on its way.'

Aboard the *Shiva*,
in the northern Arabian Sea
0321

The first missile left the *Shiva* with a thunk and hiss, steam furrowing from the rear. Two more quickly followed. The missiles seemed to stutter in the sky, as if unsure of where they were going, but their noses straightened as they reached the black edge of the night beyond the darkened ship. All three were P-700 Granits – known to NATO as SS-N-19 Shipwrecks. The Russian-designed weapons were potent, long-range cruise missiles with thousand-kilogram explosive warheads.

Memon watched as their shadows disappeared, oblivious to the chaos behind him. The carrier was simultaneously maneuvering to launch another set of fighters and to fire a round of missiles. These were P-120 Malakhits, better known as SS-N-9 Sirens. The weapons required mid-course guidance to strike their target; this would be provided by a data link with a specially designated Su-33.

'The Chinese aircraft are attempting to lock their weapons radars on us!' warned one of the officers on the bridge.

Memon felt himself strangely at peace. India's new age was beginning; the future held great promise.

Northern Arabian Sea,
offshore of the Karachi oil terminal
0323

Captain Sattari gripped the seat restraint as the submarine sank. At every second, he expected an attack. The Parvaneh was not armored at all; a few bullets through the hull would cause serious damage.

'There are many aircraft above,' the submarine captain told him. 'It may be difficult to take the course as planned.'

'What do you suggest?'

'We move farther offshore, and remain submerged for a few hours before proceeding. The nearby ships will launch a search, you see. The more we move, the easier we will be to find.'

The other submarines were already moving toward the rendezvous point. If they waited, they might miss them and the A-40 that was to pick them up in two days.

'No,' said Sattari. 'The chaos will help us escape. The Indians and Chinese will be concerned with each other. Allah is with us. Let us place ourselves in His hands.'

Aboard the *Levitow*,
above the northern Arabian Sea
0325

Mack had to scramble to stay with the Megafortress as it twisted back toward Karachi. A pair of Pakistani F-16s were flying out of the east on a collision course, but the J-13s targeting the Whiplash aircraft were his priority. He pushed his nose down, accelerating as he aimed to get between the Chinese fighters and the Osprey.

'Fighters are still not acknowledging,' said Stewart over the interphone.

'Tell them I'm going to shoot them down if they fire on my people,' snapped Mack, jamming the throttle for more speed.

Aboard *Whiplash Osprey*,
near Karachi
0326

Danny Freah flew against the bulkhead to the cockpit as the Osprey veered downward, trying to duck the Chinese fighters. The gyrations spun the Whiplash captain around like a pinball, slapping him against one of the benches and bouncing him back toward the cockpit. Danny grabbed for one of the strap handles near the opening, checking his momentum like a cowboy busting a bronc.

'Tell them we're Americans, damn it,' Danny said to the pilot.

'I keep trying, Captain. They're not listening.'

Flames leapt up in front of them.

'I'm going to stay near the fire,' said the pilot. 'They won't be able to use their heat-seekers.'

'Don't burn us up in the meantime,' said Danny, nearly losing his balance as the Osprey veered hard to the left.

Aboard the *Deng Xiaoping*,
in the northern Arabian Sea
0327

Captain Hongwu counted the enemy's missile launches as they were announced, listening with a Buddhalike patience that would have impressed his ancestors, though Hongwu himself did not put much stock in the religion's basic beliefs. He was surprised by the Indians' attack, but not caught off guard; tensions between the two countries had been increasing for years, and ships from the two nations had engaged in a bloody battle in the Pacific months before. The Chinese had not done particularly well in that battle, but Hongwu had carefully studied it, and planned now to apply its lessons.

He had another advantage besides knowledge: a considerably improved anti-cruise-missile system. The Pili, or Thunderbolt, had been developed from the LY-60 Falcon, with insights gained from the Italian Aspide. The weapon flew at Mach 4 and could strike a cruise missile at twenty kilometers.

Or so it had on the testing range. It was about to be put through a much more grueling trial.

Listening to the reports, Hongwu grasped the Indian commander's mistake; rather than concentrating his attack, he was launching small salvos against the entire fleet.

'Prepare to defend the ship,' said Captain Hongwu. 'And then answer the attack. Have Squadron One attack the *Shiva*. Direct the others to attack any target they see south of us.'

'Any ship, Captain?'

'Any ship. There are only Indian warships south of our fleet.'

Northern Arabian Sea
0327

Starship mistook the vessel that loomed ahead in his screen for the *Deng Xiaoping*, even though he knew from the sitrep that he should be at least five miles from the Chinese aircraft carrier. A flood of tracers erupted from midships, a fountain of green sparks in the screen. He started to veer away before realizing the gunfire wasn't aimed at him; it leapt far off to his left, extending toward a dark shadow that rose from the sea like a shark. Lightning flashed; the ship, fully illuminated for a moment, seemed to be pushed back in his screen. Another flood of tracers began firing, and a missile launched from the forward deck near the superstructure of the ship, which he now knew must be one of the Chinese destroyers.

Two seconds later there was another white flash, this one partially blocked by the ship. A geyser of light erupted near the destroyer's funnel. Two, three, fireballs rocketed above the ship.

'I see two missile strikes,' Starship told Eyes, 'on the Chinese destroyer – it's UNK-C-1 on my screen,' he added, using the computer's designation for the contact.

'We see it. Good work. Get over to the carrier,' said Eyes.

'Working on it,' said Starship.

Aboard the *Levitow*,
above the northern Arabian Sea
0328

'*Hawk Three* is thirty seconds from the intercept,' Stewart told Breanna. 'What do you want him to do?'

'He's going to shoot the Chinese planes down if they don't break off,' said Breanna.

Stewart nodded to herself. How could Breanna be so calm? All hell was breaking loose – besides the two J-13s, another pair of jets had just taken off from the Chinese carrier and were turning in their direction. There were all sorts of missiles in the air, radars, aircraft – Stewart couldn't keep track of any of it.

She had dealt with just this sort of chaos dozens of times in simulations. But this was exponentially different.

'Try the Chinese one more time,' said Breanna.

As Stewart went to push the communication button to broadcast simultaneously on all-known frequencies, she realized she already had set the unit to do so. '*Dreamland Levitow* to Chinese J-13s following the Osprey aircraft – that's one of ours. He's on a rescue mission. Don't fire on him, damn you. Acknowledge. Or else we're shooting you down!'

She pressed the button on the next panel down, rebroadcasting the radio transmission in Chinese. Then, trying to anticipate what Bree would want to do, she went to the weapons screen and got ready to launch an AMRAAM-plus.

Mack saw the Osprey in the long-range scan, dancing over the burning tank farm. The pilot seemed to be using the fire as a way to deke any missiles launched at him. It seemed like a good idea, though it sure looked dangerous – the aircraft dipped and disappeared in the flames, bobbing upward only to zip down again.

The J-13 appeared on his screen, coming in from the right about three miles ahead of him. Mack began angling toward its tail, his heart starting to race as the targeting bar blinked yellow. He was going to nail this sucker, and it was going to feel good.

Just as the targeting bar began blinking red, the J-13 stretched in his screen. It was an optical illusion – the plane was veering hard to the right. Mack hung with it; the bar went solid red.

'He's turning off, Mack,' said Breanna. 'The Chinese aircraft is turning off.'

Too late, thought Mack. He's dead.

But he lifted his finger off the trigger.

Aboard the *Shiva*,
in the northern Arabian Sea
0335

The guns immediately below the bridge began to fire, their steady staccato the sound of a jackhammer tearing through thin concrete. Memon stared in the direction of the steam of bullets but couldn't see their target. Then yellow light rose from below. Memon saw the shadow of a man loom before him, then heaved over, the deck suddenly cut away. He felt hot and wet, surrounded by screams, and a curtain of pain stunned his vision black.

Aboard the *Wisconsin*,
in the northern Arabian Sea
0336

'Two J-13s heading in the direction of the *Abner Read*,' T-Bone told Dog, reading the screens at his airborne radar station. 'Twenty-five feet above sea level. Not clear that they have the ship ID'd as a target. Approximately twenty-five miles from the *Abner Read*. Computer says they have very large missiles aboard, Colonel – Chinese variation of Styx, designation C-106.'

'Bay,' Dog told Jazz, changing course to intercept them.

The copilot acknowledged and the bomb bay door swung open.

'*Dreamland Wisconsin* to *Abner Read*. Two aircraft are heading in your direction. They appear equipped with versions of the Russian Styx.'

'Bastian, what do you have?' said Eyes.

'J-13s coming at you hot. Each has a Styx cruise missile. I can take them out, but you have to decide right now.'

'Stand by.'

The com line went silent. Almost a full minute passed before Storm came back on the line.

'They're homing in on our radar,' said Storm. 'They may think we're one of the Indian screening ships. We've broadcast a warning and they haven't responded. If they don't turn back in sixty seconds, shoot them down.'

'Copy that.'

Aboard *Dreamland Osprey*,
near Karachi
0336

A wall of flames appeared directly in front of the Osprey. Before Danny could blink, they'd flown into them. The aircraft shot sideways, shimmying and shaking and jerking like a train that had suddenly come off its tracks. Finally, the nose moved upward in a gentle tilt and they climbed away from the raging fires.

Danny saw figures running along a pier near the northern side of the terminal. The water around them seemed to be on fire.

'Let's see if we can rescue them,' he told the pilot. 'We'll break out the rescue basket and winch it down.'

'The whole place is on fire,' said the pilot.

'Which means we better hurry.'

Danny ran to the rear of the aircraft and told Boston and Pretty Boy that they were going to try and pull the people off the pier. As they pulled the stretcher basket out from its compartment below the web seats, Danny clicked back into the Dreamland command line.

'Whiplash leader to *Dreamland Levitow* – Bree, you there?'

'Go ahead, Danny.'

'Listen, there are some people stranded on a pier here and we're going to try helping them. In the meantime, we saw a wake west of the oil farm about ten minutes ago. We didn't see anything on the surface, and then those fighters started chasing us. Maybe it's your submarine.'

'Roger that. Thanks.'

Aboard the *Shiva*,
in the northern Arabian Sea
0336

A thousand demons roared in Memon's ears, cursing the sun, swearing that it would never rise again. Shiva, the Hindu god of war, leered before him. The god's tongue was pure fire; the flames licked at Memon's eyes, burning through the sockets.

Memon rolled away. He found himself facedown on the deck, hands so hot they seemed to be on fire. He pushed upright and struggled to his knees.

A man's body lay next to him. It seemed to have grown another arm in the middle of its chest, fingers curled around a knife. Memon struggled to comprehend what he was seeing – a sailor impaled by a huge piece of metal.

'Deputy Minister Memon! Help the deputy minister!'

Memon felt himself being pulled to his feet. A klaxon horn sounded nearby. There were shouts. Memon heard a sound like water running into a tub, then realized it was the whimper of a man dying nearby. His right arm had been sheered two-thirds off and he lay in a pool of blood.

Memon looked away. A hole had been blown in the side of the ship's island, and the compartment next to

245

them obliterated. He could see stars in the distance, twinkling white above the red-tinged sea.

'The admiral is dead,' said a sailor.

Memon shook his head, as if he might shake away the chaos and confusion. Someone was talking to him – Captain Adri – but he could not process the words. Memon tried to force himself to understand, but could not. The captain seemed very insistent, repeating whatever he was saying over and over. Finally, not sure what he was agreeing to, Memon nodded his head to make Adri go away.

Northern Arabian Sea
0336

Starship split his main screen into two views, one with the image of the Chinese carrier and the other focused on the Indian. The antiaircraft systems of both ships picked him up, but in neither case was he targeted, possibly because the human operators aboard the ships thought any helicopter this close had to be on their side. Starship knew this wouldn't last – sooner or later, he thought, he'd be shot down – but he figured that until then he'd get as good a view of what was going on as possible. He bobbed and wove, hovering for a bit and then flitting off, trying to pay equal attention to each aircraft. Two missiles had hit the Indian carrier, one just below the forward deck where its main missile batteries were located, the other, more devastatingly, at the forward part of the carrier's island, about where the bridge should be. The ship's guns had shot down several other missiles.

The Chinese carrier had been hit once, almost straight on the starboard arm of its V-shaped flight deck. Two of its helicopters were hovering above the damage, preparing to conduct a rescue mission or otherwise render assistance.

'Werewolf, see if you can get closer to the Chinese ship,' said Eyes.

'They're tracking me. If I get much closer they may fire.'

'Just do it.'

Starship put *Werewolf Two* into an orbit around the Indian ship and gave it to the computer to control. That done, he pushed *Werewolf One* forward, zigging in the direction of the Chinese carrier's stern. The carrier had a pair of twin 37mm close-in weapons and a larger caliber 57mm weapon mounted on deck bulges just below the flight deck on either side of the stern, but they were positioned in a way that made it difficult for them to strike anything approaching directly at the flight deck. Like most aircraft carriers, protection was meant to come from the escorts and the ships' planes; anything that actually made it through the screen faced relatively light defenses.

But not impotent ones – the 57mm gun on the port side began firing its large shells as the Werewolf skipped around. The stream of lead passed over the aircraft; Starship knew he was lucky. Now lined up perfectly with the stern, he took the aircraft up to fifty feet above the waves, then had a sudden inspiration: Why not fly directly over the flight deck?

'Hope this is close enough for you, *Navy*,' he said, pushing the robot aircraft forward.

Aboard the *Wisconsin*,
above the northern Arabian Sea
0338

The J-13s were flying from the northeast toward the *Abner Read*. To get them with the AMRAAM-plus Scorpions, Dog had to change course and close down the angle the missiles would have to take. Doing so, he'd make the Megafortress itself an easier target.

The real problem was that he had only two Scorpions. They'd filled the other slots on the rotating bomb dispenser with additional sonar and Piranha buoys.

'Start the turn now,' said Jazz, cuing him with the help of the flight computers.

'*Wisconsin*, I can take these guys,' said Cantor.

'There's two of them.'

'Yeah, but I can get them.'

'Do it,' said Dog.

Cantor swung *Flighthawk One* away from the Megafortress's wing, pirouetting around the bigger aircraft as it maneuvered to put itself into a firing position to attack the J-13s. The nose of the robot aircraft was now on a parallel plane to the approaching enemy fighters. The J-13s were moving very quickly; as soon as he made his first turn, the computer told him he had to turn again. He did, and found himself slightly ahead of the lead bogey. The J-13 was going so fast that it slipped right up under him in the blink of an eye; Cantor barely had time to press the trigger.

The 20mm slugs that poured from the belly of the U/MF were not the largest bullets in the world, but scattered artfully around the Chinese jet, they tore it to shreds. The outer third of the J-13's right wing seemed to fold away; the aircraft turned into an unguided missile, its nose pushing toward the sea.

So far the intercept had played out perfectly; in fact, it followed to the millimeter a training simulation based on several of Zen's real-life encounters. But the similarity to the exercise had a downside: As he recovered, Cantor expected the other aircraft to come up on his right, just as it did in the computer program. But as he edged in that direction, the display showed that the plane had already cut left. Belatedly changing course, he failed to anticipate another cut by the J-13 and sailed past the plane without a chance for a shot.

Cantor corrected, twisting back toward the weaving aircraft. The Chinese plane turned in his direction, and even though he knew he didn't have a good shot – the targeting bar was yellow – Cantor pressed his trigger.

The bullets trailed off to the left but got the J-13 pilot's attention; worried about whoever it was behind him, the Chinese pilot pulled hard left. The turn was a mistake, taking away the bigger plane's speed advantage. Cantor, with his much smaller turning radius, cut inside the other plane, narrowing the distance enough to get on his tail as he cut back. The bogey flew into the sweet spot in his targeting screen. Cantor pressed the trigger.

His bullets shot like a thick sword into his target's heart. Parts flew from the aircraft; Cantor pulled off as it exploded.

'Missile away,' said T-Bone, the airborne radar operator on the deck above. The Chinese pilot had managed to target and fire his missile, probably at the cost of his own life.

Aboard the *Abner Read*,
in the northern Arabian Sea
0340

Storm saw the warning on the holographic map table before he heard the alarm. A second later the ship's defensive weapons operator reported they were tracking a Styx missile headed in their direction.

'Distance to ship, twelve miles. Tracking. Missile does not appear to have locked onto target.'

The Chinese-made missile guided itself to the general vicinity of the target via an internal navigational system; once it got close, on-board radar would take over. The missile would descend to about twenty-five feet above the water, aiming not only to strike as low as possible but avoiding shipboard defenses. The *Abner Read*'s stealthy radar profile made it a difficult target for the missile, though anytime five hundred kilos of explosives were flying at you, it could not be taken lightly.

The missile covered roughly a third of a mile in a second. Before thirty seconds had passed, the Phalanx close-in 25mm cannon battery had zeroed in on the approaching missile and was ready to take it down. The missile had not yet found the *Abner Read*; it was tracking off to the west and still relatively high. This wasn't a problem, however: The Chinese missile flew into a cloud of nickel, cobalt, and tungsten, immolating itself about a mile from the ship.

By inclination and instinct, Storm wanted to retaliate against the Chinese. In his mind, he'd be completely justified sinking the aircraft carrier that had launched the plane. But his orders were very clear; he was to avoid conflict at all cost.

Still.

Still.

'Communications – get that Chinese carrier. I want to find out why the hell we were attacked. If they don't apologize . . .'

He let his voice trail off. If they didn't apologize, he'd sink the damn ship, consequences be damned.

'Excellent work, Weapons,' said Storm, switching into their circuit. 'Dreamland owes us one.'

Starship spun the Werewolf directly over the split in the *Deng Xiaoping*'s flight deck, the aircraft's cameras recording the scramble of the crew as it prepared to recover two of its aircraft. He felt as if he were a voyeur who'd snuck into a foreign palace. A J-13 slammed to a stop at the far side of the deck; men swarmed over it, wrestling it off the arrestor cables and wheeling it forward to an elevator.

A second J-13 appeared in the distance, making its approach.

'Werewolf, check out the escort ships in the Chinese group,' said Eyes. 'Look for the frigate. We have enough on the carrier now. Stand by for coordinates.'

The J-13 landed, and once more the crew swarmed over her. A notion seized Starship as they began pushing the plane forward: Why not get a look at the hangar deck of the carrier? Just hover right over the other aircraft as it went down, spin around, then shoot the hell out of there.

Before he fully considered the idea, Starship had pushed the Werewolf forward, skittering across the flat surface of the Chinese vessel about eight feet from the deck. The ship's lights threw a crosshatch of white and black in his face. The J-13 had just been secured on the elevator; as he approached, he saw the startled face of one of the deck crew diving for cover.

Starship thought he'd made his move too soon – the J-13 sat below him, not moving. Two figures were crouched near the folded-up wings. He spun the Werewolf around, picking up his tail slightly to give the forward camera a better view. Disappointed, he was just about to hit the gas and get out of there when the elevator began cranking downward.

Starship descended as well. He moved a little too fast – the skids smacked against the J-13. He jerked upward, then settled back down, hitting his floodlights. When the elevator stopped at hangar level, he was just above the airplane, with maybe four or five feet worth of clearance between him and the roof. He spun around once as slowly as he dared, glimpsing aircraft, people, machinery, all in a blur. Then he jerked the Werewolf straight up, praying that he was still in the same position as when he'd descended.

'What the hell are you doing?' yelled Eyes.

'Taking a look inside the sardine box,' Starship told him. 'What were those coordinates?'

Aboard the *Shiva*,
in the northern Arabian Sea
0345

The doctor held his small penlight up and told Memon he had received a mild concussion.

'You should rest,' he said.

'The ship,' said Memon. 'I'm responsible.'

'Captain Adri is in charge.'

'Adri, yes. Where is he?'

'You just came from him.'

'Someone take me to him.'

Memon pushed himself off the cot. The doctor grabbed his arm to help steady him, then passed him gently to a sailor, who led him back through the corridor, up a flight of stairs, then through another passage to the combat center. Adri and several other officers were stooped over a set of charts, discussing something.

'We have to strike them again,' said Adri, his voice rising above the din in the low-ceiling room. 'We must drive home our gains.'

Adri? Adri was talking of attack?

Memon was amazed. Adri had opposed him earlier. He and Bhaskar had done everything they could to avoid a fight.

And they'd been right.

They'd been right!

'We should not attack,' said Memon, approaching them.

Adri looked up. 'What?'

'We should withdraw.'

'You? You're saying that?'

'Yes. You were right earlier. We should withdraw.'

'It's too late for that.'

The flash had done something to his vision, Memon thought – the world had shaded deep red. Even the lights appeared to be crimson rather than yellowish white.

'Thank you for your advice,' sneered Adri. 'Someone please take Mr Memon back to sickbay.'

Aboard *Whiplash Osprey*,
near Karachi
0345

The wind whipped through the open door as the Osprey lowered itself toward the three men on the pier. Light petroleum or fuel from one of the nearby tanks had spread onto the water and caught fire; blue flames curled across the dark surface, looking like tumbleweeds in a fantasy Wild West show. But the flames were very real – when they reached the small bobbing boats nearby, they erupted in red volcanoes, consuming the vessels and everything aboard. Danny tried not to think of the possibility that there were people on some of the boats.

'One of us has to go down there,' said Boston, pulling gloves from his tactical vest. 'These guys ain't doing it themselves. Look – they're burnt to shit and scared besides. In shock.'

'Let them grab the basket,' said Pretty Boy. 'Faster.'

'Yeah, but they're not gonna.' Boston had already climbed half inside it. He had his radio unit but no wet suit, just the standard combat fatigues they'd turned out in earlier. 'You drop me, Pretty Boy, and I'm getting you back.'

Pretty Boy cursed at him but began working the controls to the winch, lowering the line as the Osprey continued to descend. Danny pulled out some blankets and the medical chest, getting burn packets ready.

The tanks were still burning nearby, and it took considerable work to keep the aircraft in a stable hover. Every so often it would twitch right or left, but they always got it back.

'Number one coming up!' shouted Boston, his voice blaring in Danny's smart helmet. He went to the door and waited as the cable cranked upward. When the basket finally appeared, the man inside forgot about the belts Boston had secured and tried to leap into the cabin. As he did, the Osprey tilted with a sudden updraft. The stretcher lurched out of Danny's reach, then swung back so hard it nearly knocked him over. Danny grappled the stretcher to a stop as Pretty Boy grabbed hold; they pulled the panic-stricken man inside and rolled him to the floor.

First degree burns covered the man's right arm. His face was putty white, and his pulse raced; he was in shock and pain, but in a relative sense not that badly off. Danny cut away his shirt and part of his pants leg, making sure there were no further injuries. Then he put a pair of ice packs on the burns and covered the man with a blanket. Color had already started to return to his face.

'Need help here, Cap,' said Pretty Boy.

Danny reached the door as the basket returned. The man inside was unconscious. Danny pulled at the stretcher but it didn't budge. Pretty Boy jumped up to help as the Osprey lurched once more. He tumbled against Danny, his head pounding him in the ribs, but he managed at the same time to pull the stretcher inside.

Danny took the man in his arms and carried him to the rear, stumbling as the Osprey continued to buck.

'Getting wicked down there,' said the pilot. 'We can't hold this much longer!'

'Just one more,' said Danny. 'Boston? Come up with this load.'

Boston's response was garbled. Danny concentrated on the new patient, whose charred clothes disintegrated as he examined them. Motley patches of crinkled black skin alternated with white blotches on the Pakistani's chest and left hand; third degree burns. Danny pulled a bottle of distilled water from the burn kit and irrigated as much of the wounds as he could. He wrapped a burn dressing over them, wincing as he worked, though his patient didn't react. He was definitely breathing, though; Danny left him to help Pretty Boy with their final rescuee.

Pretty Boy was two-thirds of the way out of the cabin, trying to secure the stretcher. The Osprey had started to revolve slowly, as if it were twisting at the end of a string, and the momentum of the aircraft seemed to be pitching the stretcher away from the cabin. One of Pretty Boy's legs disappeared. Danny leapt at the other, trying to keep his trooper inside the craft. The shoestring tackle would have made his old high school football coach proud; Pretty Boy sailed back into the cabin, along with the stretcher.

The occupant, who had to weigh close to three hundred pounds, filled the entire stretcher. Fortunately, he was conscious and seemingly not badly hurt, with a small patch of red on his cheek and a large stretch on both arms. Coughing violently, he got up slowly and made his way to the rear of the cabin.

The Osprey lifted straight up with a jerk, then began moving forward.

'Boston? Where the hell is Boston?' yelled Danny, scrambling toward the door.

The pier was now surrounded by red flames. Boston stood near the end, waving his arms.

'Get us back down there!' Danny told the pilot.

'Can't do it, Captain.'

'You got to.'

257

'The wind and flames are too intense. And we're getting torched.'

Exasperated, Danny went to the equipment locker and pulled out two LAR-V rebreather setups – underwater scuba gear intended for clandestine insertions. He pulled on the vest and fasted the small tank under his belt, still wearing his smart helmet.

'Drop me as close to the pier as you can. Meet us out beyond the fire.'

'Captain!'

Danny hooked his arm through the second bundle of gear. They were about thirty yards from the pier, up at least thirty feet. Flames covered the surface of the water.

'Take care of number two – he's got third degree burns,' Danny yelled to Pretty Boy as he threw off his helmet and jumped into the water.

Aboard the *Levitow*,
over Pakistan
0348

Breanna studied the map Ensign English had just sent to her station, showing where she proposed that Piranha control buoys be dropped. Worried about losing touch with the probe, she'd ordered it back east when the port was attacked. Now they were trying to locate the earlier contact, but hadn't had any luck. English wanted to look farther south in the direction of the Indian fleet, but that wasn't going to happen while the two sides were throwing stones at each other.

'Good map, Ensign,' she told her, 'but it's going to be a while. Put Piranha in autonomous mode if you have to.'

'I have to.'

'Two more PAF F-16s querying us,' interrupted Stewart, her voice shrill. 'They're challenging us.'

'Tell them who we are,' said Breanna. She turned inland toward Karachi at about twenty thousand feet. Even from that altitude she could see the fire at the terminal.

The Dreamland communications channel buzzed with an incoming message from the *Wisconsin*. Breanna snapped it on and her father's helmeted face appeared on her screen.

'Breanna, what are you doing that far east?'

'We're trying to get back control of the Piranha and look for that submarine,' she said. 'And I want to stay close to Danny and the Osprey.'

'As soon as the Osprey is out of there, return to base,' he told her. 'Refuel, and then get back on station. Be prepared to relocate to Diego Garcia.'

'We're bugging out?'

'The Pentagon thinks Karachi is being targeted. They want us out of there. I checked with Jed; the President agrees we should relocate. Jed's helping work out the details.'

'Just like that?' said Breanna. Using either Crete or Diego Garcia as a base would add several hours to the patrol time.

'The Pakistani defenses around Karachi won't do much against a concentrated attack,' said the colonel. 'We're sitting ducks there.'

'*Dreamland Levitow* acknowledges.'

'Our two other crews are in the process of bugging out as well,' Dog told her. 'I'll keep you advised.'

'Roger that.'

Aboard the *Abner Read*,
in the northern Arabian Sea
0355

Starship had never seen a ship sink before. Now he saw it twice, on both halves of his screen, almost in stereo – the Chinese frigate, and one of the Indian corvettes, both hit by multiple missiles, gave themselves up to the water.

The frigate went first. A good hunk of her bow had been blown away. She bent to the waves, settling like an old woman easing into a bath. The radar above the antenna mast continued to turn as the ship sank, adamantly remaining at its post. A boat pushed off from the deck near the funnel. Then the ship's downward progression stopped, as if it changed its mind about sinking; the forward section rose slightly.

Starship glanced at the Indian vessel, which was listing heavily toward its wounded starboard side. When he glanced back at the Chinese frigate, its bow had gone back down and its stern had risen from the water. The helicopter flight deck looked like a fly swatter. Men jumped from the sides, swimming toward rafts and small boats as the ship's rear continued to rise. When the angle reached about sixty degrees, the stricken vessel plunged downward, a knife stabbing the vast ocean. Steam curdled up, and then there was nothing.

Two helicopters approached from the distance. Starship fired off flares to show them where the ship-wrecked survivors were, then wheeled the Werewolf around and instructed the computer to take it back to the *Abner Read*.

The Indian corvette had an angular forward deck and a blocky midship, so that as her list increased she looked more and more like a large cardboard box that had fallen into the water. A sister ship stood nearby, pulling men from the water with the help of small boats. At least twenty men clung to the stricken vessel, waiting to be saved.

Thinking he could help the rescue operations, Starship moved *Werewolf Two* out of its orbit about a mile to the east. He lit his searchlights as he came near the stricken ship, dropping into a hover and illuminating the water. Almost immediately his RWR buzzed with a warning that he was being targeted by the radar for an SA-N-4 anti-aircraft system. Starship doused his lights and throttled away as two missiles launched.

The SA-N-4s had about a ten-kilometer range, and *Werewolf Two* had a two-kilometer head start. Starship zigged right and left, bobbing up and then jamming back toward the waves, trying to confuse the missile's guidance system. He thought he'd made it when the Werewolf suddenly flew upward, uncontrolled; before he could regain control the screen blanked.

Near Karachi oil terminal
0355

Danny pushed his legs together and covered his face as he fell from the Osprey, plunging toward a black hole in the red flickering ocean. The flames swelled up around him, then disappeared as he sank into the water. Once below the surface, he leaned forward and began stroking. He'd gone out in the direction of the pier, and figured that so long as he pushed himself forward he would eventually come to it.

The water was so dark that he couldn't see anything in front of him. After what he thought must be five minutes, he raised his hand to clear some of the oil from the surface above and went up to get his bearings. But all he could see was heavy smoke and thin red curls of flame.

Danny pushed back under the water, determined to find the pier and get Boston out of there. He still had his boots on; their weight and that of the gear he was carrying for Boston tired him as he swam. When he surfaced, flames shot over him and he quickly ducked back, swimming blindly ahead. His arms began to ache.

Finally, his hand struck something hard. Thinking it was the pier, Danny surfaced and began hauling himself upward. When he got up he realized he'd climbed on a submerged concrete pillar, part of an older pier that had been removed some years before. The pier Boston was on sat ten yards behind him, barely visible in the smoke.

Flames ran out of a long pipe about thirty yards to the north; the pipe led back to the tank farm, a roaring inferno that showed no sign of subsiding.

'Boston! Yo Boston!' he yelled as shadows danced around him. 'Boston, you hear me?'

The wind howled. Danny took a breath, ready to dive in, then remembered his boots. He doffed them and dove back into the water, the stink of oil and kerosene stinging his nose.

In three strokes he reached his hand to the metal rail at the base of the pier – then jerked it off and dove back down below the water.

By the time the pain came, a wall of flames had passed overhead. Smarting from the burn, Danny worked his way to his right, in the direction he thought Boston would be. About five yards down he had to push around another underwater pillar before reaching the wooden surface of the pier. Tired, he didn't have enough energy or leverage to make it up and fell back into the water.

'Boston!' he yelled, trying to jerk the LAR-V rebreather gear he was carrying onto the pier. 'Boston!'

A hand grabbed him from behind.

'Here, Cap,' said Boston, in the water behind him.

Danny pulled the breathing gear back down between them.

'Damn hot up there,' said Boston. 'Whole place is on fire.'

'We have to swim out beyond the fire,' Danny told him. 'So the Osprey can pick us up.'

'They told me,' shouted Boston in his ear.

'This way,' said Danny, pointing before plunging down.

Aboard the *Wisconsin*,
above the northern Arabian Sea
0407

'Looks like both navies are withdrawing,' T-Bone told Dog. 'The aircraft are staying over the ships. The Chinese have three J-13s and one helicopter over the *Deng*. Three helos west, doing search and rescue on the frigate that sunk. The Indians have two planes over their carrier. Nothing else in the air.'

Less than an hour had passed since the first shot had been fired. Two ships had been sunk, one by each navy. Each side had lost four jets; the Chinese had also lost a helicopter. Considerable damage had been done to the remaining ships and aircraft.

And then there was the oil terminal, still burning, sure to be completely destroyed before the fires were out.

'Thanks, T-Bone. Dish, you have anything to add?'

'Just that I could use some breakfast.'

'I'll take your order,' volunteered Jazz. 'As long as it's coffee and microwaved muffins.'

Dog, not quite in the mood to laugh, nudged his stick to take the Megafortress a little higher.

Aboard the *Abner Read*, in the northern Arabian Sea 0415

Toasted by the Indian ship, Starship turned his attention to the other Werewolf. The aircraft was circling alone over the survivors of the Chinese ship. The water seemed absurdly peaceful.

'*Werewolf One* heading back to the ship,' he told Eyes. '*Two* is gone.'

'You lost the aircraft?'

What the hell did you expect? thought Starship. But he kept his mouth shut, not even bothering to acknowledge.

'A thousand pardons?' screamed Storm into his mouthpiece. 'A thousand pardons?'

'That's what he said, Captain.' The radioman's voice was nearly as incredulous as Storm's. 'That was their message from their captain.'

'He sends his airplanes to sink my ship, and he says a thousand pardons?'

'They say he didn't send them. They must have mistaken us for an Indian vessel.'

'Oh, that's believable.' Storm shook his head. 'Did you tell him the two airplanes that made the attack were shot down?'

'I said they required assistance. He asked if we could render it.'

'Gladly,' said Storm. 'As soon as hell freezes over.'

Near Karachi oil terminal
0415

When Danny broke water after ten minutes of solid swimming, he had cleared the worst of the smoke. Large pieces of wood bobbed in the water nearby. The first one was too small to support him; the second, a plastic milk crate or something similar, sank beneath his weight. As he was searching for something else, Boston popped up nearby.

'There, over there,' shouted Boston, pointing to the west. 'Those lights are the Osprey's.'

Danny turned and saw two beams extending down to the water. Reaching into a pocket sewn under the Draeger vest, he took out a small waterproof pouch. Inside the pouch was a pencil flare, a small signaling device intended for emergency pickups like this. The flare was designed to work even in the water, but getting it ready was not the easiest thing in the world. He took in a mouthful of foul seawater before managing to set it off.

Boston flipped onto his back and paddled nearby.

'You look like you're in a goddamn pool,' said Danny, his teeth starting to chatter.

The Osprey's rotors kicked up a strong downdraft, and a swell pushed Danny under. He had to fight to the surface.

'Grab on, grab on!' yelled Boston, who'd already gotten hold of the cable. 'Come on, Cap.'

Danny threw himself at his sergeant, thrashing around until he managed to hook his arm around the other man's. He got another mouthful of water before the cable began winching upward.

'They told me you were out of your mind,' Boston repeated. 'Damn good thing!'

'Damn good thing,' Danny said to himself, twisting as the cable hauled them to safety.

VI

Catastrophic Events

Allegro, Nevada
1710, 12 January 1998
(0610, 13 January, Karachi)

Zen flipped through the television stations as he rested between dumbbell sets. He wished it were baseball season; baseball was the perfect sport to watch when you were only half paying attention.

He stopped on CNN, put down the remote control and reached back for the weights. He took a long breath and then brought the dumbbells forward, doing a straight pullover.

'A CNN special report – breaking news,' blared the television.

Zen ignored it, pulling the weight over his head. He'd let his workout routines slip because of the procedures. He hadn't swum since last Saturday, and the weights felt heavy and awkward.

'We have a live report from Stephen Densmore in Delhi, India,' said the television announcer.

Zen, concentrating on the exercise, lowered the dumbbells toward his waist, then pulled them back overhead.

As he brought the bars back behind him to the floor, the newsman began talking.

'Over a hundred people were reported killed and at least that number are missing following the early morning clash between Indian and Chinese naval vessels off the Pakistani coastline. An oil terminal in Karachi was said to have been destroyed in the fighting.'

'Karachi?' said Zen. He let the weights drop and rolled over to his stomach. The screen showed a still photo of an Indian naval vessel said to have been sunk.

'Where was this?' Zen asked the TV. 'Where?'

But the network cut to a commercial. Zen waited patiently through a spot for Folger's coffee, but instead of adding more details when they returned, the anchor cued the weatherman. Zen crawled toward the end table and reached for his phone.

Aboard the *Abner Read*,
northern Arabian Sea
13 January 1998
0610

'Airforce, why did you put the Werewolf down into that ship?'

Starship shifted uneasily. He'd actually forgotten all about that, sure that Storm was going to ball him out for losing the Werewolf to the Indian missile.

'I guess it seemed like a good idea at the time, sir.'

Lame, completely lame, but what else could he say?

Storm shook his head. 'Do you realize the Chinese could have grabbed the Werewolf at any moment?'

'That might be a bit of an exaggeration. I mean, they weren't expecting anything and I was only there for a minute. Not even. I was always right under the opening for the elevator. I could just escape straight up.'

'That's not the point.'

'Yes, sir.'

'You took a big risk, mister. A *huge* risk.'

Starship nodded.

'Officially, you're on report,' said Storm. 'That was a foolish thing to do.'

The furrows in the captain's brow deepened; he looked like a gargoyle about to spit stone.

'Unofficially,' added Storm, 'that was the ballsiest thing I've ever seen anyone ever do.'

Starship was confused, but he was even more confounded as Storm formed his hand into a fist and hit his shoulder with a roundhouse so powerful he was nearly knocked off his feet. The captain wore a grin that covered half his face.

'Way to go, Airforce,' Storm told him. 'The intelligence geeks back at the Pentagon are going apeshit over this. It's the coup of the year. You keep this up and you'll be a permanent member of the team.'

'Thanks, sir,' said Starship, rubbing his shoulder.

Jed Barclay knew one of his phones was ringing, but couldn't figure out which one it was until the third trill. Then he pulled his personal cell phone out of his pocket.

'Uh, Jed,' he said, unsure who would be calling on the seldom used line.

'Jed, it's your cousin Jeff.'

'Hey, Zen. How's it goin'?'

'What's going on in India?'

'Oh – jeez. All hell's breaking loose.'

'Karachi was attacked. Breanna's there,' Zen added. 'I figured you could give me some background.'

'Listen, cuz, I really can't talk about that on this line, you know?'

'Is Bree going to be OK?'

'Well, none of our people have been, uh, hurt that I know of.'

'I know that. I just talked to the base. That's not what I'm asking.'

'Yeah. Um. I still can't talk on this line.'

'What if I call you back from Dreamland?'

Jed knew that the Dreamland contingent was being pulled out of Karachi because of the volatile situation there. But not only couldn't he say so on a phone line that could be tapped, it wasn't his place to be handing out that information.

'Maybe. You don't sound like yourself,' Jed told his cousin. 'You, like, worried about Breanna?'

'Damn straight.'

'She can take care of herself, though. I mean, Bree's been –'

'I'll call you in an hour.'

Zen hung up before Jed could warn him that he might be hard to reach; the National Security Council was setting up a meeting, and he expected to be called upstairs to help his boss prepare a presidential briefing any second.

Jed went back to his computer, looking at the images that had been forwarded from the *Abner Read* following the battle. The conflict had provided a wealth of tactical and strategic intelligence, but right now he just wanted something he could show the President to illustrate both the damage and the firepower of the ships involved.

The *Abner Read* had obtained particularly interesting video of the Chinese carrier *Deng Xiaoping*, thanks to the exploits of its Werewolf. Among the images Jed paged through were clear shots of the hangar deck, showing a number of planes in storage and even what looked like a weapons area. Wondering if the information might change the Pentagon's assessment of the relative power of the two fleets – the analysts had been calling the *Deng Xiaoping* and *Shiva* about even – Jed picked up the phone and called the Pentagon.

The Navy intelligence officer he wanted to talk to was away from his desk. So were two other people he called. He was about to try someone at the CIA who specialized in weapons assessments when his friend at the Navy called him back.

'You're wondering about the *Deng*?' said the lieutenant commander.

'I'm wondering if these images are going to change your assessment that the two task groups are evenly matched, or if the battle did,' Jed told him.

'Too early to say for sure, but it looks like the Chinese have a new anticruise missile weapon. There's something else even more interesting about the *Deng,* though.'

'More interesting?'

'You got W-AB73-20 there?' asked the officer, referring to one of the image's index numbers.

'Hang tight,' said Jed, swinging around in his chair to the keyboard. He cradled the phone against his neck as he found the photo.

One of the series taken of the *Deng Xiaoping*'s hangar deck, it showed a pair of J-13 fighters, wings folded, roped off a short distance from the camera. There were two men near it; both had automatic rifles.

'OK, so I'm looking at it.'

'See those jets? They're guarded.'

'Yeah, I know.'

'Kind of strange, don't you think?'

'Yeah, definitely.' Jed zeroed in and hit the zoom. 'Are these guards? Or are these guys running up to the fight?'

'Jed, they're in the hangar of an aircraft carrier. They're guarding the plane.'

Oh, wow.

'Tai-shan?'

'That's the guess. We're studying the planes now. But, I'd say that's a real good guess. Plane types are right. We're digging into the equipment right now.'

'I'm not familiar with Tai-shan,' the National Security Advisor admitted to Jed when he took the news to his office a few minutes later.

'Two years ago, the Chinese navy conducted a series of tests in the Gulf of Tonkin, using what was then a proto-type of the J-13,' said Jed. 'They operated from a base that had been mocked up so it was similar to an aircraft carrier – the dimensions were later shown to fit one of the *Deng Xiaoping*'s arms. The aircraft dropped practice bombs over the water. One of the mock missions was tracked, and from the bombing pattern, it seemed pretty clear that it was dropping a nuclear weapon. If you recall, this was right around the time the *Xia,* their only ballistic missile submarine, was taken out of service. But –'

'Wait, Jed,' said Freeman, nearly jumping from his seat. 'You're telling me there's a nuke on that ship?'

'Maybe two. There are two planes.'

'Let's go talk to the President right now,' said Freeman, already in full stride.

The President was entertaining a delegation of church youth leaders from Minnesota on a postdinner tour of the White House when Jed and Freeman were ushered into the Oval Office. Entertaining was the right word – he was demonstrating a sleight of hand trick he'd learned on a recent trip to Florida. The President was particu-larly fond of the trick, and was taking obvious glee in making a silver dollar appear in various ears of his visitors.

'But I see, ladies and gentlemen, that duty is calling, and I'm late for my next meeting,' said the President. 'We're always burning the midnight oil here.'

He glad-handed the visitors as they left, mixing in variations of his silver dollar trick.

'Everybody loves magic,' said Martindale after they left. 'Now if I could only find a way to pull silver dollars from congressmen's ears, I'd have no problem getting my budget passed.'

'There's a new twist in the north Arabian Sea,' the National Security Advisor told the President. 'It's going to complicate things tremendously.'

Martindale's smile faded quickly as Jed told him about the images from the carrier and their implications.

'You're sure this is correct?' asked Martindale.

'The intelligence agencies are preparing a formal estimate,' said Jed. 'But I checked the original intelligence on the program. It's a real match. A Chinese agent provided photos and a procedural manual.'

'The Chinese showed restraint by not using the planes when they were attacked,' said Freeman. 'But can we count on that in the future? Maybe it wasn't a coincidence that the carrier is off the coast of India. China could be planning a first strike against the Indian leadership.'

'Are you suggesting we alert the Indians?' asked the President. 'That could backfire – they might use that as an excuse to fire nukes at the carrier. They've already tried to sink it.'

Martindale got up from his desk. He still had the dollar coin in his hand. He played with it absentmindedly, twirling it between his fingers.

'India is not our ally,' said Freeman. 'But then neither is China.'

'We can't allow a nuclear war in Asia. The consequences would be devastating,' said the President. 'Even a conventional war. We need to get some distance between the two sides, work up something diplomatically, either in the UN or on our own.'

'Neither side trusts us,' said Freeman bitterly.

'See, they have something in common,' said the President sardonically. 'How long will it take to get the *Nimitz* and its battle group into the area?'

'Two weeks,' said Jed.

'What if we sent a private message to the Chinese, telling them we know they have the weapon, and that if they try to use it, we'll sink their ship?' Martindale asked Freeman.

'For one thing, we'll be taking sides. For another, we'll be giving away intelligence that may help us down the road.'

'If they don't use the weapon.'

'True.'

'I'd rather sink it here than off Taiwan. We could blame the Indians somehow.'

'Maybe the Indians will sink it for us,' said Freeman.

'It may not be that easy to sink,' said Jed. 'It came through the battle with the Indians.'

'We can sink it,' said Freeman.

'What if we positioned ourselves to attack the carrier

once the planes appear on deck, and attack then? Could Dreamland and the *Abner Read* handle that sort of attack on their own?'

'I don't think that's wise,' said Freeman. 'We're going to risk our own people for India?'

'India and China, and the rest of southern Asia,' said the President. 'Is it feasible?'

Freeman turned to Jed.

'Um, they might. Another thing, um, they might be able to shoot down the planes.'

'All right. That might work,' said Martindale. 'We'll discuss it with the cabinet.'

He picked up the phone and told the operator to contact the other cabinet members, along with Joint Chiefs of Staff, for an emergency meeting.

'I want Bastian in charge of this,' he said when he got off the phone.

'He's attached to Xray Pop, and Captain Gale on the *Abner Read* outranks him,' said Freeman.

'Captain Gale has lived up to his nickname "Storm" once too often for my taste. Bastian is the one I trust out there. I'll talk to them personally.'

Diego Garcia
1200, 13 January 1998
(1100, Karachi)

Dog clambered down the EB-52's ladder, his throat parched and his legs aching from the long flight. Diego

Garcia was a small atoll in the Indian Ocean, south of India. Among the most secure American bases in the world – surrounded by miles and miles of open ocean – it was also a four-hour flight from their patrol area. Dog did not relish the idea of operating from here for very long.

'Hey, good to see you, Colonel,' yelled Mack Smith, hopping off a small 'gator' vehicle as it pulled to a stop. A pair of maintainers got off the golf-cart-sized vehicle, which they used to ferry tools and supplies around while working on the big aircraft. 'How was the flight?'

'Long,' Dog told him, getting his bearings.

'So was mine. I'll tell you, nothing's changed, Colonel – place looks just like we left it last week.'

Actually it had been almost two months now, back before Thanksgiving. But Diego Garcia did have something of a timeless quality to it, at least to the occasional visitor. The sand and trees and old ruins belonged to the British; everything else here was operated by the U.S. Navy. A small administrative building had already been set aside for the Dreamland force, as had six dugout revetments for the aircraft. More carport than hangar, the parking areas were more important for the shade they provided than the protection against terror attack; the closest thing to a terrorist on the island was the constable who handed tickets out to bicyclists exceeding the speed limit.

'Since I was ranking officer, I took it upon myself to contact the natives,' Mack told Dog as he walked toward a Navy jeep that had been sent to meet him. 'Base commander is Mr Cooperation.'

'That's nice, Mack,' said Dog, who'd already spoken to the commander twice while en route.

'Got our old digs, everything's shipshape.'

'Great.'

'I hear my pupil Cantor shot down two J-13s when they wouldn't turn back,' added Mack. 'Chip off the old block.'

'Your pupil?'

'He's coming along, isn't he?' said Mack, without a trace of irony.

Dog started to climb into the jeep when a bicycle ridden by a man dressed in camo fatigues appeared on the roadway in front of them. The colonel told the driver to wait a moment, realizing that the bicyclist was one of his Whiplash troopers; during their earlier stay they'd found that mountain bikes were the most effective way of getting around the base. The rider was Danny Freah, who sported a wide bandage on his left hand but otherwise showed no signs of wear from his recent ordeal.

'I thought you were going to get some rest,' Dog said.

'So'd I. You have a high-level call at the trailer.'

'Hop in,' Dog told him.

'Nah,' said the Whiplash captain, grinning as he whipped his bicycle around. 'I'll race ya.'

Breanna paused in front of the door, rehearsing what she had to say one last time. Then she sighed and raised her hand to knock. At the first rap, the door flew open.

'Captain,' said Jan Stewart, startled. 'I was just going to get something to eat.'

'Oh, good,' said Breanna. 'I'll go with you.'

Stewart shrugged, pulling the door closed behind her. Breanna realized the suggestion had been a mistake, but she was stuck with it now. She led Stewart out of the dormitory building they'd been assigned, and didn't speak until they were outside. The mess – or galley, in Navy talk – was several hundred yards away.

'I wanted to talk to you,' Breanna said. 'I've been noticing some problems you're having.'

'What problems?' snapped Stewart.

'Little things,' said Breanna. 'But a lot of them. You're having trouble processing all the systems in combat.'

Stewart stopped and turned toward her. 'Are you unhappy with my performance, Captain?'

'Yes,' said Breanna. The word blurted out; Breanna had meant to approach the topic with much more tact.

Stewart's face reddened. 'Well, thank you for your honesty,' she said, turning and continuing toward the cafeteria.

Well, that went well, Breanna thought. And now I can't even go and eat without getting the evil eye.

'Dog, it's good to talk to you under any circumstance,' President Martindale told Colonel Bastian after the call was put through. 'I hope you're well.'

'I am, sir. Thank you.'

'I'm going to let Jed Barclay fill in the details, as he has so often in the past,' said the President. 'But I want to emphasize two things. Number one: You are taking your orders directly from me. No one and nothing are to interfere with this mission. Do you understand?'

'Yes, sir.'

'Number two: You are in command. As such, you are representing me. Your judgment is my judgment. The stakes are extremely high, but I trust you. Follow your instincts.'

Before Dog could say anything else, Jed Barclay came on the line. 'Are you there, Colonel?'

'I'm here, Jed,' said Dog.

'I, um, I'm going to start with some background. I don't think you know about Tai-shan, right?'

Dog listened as Jed described the Chinese naval nuclear program and explained what the Werewolf had found.

'We're not sure whether the fact that there are two aircraft means that there are two bombs, or whether one is intended as a backup,' Jed told him. 'Navy Intelligence is preparing a dossier that will help you identify the aircraft.'

The recent showdown notwithstanding, the Megafortress was not the weapon of choice for shooting down J-13s, or any frontline fighter for that matter.

'The *Abner Read* is subordinate to you for this mission,' added Jed.

'Does Captain Gale know that?'

'The President will be telling him shortly.'

Dog could only imagine the fallout from *that* conversation.

'You have to be in a position to stop the strike if it appears imminent,' reiterated Jed, making his instructions absolutely clear. 'Whatever you have to do to accomplish that, you're authorized to do. I, um, we'll have a twenty-four-hour link set up to provide you with intelligence on the situation. I'm working on it now.'

Storm listened incredulously as the President continued. He had no problem with attacking the Chinese aircraft – he told the President that he would sink the carrier if he wanted – but putting Bastian in charge? A lieutenant colonel over a Navy captain?

An Air Force zippersuit over a sea captain?

'Sir, with respect, with due respect – I outrank Bastian.'

'Will it make you happy if I demote you to commander?' answered the President.

'No, sir.'

'Stand by for a briefing from Jed Barclay of the NSC.'

'I can sink that damn carrier now,' insisted Storm when Jed came on the line. 'Bam. It's down. Six missiles. All I need.'

'Um, uh, sir, um, you can't do that.'

'Don't tell me what I can't do,' snapped Storm, slamming the handset into its receiver.

The petty officer manning communications looked over warily from his station at the other side of the small room. 'Get me Fleet – no, get me Admiral Balboa.'

'The head of the Joint of Chiefs of Staff?'

'You got it. Get him.'

'Yes, sir. Incoming communication on the Dreamland channel. Colonel Bastian.'

Gloating already?

I'm a new man, Storm told himself. I don't get angry.

'I don't like this any more than you do, Storm,' said Dog, coming on the line. 'But we have to make the best of it. Let's come up with a plan –'

'Here's the plan, Bastian. Spot the planes on their deck, and I'll launch the missiles.'

'Listen, Storm. We don't have to be friends, but –'

'We're *not*.'

'But we have the same goal.'

'As long as you remember that, we'll be fine.'

Aboard the *Shiva*,
Arabian Sea
1213

Memon stared at the ceiling of the ship's medical center. His head pounded and he wanted to sleep, but he dared not; every time he closed his eyes he saw the severed limb on the deck before him.

Thirty-three Indian men had been killed in the brief engagement, most of them aboard the corvette that was sunk by two C-601 missiles, air-launched Chinese weapons similar to the Russian Styx. Another hundred or so had been wounded; twenty were missing and almost certainly dead. The toll aboard the *Shiva* was relatively small – seven dead, eighteen wounded. Kevlar armor at the belt line of the ship where the first missile struck had prevented serious damage. But the missile that struck the bridge area had wiped out part of the bridge and, more important, deprived the ship of many of its most important officers, including the admiral.

The list of the dead did not stun Memon anywhere near as much as the news that they had sunk only one of the Chinese ships, a frigate. The aircraft carrier *Deng Xiaoping* continued operations, and even had the audacity to send a high-speed reconnaissance flight in their direction. The *Shiva*'s fighters responded, supposedly shooting down the craft.

Memon did not trust the report. He no longer trusted anything, not even his own judgment.

He saw the blood of the victims everywhere he looked. Every spot on the wall, every shadow on the ceiling, appeared to him to be blood. His hands were free of it, but how long would that last?

'Deputy Minister?'

Memon looked to his right and found a sailor standing there.

'A message from the Defense minister, sir.'

Memon sat up. He slit the tape holding the folded piece of paper together, then read slowly.

MOVE SOUTH OUT OF IMMEDIATE CONTACT WITH DENG XIAOPING. AWAIT FURTHER ORDERS.
— ADM. SKANDAR

Memon got to his feet, then sat back down, realizing belatedly that he had taken his shoes off. The blood rushed from his head, and he had to wait for the wave to subside.

'Take me to Captain Adri,' he told the messenger.

'He's on the backup bridge.'

'Take me there.'

'Yes, sir.'

Adri was reviewing the course with the helmsman when Memon arrived.

'A note,' said Memon, holding it out. His head no longer hurt, but he still felt somewhat dazed. His eyes burned, and he saw a pattern before them when he stared at the floor.

The pattern of the explosion flash? Or of the blood surrounding the dead man's arm?

'We can't retreat,' said Captain Adri, giving him the note back. 'You have to tell him. We have to show our resolve, or they'll attack again.'

'The admiral is right. We should withdraw farther.'

'You're a coward,' said Adri. 'As soon as you see blood, you want to cut and run. You urged Admiral Kala to attack, and now you can't face the consequences.'

Dismiss him, Memon thought. That is the only option. A subordinate cannot be allowed to question orders so publicly, let alone use insults to do so.

But Memon knew he was not a sailor. He couldn't run the ship without Adri. And if he ordered someone to take Adri's place, the sailors might mutiny.

Insurrection was better than indecision. And yet he stood frozen in place, unable to say anything.

So he was a coward, then, wasn't he? A disgrace to the country.

Adri pushed his face next to Memon's. 'This is no way to win a war. We have to attack. *Attack.*'

Memon shuddered. Adri's voice sounded like his own just a day before.

'You must obey the minister's orders,' managed Memon.

'I answer to the chief of the naval staff, not the defense minister. I will follow my instincts, not yours.'

Aboard the *Deng Xiaoping*,
northern Arabian Sea
1213

Twenty-three crewmen aboard the *Deng Xiaoping* had been killed in the attack. It was Captain Hongwu's duty to write to each man's family. And so, after the damage was assessed and repairs begun, after the wounded were cared for, after the battle's success and failures were toted, he retreated to his wardroom suite. For his bottom desk drawer he removed a small wooden box and then unwrapped his calligrapher's pen and nubs. He took some rice paper and ink, commemorating each man to his family with a few well-chosen but simple words.

The Indian attack had been warded off quite successfully, due to the success of the *Pili* batteries. The weapons had struck all but two of the dozen missiles launched at the ship. It helped that the Indian attack had not been well-coordinated. Still, Captain Hongwu was now confident that the Thunderbolt could protect him from an even more intense attack; he would say so in his report to Beijing.

The overflight by the American aircraft of his deck was another question entirely. The audaciousness of the flight astounded Hongwu almost as much as its success. His ship's radar systems had tracked the aircraft intermittently when it was ten miles from the ship, but never any closer.

Both his intelligence and radar officers blamed programming in the units that controlled the radar, believing that the helicopter's slow speed had somehow confused it. Hongwu was inclined toward human error – though he had to admit that the operators had done extremely well in every other respect. Whatever the problem, it would have to be studied and fixed.

Should he report it to Beijing? If he did, his victory today would be overshadowed.

No, there was no reason to do so, at least not until the failure had been properly analyzed. He had already risked Beijing's disapproval by noting that two of his aircraft had mistaken the *Abner Read* for an Indian ship, apparently believing the radar it was using belonged to an Indian frigate. The mistake was understandable given the chaos of battle, but his superiors disapproved nonetheless.

Perhaps it would have been better if the planes had sunk the ship, he thought.

Hongwu dipped his pen and began to write:

Your son was a lion. I saw him pull another sailor from the fire, risking his life.

He shuddered at the memory, then signed his name.

Ray Rubeo rubbed his face with his hands, then looked back at the screen at the front of the Dreamland Command Center.

'We're months away from testing the long-range version of the Scorpion missile, Colonel. I can't even give you a mockup at this point,' said Rubeo. 'And the airborne version of the Razor is even further off. Funding –'

'I realize you can't perform miracles, Ray. I'm just looking for anything that can give the Megafortresses an edge here. They're not interceptors.'

'I'm well aware of their capabilities, Colonel. Now, if you want to bomb the carrier, the weapons people have studied that matter as well,' added Rubeo. 'The general consensus is that you would require nine well-placed strikes on the carrier to guarantee sinking it. Assume the Chinese weapon operates near its same efficiency, and its close-in weapon works as it has in the past: 17.3 missile launches, a minimum.'

'Or eighteen,' said Colonel Bastian.

'Yes. Eighteen would be the practical number.'

'I'm not looking to sink the carrier.'

'I have another suggestion,' said Rubeo. 'Use the EEMWBs against the planes.'

'The weapon needs further tests.'

'They'll work. You'll disable the bombs completely, without even shooting down the planes. The only drawback,' added Rubeo, 'is that the versions we currently have ready will wipe every piece of electronics within five hundred miles.'

'How many would it take?'

'One. However, I would launch two in case of the unforeseen. The weapons were due to be relocated at the end of the week in preparation for the tests anyway. We can ship them and technicians to Diego Garcia. The tests can be conducted from there following your mission.'

'How soon can you get the weapons over here?'

For Zen, it was a vibrating fever inside his chest and head, a dread and a desire – an imperative to be with his wife, to help her, save her, simply to be there. It was more important than food, more important than his legs, certainly; everything would be meaningless without her. He had to go. He had to be there. Only then would the dreams stop; only if he was with her would the fever break.

He wanted to walk – he *would* walk – but first he had to go and be with her.

He'd left a phone message for Vasin. The doctor would understand. And if he didn't – well, that was the way it had to be.

Zen rolled down the ramp of the Megafortress hangar, heading toward the door that led to the bunkers below. The doors whisked open before he reached them.

'Dr Rubeo, just who I'm looking for.'

'Major. Can I help you?'

'I hear you're putting together a flight to Crete.'

'I am sending some items to support the Whiplash deployment,' said Rubeo discreetly.

'I'm going.'

'Going where?'

'To Crete. And then Diego Garcia. I'm joining the deployment.'

Rubeo gave him a typical Rubeo look – a kind of mock befuddlement that the world was not as intellectual as he was.

'I was given to understand that you were involved in an experiment relating to your walking again,' said Rubeo.

'Yeah, well, that's on hold right now,' said Zen. 'This is more important. I *need* to be there.'

'I'm sure I'm not the one to say this to you, Major, but were I in your position –'

'You're not.'

'I'll tell the MC-17 pilots you're on the way. The aircraft is nearly ready to leave, so you'd best hurry.'

Aboard the *Abner Read*
1403

'What do these eggheads know about naval warfare?' thundered Storm. 'Eighteen missile launches? Absurd. The Pentagon people tell us we can do it with three. Well, all right, that's ridiculous, too. We figure six hits, which at most calls for eight launches. Eighteen? That's ridiculous.'

Storm glanced at Eyes and his weapons officers as he

waited for Colonel Bastian to respond via the communications system, which was being piped over the small conference speaker on his desk. His quarters was the most convenient place for the secure conference, but if there had been one more person in the cabin, they wouldn't have been able to move.

'I'm just telling you what their simulations showed,' said Dog. His face jerked in the video feed, not quite in sync with the sound. 'I thought you'd appreciate knowing.'

'Well, let's get on with it,' said Storm. 'Where are we to position ourselves for this intercept?'

'I need you to sail west.'

'West?'

'Two hundred miles west.'

'Two hundred miles west?'

'We're going to use a weapon that will fry their electronics. It'll affect yours as well. The radius is roughly five hundred miles, but to be safe –'

'No way, Bastian. No way.'

'Listen, Storm –'

'I can understand you wanting to grab all the glory for yourself. I really can. You're ambitious, and you have the track record to prove it. But telling us to leave the area when we have a mission here? No way.'

'I'm telling you for your own protection.'

'Our vital systems are shielded against magnetic pulses,' said Eyes.

'Not like this.'

'I'm not moving, Bastian. You can take that to the bank.' Storm folded his arms and scowled at the screen.

As soon as this call was over, he was calling Balboa personally, before Bastian got his version of the story in.

'I can't guarantee that we can detonate the weapons far enough away from you not to harm you,' the colonel told him.

'I'm not looking for guarantees. I'm telling you: *I'm not moving.*'

Northern Arabian Sea
2010

Captain Sattari climbed onto the deck of the Parvaneh submarine, legs wobbly from the long day and night below the water. A breeze struck the side of his face, tingling it; his scalp bristled, and his lungs – his lungs luxuriated as they sucked in *real* air. The rest of his men crowded up behind him, anxious to breathe and move freely after hours of drowsy confinement. A few dropped to their knees, praying in thanksgiving. Sattari did not remind them that they were very far from being safe.

'*Boat Four*, dead ahead,' said the Parvaneh's mate. He held up the signal lamp.

Captain Sattari pulled up his night glasses to scan the ocean around them. Between the darkness and the fog, he could see only a short distance; the shoreline, barely four miles to the north, was invisible, as were the towering mountains beyond.

The Parvaneh had sailed roughly 140 miles, but they

were still in Pakistani waters; Iran lay another 150 miles to the west, and their home port was three hundred miles beyond that. The Parvanehs carried enough fuel to reach Iranian territory, but only if they traveled mostly on the surface, where they would be easy to detect. Rather than taking that risk, Sattari had arranged a rendezvous with the *Mitra,* the tanker that had been altered to take them into its womb. It was to meet them twenty miles southwest of here in exactly three hours; they had barely enough time to put a small charge back in the batteries before setting out again.

Sattari continued to hunt for *Boat Two* and *Three.* They had started before his; surely they must be lurking nearby.

And yet, neither had been found twenty minutes later. A light rain started to fall, making Sattari's infrared glasses nearly useless. He paced along the narrow deck, weaving around his men. To make their rendezvous with the oil tanker, they would have to leave within a half hour.

Ten more minutes passed. Sattari spent them thinking of the soldiers in the midget submarines. He saw each of their faces; remembered what they had done by his side.

The submarine commander came up from below.

'Twenty minutes more, Captain. Then we must leave.'

'Have you heard anything on the radio?'

The commander shook his head. They were far from the world here.

Five minutes passed, then ten.

'Signal *Boat Two* to start,' Sattari told one of his men. 'We will follow shortly.'

The signal given, Sattari scanned the waters once again. He saw nothing.

'Sound the horn,' he told one of his men.

'A risk.'

'It is.' The captain folded his arms in front of his chest, listening as the handheld horn bellowed.

A light flickered to the west. One of his soldiers spotted it and shouted, 'There!'

The mate signaled frantically with his light. The light in the distance blinked back and began to grow. It was *Boat Four*. Signals were passed; the submarine turned and began to descend, heading toward the rendezvous.

Three was still missing; Sergeant Ibn's boat.

Sattari ordered the horn sound again. Two more times they tried, without response.

'Time to go below,' the captain told his men. They got up reluctantly, walking unsteadily to the mock wheelhouse that held the hatchway and airlock. The last man began folding the wire rail downward. Sattari helped him.

'The horn once more.'

A forlorn *ba-hrnnn* broke the stillness. Sattari listened until he heard only the rhythmic lapping of water against the Parvaneh's hull.

'With God's help, they will meet us at the *Mitra*,' he told the submarine captain below. 'But we can wait no longer.'

Aboard the *Wisconsin*,
over the northern Arabian Sea
2222

'Still no sign of the Piranha, Colonel,' Cantor told Dog as they reached the end of the first search grid. 'Sorry.'

'Not your fault, son. All right, crew; get ready to drop the second buoy. Mack, stay with me this time.'

'I was with you the whole way, Colonel.'

Cantor's attempt to stifle a laugh was unsuccessful.

'Concentrate on your tinfish, kid,' snapped Mack.

'Trying.'

Cantor had been pressed into service as an operator for the robot undersea probe so the Megafortresses could extend their patrol times. Gloria English and *Levitow* were en route to Crete to pick up EEMWBs before starting their patrol. The *Wisconsin* would go to Crete at the end of this patrol as well so that it, too, could pick up the weapons.

Cantor didn't mind 'driving' the Piranha, though until now he had done so only in simulations. The hardest part of controlling the robot probe was reminding yourself not to expect too much. It moved *very* slowly compared to the Flighthawk; top speed was just under forty knots.

The question was whether they would find it. The probe hadn't been heard from since English put it into autonomous mode. The last patrol had taken advantage of a lull in the fighting between the Indians and Chinese to drop buoys south of Karachi, without any luck. The

Wisconsin had flown back through that area, up the Indian and then Pakistani coasts and around to the west before dropping its own buoys. Batteries aboard the buoys allowed them to be used for twenty-four hours; after that they were programmed to sink themselves into the ocean. Their limited contact range with the Piranha was their one drawback, a by-product of the almost undetectable underwater communications system the devices used to communicate.

Gravity gave Cantor a tug as the Megafortress began an abrupt climb after dropping the fresh buoy.

'See, I'm just about right on top of him,' said Mack.

'Sure,' mumbled Cantor.

'I know what you were trying to tell me the other day,' Mack added. 'And you know what – I appreciate it.'

Cantor was so taken by surprise by Mack's comment that he thought he was being set up for some sort of joke.

'I was thinking about these suckers all wrong. I have the hang of it now,' said Mack. 'I'm on top of the game.'

'Good,' said Cantor, not sure what to say.

'You were right. I was wrong.'

An apology? From Major Mack 'the Knife' Smith? Cantor wondered if he should record the date for posterity.

'If we have to tango and you're watching Piranha, don't sweat it,' added Mack. 'I can take two.'

Flighthawk Two was on *Wisconsin*'s wing, ready to be launched in an emergency.

'It's a lot easier one at a time,' said Cantor.

'Ah, I can handle it. Piece of cake,' said Mack.

Before Cantor could consider what, if anything, to say, he got an alert from his console. He turned his head back to the screen and saw a message: PIRANHA CONNECTION ESTABLISHED.

'I've got Piranha!' he shouted. He flipped from the master control screen to the sensor view, which synthesized the sensor data and presented it to the screen as an image, much the way the sensors on the Flighthawk were used to give the pilot an image. The Piranha carried two different sensors in its nose. One was an extremely sensitive passive sonar; the other made use of temperature differences to paint a picture of what was around it. An operator could choose one or the other; passive was generally easier to steer by, and that was where Cantor started, flipping the switch at the side of the console. A sharp black object appeared dead ahead, marked on the range scale at five hundred yards.

'Piranha has got a target, dead in the water. I'm transferring the coordinates to you now.'

Dog double-checked his position, then hailed the *Abner Read* on the Dreamland Command circuit. Storm came on the line almost immediately.

'We've reestablished a connection with Piranha,' Dog told him. 'We think we found that special operations submarine. It's fifteen miles off the Pakistani coast, about a hundred miles from Karachi. It's about eighty miles north of you.'

'Excellent. I'll send the Sharkboat to trail it.'

'How long will that take?'

'About three hours.'

'Good. Listen, Storm, about your position –'

'I've spoken to Admiral Balboa. He agrees that there's no reason for me to move that far west. In fact, he wants me to keep the carrier within range of my Harpoon missiles, just in case it becomes necessary for us to sink it. Backing you up,' added Storm.

'Do not attack the carrier.'

'I didn't say I was going to, did I?'

Dog bit his cheek to keep from responding.

Cantor eased Piranha closer to its target, moving as slowly as he could. The probe literally swam through the water, using a series of expandable joints to wag its body back and forth as a fish would. The sound and wave patterns that the movement created would seem to all but the most discerning observer to belong to a medium-size shark – assuming they were detected at all. But Cantor was loath to take chances. At a dead stop, a submarine could generally hear quite well, and it was preferable that it did not know it was being observed.

When he had eased to two hundred meters, Cantor eased Piranha into a hover and changed his sensor selection. A blur of colors appeared before him; the computer then adjusted the colors, shaping them into an image of a small, odd-looking vessel. The computer analyzed the object, giving its approximate dimensions: twenty meters long, and only 2.65 wide, or at beam, according to the nautical term. Its height was 2.2 meters. It looked more like a sunken pleasure cruiser than a sub.

The smallest non-American military submarine listed

301

in the computer reference for Piranha was the Russian Project 865, a special operations craft. The 865 had a crew of nine and carried only two torpedoes. It was 28.2 meters long, 4.2 at beam, and looked very much like a down-sized conventional sub.

Cantor wasn't sure how well the image corresponded to the actual vessel. He started to move again, circling the sub to get a fuller view. When Piranha had gone about two-thirds of the way around the submarine, the computer made a light clicking noise – the sub was starting to move.

Upward.

'Piranha to *Wisconsin*,' said Cantor. 'Looks like he's headed toward the surface.'

'Roger that. Thank you, Piranha. Mack, stand by.'

Souda Bay U.S. Navy Support Base, Crete
1922 (2222, Karachi)

Aided by a strong jet stream and powerful Dreamland-modified supercruise engines, the MC-17D 'Fastmover' carrying Zen took just under eight hours to get from Dreamland to Crete, but every minute seemed an hour to him. He was so happy to finally get there that he didn't mind being carried ignobly down the ramp to the runway. Two sailors – the base was a Navy supply facility – carried him between their arms. After the humiliation of the past week involving the tests, it was a minor annoyance. They even set him down gently in his wheel-chair.

'*Jeff?*'

'Hey, babe, how's it going?' he said as Breanna came toward him.

'I can't believe you're here.'

'Believe it.'

'You're supposed to be at the medical center.'

'This is more important.' She got a funny look on her face, so he added, 'It wasn't working. They need more research. And you guys need me right now.'

'But . . .'

Zen rolled his wheelchair forward. 'Can we get some chow? I'm starving. And if there's any coffee on this base, I want to start an IV.'

Aboard the *Wisconsin*, over the northern Arabian Sea 2242

Dreamland was a developmental laboratory, not an intelligence center. Still, they had access to some of the most brilliant minds in the country, as well as experts in just about every weapon or potential weapon imaginable – and it still took more than an hour for them to tell Dog what they had found.

'Civilian submarine. Nautilus Adventure 2000. Heavily modified,' said Ray Rubeo. 'But hardly cutting edge.'

'I've never heard of civilian submarines,' said Dog.

'Yes.' Rubeo's tone implied that everyone else in the world had. 'It's a small market. Primarily for tour boats, though for the well-heeled it's a status symbol. I suppose you can park it next to the yacht. This would seem to be from a German firm. We'll have to rely on the CIA for additional data, but we have a spec sheet of the base model for you. It's powered by batteries and diesel.'

'Have you tried to trace it?'

'Colonel –'

'I realize you have a lot to do, Ray. Pass the information along to the NSC. I'll tell Jed to expect it.'

'Very good.'

'Sub is moving again, Colonel,' said Cantor. 'On the surface.'

'Thanks, Cantor.'

'Jazz, get hold of that Sharkboat and find out how long it's going to be before they get up here. And tell them the sub's moving.'

'Just did, Colonel. He's five miles due south. Roughly ten minutes away.'

'Making sounds like it might be starting to submerge,' said Cantor. 'Taking on water.'

'Mack, see if you can get some close-ups and maybe distract them.'

'I'll land on them if you want.'

'Just annoy them,' said Dog. 'You ought to be good at that.'

Mack brought the Flighthawk down through the clouds, clearing a knot of rain as he headed for the midget submarine. The vessel was about a half mile away, gliding across the surface at two or three knots. He swung to his left, arcing around so he could approach it head-on. He took the Flighthawk down to five hundred feet and saw figures near the wedge-shaped conning tower.

'Smile down there, kiddies,' said Mack, passing overhead.

He looped back, pushing *Hawk One* down through three hundred feet, passing two hundred and still descending. He leveled off fifty feet above the waves as he began his second run. Two men were still on the deck of the sub as he approached. The submarine seemed to have stopped descending.

'Stand still and I'll give you a haircut,' he told them.

One of the figures on the submarine jerked something out of the tower structure. Instantly, Mack hit the throttle and reached for his decoy flares.

'Missile launch!' warned the Flighthawk's computer.

Souda Bay U.S. Naval Support Base, Crete
2000 (2300, Karachi)

Jan Stewart climbed up onto the darkened flight deck of the *Levitow,* her way lit only by the glow of the standby power lights and a few instruments. She was just approaching her seat when something moved beside it. She leapt back before realizing it was Breanna Stockard, sitting alone in the airplane.

305

'Just me,' said Breanna.

'Jesus, you scared me,' said Stewart. Annoyed, she pulled herself into her seat. 'I thought you were with your husband.'

Breanna didn't answer. Stewart glanced at her, then took a longer, more careful look. Even in the dim light, she could tell Breanna's eyes were red.

The Iron Bitch crying?

Stewart put her mission card – a flash memory unit with recorded data about their mission – into its slot and powered up her station. She couldn't imagine Breanna Stockard crying about anything, and surely with her husband here – but those weren't tears of happiness.

The copilot busied herself with checking the computer data on the flight computer. Breanna made no pretense of working, continuing to sit silently and stare out the windscreen.

'We could go to the checklist on the engine start, even though it's a little early,' said Stewart when she ran out of things to do.

'I can't believe he gave up.'

'Who?' asked Stewart.

'Zen.'

'What did he give up?'

A tear slipped from Breanna's eye as she turned toward her. Stewart felt not only shocked but afraid. Breanna's pain somehow made her feel vulnerable.

'Zen left – he was in a program to rebuild his spinal cord. He left it because he thought we were in trouble.'

Stewart, still not understanding, said nothing.

'He's always wanted to walk again,' explained Breanna. 'He's fought for it. Now he's giving up. For me. He shouldn't give that up. He shouldn't be afraid for me.'

'Maybe he just wants to do his job,' said Stewart, not knowing what else to say.

Another tear slipped from Breanna's eye. How difficult – how *impossible* – it must have been for her to see her husband crippled, thought Stewart. How impossible it must be every day to live through it.

'The tests they're doing or whatever,' said Stewart. 'They're going to make him walk?'

'They're a long shot at best. Really a long shot. But walking or not walking – it's not as important as who he is. He can't surrender. That's not who he is. I don't want him to give himself up for me. It's not a trade I'd take.'

To her surprise, Stewart realized her own cheek was wet. 'I'm sorry,' she told Breanna.

Not because of Zen, but because of everything – bad mouthing her, grousing, resisting her attempts to help.

And not being able to handle the job in the stress of combat. That especially.

'We should get moving. You're right,' said Breanna suddenly, as if Stewart had suggested it.

'Hey.' Stewart reached over and touched Breanna's shoulder. 'If you need anything.'

Breanna turned back to her. Her eyes glistened in the reflected light and she gave a forced smile. 'Just the checklist for now. Thanks. Thanks.'

Mack let out a long string of curses – a very long string of curses – as he fought to outrun and outfox the shoulder-launched SAM. Caught at low altitude and low speed, there wasn't that much he could do, and his response would have been the same no matter what he was flying: toss decoy flares, jink back and forth, hit the throttle for all it was worth.

And pray, though Mack Smith had never found that particularly effective.

The missile sniffed one of the flares and rode off to the right, exploding more than half a mile away when it realized its mistake. Not entirely sure he was safe, Mack continued to the south until he saw the Sharkboat ahead.

'*Hawk One* to *Wisconsin* – that scumbag just tried to shoot me down.'

'Copy that, we saw it Mack.'

'Permission to give him his just reward,' said Mack, pulling up the weapons screen. 'I'll send him to the bottom.'

'Hold on, Mack. We want him disabled, not sunk. Stand by so we can coordinate with the Sharkboat. We want those people alive if at all possible. They're very valuable.'

'Sharkboat has them in sight,' said Jazz. 'Radioing to them to surrender.'

'Mack, take a pass,' Dog added. 'Fire into the water near the bow. Don't hit them.'

'Jeez, Colonel. I don't know if I can miss.'

'Not very funny, Mack.'

Actually, he wasn't making a joke. Mack had never tried *not* to hit something when flying a Flighthawk.

'Warning fire,' Cantor said. 'Designate the target, then give a verbal command. Computer will make sure you miss.'

'Thanks, kid.'

Still a little dubious, Mack accelerated back toward the submarine. Sure enough, after giving the verbal command, the bullets sailed near the vessel's path.

'Got their attention,' said Mack.

The submarine had stopped moving; it was still half submerged, with water lapping over the deck.

'Colonel, something's going on with the sub,' said Cantor. 'Strange noises – bubbling like they're taking on water.'

'Mack, did you hit them?'

'Negative.'

'It's going down, almost straight down,' said Cantor.

Mack banked back. Sure enough, the submarine had sunk below the waves.

'I think they're trying to make a run for it,' said Mack.

'Big explosion!' reported Cantor. 'Wow – they're going down straight to the bottom!'

VII

Coming to Their Senses

Aboard the *Abner Read*,
northern Arabian Sea
13 January 1998
2310

Storm kicked at the deck as he listened to the chatter from the Sharkboat. The technology that made it possible to coordinate actions over a wide-ranging area also made it possible to be incredibly frustrated. They'd missed their chance to catch the commandos. The submarine had seen the Dreamland aircraft and the Sharkboat. Realizing the jig was up, they'd hari-karied themselves.

'*Sharkboat One* is asking for further instructions, Storm,' said Eyes. 'Water's too deep for any sort of recovery operation. They've picked up what they can from the surface. Bits of plastic. Nothing significant.'

'Let's have them stay until morning light,' Storm told him. 'Pick up whatever they can find.'

'Yes, sir.'

'That Piranha unit – tell Bastian to send it south. Might as well get an eye on the Chinese Kilo.'

'We have that ourselves with the array.'

'Do you have anything better for the Piranha to do?'

'Can't think of anything.'

'All right, then. Let's get it down where it might do some good.'

Now everyone was questioning his orders. Storm looked at his holographic display. The Chinese aircraft carrier was a little over seventy-five miles away. A U-2 was nearby, keeping watch for the Tai-shan aircraft; it would alert Bastian if the planes came on deck, and he'd get his people into position to intercept.

The Indian carrier had moved north again. Maybe they were looking for a rematch.

'What do you think the submarine was?' Eyes asked him.

Bastian's theory that it was some sort of civilian craft put to military use by the Iranians made a hell of lot of sense, but there was no way Storm was going to admit that.

'Wouldn't even want to guess,' he told Eyes. 'Have intel prepare details on what the Sharkboat finds for Fleet and Pentagon intelligence.'

'Aye aye, skipper.'

National Security Council Conference Room 2A, Washington, D.C.
1800

'The Pakistanis have put Missile Site Two on its highest alert,' CIA director Robert Plank told the President as they briefed in the high-tech conference room beneath the West Wing. 'That's the site with their nukes, you see it here on the map. Four missiles, four warheads, each aimed at an Indian city.'

'What about the Indians?' asked Secretary of State Hartman.

'They're also on alert. We have satellite photos.'

Jed glanced at the satellite photos on the flat screen in front of him, even though he'd seen them earlier. The Indians and Pakistanis had engaged in serious shooting wars several times over the past decade, but those actions were mostly confined to the disputed regions in the North, near Kashmir and Jamu. They also had not involved nuclear weapons, or other countries. The Chinese were taking an aggressive tack to help the Pakistanis. Not to be outdone, the Russians were voicing support for the Indians and had ordered three ships to set sail for the Indian Ocean. An NSA intercept two hours ago indicated that a pair of Russian attack submarines were also en route.

'I have no confidence that the ceasefire will hold,' said Secretary of State Jeffrey Hartman. 'Quite the contrary.'

'I agree,' said Jed's boss, National Security Advisor Philip Freeman. 'We're very close to war. If the two sides use their missiles, the weapons aboard the *Deng Xiaoping* will be almost beside the point.'

'Yes, I want to talk specifically about that plan,' said Admiral Balboa.

'Jed, tell us about the weapons Dreamland wants to use,' said President Martindale. 'The EEMWBs.'

Jed tried to speak but couldn't. His tongue seemed to have shriveled and gone into hiding.

It wasn't that he hadn't been expecting the question. In fact, he'd rehearsed the answer for nearly a half hour. It was just that speaking in front of this many people – this many *important* people – was always a struggle.

He pushed a few words out of his mouth, stuttering as he went.

'Um, we, um, the EEMWB is an electronic bomb, like an E bomb. It uses T-Rays to disrupt electronic devices. The weapons would be much more efficient against the aircraft carrier than the Harpoons.'

'Another pie-in-the-sky Dreamland program,' said Balboa.

'Um, they've been used in tests and were supposed to be tested in two weeks in the Pacific.'

'Yes, I know about the weapons,' said Balboa. 'This isn't the place to be taking chances. We should have the *Abner Read* take the lead on this – position it between the Chinese and the Indians, as I argued yesterday. And who told Bastian he could use these weapons?'

'I told him he could use whatever he needed to get the job done,' said the President. 'Jed, could these EEMWBs stop the Indian and Pakistani missiles?'

Jed nodded. 'It would depend on the flight paths and everything. In theory, yes.'

'Talk to Bastian. Make it work,' said Martindale. He turned and looked at Balboa. 'The *Abner Read* will continue to be subordinate to Colonel Bastian on this aspect of the mission. If Storm wants to move, he's to clear it with the colonel.'

Jed played nervously with his pencil as he waited for the call to Colonel Bastian to go through on the Dreamland communications channel. The ultra-high-tech Situation Room in the basement under the White House had just undergone new renovations, increasing the available information stations and adding several security features. The situation room seemed to be a constant work-in-progress; this was at least the fourth major renovation it had undergone since Jed joined the NSC.

'Bastian,' said Dog, appearing in the screen.

'Colonel, your mission has been altered,' said Jed. As he relayed the President's new commands, he hit a switch that popped a map onto the screen so he could show Bastian where the missile sites were located.

'Pretty far inland,' said Dog.

'Can you strike those spots?'

'In theory, yes. Looks like you'd need three missiles, more or less in a straight line almost directly over the border. The weapons scientists will have to run some simulations to be sure. When is this taking effect?'

'Immediately.'

'We'll work something out. What about the carrier?'

'Not as important, but still –'

'I get the picture.'

'If this isn't doable, Colonel . . .'

'It's a stretch, Jed. I have to be honest. But we'll do our best. Technically, it's nothing we're not capable of.'

'The diplomats are working around the clock to calm things down.'

'I hope to hell they succeed.'

Northern Arabian Sea
14 January 1998
0400

When the sailor aboard the *Mitra* woke him, Captain Sattari did not know where he was. For a moment he believed – or perhaps wanted to believe – he was at his family's old house on the shore of the Black Sea, huddled with his wife Zenda. But she had died only three years after their marriage and lay enshrined in his memory as the perfect beauty, the flawless young bride he returned to whenever reality's storms were severe.

'Captain, an important message for you,' said the sailor.

Sattari took one last breath of Zenda's perfume, then opened his eyes. The man was holding a folded piece of paper in his hands. Pulling himself out of the narrow bunk, Sattari steadied his sockless feet on the floor and took the paper.

'Bring me coffee,' he told the sailor.

'Yes, sir.'

The message had been relayed by radio and contained only two words: 'Excellent. Accelerate.' It could only have come from Pevars, the oil minister, as he was the only one in the world who knew how to contact him.

Sattari rubbed his chin, eyes focused on the thin carpet

318

of the floor. He reached to the side of the bed, where he had left his shirt and a fresh pair of socks. He knew that *Boat Three* had not shown up during the night, for otherwise he would have been woken sooner.

Another argument for stepping up their schedule, if he had needed one.

In truth, he had hoped after Karachi it would not be necessary. The *Mitra*'s master said the Indians had attacked the Chinese aircraft carrier meant to reinforce the Pakistanis; surely that alone would mean war.

Sattari buttoned his shirt, then pulled on his socks. As he reached for his shoes, the sailor returned with his coffee.

'Is the ship's captain awake?' Sattari asked.

'Usually not for two more hours.'

'Go and wake him,' said Sattari. 'There has been a change in plans.'

Diego Garcia
0740 (0640, Karachi)

Danny Freah shuffled the cards and began laying out a solitaire hand on the table in the middle of the Command trailer's main room. He knew he ought to be enjoying the easygoing pace of the deployment, where Whiplash's only task was to provide security inside an installation that probably rated among the most secure in the world. Diego Garcia was literally an island paradise, and aside from the fact that he didn't have his wife with him, it would be the perfect place to while away a few days or even

319

weeks. He didn't often get a lull, and after his adventures in Karachi he deserved one.

But one man's vacation was another's purgatory. Danny Freah couldn't kick back while other people were putting their lives on the line. Besides, his night swim in the fiery waters was already receding in his memory, like the light burns on his hands.

A buzzer sounded from the Dreamland communications section, indicating there was an incoming message. Danny grabbed his coffee and went to the small station in the next room. Ray Rubeo's pale face appeared in the screen when he authorized the link.

'Captain Freah, we have information regarding the submarine that sank itself. Colonel Bastian requested a copy. I'd like to upload it to you now.'

'Go for it,' Danny told the scientist. 'So what is it? Russian Special Forces?'

'Hardly,' said Rubeo. 'It's civilian craft made by a Polish company. Some of the members of our Piranha team have done a little digging.'

'Whose sub is it?'

'Good question. We've asked the CIA, which means we will never know.'

Danny laughed. When the download was finished, he opened the file to make sure it had transferred properly. He found himself looking at a brochure of a craft that looked more like a pleasure boat with portholes in the bottom.

'It has windows?' asked Danny.

'No. Those would have been filled in. Flip to the end

of the file and you will see a schematic diagram one of the Piranha people did based on this and the findings from the probe. The basic systems from the commercial design appear intact, much as the chassis of a General Motors car would be similar across divisions.'

'Gotcha,' said Danny, toggling through to the diagrams. 'Say, Ray – if I was going to disable the submarine, what would I do?'

'What would be the purpose?'

'Just say I wanted to disable it. To capture it, and the people inside. What would we do?'

Rubeo gave Danny one of his what-fools-these-mortals-be sighs. 'I am not an expert on submarine warfare, Captain. I can get one of the Piranha people to talk to you if this is of more than theoretical interest.'

'Oh, it's very theoretical. But I'd like to talk to him anyway.'

'Very well. One area to question him on – this being a civilian submarine, it has many safety features incorporated into the design. The most interesting is an external emergency blow device.'

'You're losing me, Doc.'

'It forces the tanks to blow, raising the submarine to the surface. It's apparently intended to be used in the case of an emergency where the crew is completely incapacitated. If you were looking to recover the submarine, you might build a strategy around that device. Theoretically.'

'Oh, very theoretically,' said Danny. 'How soon can you get one of those Navy guys to talk to me?'

Aboard the *Shiva*,
off the coast of India in the northern Arabian Sea
0640

The helicopter was ancient, a Coast Guard Chetak that had first flown in the 1960s. Its engine sounded like a rasping buzz saw as it headed for a landing on the *Shiva*'s deck. But its white skin glistened in the sunlight, and the aircraft steadied herself with what seemed to Memon fitting dignity before settling to a landing on the deck. No sooner had the pogo-stick wheels touched down than the cabin flew open and Admiral Skandar emerged, stooping low to clear the blades, then straightening into full stride. He ignored the honor guard standing at full attention and walked to Memon and Captain Adri, who along with the deputy air commander and weapons officer had come out to meet him. Skandar walked directly to Captain Adri, ignoring Memon completely; Memon felt his heart sink.

'Captain,' said Skandar. 'You are prepared to launch an attack?'

'Our forces are ready and well-prepared,' said Adri. 'We are positioned to strike.'

'You did not receive my order to pull back?'

'Sir, I complied with your order not to attack when it was confirmed by the Chief of the Navy, but upon reflection concerning my positioning, I believed that you had erred. So I adjusted accordingly.'

'Captain, you will board my helicopter and return to Mumbai. I am in command of this vessel now.'

'But –'

'If necessary, you will be arrested.' Skandar turned and addressed the other two officers. 'If you are not prepared to carry out my orders without question, you may join him.'

The men stiffened, but said nothing.

'Admiral,' said Adri. 'I wish to apologize.'

'Why are you not aboard the helicopter? Leave now – your personal belongings will follow. Take me to the bridge,' Skandar told the others. 'Then I wish to inspect the damage and the wounded. After that, we will gather our commanders and prepare for the next stage of battle.'

Aboard the *Abner Read*,
northern Arabian Sea
0710

Storm grunted when the seaman knocked at the entrance to his cabin.

'Encrypted message from the Pentagon, Captain,' said the sailor.

'I'll take it here,' said Storm. He glanced at his watch. A light sleeper by nature, he rarely got more than four hours of sack time in a row during a cruise; he'd already had nearly three.

'Brought you coffee, sir,' added the seaman.

'Johnson, you are a tribute to the service.'

The sailor chuckled. Storm, who slept in his uniform, padded to the nearby door. He opened it, took the carafe, and then went to the small communications set on his desk opposite the foot of his bed. The set consisted of a small flat-screen monitor, video cam, speakers, microphone, and keyboard; it was essentially a computer with dedicated circuitry. Storm took the unit out of stand by, typed in a generic system code, then his own password. As the unit came to life, he opened the carafe and refilled the mug that sat in the indentation on the desk, not bothering to dispose of the coffee that filled its bottom.

The screen turned blue. Storm pecked in a second code word to clear the transmission. He found himself looking at an empty communications station in the Pentagon Situation Room. As he took his first sip of coffee, the top of a head appeared. Then a face came into camera range.

Storm had expected an intelligence officer. Instead, the face belonged to Admiral Balboa.

'Storm, I've just come back from the White House,' said Balboa. 'I've been in meetings all day and night over there.'

'Yes, Admiral?'

'Your mission's being altered. Has Bastian gotten a hold of you yet?'

Please tell me he's no longer in charge, prayed Storm.

'No, sir.'

'Typical. The President wants to stop World War Three. Bastian and his Dreamland people are going to use their weapons to do it. That means you're going to be on the front line against that carrier.'

'I already am, sir. I'm ready to sink it at a moment's notice.'

'I want you to shoot down the planes, Storm. You don't have to sink the carrier.'

'I can do both.'

'Don't go overboard. Take the planes.'

'Aye aye,' said Storm, speaking into his mug.

'However –'

Storm's ears perked up.

'If circumstances warranted – if you were to come under attack again,' said Balboa, 'then the carrier would be a legitimate target.'

'Damn straight it would, Admiral,' said Storm.

'Since they've already been warned once, no one could accuse you of being trigger happy. Sinking the Chinese super carrier – so-called super carrier – would be quite an achievement. If the circumstances were right.'

'I understand completely, Admiral. I appreciate your guidance.'

'Merely stating facts,' said Balboa. 'That Indian ship – is it as potent as they claim?'

'It didn't do very well against the Chinese,' said Storm.

'Best thing would be for them both to go down,' said Balboa. 'Not that they're competent enough to sink each other. Now, what's this theory about an Iranian submarine? We have all their Kilos under observation in the Persian Gulf. You're telling me the *Navy* missed one?'

'No. The theory is – Bastian's theory – is that the Iranians are trying to instigate a conflict using civilian-style aircraft converted to military use. He thinks a civilian-style aircraft may have launched the torpedo that struck the Indian ship en route to Port Somalia.'

'Preposterous. Bastian sees Iran behind everything.'

Storm found himself in the unusual position of actually thinking the Air Force lieutenant colonel was correct. But now wasn't the time to push the issue with Balboa.

'The attack on Karachi may have been carried out – definitely was carried out – by a commando team, some sort of SpecWar unit,' said Storm, treading carefully. 'We did find a submarine in Pakistani waters following the attack. The curious thing –'

'I've seen the report. So *your* theory is that Iran is behind this, trying to instigate a war?'

'That's Bastian's theory. I don't have an opinion.'

'Well, get one.'

'Yes, sir.'

Balboa frowned, then raised one of his bushy eyebrows. 'Stand by for Captain Connors and the intelligence updates.'

Souda Bay U.S. Navy Support Base, Crete
0915 (1215, Karachi)

Dog leaned in under the Megafortress's outer wing and examined the EEMWBs that had just been installed on the *Wisconsin*'s wing. The weapon's elongated and rounded nose added several feet to the overall length of the AGM-86C it had been attached to, making it impossible to carry inside the bomb bay. Two apiece were loaded on the Megafortress's outer wing, beyond the

Flighthawks. While they had a negligible effect on the Megafortress's general performance, they increased her radar profile, making the planes easier to detect.

Unlike the *Levitow*, the *Wisconsin* had not been shielded against the weapons; if she exploded them nearby she would lose her electric systems. But the *Levitow* couldn't stay on station indefinitely, and the only other aircraft in the world that was shielded against T-Rays was *Dreamland Raptor*, currently in several thousand pieces on the floor of one of the Dreamland hangars, being examined and overhauled. A crew of techies was heading toward Diego Garcia, where they would retrofit the *Bennett* with protective gear and shielding in the wings and fuselage; when they were done, that plane would be equipped with the missiles and alternate with the *Levitow* on patrol. For now, *Wisconsin* would play relief.

The weapons people at Dreamland had studied the possible paths the ballistic missiles would take, and they decided that only two explosions would be needed to disrupt the missiles. But to guarantee success, they wanted four launches in an overlapping pattern; that way, if one or even two failed to work or the yield was unexpectedly low, the plan would still succeed. That complicated matters for Dog, since to take out the carrier plane, he had to keep a second Megafortress in the area. He'd also told Storm to stay close to the carrier as well, a directive that was met with a grunt, which in Dog's experience represented almost euphoric enthusiasm on the naval commander's part.

Dog continued his walk-around, escorted by Chris Morris, the airman first class who was acting crew chief for the plane while it was 'pitted' at Crete. The young man had come from Dreamland with the missiles; this was not only his first deployment with the unit, but the most responsibility he'd ever been given in his life. He'd had a great deal of help prepping the plane from the Navy and from an experienced Air Force crew of maintainers that had flown in from Germany to help out. Still, as a Dreamlander he was the one ultimately responsible for the plane. He wouldn't have been sent if he wasn't up to it, but Dog could sense the butterflies in Airman Morris's stomach every time he stopped to look at something. Finally, when they'd done a complete circuit around the aircraft, Dog folded his arms in front of his chest.

'Something wrong, Colonel?' asked Morris.

'I've never seen aircraft more ready to fly,' Dog told him. 'Job well done.'

The kid's smile could have lit half the island. Dog ducked back under the wing, heading toward the ladder.

'Colonel!' shouted the airman.

Dog turned back.

'Um, Greasy Hands said I, um, I wasn't supposed to let you go without telling you.'

'Telling me what?'

'Don't break my plane. Sir.'

Dog laughed. 'I'll try not to. Go get yourself some sleep.'

Cantor watched from his station as Mack completed the launch procedure with *Hawk One* and took control of the aircraft. He rolled right, swinging the UM/F out ahead of the Megafortress as they flew over the eastern Mediterranean. They would fly over Israel, Jordan, and then Saudi Arabia en route to their station over the Arabian Sea. *Hawk Two* remained on the wing. Colonel Bastian had modified his one pilot-one Flighthawk rule slightly, allowing two planes to be used 'in an emergency,' but it was highly unlikely the plane would be launched on their way to the patrol area. Cantor thus had nothing to do until they got to the Arabian Sea, where he would take over control of the Piranha from Ensign English aboard *Levitow*. Piranha had gone south and was searching for the Chinese Kilo submarine escorting the *Deng Xiaoping*.

Cantor found himself wishing for an alert – scrambling Syrian MiGs as they approached the coast, an over-anxious Yemen patrol – to break the monotony.

'So what do you think, kid?' said Mack as the flight dragged on. 'Would you rather face two Su-35s? Or one F-15?'

'One F-15.'

'An F-15? Why?'

' 'Cause I know what he'll do. The Indians I'm still studying.'

'Fair enough. We won't be fighting against them anymore this time around, though.'

'Why do you say that?'

'Because now that the Indians and China have gotten their taste of what real action is like, they'll back off. I've seen this before. They don't want to lose any of their toys.'

* * *

329

Dog cleared the transmission. Danny Freah's face appeared in the Dreamland communications panel.

'Hey, Colonel, I've finished analyzing the attack on the Karachi terminal,' he told Dog. 'Definitely done by explosives. I'd say they used a dozen people, maybe more.'

'Twelve is a few too many for that submarine,' Dog said. 'Rubeo says they're figuring maximum capacity at about eight, maybe ten.'

'Yeah. But working out the way the explosives were set and the time of that first contact, there had to be at least twelve guys, like I say. I think it's likely there's at least one more submarine.'

'All right. Thanks, Danny.'

'Hey, Colonel?'

'Yes?'

'I'd like to draw up a mission to take the sub.'

'What do you mean?'

'Capture it. I've studied the data Ray Rubeo gave us, and talked to some submarine people on how to do it. There's a kind of a safety valve we can use to blow the tanks to get it to surface. When it does, we drop tear gas inside, get in and disarm whoever's aboard. Can't be more than eight people, maybe less.'

'First of all, Danny, I'm not sure you'd be able to disable everyone aboard before they blew it up.'

'There's also an external air fitting for emergency air – we could pump in nitrous oxide. There's a dentist over here who –'

'Second of all – and more to the point – you're four hours flying time from the general area in a Megafortress traveling at top speed. The Osprey would take twice as long, to have enough fuel to make it.'

'Be worth the trip. You have to find out where these guys are coming from, right? This is the best way to do it.'

'You're assuming we're going to see these guys again.'

'If I had a weapon like that, I'd use it until it broke,' said Danny. 'We should be ready, right?'

'I'll discuss it with Storm,' Dog told him. 'Don't hold your breath.'

Aboard the *Levitow*,
over the northern Arabian Sea
1230

It felt as if it had been months since he'd flown. Zen had trouble lining up for the refuel, coming on tentatively and then rushing into the furling turbulence behind the big plane. *Hawk Three*'s nose shot downward and he aborted, riding off to the right, more bemused than angry. He came around again, easing his hand forward on the stick.

His muscles began to spasm – a side effect of the treatments?

Forget the treatments, he told himself.

He pushed his body down in the seat, trying to ease the cramps without actually affecting his control of the airplane. He drove the Flighthawk into the hookup, then let the computer take over. By now his arm felt as if it had been mangled in a wheat thresher.

331

'*Levitow* to Flighthawk leader,' said Breanna. 'We have two J-13s coming at us hot out of the east. Distance is sixty miles.'

'Yeah, OK, I got 'em on the sitrep,' said Zen. 'I'll say hello.'

Zen took *Hawk Four* over from the computer and began cutting north. The Chinese aircraft were not part of the normal patrol over the carrier; these were sent here to get a look at the Megafortress. With the help of C³ he started back south at the very edge of his control link with the *Levitow*, putting himself in position to pull up behind the J-13s as they closed in.

'*Hawk Three* refueled,' said the computer.

Zen popped back into *Hawk Three* and slid her out from under the mother ship's refueling line. Then he ducked under the Megafortress's flight path, aiming at the oncoming J-13s. He had the robot planes positioned to sandwich the Chinese craft; he'd also be able to follow if they split up or did something unexpected.

'Looks like they're going to draw up alongside you and take pictures,' Zen told Breanna.

'*Levitow*.'

She was angry at something. Zen wondered if she was having more trouble with Stewart; the copilot had had trouble adjusting to the program.

When they were about seven miles from the Megafortress, the J-13s turned so they could come up alongside either wing. As they did, Zen slid *Hawk Three* between them, twisting into a roll and making it obvious that he was there. Their attention consumed by the approaching

332

plane, he pushed *Hawk Four* within spitting distance of *Bogey Two*'s tail. The Megafortress turned as it approached the end of its patrol track; Zen pulled *Hawk Three* around so he had a Flighthawk on each J-13. If they did anything hostile, he could take them down in an instant.

'The jerk on my side has a camera,' said Stewart as the Chinese planes pulled up alongside the *Levitow*.

'Well, make sure you wave,' Zen told her.

Stewart turned her head back to the glass 'dashboard' in front of her, scanning the sitrep map to make sure nothing new had appeared. There were two dozen aircraft in the Megafortress's scanning range, including a flight of Pakistani F-16s and an Indian long-range radar plane about a hundred miles inland. She worked through it quickly, top to bottom, then turned her attention to the systems screens, checking the engines to make sure everything was at spec. The computer made this easy for her by color coding the readings – numbers in green meant things were fine, yellows were cautions, red was trouble. The computer was also set to provide verbal alerts.

As she scanned the settings, Stewart realized that she had a tendency not to take the computer's word for things – to read each instrument's data and query for exact details, which would be provided on many of the sensors by tapping the screen. That was the right way to do it, certainly – but in a combat situation it added greatly to the information overload that had been messing her up. Glance and move on – rely on the technology.

If the J-13s tried anything, what would she do?

The Flighthawks would take them out.

If they didn't?

The Chinese planes would drop back, angling to get behind the Megafortress and use their weapons. Go to weapons screen, activate Stinger air mines.

They'd turn off or roll out, looking to get a little distance to make a missile attack. Evasive action, ECMs, flares, chaff, then AMRAAM-pluses.

SAM missile alert?

ID threat first. Then countermeasures.

Staying calm was the important thing.

'How you doing over there, Jan?' asked Breanna.

'All indicators in the green. Tweedledee and Tweedledum are right at our sides.'

Stewart felt a wave of anxiety rush over her. What had she missed? Was Breanna grilling her about something she'd screwed up?

No. She really wasn't like that. She was human.

'Nothing else in the air for fifty miles,' Stewart added, looking at the sitrep. 'CAPs are still over their carriers.'

'Good. Feeling tense?'

Another trick question? The Iron Bitch probing weaknesses?

Or just an honest one?

'A little. And tired,' she admitted.

'I know the feeling. Boy, do I know the feeling,' said Breanna.

Somehow, the reply felt like a compliment.

Diego Garcia
1640 (1540, Karachi)

Danny Freah carefully aligned his fingers on the stitches of the football, gently rolling the pigskin against his wide palm.

'Down, ready, set,' he yelled, his voice sharp and loud. He glanced to the right at his teammate – Boston, whose right hand was still bandaged, lined up at split end – then at their opponents – Liu, who was playing defensive back, and Pretty Boy, who was rushing.

There had to be some way to get up to the target area quickly.

Deploy the Osprey from the *Abner Read*?

They'd done that before. That would lower the response time considerably; it'd be an hour at most.

'Hut, hut, hut.' Danny took the ball and dropped back. Boston shot down the field. Danny waited for him to stop and fake right. He pumped, then lofted a bomb over the middle just as Pretty Boy finished his Mississippis and leapt into his face. Ducking away, he saw Boston get a hand on the ball but miss it, batting it into the air – where it was promptly snatched by Liu.

'Son of a bitch,' he growled, dodging Pretty Boy and heading toward Liu. Knowing from experience that the short and skinny Liu was a master of feints, Danny ran at three-quarter speed, waiting for the dance to begin. Sure enough, Liu did a stutter step as he approached, faking left then right then left. Then just as Danny grabbed for him, Liu tossed the ball backward – to Pretty Boy, who'd circled back and now had an open field to the goal. Danny turned on the jets in pursuit, but Pretty Boy lumbered across the goal before he could get two hands on him. Both men collapsed in the end zone, next to the nearby sidewalk that marked the end of their playing field.

'I had it,' griped Boston, coming over. 'Damn bandages got in the way. I don't even need the stinking things.'

Liu grinned as Boston pulled the gauze wrappings off. He'd applied the fresh dressing just before the game, no doubt figuring out some way to make them extra slippery.

The problem with the Osprey was that the submarine might see it coming. Ditto with the Sharkboat that accompanied the *Abner Read*. If they had *any* sort of warning at all, they might blow the submarine up.

He had to strike quickly, make it seem as if it were a malfunction, immobilize them before they could react.

'Spot pass on the kickoff,' whispered Boston. 'You receive, call pass while I run down the sideline. Just throw. We'll catch them off guard.'

'Spot pass?'

'Boston city rules,' said the sergeant. 'Allowed on a kickoff if you call it. Grab the ball, don't move, yell spot pass when they're close and bomb it. Let's do it and let them argue about it later.'

'Yeah,' said Freah. 'A long bomb.'

He started trotting toward the Command trailer.

'Cap?'

'You guys play without me for a while. I gotta go talk to the colonel.'

Aboard the *Wisconsin*,
over the northern Arabian Sea
1555

Dog sipped a coffee at the pilot's station as Jed Barclay continued to update him on the situation. He'd turned the plane over to Jazz and was enjoying the closest thing to a break he was going to have for the next eight hours or so. The *Levitow* had just left for Diego Garcia, where she'd get a fresh crew and a full load of fuel before returning to duty.

'Pakistan's missile batteries are on their highest alert. Same with India's,' said Jed Barclay. 'Nobody's backed off or stood down.'

'I thought the UN was sending a mission.'

'They have. The President's been talking to the different governments as well. The Indians say they're willing to negotiate, but both Pakistan and the Chinese blame them for the last round of attacks, both at Karachi and on the carrier. The Russians are egging the Indians on.'

'What about the Iranians?'

'Um, not following you there, Colonel.'

'I think they're the ones behind this. The aircraft –'

'We need proof. Like, something tangible. The airplanes weren't even flying toward Iran, and the CIA hasn't found any connection with the government yet.'

'The submarine?'

'No information's been developed that I've seen. Um, problem is, Colonel, a lot of people won't believe Iran's involved without real hard evidence and, um, the Secretary of State would never go out on a limb to charge them without something tangible, real tangible.'

'Yeah, all right. Thanks, Jed.'

Dog was just getting up to stow his coffee cup when the Dreamland channel buzzed with another incoming message, this one from Danny back on Diego Garcia. Dog sat back down and cleared it through.

'I have a plan to take the second submarine,' Danny said as soon as he came on the screen. 'We stage the Osprey off the *Abner Read*. In the meantime, two of us are orbiting in manpods aboard the Megafortress watching for the Tai-shan aircraft. When the submarine is sighted, we do a drop into the water, pump my laughing gas in, and do an emergency pop to the surface.'

'Manpods? Those one-man coffins that barely fit on the EB-52's wings?'

'No. Manpods, the one-man clandestine insertion devices that will give us a stealthy strike capability and allow us to grab the key actors in this international crisis.'

'Pretty risky, Danny. Assuming there *is* another submarine.'

'I think it's worth a shot. We ought to at least be in position.'

It was a no-brainer, wasn't it? If the Pakistanis, Chinese, and Indians were given evidence that they were being provoked into war, surely they'd stand down. And if the President was willing to risk the crew of a Megafortress to stop that war, then he'd be willing to risk the Whiplash team and an Osprey as well.

'Danny, tell you what,' said Dog. 'Let me get Storm on the line and have you run the plan down for him. Stand by.'

Aboard the *Abner Read*, northern Arabian Sea 1600

The sea air pepped him up as soon as Storm stepped out on the fantail of the *Abner Read*. Squinting at the late afternoon sun, he walked over to the two seamen who were prepping the Werewolf for another sortie. He watched as the men went silently about their business, working together as if they'd done this for years, though they had never even laid eyes on a Werewolf until two months ago.

Starship appeared from the hangar entrance, walking toward the aircraft on unsteady legs. Storm watched approvingly as the Dreamland pilot checked with each of the men, then ducked under the rotors of the craft, kneeling over some part of the control unit, giving it his own personal check.

Storm stepped forward to talk to the men, but before he reached the flight area the com unit on his belt buzzed. He pushed the headset forward, then hit the switch to connect.

'Storm.'

'Captain, incoming communication from the Dreamland aircraft *Wisconsin*. It's Colonel Bastian.'

'All right. Tell him to wait for a minute until I'm on the bridge.'

Starship pulled back the panel on the self-diagnostics unit of the Werewolf, punched in his code, and then keyed PrG-1, the main diagnostics program, to start. The LEDs began to blink furiously. He backed out from under the rotors; the checks took thirteen and a half minutes, and there was no sense waiting on his knees.

'You really flew this thing into the Chinese aircraft carrier?' asked one of the maintainers.

'Yup,' said Starship, trying to remember the sailor's name. He thought it was Tony, but he didn't want to say it in case he was wrong.

'Could've shot them up pretty bad, I'll bet,' said the other sailor.

'You're probably right. Sure scared the hell out of them,' said Starship.

'Probably peed in their pants, I bet,' said the man he thought was Tony.

Tony or Tommy. Starship had always been lousy with names.

The other was Jared. Definitely Jared.

'So you like being aboard the ship?' asked Jared.

'It takes some getting used to,' Starship admitted. 'I mean, I'm used to, well, moving around more.'

'It's not too bad once you get used to it,' said the sailor

he thought was Tony. 'On the bigger ships, you have more facilities and stuff, but the thing with a small boat like ours? Everybody pulls together. It's like a family.'

'Yeah, the people are pretty good,' said Starship.

'Captain can be a bit of a pill,' said Jared.

'Storm? Nah. His bark is worse than his bite,' said Starship. 'Tough guy, but fair.'

Jeez, listen to me, thought Starship. Guy says a few nice words to me and all of a sudden I'm running his campaign for President.

'I can use another aircraft, that's for sure,' Storm told Dog and Danny after they finished presenting the plan to take the commando submarine. It involved basing an Osprey on the *Abner Read* and having two Whiplash troopers dive into the water from a Megafortress using a special deployment device they called a manpod. Storm wasn't familiar with it, but it sounded a bit like a hollowed out bomb. 'But I'll be honest with you, Captain Freah. I'm not positive that there is another submarine out there, and I'm not sure you can pull this off, even if there is.'

'If we're supposed to be trying to stop a war,' said Danny, 'then it seems to me grabbing the people who are trying to start it ought to be a priority.'

'I'd rather sink the bastards and be done with them,' said Storm.

Then, as he often did after he'd shot from the hip, he considered the situation more carefully. First the negatives: The Osprey did not fit in the *Abner Read*'s low-slung hangar, negating much of the ship's low radar profile. They had not been resupplied for three weeks and were already starting to get low on fuel for the Werewolf.

Then the positives: Capture the submarine and its crew, and they'd have all the information they needed about who was trying to instigate the war. The commanding officer of the unit responsible would get considerable glory . . . and maybe an admiral's gold braid.

Same thing would happen if he sank the Chinese carrier, only faster. But that chance might not come, especially if Bastian found some way to muck things up.

Bastian was trying to be nice, deferring to him on this. It didn't fit him particularly well.

'What are the logistics?' snapped Storm. 'We haven't resupplied our jet fuel for the Werewolf, and we're pretty deep into our supply. How much fuel are you going to need?'

'I have to get a tanker to refuel the Osprey while it's en route,' said Dog. 'It may take me a few hours. If we can set that up, we may be able to arrange for a tanker to orbit outside the combat area to the west. If the Osprey is needed, it can tank before returning to the ship.'

'How long before you can get the Osprey up here?' asked Storm.

'We still need some gear and the manpods,' said Danny. 'But I would say we can launch within twelve hours, just before dawn our time here. We stay on station for the whole EB-52 shift, then the next group comes in. Two of our guys will be with the Osprey, and you can supplement them with your SITT team. Worst case with this whole deal, you have my whole team aboard your ship and we stage from there.'

'Let's do it. Captain Freah, I look forward to welcoming you aboard.'

Dreamland
1055 (2355, Karachi)

Jennifer Gleason looked at the computer screen and shook her head. 'The problem is that last set of missiles, Ray. If they don't launch simultaneously, they'll be too far from the initial explosion to guarantee they'll be affected.'

Rubeo sighed. 'With all due respect, Dr Gleason,' he said, in the tone he always used when he disagreed, 'your expertise is with computers.'

'Listen, Ray, I'm telling you – if you want to reach that set of missiles, you have to launch another missile. And change the launch coordinates.'

Jennifer knew why Rubeo was hesitating – her recommendations meant two planes, not one, would have to undertake the mission, and both aircraft would have to fly deeper into Indian territory. Besides Russian-made SA-6s and improved SA-2s, the Indian antiair batteries in the flight paths had recently been equipped with Russian SA-10s and SA-12s. The latter was considered especially advanced, roughly on a par with the American Patriot.

'I suppose I had best tell Colonel Bastian of your findings,' said Rubeo finally.

'I'll do it, Ray,' Jennifer told him.

'As head scientist, the job is mine. Besides, delivering

bad news enhances my image as a killjoy.' He got up from the console. 'You might accompany me to the Command Center, in case technical data is needed.'

Twenty minutes later Dog's tired face appeared on the large screen at the front of the Command Center in the Tac subbasement. Jennifer felt her chest clutch.

'Ray, what's up?'

'Colonel, I asked Dr Gleason to refine our computer simulations on the effects of the EEMWB. As you recall, we based our original assessments on the programs we used to design the tests, rather than the tests themselves.'

'Uh-huh.'

'After using the data from the tests to update the simulations, it would appear that a change in strategy would be desirable. I'm going to transmit a map for you. You'll notice it requires seven missiles launched at two separate intervals. This is to achieve the proper overlap to account for any malfunctions.'

'Seven missiles? That's two aircraft.'

'Yes.'

Jennifer watched Dog as he studied the screen. She longed to be there with him, though truthfully she was probably of much more use here.

'This is going to change things for us quite a bit,' said the colonel finally.

'I realize that. I'm sorry we didn't develop this information sooner. I take full responsibility.'

The corner of Dog's mouth curled up just a bit. But

instead of the sardonic comment Jennifer expected, he told Rubeo not to worry about it. Then, before she could say hello, he killed the connection.

Northern Arabian Sea
2355

Sattari took the night glasses and scanned the ocean to the south. He could just make out the mast of the Pakistani warship the *Mitra*'s captain had pointed out.

'It is the *Babur*,' said the captain. 'A destroyer.'

The *Babur* was more than twenty years old; it had begun life as the British Royal Navy frigate *Amazon*, before being sold to Pakistan a few years before. Cramped, not a particularly good seakeeper, and far past its prime, the vessel had an accurate and deadly 55mm gun at its bow that could tear through the tanker's skin like a staple gun chewing through paper. It also had potent antisubmarine torpedoes that could send a Parvaneh to the bottom with even a near miss.

Sattari's plan called for the three Parvanehs to leave the oil tanker in thirty minutes. Sailing at top battery speed, they would reach the Indians' offshore early warning radar platform off Dwārka in five hours. That would allow them to launch the attack just before dawn. If successful, the strike would convince the Indians that the Pakistanis or the Chinese were clearing the way for a bombing attack on India itself.

The platform had been constructed on a rock

345

outcropping in water so shallow that not even the Parvaneh submarines could get closer than three-quarter miles; to succeed, the commandos would have to approach in darkness. Delaying for too long now would scrub the mission for tonight.

Sattari did not want to delay. The transmissions they'd been monitoring all day showed that the antagonists were primed and ready for battle. But there were news reports that diplomats had begun shuttling around the subcontinent, trying to get the sides to stand down. The longer he waited, the greater the chance that the conditions he needed for success would slip away.

Could he take the chance that the Pakistanis' antiquated sonar systems would miss the Parvanehs? Perhaps this very frigate had been responsible for the disappearance of his other boat.

'We will wait,' Sattari told the *Mitra*'s captain. 'Continue on the course you have set. We will review the situation every twenty minutes.'

Aboard the *Shiva*,
northern Arabian Sea
2355

'The Chinese aircraft presented the most difficult challenge,' said Admiral Skandar, pointing to the chart. 'Their missiles were the ones that struck the *Shiva*. By coordinating their attack with the salvos from the destroyers, they were able to swarm our defenses. That must not happen again. The screening vessels must be placed here and here, to deal with the Chinese.' Skandar jabbed his thumb at the map. 'And a more aggressive air patrol sent to combat the attackers. They were too late to prevent the missile launches – that was their first duty.'

Memon listened as the Defense minister continued to lay out the battle plan. Two more destroyers had joined the *Shiva* in the past two hours, and their captains – along with officers from the other escorts and the warfare commanders of the *Shiva* – had assembled in the warfare briefing room aboard the carrier. The admiral had eschewed the array of multimedia equipment available, preferring a large sea chart with the positions of the ships penciled in by hand. He spoke without notes, his knowledge of the ships, weapons, and strategies available to both sides evident as he prioritized the targets – the radar helicopters first at long range, then the carrier.

This was a different man than the one Memon had seen in the political halls of New Delhi; this was the man who matched the reputation that had brought him to congress and the ministry. His voice remained gentle, and yet he was neither reticent nor compromising. He had begun the meeting by saying that he hoped dearly for peace – and then plunged straight to war making.

A week ago such talk would have filled Memon with confidence and excitement. Now he felt dread. He was afraid that the missile attack had revealed his true nature as a coward. The memory of the dead man vibrated in the air before him, a storm just outside his flesh.

Skandar had quieted the panic he felt, but this was

not to say that the Defense minister had restored him to the man he had been before the attack. On the contrary. Memon's great fear now was that the admiral knew he was a coward, and was merely biding his time before denouncing him. Then his despair would be complete.

Adri had been banished for being too aggressive, if only by a hair; how much more extreme would the punishment be for a man who was a coward and a disgrace? If Admiral Skandar saw his true nature, would he not react with disgust?

Memon's eyes followed as Skandar pointed to the map west of the *Shiva*'s position.

'And where is the American ship?' he asked.

The intelligence officer who had plotted the positions for him said the *Abner Read* had moved to the west overnight, and its location had not yet been ascertained.

'It must be known at all times,' said the admiral, his tone still mild. 'In the event of action, it must be targeted immediately.'

'The Americans?' said one of the destroyer captains.

'Yes. They must be attacked at close range. The design of their vessel is well-suited to warding off radar-guided weapons, but an old-fashioned attack, launched with bombers at close range – that is how to defeat them. The aircraft must be close to them before the fighting begins. Their radar planes, too, must be attacked. This task we will assign to the shore batteries.'

Attack the Americans? Memon glanced around the room, waiting for someone to object. But no one did.

Skandar looked up at Memon. 'And now, a late snack for all before you return to your ships.'

The others began filing out. As Memon turned to join them, Skandar settled his hand on his shoulder.

'Deputy Minister, a word.'

They waited until the others were gone.

'You are anxious about attacking the American ship,' said Skandar.

'I am not questioning your orders.'

'There are situations when questions are appropriate, and situations when they are not. Express your thoughts.'

Was this a trap? Memon wondered. A test to see if he was a coward?

But if he spoke falsely, would Skandar detect that?

He resigned himself to telling the truth. 'If we attack the Americans, won't they retaliate?'

'If we strike fiercely enough, they will not be in a position to attack us.'

'I meant, after this battle –'

'We must survive the battle first before worrying about the future. Do you not think the Americans are a threat?'

'The Americans have been neutral.'

'Do you think it is a coincidence that they have been nearby when the other attacks occurred? If they have not launched the attacks themselves, is it not possible that they provided intelligence to those who have?'

Memon had made this point, or one similar, to Admiral Kala. But now the idea filled him with fear.

'During the 1967 war between Israel and Egypt, the Israelis had a similar situation with an American vessel in the war zone,' continued the admiral. 'The ship was attacked as a necessary expedient. There was no retaliation.'

'Yes,' managed Memon, not knowing what else to say.

'American policy in Asia is best served if neither China nor India are superpowers,' continued Skandar. 'They want us to destroy each other. Their diplomats pretend otherwise, but it is a logical conclusion on their part. Their vessel may supply information, directly or indirectly, to our enemies. It cannot be ignored.'

The harsh fluorescent light made Skandar's face appear somewhat paler than normal. But the effect, harsh on so many others, made the minister seem years younger. Only his eyes, with their crinkled corners, stayed old.

'You are afraid of attacking the Americans?' Skandar asked again.

'I worry about the consequences.'

Skandar nodded. 'In a battle, many things happen. The diplomats will excuse it. They will say that the government did not order the attacks. I have consulted with our friends in congress on this; we have weighed the consequences. The loss of the ship will be overshadowed by other events. If the Pakistanis or their Chinese allies attack, the response will be devastating. And they *will* attack. This is a moment of history, Anil. It is the opening of a struggle for dominance in Asia, a new era. But you recognized this moment would come. You've spoken of it often.'

'Are we ready?' Memon asked weakly.

'We are prepared. You've helped see to that,' said Skandar. 'The war will come. It is an inevitability.'

'Inevitable,' repeated Memon.

'You tasted blood.' Skandar's voice rose slightly. 'The encounter was more than you had thought it would be.'

Memon nodded.

'I could not hold food in my stomach for two weeks after my first battle, and the only dead men I saw were the enemy,' Skandar said. 'You will be fine. Come.'

Memon followed along, as unsure as ever.

VIII

Inevitability

Diego Garcia
0055, 15 January 1998
(2355, 14 January, Karachi)

Breanna pushed the lock of hair away from her eye, arranging it behind her ear with her fingers. The mirror in the tiny bathroom wasn't big enough to show more than a quarter of her face, let alone the rest of her. Her nightshirt – actually an oversized T-shirt she'd appropriated from Zen months ago – was hardly sexy, but it was marginally more alluring than the heavy sweats she usually slept in.

Not that she wanted to be alluring, or felt a need to be. What she wanted to be was honest and easy and uncomplicated, not wracked with guilt and fear, if that was the right word. She wanted to talk with her husband without worrying about landmines, to be able to say she loved him and wanted the best for him, and ask why he was giving up.

Why *was* he giving up?

'Hey,' Zen grunted from inside the room. 'You comin' to bed?'

Breanna snapped off the light. 'I'm thinking about it,' she said, forcing her voice to be cheerful.

She opened the door and stepped into the darkened room, nearly tripping over the cots they'd pushed together to form a double bed. She slipped in beside him, wrapping her arm around his chest and then gently resting her head on his shoulder.

'I missed you,' she whispered.

'Missed you too. More than ever.'

'You think you'll be able to sleep? My body clock's all messed up.'

'I have some Ambien if you need it.'

'Thanks.'

I'm being a coward, she told herself. Just blurt it out.

'Jeff?'

'You feeling frisky?' he asked, leaning his body to the side and starting to fondle her breast.

'I –'

Before she could continue, there was a knock on the door.

'Major Stockard? Captain?' said Boston from the hallway. 'Uh, sir, ma'am? You awake in there?'

'We're busy, Boston,' growled Zen. 'Come back next year.'

'I really wish I could, sir. I really wish I could. But the colonel needs to talk to you ASAP over at the Dreamland Command trailer.'

'He's back already?' said Breanna. She glanced at her watch. The original plan called for the *Wisconsin* to stay on station until the *Levitow* returned to the area. It wasn't supposed to be ready to take off for another hour yet, at least.

'Uh, no, ma'am. He's on the secure line.'

'All right. We'll be right there,' said Zen, pushing himself upright.

Ten minutes later Zen and Breanna joined the other Dreamland officers crowding into the Dreamland Command trailer. Zen had to squeeze past the door and pivot to his right, never easy in these cramped quarters as he came up the ramp, and harder today, not so much because of the crowd as the fact that he was tired.

Danny had folded back the divider between the secure communications area and the main room, making it possible to swing the video conferencing unit out where everyone could see – or at least pretend to see. He'd also jacked up the volume, though even at its highest level it was just barely audible at the far end of the trailer.

'We've had some more simulations done at Dreamland,' Dog told them after briefly recounting their mission and the general situation. 'The computer models show that we need more detonations to be successful than we thought earlier. That means, for practical purposes, seven missiles, fired in a preplanned sequence. And from somewhat farther over Indian territory than we had originally planned.'

Zen guessed the rest: The *Levitow* and *Wisconsin* would have to stay on station until the crisis passed, or until more EEMWBs were manufactured. The *Levitow*, due to take off within the hour, would have two sets of pilots and an extra radar operator; the crews would rotate, with those off-duty trying to catch some z's in the compartment behind the flight deck. Used by the defensive team in a 'stock' B-52, the compartment was designed for another set of Flighthawk operators, but in Dreamland EB-52s it was usually empty or else crammed with test gear. Cots had been installed during some deployments and long sorties. There was no confusing the accommodations with a deluxe hotel, or even a sturdy Army cot, but they were serviceable.

'What about the Flighthawks?' asked Zen.

'Two per plane. They're not shielded, so Zen, you'll have to work out a strategy to maximize protection if we have to move ahead. We'll exchange Ensign English for a Flighthawk pilot on *Levitow*. The Piranha unit is nearing the end of its patrol time anyway; its fuel cell is almost used up. The second pilot will control it for as long as possible, then put it into autonomous mode.'

'What about the planes on the Chinese carrier?' asked Breanna.

'The *Levitow* will target them, with the *Abner Read* backing her up.'

'I think *Dreamland Fisher* ought to be dedicated to the targeting mission,' said Tommy Chu, the aircraft's pilot. 'If the *Levitow* can't get back in time, it will be in position.'

'We can use it for the Whiplash mission as well,' said Danny.

'All right. Let's do it. *Wisconsin* will return to base as soon as the *Levitow* is on station. *Bennett* is en route home right now; they'll try and grab some rest and then form the backup crew on *Wisconsin*. We want a hot pit – basically just long enough for our backup pilots and crew to jump aboard. The diplomats are working overtime,' added the colonel, trying a little too hard to sound positive. 'If we can get past the next forty-eight hours or so, tensions should calm.'

A big if, thought Zen, though he didn't say it.

Fifteen minutes later, out on the apron near the runway, Danny wondered what he'd gotten himself into. The manpod – actually a large, flat, pressurized container designed to fit under a B-2 or a B-52's wing – did not want to align properly with the detents that would allow auxiliary power to be pumped into the unit from the *Fisher*. The power was necessary for several reasons, not least of which was the fact that without it the pod would not pressurize.

It wasn't as if Danny could do an awful lot about the problem – he and Boston were packed inside their respective pods, talking through the 'smart helmet' com links to Sergeant Liu, who was supervising the 'snap in' – or trying to.

The lift truck lowered him again.

'Hey, guys, I'm supposed to be part of the plane, right?' said Danny.

No one answered for a second, then Danny overheard a muffled grumble through Liu's microphone. He couldn't make out the words, but the grumble had a familiar snarl to it.

'Good morning, Captain,' said Greasy Hands – aka Chief Master Sergeant Al Parsons – a moment later. 'We seem to be having a little difficulty here.'

'You're telling me.'

'Well, you just hold on for a second, Captain, while I straighten these boys out.'

A moment later Danny felt the manpod being lifted off its carrier. Over the com system he heard someone – it had to be Greasy Hands – counting off in the background. Then the manpod was thrust upward against the wing, slapping into the brace with a resounding *clunk*.

'There you go,' snarled Greasy Hands. 'We'll have Boston on in a minute. *Less time* if someone here would get me my *coffee!*'

'Pretty Boy, get the chief a pot of coffee, on the double,' said Danny to Sergeant Jack Floyd, his ears ringing.

Northern Arabian Sea
15 January 1998
0115

'God is great,' the *Mitra*'s captain told Sattari. 'The destroyer has changed course and is heading west.'

'You're sure?'

'Look for yourself. His stacks are billowing – he must be off to meet one of the Chinese ships. I've sent to the radio room to see if they have intercepted any messages.'

Sattari took the night glasses. He saw the cloud of warm exhaust rising in the distance, but not the Pakistani ship.

'We will leave immediately,' Sattari said. 'With the protection of God, we will do our duty. Protect yourself,' he added, handing the glasses back.

'We will do our best,' said the captain. 'May God be with you.'

Aboard the *Wisconsin*,
over the northern Arabian Sea
0330

Cantor stared at the Piranha's screen, trying to blink away some of the burn he felt in the corner of his eyes. The milky representation of the ocean was supposedly a huge advance over the displays used by conventional passive sonar systems, but the only thing he had to compare it to was the Flighthawk's synthesized radar images, and that was like comparing shadows reflected from a camp-fire to an iMax movie.

Piranha had followed the Chinese submarine into Pakistani waters south of Karachi, close to the border with India. This happened to suit them well, taking them within six minutes' flying time to the spot where they would cross the border if they had to fire their EEMWBs. For the past two hours, the Kilo-class sub had sat a hundred feet below the surface of the water, silently waiting. But now that the Chinese submarine began to move westward, Colonel Bastian would have to decide whether they would drop another control buoy and follow or pull the Piranha back.

Besides the submarine, there were two surface ships in the vicinity. One – too far away to be identified by the Piranha, but ID'd by the surface radar as a Pakistani patrol craft – was sailing south. The other was a civilian ship. Cantor could see both vessels on the large surface radar plot in his lower left-hand screen.

The computer gave an audible warning that the Piranha was approaching the limit of the buoy's communication system. Cantor throttled the robot back, then asked Colonel Bastian what he wanted to do.

'Tell you what, Cantor – *Levitow* is about two hours' flying time away. Let's put down one more control buoy and move south. They can pick it up when they come on station.'

'Copy that, Colonel. We could swing south about six miles and drop it there.'

'I have to watch out for traffic,' said Dog. 'Stand by.'

While he was waiting, Cantor swung the Piranha around, doing the robot submarine's version of 'checking six' to see what was behind it. The merchant ship showed up on the screen – a long blurry shadow, with a set of numbers giving data on the direction the contact was moving and categorizing the sound it made. Cantor moved his cursor to select the contact, directing the computer to check the sound against its library of contacts. The computer classified the vessel as an 'unknown oil tanker type,' as had the system tied into the Megafortress's surface radar.

As the Piranha continued to swing through the circle, its passive sonar picked up another contact, this one underwater. The contact was so faint the robot's gear couldn't tell how far away it was.

Was it really there? The irregular coastal floor nearby played tricks with sound currents, and it was possible that Piranha was 'seeing' a reflection of the submarine or one of the surface ships. The only way to tell was to get closer.

Cantor halted the Piranha's turn, sliding the stick forward and moving gingerly in the direction of the contact. The scale showed the contact was at least twenty miles away, just about in territorial waters.

'Colonel, I think I have something, another sub maybe,' Cantor told Bastian. 'It's a good twenty miles east of us. I wonder if we should check it out.'

'You're sure it's a sub?'

'I'm not sure at all,' Cantor admitted. 'But if I follow the Chinese Kilo, I'll definitely lose it. Very faint signal – extremely quiet.'

'Give me the coordinates,' said Dog.

Aboard the *Shiva*,
in the northern Arabian Sea
0340

Memon watched as the last Su-35 exploded off the deck of the carrier, its rapid ascent into the night sky belying the heavy load beneath its wings. Six new jets had arrived last evening, bringing the carrier's flyable complement to eighteen. All but two were now in the air; if the order was given to attack, it would take no more than ten minutes for the first missile to strike its target.

He hoped it would not come to that.

Did this mean he was a coward? Or was Skandar right – was it just a matter of experience, of getting past the first shock?

'A beautiful sight, isn't it?'

The voice sounded so much like Admiral Kala's that Memon turned around with a jerk. But it wasn't the dead admiral or his ghost, just one of the NCOs, an older man who supervised the radar specialists.

'Yes, it is beautiful,' managed Memon. 'Incredibly beautiful.'

NSC Situation Room
1740, 14 January 1998
(0340, 15 January, Karachi)

Jed Barclay wheeled his chair back from the communications console and surveyed the screens arrayed before him. Twenty-three different computers were tied into various intelligence networks, allowing him almost instantaneous information on what was happening in India and Pakistan. Updated feeds from satellites designed to detect missile launches took up four screens at the left; the coverage overlapped and had been arranged so the entire subcontinent was always in view. A pair of screens collated feeds from a pair of U-2s covering the Arabian Sea. The

364

planes' sensor arrays, dubbed 'Multi-Spectral Electro-Optical Reconnaissance Sensor SYERS upgrades,' provided around-the-clock coverage of the region, using optics during the day and in clear weather, and infrared and radar at other times.

The next screen provided a feed from an electronic eavesdropping program run by the National Security Agency; the screen filled with updates on intelligence gathered by clandestine electronic listening posts near India and in Pakistan. Interpretations on captures of intelligence on Pakistani systems filled the next screen. Then came a series of displays devoted to bulletins from the desks at the different intelligence agencies monitoring the situation. Finally there was the tie-in to the Dreamland Command network, which allowed Jed to talk to all of the Dreamland aircraft and share the imagery.

Six people were needed to work all of the gear. Jed was the only one authorized to communicate directly with the Dreamland force. He would be relieved in the morning by his boss, who had just gone to dinner and who expected to be paged immediately if things perked up.

'I say we send out for pizza,' said the photo interpreter monitoring the U-2 and satellite images.

'How about Sicilian?' suggested Peg Jordan, monitoring the NSA feed.

'Sounds good,' said Jed.

'Let's call Sicily and have it delivered,' deadpanned Jordan.

Everyone laughed. As lame as it was, Jed hoped the joke wouldn't be the only one he heard tonight.

Dog double-checked his position, making sure he was still outside Pakistani territory. A pair of Pakistani F-16s were flying thirty miles due east of him, very close to the country's border with India. The planes had queried him twice, making sure he wasn't an Indian jet. Even though that should have been obvious, Dog had Jazz reassure the pilots, telling them they were Americans hoping to 'help keep the peace.' There was no sense having to duck the planes' missiles prematurely.

Besides the Pakistani flight, the Megafortress was being shadowed by a pair of Indian MiG-21s. Much older than the F-16s, they were farther away and less of a threat. But they were clearly watching him. Probably guided by a ground controller, they changed course every time he did. He knew this couldn't go on much longer – the small fighters simply didn't carry that much fuel – but it was an ominous portent of the gamut they'd have to run if things went sour.

Jed had warned that they couldn't expect the Pakistanis to be friendly. Annoyed at the neutral stance of the U.S., the government of Pakistan had specifically warned that the Dreamland aircraft were 'unwelcome' in Pakistani airspace for the length of the crisis.

If ballistic missiles were launched, Dog would know within fifteen seconds. Ideally, he would then rush over the Thar Desert, flying at least twelve and a half minutes before firing the first salvo of three missiles, which would detonate roughly seven minutes later. Seconds before they did, he would fire his last missile. Soon afterward, he would lose most if not all of his instruments and fly back blind. And while the radars and missile batteries along the route he was flying would be wiped out, the closer he got to the coast, the higher the odds that he'd be in the crosshairs. The *Wisconsin* might never know what hit her.

The worst thing was, if the new calculations were correct, the mission might be in vain. And the same went for the *Levitow*. It was going to be ten or twelve hours before they could have both aircraft on station.

'J-13s from the carrier are headed our way,' said Jazz.

Dog grunted. The Chinese seemed to be working on an hourly schedule – every sixty minutes they sent a pair of planes to do a fly-by and head back to the carrier.

'*Wisconsin*, this is *Hawk One* – you sure you don't want me to get in their faces?'

'Negative, Mack. Conserve your fuel. And your tactics.'

'Roger that.'

Dog thought Mack must be getting tired – he didn't put up an argument.

'Colonel, Piranha is within ten miles of that under-water contact,' said Cantor. 'Computer is matching this to the other craft. The one that scuttled itself the other day.'

'You're positive, Cantor?'

'Computer is, Colonel. Personally, I haven't a clue.'

'All right. I'll contact Captain Chu and Danny in *Dreamland Fisher*. Good work.'

Aboard the *Abner Read*,
in the northern Arabian Sea
0348

Storm watched the plot on the radarman's scope, tracking the Indian jets as they circled to the east.

'Keeping an eye on us,' said the sailor. 'Every fifteen minutes or so they split up. One comes straight overhead.'

Storm scratched the stubble on his chin, considering the situation. The planes were well within range of the Standard antiair missiles in the forward vertical launch tubes.

The problem was, his orders of engagement declared that he had to wait for 'life-threatening action' before he could fire. That meant he couldn't launch his missiles unless the Sukhois got aggressive – which at this close range might be too late. Storm decided that when he got back to the bridge he would radio Bastian and see if he couldn't get one of his little robot fighters over to run the Indians off.

Continuing with his tour of the Tactical Center, Storm moved over to the Werewolf station. Starship had gone off to bed, and one of Storm's crewmen – Petty Officer Second Class Paul Varitok – was at the helm of the robot. The petty officer was one of the ship's electronics experts and had volunteered to fly the aircraft when it came aboard. He was still learning; even discounting the fact that Storm's presence made him nervous, it was obvious to the captain that he had a long way to go.

Storm completed his rounds and headed over to the communications shack. After checking the routine traffic, he made a call to Bastian. The Air Force lieutenant colonel snapped onto the line with his customary, 'Bastian,' the accompanying growl practically saying, *Why are you bothering me now?*

'I have two Indian warplanes circling south at five miles,' Storm told him. 'What are the odds of you chasing them away?'

'No can do,' said Dog. 'Stand by,' he added suddenly, and the screen went blank.

It took the Air Force commander several minutes to get back to him, and he didn't offer an apology or an explanation when he did. If he wasn't such an insolent, arrogant, know-it-all blowhard – he'd still be a jerk.

'Storm – we have a contact we think may be another midget submarine. It's similar to the one that blew itself up. We're going to track it. My Whiplash people will be en route shortly.'

'Where is it?'

'A few miles off the Pakistani coast, just crossing toward Indian territory.'

Dog gave him the coordinates, about sixty miles to the east of the Sharkboat, which was another forty to the east of the *Abner Read*.

'It will take about two hours for the Sharkboat to get

there,' Storm told him. 'But those are Indian waters. If we're caught there, it will be viewed as provocative. The Indians will have every right to attack us.'

'You're telling me you won't go there?'

'This has nothing to do with the aircraft carrier, Bastian. You can't give me an order regarding it.'

'I'm not. But if we want to get the submarine, we have to do it now. I would suggest – *suggest* – that you position your Sharkboat several miles offshore so it can come to the aid of the craft when it begins to founder.'

'You know all the angles, don't you?' snapped Storm.

Dog didn't respond.

'Yes, we'll do it,' said Storm. 'Get with Eyes for the details.' He jabbed his finger on the switch to kill the transmission.

Aboard the *Levitow*,
over the northern Arabian Sea
0430

Zen watched as Lieutenant Dennis 'Dork' Thrall finished the refuel of *Hawk Three*. Dork backed out of *Levitow*, rolling right as he cleared away from the Megafortress. *Hawk Four* remained on the wing; Zen would have to take the Piranha when they arrived on station, and didn't want to leave Dork to handle two planes.

Dork steered the Flighthawk out in front of the Megafortress, climbing gradually to 42,000 feet, about five thousand higher than the EB-52. They were still forty-five minutes from the *Wisconsin*'s position, but already they'd encountered three different Indian patrols. They had also passed a Russian guided missile cruiser steaming northward with two smaller ships. If tempers were cooling, Zen saw no evidence of it.

He heard something behind him, and turned to find Breanna climbing down the metal ladder at the rear of the deck.

'I thought you were sleeping,' he told her.

'I fell asleep for, oh, twenty minutes,' she said. 'Hard to sleep with Stewart snoring in my ear. She's louder than the engines.'

'Dork's flying *Hawk Three*,' said Zen.

'So I gathered. You're just surplus?'

'Nothing but a spare part. You too?'

'Actually, I'm going to switch with Louis and take the stick. He's feeling the aftereffects of the Navy food.'

'You sure you shouldn't get more rest?'

'Nah,' said Breanna. Then she added cryptically, 'Hardly worth giving up your treatments for.'

'Huh?' Zen looked up at her, shocked – almost stunned – by what she'd said.

'You want anything? Coffee?'

'I'll take a cup.'

He watched her disappear upstairs and felt a pang of regret at not being able to get up and go with her – at not being able to *walk* up with her.

She thought he'd made a mistake. That's what she'd meant. She wanted a whole man for a husband: one who walked.

Zen forced himself to go back to watching Dork. The Flighthawk pilot checked his sitrep, keeping a wary eye on a pair of Indian MiG-29s that the *Levitow*'s radar painted about 150 miles to the east. He had a good handle on what he was doing; while there were no guarantees, Zen thought he'd do well in combat once he got a little experience under his belt.

Maybe no one really needed him here at all.

'Coffee,' said Breanna, returning with a cup.

'Where's yours?'

'I have to get back. Lou's whiter than a ghost.'

'All right. See you around.'

'Something wrong, Jeff?'

'Nah. I'll be talking to you.' He tried to make it sound like a joke, but couldn't quite manage it.

Aboard the *Wisconsin*,
over the northern Arabian Sea
0450

'Piranha to *Wisconsin*.'

'Go ahead, Cantor,' said Colonel Bastian, checking his position to make sure he was still in international airspace, about fifteen miles to the west of shore.

'The submarine is surfacing, Colonel. I think they're going to that radar platform. And I think there's another one nearby, closer to the coast but behind us. I'll have to circle around to find out.'

The platform held one of a series of large radar

antennas used to detect aircraft by the Indians. It would be a perfect target for a covert operation.

There was also a small building and shed at the base – a good place to resupply a small vessel.

'*Wisconsin* to Flighthawk leader – Mack, I want you to take a pass at the radar platform and give us some visuals. I want to see if that platform is expecting them.'

'On it, Colonel.'

Aboard the *Deng Xiaoping*, in the northern Arabian Sea 0450

Captain Hongwu, the master of the *Deng Xiaoping*, reviewed the movements of the Indian ships over the past several hours. The *Shiva* and her escorts had spread out, and at the same time come closer to him. Clearly they were positioning themselves for an attack.

While he had expended most of his anticruise missiles in his earlier engagement, Hongwu felt confident he could handle the Indians by overmatching their aircraft with his larger squadron, allowing him to reserve the missiles for use against ship-launched weapons. He would devote his planes to defense initially, counter-attacking only after he had broken the enemy's thrust.

But he worried about what role the Americans would play. Besides the warship his pilots had misidentified, they were flying Megafortresses above the Arabian Sea. One seemed to be tracking his fleet. He thought it unlikely that they would help the Indians, but he knew he had to be prepared.

'The American aircraft should be kept at least fifty miles from us at all times,' he told his air commander. 'We must keep their air-to-air missiles out of easy range of the radar helicopters. And if fighting starts again, they should be moved back beyond the range of the standard Harpoon missiles they carry – eighty miles.'

Hongwu immediately noted the concern on the air commander's face.

'If necessary, assign four aircraft to escort them,' added Hongwu. 'Escort them at very close range, where their air-to-air missiles will not be a factor.'

'It will be done, Captain.'

Northern Arabian Sea
0455

Captain Sattari rolled his neck sideways and then down toward his chest, trying to stretch away the kink that had developed there in the past hour. They were almost at their destination; he wanted to be out, and so did everyone else aboard the submarine.

'We are a little ahead of schedule, Captain,' said the Parvaneh's captain. 'The others may be well behind us.'

'Good. We will lead the charge.' Sattari got up and turned to the rest of the commandos. 'Be prepared to fire your weapons the moment we are out of the submarine.'

Aboard the *Shiva*,
in the northern Arabian Sea
0500

'The radar platform at Dwārka reports that an American Megafortress is orbiting it to the west,' the radar officer told Admiral Skandar. 'A flight of air force interceptors is being scrambled to meet it.'

Skandar nodded, and turned to Memon. 'Do you still think the Americans are neutral?'

'No, Minister,' said Memon, though the question was clearly rhetorical.

'They are targeting the radar platform. You will see – it will be attacked at any moment.' Skandar turned to his executive officer. 'Warn the platform to be on its guard. Have the men move to their battle stations. The showdown is about to begin.'

Aboard the *Wisconsin*,
over the northern Arabian Sea
0501

Mack Smith accelerated as he approached the platform, taking the Flighthawk down through fifty feet. He was too low and close to be seen by this radar system, but human eyes and ears were another matter. He had the throttle at max as he rocketed by the platform at close to 500 knots, banking around to the north and making another pass.

'If there's a sub pen or docking area under that platform somewhere, I can't see it,' he told Dog. 'Cantor, where's that submarine? Let me do a flyover as he comes up.'

'He's just coming to the surface, about a mile north of the platform, in very shallow water.'

Mack slid the Flighthawk around, slowing down now to get better images. Nothing showed on the screen, though, as he passed.

'Two MiG-29s coming off Bhuj,' warned T-Bone, naming an airfield along the coast. 'And we have another flight coming in from the south – they're going to their afterburners.'

'Want me to go cool their jets, Colonel?' asked Mack.

'No. Take another pass where that submarine is coming up. I want pictures.'

'Just call me Candid Camera.'

'The MiGs out of Bhuj are looking for us,' said Jazz. 'Carrying AMRAAMskis. They're about a hundred miles away, speed accelerating over five hundred knots. Think the radar station picked up the Flighthawk?'

'I doubt it,' Dog told him. 'They probably just got tired of us orbiting so close to them.'

Dog checked his watch. Danny and Boston in the *Fisher* were still twenty minutes away.

'Let's do this,' he told Jazz. 'Try and raise the Indian controller on his frequency. Tell him that there's a submarine surfacing near his platform in Indian territory.'

'How do I explain that we know that?'

'Don't,' said Dog.

'Southern flight of MiGs has also gone to afterburners,' said T-Bone at the radar station. 'Now approximately seven minutes away.'

'Mack, do you have any visuals for me?'

'Negative, Colonel. Submarine hasn't broken the water yet.'

'All right. Come north with me. We're going to run up toward the end of our patrol track and turn around. On the way back south we'll launch *Hawk Two*.'

'You want me to take it?' interrupted Cantor.

'No. Stay with Piranha. Mack will have to handle both planes for a while.'

'No sweat,' said Mack.

'If the Indians don't back off, set up an intercept on the group coming out of the east, from Bhuj,' Dog told him.

'Got it, Colonel.'

'And Mack – don't fire at them unless I tell you to.'

'Your wish is my command, Colonel. But say the word, and they're going down.'

Aboard the *Levitow*, over the northern Arabian Sea 0503

Stewart opened her eyes and saw that Breanna had left the bay. She rolled out of the bunk and pulled on her boots, then went out into the Megafortress's galley area. The restroom – imagine *that* in a B-1B! – was occupied.

'I'd like to brush my teeth,' she joked.

'I'll be a while,' moaned the occupant.

It wasn't Breanna. Stewart looked toward the front and realized that she had taken over as pilot four hours ahead of schedule.

Just like her.

Stewart grabbed her helmet and walked up past the radar stations to the first officer's seat.

'Sorry I overslept. Mom forgot to set the alarm clock,' she told the copilot, Dick 'Bullet' Timmons. 'Thanks for covering, Bullet.'

'I'm still on, Stewie. Lou's stomach just went ballistic on him.'

'Bree and me are partners,' she told him. She glanced at Breanna. 'Don't want to break up the act.'

'Yeah, the teams ought to stay together,' Bree said.

Stewart felt her face flush. Finally, she thought, she'd been accepted.

'Your call, Captain,' said Bullet. 'Time I stretch my legs anyway.'

'Just don't try the bathroom for the next hour,' added Stewart.

The *Levitow's* long-range radar plot showed the two MiGs on afterburners, heading north to intercept *Wisconsin*.

Breanna clicked into the Dreamland communications

channel. '*Dreamland Levitow* to *Wisconsin*. I assume you see those MiGs coming at you from the south.'

'Roger that, *Levitow*,' said Dog. 'We're moving north. What's your estimated time to station?'

'Still a good fifteen minutes away from the designated patrol area.'

'Be advised, Piranha's contact has stopped about a mile from the radar platform. We think they may be planning a raid. We're trying to alert the Indian authorities. Piranha is about a mile and a half from the stopped sub and is approaching another contact, apparently a similar submarine.'

'Do you still want us to take over Piranha when we get closer?'

'Let's play that by ear. It may depend on what these MiGs do. I'm going to launch *Hawk Two* right now.'

'Roger that.'

'Turn *Hawk Three* over to the computer and then swap stations with me,' Zen told Dork.

'You sure, Major?'

'Yeah, I'll take *Three*. You launch *Hawk Four* from this station. Then if we're in range and have to take over Piranha, you can do it while I fly both U/MFs. You can't control Piranha from the left station.'

'I've only flown – I mean, sailed – Piranha in simulations.'

'It'll be easy,' said Zen.

Far easier than flying two Flighthawks in combat, he thought, though he didn't say that.

Dork put *Hawk Three* into one of its preset flight patterns, turned its controls over to the computer, then undid his restraints and got out of his seat. Zen levered himself close enough to the other station so he could swing into the unoccupied chair. He landed sideways, then dropped awkwardly into position.

Blood rushed from his head. Whether it was an aftermath of the treatments or sleep deprivation, he felt zapped.

'Here's your flight helmet,' said Dork.

'All right, thanks,' said Zen. 'Let's do the handoff, then get ready to launch. I'll talk to Bree.'

Aboard the *Fisher*,
over the Arabian Sea
0505

Lying in the manpod was like being in an isolation chamber. A very *cold* isolation chamber. There were supposedly heating circuits in the damn things, but Danny had never used one yet without freezing his extremities off.

Not that he had all that much experience with the manpod. In fact, he'd only used it in training missions, and only once on a water jump.

The manpod could be ejected from either high or low altitude. In this case, the plan was to go out very low, so the EB-52 wasn't detected. The pod would be more projectile than package, its descent barely retarded by a special drogue parachute.

'Danny?'

Colonel Bastian's voice reverberated in his helmet.

'What do you need, Colonel?'

'I just want you to know that we have fighters approaching the area where the submarine is. I've told Lieutenant Chu that he's to stay out of the area unless I instruct him otherwise.'

'Aw, Colonel, it's cold in here. You have to let me jump or I'll freeze to death.'

'We'll play it by ear, Danny. Sorry,' added Dog, the word echoing in Danny's helmet.

Lieutenant Chu checked his altitude on the heads-up display, keeping the Megafortress at precisely thirty-eight feet above the waves. The aircraft's powerful surveillance radars were off, allowing it to slip undetected like a ghost in the night.

His adrenaline had his heart on double-fast forward. It had been like this the whole deployment, almost a high.

Chu had been thinking of trading in his pilot's wings and going to law school before he got the Dreamland gig. He still hoped to be a lawyer someday, but this deployment had convinced him to push someday far into the future. Driving a Megafortress was the most fun you could have with your clothes on.

'Whiplash to *Dreamland Fisher* – yo, Tommy, what'd you tell the Colonel?' asked Captain Freah, who could communicate through a special channel in the Dreamland com system.

'Told him we were ready to kick butt and not to worry about the fighters.'

'Keep singing that song.'

'I will, Danny. Hang loose in there.'

'I am, but next flight, I want stewardesses and a better movie.'

Northern Arabian Sea
0508

The sea air pulled Captain Sattari out of the Parvaneh submarine, up to the deck behind the lead commando and the mate. He moved toward the rubber boat, AK-47 in one hand, grenade launcher in the other. His lungs filled with the sweet, wet breeze.

They were farther from the platform than he thought.

There were planes nearby, jets flying somewhere in the dark sky. He twisted his head back and forth but couldn't see anything.

'Bring the SA-7s!' he yelled, telling the others to take the antiaircraft missiles. 'Quickly! Into the boat. We have to paddle at least three hundred meters to reach the rocks! Hurry, before we are seen!'

Aboard the *Wisconsin*,
over the northern Arabian Sea
0508

'Midget sub is on the surface,' Dish told Dog. 'Very small. Similar to the vessel that sank itself.'

'Jazz, have the Indians responded to our warning?'

'Negative,' said the copilot.

Dog toggled into the Dreamland Command line. *Wisconsin* to *Abner Read*. Eyes, I need to talk to Storm.'

'I'm here, Bastian. Go ahead.'

'The submarine we were tracking has surfaced about a mile north of the platform. Looks like an attack. I've tried contacting the Indians but gotten no response. I have two MiGs coming at me from the east. They may think we're attacking the radar.'

'We'll try notifying the Indians,' said Storm. 'Don't put yourself in danger for them.'

Jeez, thought Dog, he sounds almost concerned.

'Colonel, the lead MiG's radar is trying to get a lock on us,' warned Jazz. 'Threat analyzer says he has a pair of AA-12 Adder AMRAAMskis.'

'Storm, the Indian fighters are using their weapons radars to lock on us,' Dog said. 'I'm not in their territory. I can't tell if it's a bluff or not, but if I have to defend myself, I will.'

'Understood.'

Dog killed the circuit.

'Jazz, try telling the Indian fighters their radar station is being attacked by commandos. Maybe they can talk to the station.'

'I'll give it a try, Colonel.'

'*Wisconsin* to *Hawk One* – be advised the MiGs are trying to lock their radar weapons on us,' Dog told Mack.

'On it, Colonel.'

Aboard the *Abner Read*,
in the northern Arabian Sea
0510

Storm glanced at the holographic display. *Sharkboat One* was still a good twenty miles to the east of the Indian radar station's atoll; it would take the small patrol boat another forty-five minutes to reach the platform, assuming he authorized it to enter Indian waters.

'Eyes, what's the status on Werewolf?' he asked.

'Should be just finishing refuel.'

'Good – get it up and over to the radar station. The submarines have surfaced. And Airforce – where the hell is he?'

'Sleeping, Captain.'

'Get him out of bed. I want him at the wheel of that helicopter.'

'But –'

'Pour a pot of coffee down his throat and get him up. I want him flying that bird. Got me?'

'Yes, sir.'

Belatedly, Storm realized that Eyes was concerned not about getting Starship up but about breaking the news to Petty Officer Varitok, the man who was flying Werewolf now.

'I'll explain it to Varitok,' he added. 'It's nothing personal. Have him come up to the bridge as soon as Airforce has taken over.'

'Aye aye, Captain.'

Dwārka Early Warning Radar Platform One, off the coast of India
0510

Captain Sattari's oar struck the rocks about midstroke. The jolt threw him forward so abruptly he nearly fell out of the raft. He pulled himself back, aware that his mistake had thrown off everyone else in the boat.

'I'm sorry,' he whispered, pushing the oar more gingerly this time. It hit the rocks about a third of the way down this time, and he was able to push forward, half paddling, half poling.

Two more strokes and the bottom of the raft ran up on something sharp – a wire fence just under the water-line. Before Sattari could react, the water lapped over his legs. He could feel the rocks under his knees.

'Wire,' said the man at the bow in a hushed whisper. 'I need the cutters.'

'Push the boat forward and use it to get over the wire onto the rocks,' said Sattari. 'We can just go from here.'

The man at the bow stood upright in the raft. Holding his AK-47 above his head, he stepped over onto the nearby rocks, then reached back to help Sattari. The captain fished the grenade launcher that had been next to him from the water and then got up, stumbling but managing to keep his balance.

The others splashed toward him, carrying their water-proof rucks with explosives. The legs of the platform loomed in the darkness just ahead. At any moment Sattari expected to hear gunfire and shouts; it seemed a miracle that the Indians had not detected them so far.

'The ladder is here,' said someone, not bothering to whisper.

Sattari moved toward the voice, slipping on the rocks but keeping his balance. He reached a set of metal bars that had been planted in the rocks to hold part of the grid-work of a ladder. The captain grabbed the rail with his right hand and pulled himself up. He still clutched the grenade launcher with his left hand.

Eight feet above the rocks, the ladder reached a plat-form. A set of metal stairs sat at one end; the other opened to a catwalk that extended around the legs.

'Place a signal for the other boats,' Sattari told the men who clambered up behind him. He did not single the men out as he spoke, trusting that they would divvy up the duties on their own. 'Place your charges on the leg posts, then follow me.'

As he pushed toward the metal stairway, he heard a shout from above, then a round of gunfire.

Finally, he thought. It hadn't seemed real until he heard the gunfire.

Aboard the *Wisconsin*,
over the northern Arabian Sea
0515

Mack Smith throttled *Hawk One* back toward the Mega-fortress, banking in the direction of the MiGs. If they were looking to play chicken, he was ready for them; he'd have them breaking for cover in a few minutes.

Ten miles from the Megafortress he began another turn, aiming to put himself between the two bogies and the mother ship at roughly the distance they could fire their radar-guided missiles. As he got into position, Jazz gave an update.

'*MiG One* is breaking off,' reported the copilot. 'Heading east. *MiG Two* – Whoa! Watch out! *MiG Two* is firing.'

'He's mine,' said Mack, checking the sitrep. The Indian plane was three miles behind his left wing, closing fast. Mack brought up his weapons screen, readying his cannon.

Besides the midget submarine they'd found on the surface, there were two others, still submerged, but rising. They were about three miles northeast of the radar platform, within fifty yards of each other. Cantor put the Piranha into the underwater robot's version of a hover, its motor pushing just hard enough to keep the current at bay and stay in position.

He got a connection warning that the Megafortress was going outside the range of the control buoy.

'Piranha to *Wisconsin* – Colonel, we have a total of three submarines, one on the surface and two more coming up. Should be on the surface in less than a minute. But we're coming up to the edge of communications range with the buoy.'

'Roger that, Piranha, but I have other priorities – we

have a missile on our tail and two apparently hostile aircraft pursuing us. Can you hand off to *Wisconsin*?'

'Negative. They're not close enough.'

'Park it,' Dog told him. 'Prepare to launch *Hawk Two* as soon as you can.'

Until now, all of the aircraft Mack had encountered while flying the Flighthawks had acted as if he wasn't there. The small planes were invisible to their radar except at very close range, and in the dark they were almost impossible to see. Mack planned his move against the Indian MiG as if that were the case now, expecting the aircraft to clear right after firing a second missile, at which point he could tuck into a tighter turn and get *Hawk Two* on its back. Alternatively, he might continue behind the Megafortress, positioning himself to fire heat-seekers if the radar-guided missiles failed to hit.

But the MiG didn't fire another missile, nor did it turn off or even speed past him. Instead Mack found himself roughly a half mile in front of the MiG, well within range of its 30mm cannon. Seconds later tracers flew past *Hawk Two*'s nose.

Mack pickled flares as decoys and swung the Flighthawk into a shallow dive to his right. When he realized the MiG hadn't followed, he tried to pull back up and come up behind it. As he started to accelerate, the Indian pilot fired another AMRAAMski at the *Wisconsin,* then pulled hard to the right. Mack finally had his shot, but it was fleeting and at a terrible angle; he spit a few shells at the MiG's fat tailfin, but lost the target in a turn. He tucked a little too hard to the right trying to stay with him and within seconds lost the plane completely and had to swing back in the direction of the Megafortress to keep from losing his connection.

Not exactly auspicious. But as he glanced at the sitrep, he saw that *MiG One* was flying almost directly at him.

If you've been handed a lemon, make lemonade, he thought, setting up for an intercept.

Aboard the *Shiva*
0516

Memon's legs trembled as he stepped onto the deck of the *Shiva*'s backup bridge, a space at the seaward side of the carrier's island that had not been damaged by the earlier attack. Even though it bore only a passing resemblance to the main bridge, Memon felt as if it were inhabited by ghosts. The fear that had hovered around him earlier pressed close to his ribs.

'A message, Admiral!' one of the men on watch shouted to Admiral Skandar. 'From the radar platform!'

A commando team had been spotted trying to make an attack. A small American patrol craft was sailing in the general vicinity, and a flight of Indian landborne fighters were engaging the Megafortress nearby. It was assumed that the Americans had launched the attack.

'You see, I was quite correct about where the true danger lay,' Skandar told Memon. 'They are honoring their commitments to Pakistan. This is the prelude to an attack by their aircraft on our bases.'

He picked up the phone connecting him to the ship's combat center. 'Launch the attack. Do not neglect the American ship.'

Aboard the *Wisconsin*, over the northern Arabian Sea 0517

The Indian's first missile had been fired from extremely long range, so far in fact that Dog knew from experience that he could simply outrun it. But the second missile was a different matter. He jerked the Megafortress's stick sharply, turning the bomber to the east. The radar tracking the Megafortress lost its slippery profile, and the missile flew on blind for several miles, vainly hoping that the ghost it was chasing would materialize in front of it when it used its own radar for terminal guidance.

The sharp maneuver took Dog into Indian territory, where a host of ground radars that had been tracking them at long range suddenly sharpened their eyes and ears.

'That SA-10 battery inland is trying to get a lock,' said Jazz.

'Tell these idiots we were in international airspace and are not hostile.'

'I've broadcasted that six ways to Sunday. I'll try again.'

'Cantor, you ready to launch?'

'Booting the command sequences now, Colonel. Screens are just finishing their diagnostics.'

'Emergency launch of *Hawk Two* in sixty seconds.'

'*MiG One* is turning toward us from the east, roughly forty miles away,' warned Jazz.

'I've been expecting him,' said Dog. 'Get ready to launch.'

Cantor took control of *Hawk Two* and immediately pushed east, figuring he could cut off the Indian fighter *MiG One*. But a glance at the sitrep showed that Mack and *Hawk Two* had gone in that direction, leaving the other plane free – and much closer to the *Wisconsin*.

'I have *Hawk Two*,' Cantor told Mack. 'I'll get *MiG One*. You concentrate on *MiG Two*. He's off your left wing, two miles.'

'No, I have *MiG One,*' said Mack.

There was no point in arguing. Cantor immediately changed course, dipping his wing and plotting an intercept.

Dog swung the *Wisconsin* out to sea, still pursued by the AMRAAMski. The missile had a finite load of fuel; by rights it should have crashed into the sea by now.

Or maybe time just seemed to be moving at light speed. Dog pitched his big aircraft on its wing in another sharp cut, trying to take advantage of one set of physical principles – those governing radio or radar waves – while defying another – those governing motion, mass, and momentum. In this case radio won out – the missile shot wide right and immolated itself.

'*MiG Two* is swinging south,' said Jazz. 'Looks like he and his partner are going to try and sandwich us.'

'They can try if they want,' said Dog.

'At what point do we go to the Scorpions, Colonel?'

'I'd rather hold on to them as long as we can,' he told the copilot. 'We may need them.'

And pretty soon too. This looked suspiciously like the start of all-out war.

Dog turned back to the communications screen, activating the link with Jed Barclay in the NSC's Situation Room.

'Jed, we've been fired on here by Indian MiGs,' he told the NSC deputy as soon as his face appeared in the screen. 'We've detected three submarines that we believe are trying to launch a commando attack on an Indian early warning radar platform near the border with Pakistan.'

'Are they Pakistani submarines? Or Chinese?'

'We haven't identified them, but they match the sound profile Piranha recorded for the submarine that scuttled itself, which we believe was involved in the attack on Karachi.'

'Understood, Colonel. We're starting to get some alerts here now.'

Jazz broke in to tell Dog that there were four F-16 Pakistanis coming from the east.

'Jed, things are getting a little crowded at the moment. I'll check back with you in a few minutes.'

'I'll be here, Colonel.'

'*MiG One* is launching missiles,' warned Jazz. 'AMRAAMskis! Long range – sixteen, seventeen miles. Guess these guys believe the advertising.'

'ECMs. Stand by for evasive maneuvers. Mack, I thought you said you had this guy.'

* * *

Mack had just made a turn and started to close on the MiG's tail when he saw the flare under its wings. Two large missiles ignited, steaming off in the direction of the *Wisconsin*. Mack's weapons screen indicated that he was not in range to fire; all he could do was wait for the tail of the Indian warplane to grow larger at the center of his screen. The targeting bar went yellow, then flickered red before turning back to yellow; the MiG pilot had punched his afterburner for more speed.

Mack cursed as the aircraft steadily pulled away.

'*Hawk One*, I'm turning back south,' said Dog.

'Yeah, OK,' said Mack. He started to follow, then realized that if he kept his present heading he could catch the MiG when it made its own turn to follow the Megafortress. Sure enough, a few seconds later the Indian aircraft appeared at the top corner of his screen. He closed in, then just as the targeting bar turned red – indicating he had a shot – the computer warned that he was going to lose his connection. Mack fired anyway, putting two long bursts into the underside of the MiG's fuselage. There was no doubt that he got a hit this time – flames poured out of the aircraft. Mack jerked his stick back just in time to keep the link with the *Wisconsin*.

'Splash one MiG. Finally,' he said. 'And about time, if I do say so myself.'

'One of those missiles is still coming for us, Colonel.'

Dog pulled the Megafortress into a tight turn, trying to beam the guidance radar by flying parallel to the radar waves. The tactic didn't work this time; the missile continued to close. They threw chaff and sent a wave of electronic countermeasures into the air to scramble the missile's brains. Dog, sensing he was still being pursued, rolled the big plane onto its wing, dropping and twisting behind the fog created by the countermeasures. This finally did the trick; the missile sailed overhead, exploding a mile away.

'Action near the Chinese carrier,' said T-Bone. 'Air groups from the *Shiva* – they're coming north at a high rate of speed. Missiles being fired! Jesus – they're throwing everything at them!'

Dog went on the Dreamland Command line to warn Storm.

Aboard the *Abner Read*, in the northern Arabian Sea 0523

'Multiple missile launches from the *Shiva* and other Indian ships,' Eyes told Storm. 'Dreamland aircraft *Wisconsin* reports Indian aircraft moving toward the *Deng Xiaoping* in apparent attack formation.'

'Where are our shadows?'

'Still circling overhead.'

'If they turn their weapons radars on, shoot them down.'

'We're ready, Captain.'

Storm took his night vision binoculars and stepped out onto the flying bridge, scanning the air above, and then the horizon in the direction of the Chinese carrier sixty miles away.

Too far to see the results of the Indian attack. A pity, he thought. A real pity.

Starship rubbed his eyes furiously as he waited for Petty Officer Varitok to put the Werewolf into a hover so he could take over. The Tac Center, never a picture of calm, looked like a commodities exchange on steroids behind them. The Indians were launching dozens of missiles, and the Chinese were starting to respond.

'All yours, Airforce,' said Varitok, leaping out of the seat. 'You're right over the Sharkboat.'

Starship pulled on his headset and dropped into the chair. There was a flash of red on the main screen. 'Is that coming from the radar platform?'

Varitok looked at the screen. 'Can't tell. It's ten miles east, two miles from shore.'

Starship pushed the Werewolf forward, accelerating from zero to 200 knots in a matter of seconds. He saw a second flash, and realized the explosions were too high to be from the radar platform.

There were fighters nearby – a pair of Su-35s far overhead, and a MiG-29 at about ten thousand feet, fortunately heading north. A missile launched from a boat to the south, crossing within a half mile.

'Tac, it's getting ugly out here,' Starship told Eyes. 'You want Werewolf to continue this mission, or come back to the *Abner Read*?'

'Continue your mission until told not to.'

'You got it.'

* * *

Storm listened as Radar updated him on the Su-35s. They'd begun to descend rapidly in the direction of the ship, but still had not activated the radars normally associated with air-to-ship missiles.

What were they doing? Sightseeing?

The hell they were.

'Eyes – take down those planes!' shouted Storm. 'They're going to either switch their targeting radars on at the last minute or hit us with iron bombs.'

'Aye aye, Captain, firing missiles.'

Two Standard SM-2 AERs spit out of the vertical launch tubes. Storm tracked their flares as they arced upward. Thirty seconds later the sky flashed white. A loud boom rent the air. Another flash. *Boom! Bar-oom!*

'Both planes hit,' Eyes reported.

'Good work.'

As Storm turned to go inside, the Phalanx close-in air defense gun on the starboard side of the ship began firing. Storm gripped the rail, and in the next moment the ocean erupted beneath him.

Dwārka Early Warning Radar Platform One
0523

Captain Sattari felt his heart pound as he ran up the stairs, a few steps behind the team's point man. Bullets flew down from above, but they were unaimed, falling into the nearby water. Sattari's chest heaved as he reached the landing. The other soldier had stopped to wait for him and the others.

'One more set of steps and we are at the main level,' said the point man, repeating the brief Sattari himself had delivered before the mission. 'There will be four men there, no more.'

Sattari grunted, too winded to reply. He pulled up the grenade launcher while he caught his breath, making sure it was ready to fire.

Had the water ruined it? The only way to find out would be to use it.

Two more men reached the landing.

'Let us take them now,' said Sattari, his wind back. He pushed to the nearby steps. By the time he got halfway up the flight, the others had run ahead of him, his age finally starting to tell.

Gunshots peppered the air as they reached the turn. Two of the men threw themselves down, answering with their own gunfire. The third – the point man who had just been leading Sattari upward – tumbled down, shot several times.

Sattari slid close to the railing and went up, stopping below the crouching men. Once again he checked the grenade launcher.

'All right,' he said, crawling next to them. 'Wait until I fire.'

If only he could have one of the black robes who'd questioned his courage with him now – he would use him as a shield.

When the rattle of the automatic guns above started to die, Sattari leapt to his feet, raised the launcher and fired.

Aboard the *Levitow*,
over the northern Arabian Sea
0525

Breanna checked their position again. They were not quite ten minutes from their patrol area. The Indian aircraft carrier *Shiva* was forty miles to the northeast.

'All hell's breaking loose up there,' said Stewart. 'Multiple missile firings from the *Shiva* and their task group.'

'Plot a course to the EEMWB launch point,' said Breanna. 'I'm going to turn east. There's no sense going through the middle of this.'

'But we haven't gotten the order yet.'

'I want to be in a position to respond if we do. Long-range radars off,' added Breanna, adopting the mission plan. 'Prepare to penetrate hostile territory.'

'Roger that.'

'*Dreamland Levitow* to *Hawk Three* and *Four* – we're changing course and descending. Stay with me.'

Aboard the *Abner Read*,
in the northern Arabian Sea
0525

Storm flew against the side of the littoral destroyer's superstructure, slamming back and recoiling onto the deck. He slid on the gridwork, grappling for a handhold to keep from falling into the sea.

The *Abner Read* lurched away from the explosion

– and then back toward it. Storm's legs shot over the edge of the flying bridge as his fingers dug into the grating. He got enough of a hold to get to his knees before he lost his grip and slid as the ship bobbed violently, rolling him toward the portal that led back inside to the bridge. He caught the side of the opening with his wrist, slid his hand there for a grip and, finally, with the boat still rocking violently, managed to push his right knee up under him and throw himself inside the ship.

He only got two-thirds of the way in, but it was far enough to grab hold of one of the legs of the instrument console. He clutched it as tightly as he could, squeezing with all of his might. Then he pulled himself upward, smacking his head on the shelf as he did.

'Captain!' yelled one of the men on the bridge. He too was on his knees.

Dazed, Storm struggled to his feet.

'Damage Control, report,' he said. 'Damage –'

Storm put his hand to his face; his headset was gone.

One of his men grabbed him, steadying him on his feet. It was Petty Officer Varitok, the Werewolf pilot he'd ordered replaced.

'You all right, Captain?'

'Yes, I'm fine. Get me the backup headset. In my cabin – go.'

Storm went to the holographic display, activating the damage control view. One of the compartments on the starboard side had been breached.

It was too soon to tell how bad the damage was, but

already the automatic damage control system had cordoned off the area. Even if the compartment was a total loss, the ship would not sink.

His heart pounding in his chest, Storm turned his attention to the helmsman, who was still at his post. 'Keep us steady, Helm,' he said. Then he clapped the man on the back. 'Damn good job, son. Damn good job.'

'Are you all right, sir?'

'I'm sure I look worse than I feel,' said Storm. He wiped his face again, and discovered that what he'd assumed was seawater was actually blood.

'Captain!' yelled Varitok, returning with the headset. 'Your face. You're bleeding.'

'It never looked that good to begin with,' said Storm, pulling on the headset. 'Eyes – if any other aircraft get within ten miles of us, shoot them down.'

Dwārka Early Warning Radar Platform One
0525

The Grenade seemed to fly in slow motion from Captain Sattari's launcher, spinning in the direction of a low wall of sandbags. Sattari saw everything that was happening, not merely on the platform, but in the ocean and the world around him: the ships and airplanes charging into war, the missiles that the Indians would fire against the Pakistanis, the Chinese weapons that would retaliate. He saw himself standing at the center of it all.

He turned his attention to the area in front of him. Two men with rifles leaned over the sandbags above. Bullets spewed from their weapons – he could see each one as it flew from the barrel, a dark cylinder coming for him. The Russian-made RPG-7 grenade he'd fired flew toward them, nudging against the top of the uppermost sandbag protecting the enemy's position. Deflected slightly, it continued over the bag toward an upright grating behind the position.

The bullets stopped coming toward him. The grenade halted in midair. It was the greatest moment of his life, an instant that filled him with a sensation that went beyond pleasure: an infinite grandeur, a knowledge that he had fulfilled the wish God had for him when he was created.

Then light cracked open the sky, and the world returned to its chaotic tumble. The grenade exploded directly behind the Indian soldiers guarding the station, and the platform jolted with the explosion. Sattari found himself facedown on the metal steps, his breath taken away by the shock. By the time he managed to fill his lungs, the others had run up to the landing and finished the wounded Indians off. Dazed, Sattari followed without completely comprehending what was going on. His men ran past him to set their charges.

'Helicopter!' yelled someone.

The word cleared Sattari's head.

'Quickly! Set the explosives and back to the Parvanehs,' he shouted. 'Go!'

The *Abner Read* rocked so violently that Starship was yanked half off his seat. He grabbed the handhold at the side of the station, gripping it as the vessel shuddered from the effects of an explosion somewhere nearby. If he'd been a little sleepy before, he was wide awake now.

Bracing himself against the seat with his legs, Starship let go of the handhold and put his hands back on the Werewolf controls. The aircraft was programmed to drop its speed and glide into a hover when pressure was suddenly removed from the controls; Starship reasserted control gingerly, picking up speed and increasing his altitude as he hunted for the radar rig.

He saw it three miles away, five degrees south. The platform looked like a squat oil drilling rig with thin derricks jutting from the top. He spotted pinpricks of light as he approached – tracers. A white flash swallowed the gunfire, then blackness returned.

'Action on the radar platform,' he told Eyes. 'I have three vessels on the surface, at the north end.'

People were yelling behind him. If Eyes answered, Starship couldn't hear. He dipped the Werewolf in the direction of the vessels. From two miles off they looked like speedboats or pleasure cruisers very low in the water.

'I think I have the midget submarines,' he told Eyes. 'Werewolf to Tac – I have the submarines in view, north of the tower, on the surface.'

He steadied the aircraft and switched his main view from infrared to light-enhanced mode, which gave a sharper digital photo. He was still too far to get a good shot, and began moving forward slowly, filling the frame with one of the vessels at maximum zoom. He took the photo, creating and storing an image in standard, low resolution .jpg format; then he moved in to get a close-up of what looked to be the sub's conning tower.

When he backed the zoom off, Starship saw small boats in the water. Before he could figure out if they were leaving or returning, the screen went white at the right side. Starship jammed the Werewolf controls to race away from the explosion, though he knew he was already too late.

NSC Situation Room
1934, 14 January 1998
(0534, 15 January, Karachi)

Things ratcheted up so quickly it seemed to Jed that a hidden fast forward switch had been thrown. One moment the screens with information from the U.S. intelligence agencies were mostly blank or filled with log entries indicating 'nothing new.' Then bulletins and updates began scrolling onto the screens in rapid succession.

Jed grabbed the direct line to the NSC Advisor before it finished its first ring; he had paged Freeman via his Blackberry a few minutes before.

'It looks like the Indians are launching an all-out attack

on the Chinese and Pakistani ships in the northern Arabian Sea,' Jed told his boss. 'One of their radar platforms has been attacked. Pakistani aircraft are being vectored to meet Indian flights near the border. One of our Megafortresses has been shot at.'

'Are they OK?'

'Yes. I think the attack on the platform may have started things off, but it's hard to sort it out,' Jed added.

'That's immaterial right now, Jed. What's the status of the Indian nuclear units?'

'They're one step below launch.'

'Is the Dreamland mission still viable?'

'Yes, sir.'

'I'm on my way back. I'll alert the President. He may arrive before I do. Hang in there, Jed.'

Barclay put down the phone.

'Indian missile site at Bhatinda has just gone to launch warning,' said Jordan, reading from the NSA screen.

'Warning? Do we have that area on satellite?'

'There,' said the image interpreter, pointing to the display. 'They're getting ready to launch.'

Jed reached for the button to key into the Dreamland communications network.

'Launch in Pakistan!' yelled Jordan. 'My God, they're really going to try and end the world!'

IX

End Game

Clear of the Indian fighters and their missiles, Dog began climbing over the water, trying to sort out exactly what was going on. More than a dozen missiles had been launched at the Chinese aircraft carrier, which was beginning to respond with anticruise missiles.

The Dreamland circuit buzzed.

'Colonel, we have a missile launch,' said Jed Barclay, his words running together. 'Go to End Game. I will stay on the line and update you.'

'Bastian acknowledges, End Game is authorized,' said the colonel calmly. 'I need the status of Chinese aircraft carrier *Deng Xiaoping*.'

'Tai-shan order has not been given. Repeat, Tai-shan has not been given.'

That meant that the electronic 'ferret' satellite had not yet picked up the order authorizing the launch of the nuclear-equipped aircraft. But that wasn't enough.

'Jed, I need to know specifically that those aircraft are not on the hangar deck,' said Dog.

'I am looking at the U-2 image now. Neither plane is on deck.'

'Then I'm proceeding with End Game,' said Dog.

'Acknowledged,' said Jed.

Dog hit the preset under the screen; Tommy Chu, the pilot of *Dreamland Fisher*, appeared on the screen.

'Tommy, End Game has been authorized. *Wisconsin* and *Levitow* will proceed overland. I want you to take up station and be prepared to deal with the *Deng Xiaoping*'s planes if the Chinese order Tai-shan to proceed.'

'*Fisher* acknowledges. Colonel, I'm roughly ten minutes from the radar platform on my present course. Should I go ahead with the drop or not?'

'I don't want you taking unnecessary risks. Tai-shan is higher priority.'

'Understood, Colonel. But my best course at this point to avoid both aircraft carrier groups will take me right past the platform. And frankly, I think I'd do better without the manpods on my wings.'

'Have Danny check with Captain Gale on the *Abner Read* and find out the status of the Sharkboat he sent. Danny's not to proceed without coordination from the Sharkboat, and approval from Gale. Understood?'

'Yes, sir.'

'If it looks too risky, call it off. Drop the pods near the *Abner Read*. If Danny gives you grief, refer him to me.'

'You got it, Colonel.'

'Bastian out.' Dog hit the preset to connect with *Levitow*. Breanna's face appeared on the screen.

'End Game has been authorized,' he told her. 'What's your position?'

'We're approaching the Indian coast, thirty miles north of Mumbai. We'll go from here.'

Dog realized she was much farther south than they'd planned. Distancewise, that wouldn't be much of a problem. But it would take them much closer to the Indians' most fearsome antiaircraft defenses.

'We've turned off our radar,' she added. 'We'll make it, Daddy.'

For once he didn't mind that she called him that.

'I know you will. Check back in five.'

'Roger that.'

MiG *Two*'s nose had just come into Cantor's view screen when Colonel Bastian announced that they were going back over India. He stayed on course, closing to a mile before he got the signal from the computer that he had a shot. He pressed the trigger, releasing a hail of bullets for the MiG to fly into. Rather than turning to finish off his prey as he'd planned, he pulled back east, racing parallel to the *Wisconsin*.

'Didja get him, kid?' asked Mack.

'No.'

'You got him away from us. That's the main thing.'

'Thanks,' said Cantor, surprised that Mack was trying to sound encouraging.

The Megafortress's flight plan would take them toward the Thar desert, a vast wasteland between Pakistan and

India. They would be crossing Pakistani territory as well, which meant that they would be exposed to two American I-Hawk antiaircraft batteries as well as a number of Russian-made ones on the Indian side.

A more immediate threat, especially as far as Cantor was concerned, were the fighters both sides were hurling into the air. The second flight of Indian MiGs that had scrambled earlier were coming north, and the four Pakistani F-16s they'd detected were approaching the border directly in their path.

'I'll worry about the Indians,' Cantor told Mack. 'You've got the F-16s.'

'Yeah, I was about to say the same thing, kid.'

'You remember the Fort Cherry exercise? Same thing. You can let the computer program the attack route, because it'll look that encounter up. It's based on Pakistani tactics in a four-ship group that Zen taught during –'

'I don't need Professor Zen's pointers, kid,' said Mack.

Typical Mack, thought Cantor. Just when you thought he'd stopped being a jerk, he rubbed your nose in it.

Aboard the *Abner Read*,
in the northern Arabian Sea
0538

The explosion buffeted the Werewolf, but was too far away to do any damage. By the time Starship recovered and circled back to see what had happened, two of the legs holding the radar platform had collapsed. The structure tilted forward, as if about to dive head first into the water. One of the large antenna towers had fallen; the other two were twisted sideways.

The submarines sat on the surface between a mile and two miles from the platform. Starship dropped his speed and began a slow arc around them to the northeast. There were several aircraft nearby, Pakistani and Chinese, but as yet no one seemed to have reacted to either him or the boats.

'Eyes – they've hit the tower. The radar platform has been destroyed. You want me to stop these guys? They're boarding the submarines. I see two more small boats. One of the subs is moving.'

Starship could choose between six Hellfire missiles, two 30mm chain guns, and a pair of 7.62 machine guns to use against the submarines. He opted for the Hellfires, whose shaped warheads would slice easily through their hulls. But he still needed permission to fire.

'Werewolf to Tac Commander, am I authorized to fire on these submarines? Am I supposed to stop them from getting away or what?'

'Go ahead,' said Eyes finally.

Starship reached his right hand to the rollerball controlling the cursor for the laser designator, zeroed in on the nearest sub, and clicked to lock the target. Then he fired two missiles. The missiles rode a laser beam from the Werewolf down to the sub, zeroing in on the cue like a Walker foxhound chasing its prey in an overgrown field. The first Hellfire hit with a wallop of steam; the second Hellfire rolled into the fog.

'Starship, what the hell are you doing?' yelled Eyes.

'Taking out the submarines.'

'Belay that – *stop!* I haven't given you the order. Hold your fire.'

'You just said go ahead.'

'I wasn't telling you to attack. I thought you wanted to talk to me. We need authorization from the captain.'

'I don't have it?'

'Negative, negative. Hold your fire.'

'Roger that. Holding fire.'

Starship circled the Werewolf farther from the submarines. The first craft had disappeared. The other two were moving to the north.

He knew he'd asked, and he knew what he'd heard. The stinking Navy could never make up its mind.

No, it was just Eyes.

'What's your situation, Airforce?' asked Storm, coming on the line.

'Captain, the radar platform has been destroyed by a commando attack. There are three submarines to the north. I fired on one thinking I had been ordered to do so.'

'What are the others doing?'

'Moving to the north.'

'Our intention is to seize the submarines. See if you can keep them on the surface.'

'I'll try, sir. But it's possible my gunfire will sink them.'

'Do your best, Airforce.'

'Aye aye, Captain.'

Storm's uniform was soaked from the blast and he'd cut his face and hands. Two other men had been hurt; one had a severe head wound and was in serious condition in sickbay.

The blast started a very small leak above the belt line of the ship. The damage had already been repaired, and only a small amount of water had gotten in.

Storm wanted to launch an immediate counterattack on the Indian carrier – he wanted to show the bastards what happened when you attacked a U.S. Navy ship. But they were out of range for the Harpoons.

That could be fixed.

'Eyes, we're going south,' he said over the intraship com system. 'Where is that Indian aircraft carrier?'

'Storm, we have to stay in range of the Chinese carrier's aircraft, to back up the Dreamland people.'

'I know what my damn orders are, Commander.' Storm's head began to pound. His anger was flaring. This is what happens when you're a nice guy, he thought. Your subordinates take you for granted.

He would get his way, no matter what. But he had to be careful about it, had to be clever – yes, the way Bastian was clever, always covering his butt and making it seem as if he was in the right.

He'd already been fired on, and feared for the safety of his people.

His head pounded.

And he had a mission – he was supposed to get that submarine.

'We have an operation under way,' Storm told Eyes, gritting his teeth against the pain. 'I want to protect my Sharkboat.'

413

'Should I order them to come back?'

'No – I want that submarine. They're to get it.'

'Captain, I'd advise calling the mission off.'

'Thank you for your advice, Eyes.' Storm turned to the helmsman. 'Take us east. Stay close enough to launch on the *Deng*'s aircraft if we have to.'

'Heading, Captain?'

'South.' Storm looked down at the holographic display. The Megafortress had gone inland; there was no more long-range view of the ships and aircraft in the area. He thumbed the display back, found the *Shiva*'s last known position and gave the heading to Helm.

His headset buzzed.

'Dreamland Whiplash team trying to contact you, Colonel,' said the communications officer. 'Looking for a go/no go on the platform.'

'It's go.' Storm punched into the line. 'Is this Freah?'

'Freah.'

'This is Captain Gale aboard the *Abner Read*. What's your status?'

'We're roughly ten minutes from the radar platform,' said Danny. 'I need your approval to proceed.'

Storm checked his impulse, but just barely. He knew he had to think, to consider, not react – but it was damn hard with his head pounding.

'You're aboard a Megafortress or the Osprey?' he asked.

'Megafortress. The Osprey is three hours behind,' said Danny. 'Do you want us to proceed?'

'Damn straight I do.'

'Good. We're on a low-altitude approach, flying

without our long-range radar,' continued the Air Force Whiplash leader. 'We don't believe we've been detected. What's the status of your Sharkboat?'

'I'm going to order them in,' said Storm.

Had he already done that? He couldn't remember.

Think. Make your decisions in a calm, reasonable manner.

Ten minutes might be too long. The submarines would be under the surface by then, and the Sharkboat lacked the sensors needed to pick it up.

'If the submarines dive, the Sharkboat won't be able to find them,' Storm said. 'We need Piranha to locate them. *Wisconsin* was operating them but had to leave the area.'

'Ensign English will take control of the probe,' said Danny. 'She'll find it.'

He couldn't control every variable. If Freah was willing to take the chance, so was he.

He was *more* than willing. He wanted that sub.

And he wanted the Indian carrier as well. Which he was going to get.

'Very good, Captain,' said Storm. 'Proceed. I'll let the Sharkboat know you're on your way. Eyes will liaison in Tac.'

Aboard the *Shiva*,
in the northern Arabian Sea
0538

Memon stared at the shadowy sea, his eyes losing their focus. Reports from the first wave of attacks on the

Chinese carrier were just coming in. Remembering how overly optimistic the news had been during the last attack, Memon resolved not to believe them. He made his face into a stone mask, impassive.

'First missile has missed. Second missile – we've lost contact.'

'Aircraft are attacking the Chinese helicopter – one shot down.'

One of the Chinese escort ships fired back. Two flights of Chinese aircraft had made it past the Indian screening aircraft and were attacking. A flight of Pakistani F-16s was being engaged to the north by shore-based planes.

Admiral Skandar listened impassively to the chatter from the radio and the ship's intercom systems. 'Battle is a struggle against chaos,' he told Memon.

'Enemy missiles launched! On their way!'

Something squeezed Memon's stomach, and he felt tears stream from his eyes.

Aboard the *Wisconsin*, above the northern Arabian Sea 0540

At first the Pakistani F-16s showed no interest in the *Wisconsin*. Mack stayed close to the Megafortress; he was starting to get low on fuel and was more than willing to let the planes go if they didn't want to tango. But as the F-16s got to within twenty miles, a pair veered in the direction of the EB-52, starting what Mack interpreted as a maneuver to get behind the Megafortress. He swung out to meet them.

The PAF aircraft stayed together, closing quickly. The two groups of planes were rushing toward each other so fast that within thirty seconds they were separated by less than ten miles. Mack, descending from thirty thousand feet, had barely enough time to get his gun ready before the closest aircraft raced into his targeting pipper. He slammed his finger onto the trigger, ripping through the left wing root and into the fuel tanks and engine of the aircraft. He pumped his cannon twice more, catching a bit of the wing as the aircraft rolled downward. Then he tucked left, trying to line up to take the stricken Viper's wingman. But the other F-16 had veered back northward, and by the time Mack found him, he was too far off to engage.

He banked *Hawk One* to the east, pushing back closer to *Wisconsin*. He glanced at the sitrep to find out what had happened to the other F-16s. He found out a lot sooner than he would have hoped – a launch warning sounded; he'd turned almost directly in the path of the second element of PAF fighters.

The Indian MiGs were twenty miles behind the Mega-fortress, and roughly ten behind Cantor. But rather than closing, the Indians were losing ground. Cantor waited for a minute or so; when the MiGs still didn't make a move to catch up, he decided to ignore them for the time being. He hiked his speed up, then checked the sitrep to see how Mack was doing.

In the exercise Cantor had mentioned, the four-ship formation broke into two pairs. One group flew parallel but in the opposite direction to the course of its target, while the other continued at a right angle to it. The elements would then launch separate attacks from either the sides or, more often, the rear quarter.

While there was no perfect solution, the best strategy for the Flighthawks was to avoid going too far from the Megafortress to take the first attack, even if you had a good opportunity to make a kill. Any defensive move by the fighters would leave the robot too far away to take the second element on.

Mack seemed to have avoided the first pitfall, and had gotten himself tangled up with one of the F-16s in the second group. Meanwhile, his wingman was angling to the north, trying for an end run.

Cantor pushed the throttle guide to max power, leaning forward as he tried to get into position to cut it off.

Mack pickled flares and flicked the Flighthawk to the left, rolling out of the way of the American-built Sidewinder AIM-9s fired by the Pakistani fighter. As good as the Sidewinders were, they couldn't resist the flare, which burned hotter than the Flighthawk's masked engine heat. By the time the missiles exploded, Mack had leveled off and was looking for a way to get at his antagonist.

The Pak jock was still behind him, trying for another shot. Mack started a turn to the right, hoping to use his superior turning ability to throw the F-16 out in front of him. Belatedly, he realized that the Viper's real purpose was to keep him busy while his wingman went for the *Wisconsin*. He was committed now; even if he turned back, he'd never catch the other airplane, which was flashing across the top corner of his screen.

'*Hawk One* to *Wisconsin* – I let one of those suckers get by.'

'I have him, Mack,' said Cantor, breaking in.

Mack was too busy dealing with the Viper behind him to ask how Cantor had managed to get into position to fight the PAF plane. Refusing to get into a turning battle with the Flighthawk, the F-16 fired another Sidewinder and swung back in the *Wisconsin*'s direction. Mack went for his flares again, rolling out and changing course in time to get a shot on the F-16's tailpipe. But the Viper pilot managed to jerk out of the way, and Mack found himself too high and fast to fire again.

Cantor saw the missile flare under the F-16's wing just as he got the cue to fire from the computer. He laid into the Viper, signing his name in the left wing and tailplane. The canopy flew off, and the pilot quickly followed, projected upward by the ACES II ejection seat – but not before another missile flew out toward the Megafortress three miles ahead.

'Missiles!' yelled Cantor. 'Sidewinders! Watch it!'

'We're on it,' replied Dog calmly.

Cantor felt the Megafortress jerk hard to the right. He saw the aircraft in his screen, a shower of flares erupting from her belly. The *Wisconsin* pushed hard to the left; Cantor saw the Sidewinder that had been fired at it explode about three-quarters of a mile beyond the plane, too far away to do any damage.

'*Hawk One* is clear,' said Mack.

'*Two* clear,' said Cantor. '*Wisconsin*, your tail is clean.'

'Thank you, *Hawks One* and *Two*.'

'Thanks for the assist, Cantor,' said Mack.

'You're welcome.'

'That second element cut back quicker than I thought they would,' Mack said. 'Better get Zen to change the programming on that simulation.'

Cantor smirked – but only to himself. 'I will, Major. Consider it done.'

Aboard the *Abner Read*,
in the northern Arabian Sea
0540

Starship skipped the Werewolf toward the two submarines, which were moving at three or four knots northward. Stopping them without sinking them was going to be tricky, if not impossible. Obviously, the Hellfire was not the weapon to use – he switched to the light machine guns, which were locked to fire in line with the Werewolf's nose. The aiming cue showed he was high; he angled down accordingly and sent two rows of shells across the bow of the sub.

The vessel, continuing on, gave no sign that it was

impressed. Starship let off on his trigger and flew toward the craft, buzzing within ten feet of its topside. He could see two men diving into the craft's conning tower as he passed; they went in the side, as if it were a speedboat rather than a submarine. By the time he spun around it had started to dive under the water. It moved forward, gliding down a long, gentle escalator. Starship aimed for the tail of the sub this time, firing his bullets into the water directly behind the disappearing body. When that didn't stop the boat, he fired a long burst at the rapidly disappearing conning tower.

Then he got another idea.

He switched over to the Hellfires and zeroed in on the water about fifty yards ahead of the submarine. Then he fired, hoping the missile would act something like a depth charge, damaging the submarine just enough to bring her back to the surface.

If the missile had any effect – if it even exploded – he couldn't tell.

Starship turned his attention to the other submarine, which was just disappearing underwater. He laced it with bullets, pouring them into the shadow as it slid down below the waves.

'Both submarines are under the water,' he told Eyes. 'I can't see them anymore.'

'Stand by. We hope to have Piranha on line any minute now. Be alert for the approaching Megafortress.'

Everyone but Jed jumped to attention as the President walked into the room.

'No, no,' said Kevin Martindale. 'As you were. Keep working. Jed, what's the situation?'

'We have alerts all across the board. India and Pakistan have fired on each other.' Jed pointed to a screen from a Pentagon launch alert system set up to summarize what the analysts blandly called 'launch events.' As predicted, the Indians had reserved their longest range missiles, undoubtedly for use against China if she came to Pakistan's defense.

'What's the status of the E-bombs?'

'The Dreamland aircraft with the EEMWBs are on course,' said Jed, gently correcting the President as he pointed to the screen where End Game's status was updated. 'The plot here' – he toggled into a new window– 'is from Dreamland Command and gives an approximate location of the bombers. It's accurate to within a mile.'

'Good.'

Martindale folded his arms and surveyed the rest of the room. Jed had seen the President in many tense situations; always, he was calm and almost detached. But clearly he recognized the tension in the room.

'The technology down here is great,' said Martindale.

He winked at Jed. 'But what we really need is a good coffee machine.'

Aboard the *Fisher*,
near Dwārka Early Warning Platform
0543

Danny clicked the control for his smart helmet's visor, selecting the image from the low-light camera in the *Fisher*'s nose. The wrecked platform was dead ahead.

Tommy Chu's voice boomed in his ear. 'We're sixty seconds from drop,' said the *Fisher*'s pilot. 'The Sharkboat is eight miles to the west. The targets are diving. I'm going to drop you approximately five hundred yards ahead of their route calculated by the computer.'

'What happened to Piranha?' Danny asked.

'We haven't reconnected yet,' said Chu. 'Ensign English is working on it. Things are pretty hot down there, Danny. Are you sure you want to go ahead?'

'No doubt in my mind.'

'All right. One of our Flighthawks will orbit to assist if you need it. Thirty seconds.'

'Boston, you ready?' Danny asked his sergeant on the other wing.

'Born ready, Cap. Can't wait to get in the water. Goin' stir crazy here. And freezin' my nuts off.'

Danny switched the screen view to the manpod's rear camera, figuring that would be the one he'd want to use after the drop. Then he took a long breath, gripped the rails near his head, and closed his eyes.

Aboard the *Levitow*, over northwestern India 0545

Flying the Megafortress at high speed and low altitude was the ultimate thrill ride, the sort of attraction roller coaster designers could only dream about. The scenery north of India's largest city added to the sensation; exotic rooftops flew by the windscreens, giving way to yellowish fields, then more houses and factory buildings.

Breanna wasn't interested in the scenery, except as a reference point to make sure she was flying as low as possible. The thrills she could take or leave, though at the moment she couldn't live without them.

She hurled the Megafortress forward at 500 knots, counting on her reflexes to keep her out of trouble. They were less than fifty feet above ground level, so close to some of the buildings that if she extended her landing gear she could have scraped off shingles.

'Terrain rising!' warned Stewart.

'Thanks,' said Breanna, even though she was already pulling back. '*Levitow* to Hawk leader – we're approaching Omega point.'

'Roger that, *Levitow*. We're getting ready to say goodbye right now.'

* * *

Unlike their mother ship, the Flighthawks were not shielded against the EEMWB's electromagnetic waves. To avoid the effects of the blast, *Hawk Four* would be sent to a rendezvous point south, piloted completely by the onboard component of its C^3 flight-control computer. The Megafortress would pick it up on the way back. If for some reason they were unable to return within an hour, C^3 would fly the plane westward and ditch in the ocean.

The other aircraft, *Hawk Three*, would stay with the *Levitow* until the EEMWBs went off. That would leave the Megafortress temporarily without an escort, but in theory anything nearby would have been zapped out of order anyway.

'Thirty seconds to disconnect,' Dork told Zen.

'Hard to let go, huh?' Zen asked the other pilot.

'You got that, Major.'

Zen kept *Hawk Three* five miles ahead of the Megafortress, flying at thirty feet. He was so low not simply to avoid detection – the Flighthawk's radar profile was considerably stealthier than the Megafortress's – but as a kind of terrain bird dog to alert Breanna to anything unexpected.

'*Hawk Four* is no longer under my control,' said Dork, sounding a little sad.

Zen leaned forward in his seat, eyes scanning the screen as the ground whipped by.

He'd made the right decision. This was exactly where he needed to be.

Northern Arabian Sea
0548

The concussion threw the midget submarine sideways. Sattari lurched against his seat belt, then fell back, suddenly weightless in the small craft.

He waited for a second blast, sure that the aircraft they had seen above would finish them off. He felt his heart pounding at the top of his chest, near his collarbone.

A minute passed, then another. There were no more explosions. Sattari bent his head and uttered a prayer of thanksgiving.

'Captain, we are losing power,' said the submarine's commander. 'We're losing speed.'

The soft light from the instrument panel turned the man's face a brownish red; he looked like a demon.

'We will wait, then.'

'If the Parvaneh has been seriously damaged, we may not be able to stay under very long.'

'Let us examine the damage and discover what else we can do. Trust yourself, and Allah.'

'Yes, Captain.'

The manpod hit the water with a teeth-rattling smack and shudder. The nose – where Danny's feet were – shot downward, then flipped abruptly toward the surface. Danny hung onto the handles near his head, expecting the pod to spin or, worse, flip over. But it did neither. A buzzer sounded in the cabin as the pod's automated raft system prepared to inflate. He didn't override, and three seconds later a shrill hiss told him compressed air had filled the bladders at the sides, stabilizing the craft.

The feed from the rear cam showed nothing nearby. Danny reached to the back of his helmet and cued in the front view. Water lapped the top two-thirds of the screen; he couldn't see anything else.

Balling his hands into fists, he reached down and pounded the recessed handles above his stomach, blowing the top half of the pod off. He pulled himself upright, punching his visor into its low-light mode.

There was nothing nearby – including the other manpod.

'Boston?'

No answer.

'Boston?'

He was just about to switch back into the Dreamland circuit and make sure that Chu had dropped his sergeant when something broke the water a few yards away.

'Boston?' he yelled.

The figure waved. It *had* to be Boston, he decided, and reached down to his pants leg to take out the flashlight. He gave a quick flick of light to help the man find his way over, then pulled off his helmet.

'Boston?'

'Yo, Cap,' said the sergeant, grabbing onto the side of the pod. 'Had a little trouble. The stabilizer raft didn't inflate right, and I guess I blew the lid too soon.'

'Where's your helmet?'

'Bottom of the sea. Lost the laughing gas too. Got my

dive gear and weapons, though.' Boston hauled the water-proof sacks up to Danny.

'All right. Let me see where our submarine is,' Danny said, pulling his helmet back on.

Aboard the *Abner Read*,
in the northern Arabian Sea
0555

Starship stayed in an orbit between the Sharkboat and his last sighting of the submarines.

'Werewolf, the Dreamland team is in the water,' said Eyes. 'Approach the area and give them cover.'

'Copy that. I see them. Do you have a location on the submarine?'

'*Dreamland Fisher* is still working on that.'

Starship sped forward. He saw a dark smudge in the water at about a mile. Thinking it was the Dreamland Whiplash team, he started to slow down, then realized it was one of the commandos' empty rafts. Tracking north, he found a small missilelike raft nose down in the water – one of the manpods.

'Werewolf has Whiplash manpod in sight,' he told Eyes.

'I'm switching you over to the commander of *Sharkboat One*. You have a direct line on your channel two.'

Starship gave the commander the GPS coordinates for the manpod. One man clung to the side and the other was in the tiny vessel.

'Stand by for the location of the submarines, via *Dreamland Fisher* commander,' said Eyes, breaking in.

Northern Arabian Sea
0558

The global positioning cue in the smart helmet indicated that the submarine was four hundred yards almost directly south. It appeared to have stopped moving, drifting less than twelve feet below the surface.

'Quarter mile,' Danny told Boston. 'Just below the surface. Probably trying to lay low until things quiet down. Let's paddle as close we can. We'll skip the laughing gas, do everything else like we drew it up.'

Boston moved to the back of the raft and began kicking. Danny picked up a paddle. The wind was gentle, but it was in his face, and it took quite an effort to reach the spot where the submarine was. Finally, Danny grabbed the waterproof packs from the inside of the manpod and gave one to Boston. He traded the smart helmet for a dive mask with a light and breather, and pulled on flippers.

'Ready?'

'If you say so,' replied Boston.

Danny took out his survival radio and held it to his face. 'Whiplash to Werewolf and Sharkboat. We're ready to go below.'

'Sharkboat is fifteen minutes away,' replied the boat's captain.

'Great. We'll meet you on the surface.'

429

'Whiplash, you got a fighter coming at you out of the north. He's at low altitude and slow.'

'Roger that. We're in the water,' said Danny, tossing the radio behind him and slipping over the side.

The water was much darker than he had imagined it could be. Even with the light, he couldn't see more than a few feet away.

Just when he thought he'd swum right by the sub, he spotted a black shadow looming a few yards to his right. A strong kick took him to the side of the vessel. He looked back and saw Boston's light approaching.

Fearing that any noise outside the submarine might alert the people inside, he stayed off the hull, swimming above the deck to locate the emergency blow device. The sub expert had warned that the device might have been removed, but the door covering it was exactly where he'd seen it on the diagram. He reached gingerly to the panel, running his fingers around it. There were two latches. He slipped them to the sides and pried the panel upward. The large red lever sat inside, exactly as in the brochure advertising the civilian version of the submarine's safety features.

Not ready to activate the system, Danny turned and worked his way to the rear of the vessel, looking for the stern planes. Resembling a pair of airplane wings, the planes helped hold the vessel at the proper angle in the water; blowing them would make the submarine bob forward, further disorienting the passengers and making it harder for them to get away if something went wrong. He placed the small packs of explosive, then waited for

Boston to put his on the propeller shaft. They pressed the timer buttons almost simultaneously. Then Danny swam back to the rescue device while Boston went to see if there were forward fins.

Captain Sattari listened as the creaks and tremors of the great ocean rippled through the submarine, the sounds magnified by fear as much as acoustics.

If Allah permitted, they would stay here all day until the sun set. Then they could surface and repair whatever had caused the engine to fail. If unsuccessful, they would board the raft and head to shore.

It was possible. It would be done.

Sattari heard a loud clunk above him, so close it sounded as if someone had kicked the submarine.

'There may be patrol vessels searching for us,' said the Parvaneh's commander. 'We should be prepared to scuttle.'

Even as Sattari nodded, he found himself hoping it wouldn't come to that. He wanted to stand before his father and tell him of his great victory.

The handle refused to budge. Danny put his feet as gingerly as he could on the deck of the submarine and pushed, but still couldn't get it to turn.

Boston swam up next to him and pointed at his watch. The charges were set to go off in another sixty seconds.

Danny motioned to him to get near the hatchway, located inside the low-slung conning tower, so he would be ready to throw the grenades inside when the sub surfaced. Glancing at the timer on his watch – forty-eight

431

seconds – he balled his hand into a fist, measuring his aim. As he did, he saw a long plastic knob next to the handle. It looked like a screwdriver, but turned out to be a release for the handle.

Before he could try the handle again, the charges exploded. Small as they were, they rocked the submarine upward. Danny jammed his hand against the lever as the top of the sub smacked him into his face mask. He felt himself propelled upward, as if he were sitting on an underwater volcano. He lost his grip on the handle but grabbed the device door, holding on as the submarine surfaced with a roar.

Aboard the *Wisconsin*,
over India
0610

There were times when flying the EB-52 was like being the engineer on a high-speed train riding on a dedicated rail, with relatively few decisions to make and a predictable program ahead of you.

This wasn't one of those times.

Dog was being tracked by no less than six different missile batteries. He tried to zigzag between them and still stay on course.

'SA-12s to the right, SA-10s to the left,' said Jazz. 'Pick your poison.'

'Tens,' said Dog.

'Flap Lid radar,' said the copilot, telling Dog that the

SA-10's engagement radar had locked onto them. 'Breaking. I'm using every ECM we've got, Colonel.'

They were roughly seventy miles from the missile site, just outside its maximum reach. But their course was going to take them down to thirty miles from the battery.

'SA-12s are launching!' shouted Jazz. 'I don't think they have a lock.'

Dog immediately changed his course, dodging back to the north, closer to the SA-12 battery – if they were going to fire at him anyway, there was no sense getting too close to the SA-10s.

The Russian SA-12 – known to its makers as the S-300V – was a versatile missile that came in two different versions, depending on its primary use. The SA-12A – code-named Gladiator by NATO – was a low-to-high altitude missile that could reach targets up to fifteen and a half miles in the sky, with a range of just over forty-five miles. The B version was optimized as an antiballistic missile, with a higher altitude and longer range. Both missiles were incredibly fast, in the league of the American Patriot, which could hit Mach 5.

'He's coming for us, Colonel. Forty miles.'

They had less than a minute to dodge the missile. Dog shoved the Megafortress hard to his left, trying to beam the Grill Pan missile radar.

'Still coming.'

'ECMs,' Dog told Jazz.

'I'm playing every song I know.'

'Chaff. Hang on, tight.' Dog veered down, trying to

433

stay at a right angle to the radar and get the missile to bite on the tinsel.

'We're clear! We're clear!' said Jazz.

The missile's warhead exploded a few thousand feet above them, two miles away. Dog kept the Megafortress level as he tried to sort out where he was relative to his original course. He'd strayed farther south than he wanted; as soon as he corrected, Jazz called out a fresh warning.

'We're spiked! More SA-12s. The whole battery, looks like. This time they have a lock.'

Northern Arabian Sea
0612

The Parvaneh submarine shook with the sharp thud of multiple explosions. Captain Sattari ripped the seat belt from around his waist and grabbed his AK-47 from the floor. He started to run toward the ladder to the deck above – the charges for the explosives that were sealed in the vessel's hull were set off from the panel there.

After his third step he heard a loud roar, the sound of an old-fashioned locomotive letting off steam. Then he flew forward, knocked off his feet by the submarine's sudden and unexpected rise toward the surface.

Danny was thrown off the side as the submarine popped up. His foot grabbed in the side rail and he slammed against the hull, caught on the deck. He pushed himself back toward the conning tower, half swimming, half stumbling, in the direction of Boston, who was already at the hatch. The submarine twisted, whirling as the waves frothed and steamed. Danny lurched to his knees and slid into Boston's back just as the sergeant dropped his tear gas canisters down into the vessel. Catching his balance, Danny gripped the edge of the conning tower. He tossed off his knapsack and unzipped the outer and then the inner skins, exposing the CQWS shotgun.

The close-quarters weapon – developed by Dreamland's weapons lab, the letters stood for Close Quarters Whiplash Shotgun – looked like a Pancor jackhammer shotgun that had been sawed off just fore of the trigger. It held twelve rounds of plastic pellet-filled shells, designed to incapacitate but not kill a person. The shells were expelled with enough force to knock down a 250-pound man.

Danny grabbed the gun and leapt down into the submarine. He saw only smoke in front of him, but immediately fired two rounds. Something fell at his feet – a man. Danny sidestepped him, then raised his gun as something moved a few feet away. He fired point-blank and it went down.

Boston was right behind him. Danny pushed through the thick haze, still using his dive pack to breathe. The submarine had an aisle down the middle, with a seat to each side. He saw a station with a wheel at the front, a shadow moving next to it. He put two shells into the shadow.

Someone grabbed at his side. A sharp elbow got rid

of his assailant, but as he brought his gun up, a bullet rico-
cheted nearby. Before Danny could react, he felt a burning
sensation in his calf. He fired toward the front of the
submarine, heard another bullet, and found himself falling.

Aboard the *Wisconsin*,
over India
0613

Dog veered to the south as soon as Jazz gave him the
warning about the SA-12s. The Megafortress groaned with
the strain, pulling nearly eight g's. Engines at max power,
he pushed his nose down, increasing his speed.

'Colonel – you're heading straight for the SA-10 site.'

'Turn off the ECMs.'

'Colonel?'

'Jazz.'

'ECMs off. Clam Shell acquisition ra – They have
us! They have us! They're launching – two, four missiles.'

Three behind them, four in their face. Dog continued
on a beeline for the Indian site that had launched the SA-
10s for another twenty seconds.

'Give it everything you got, Jazz,' he said. 'Chaff,
ECMs, the kitchen sink. Crew – stand by, this one's going
to be close.'

Though the Flighthawk was several times more maneuverable than the EB-52, Mack had trouble keeping
Hawk One close to the *Wisconsin* as she jinked and jived

toward the ground, rolling on her wing and then heading almost straight down. It wouldn't have been half bad if he hadn't actually been in the plane – the hard maneuvers while he was flying in a different direction threatened to tear his head from his body. His stomach felt like it was where his legs should be, and the g forces tried to jerk his arms out of their sockets.

One of the Indian missiles was beelining for the Flighthawk. That wasn't a bad idea, he thought – intercept the missile before it hit the Megafortress. But the telephone-pole-sized weapon flew by him at the last second.

Dog powered the Megafortress into a dive. He glanced at the sitrep, then back at the windscreen.

'SA-12s are following – no, he's off – he's going for the SA-10,' shouted Jazz.

'Hang with me, son.'

Confused by the jamming gear and the apparent disappearance of their target, the two sets of missiles quickly found alternatives – each other. None managed to complete an exact interception, but when the first missile detonated, the others quickly followed suit.

The plane shuddered, and the computer warned that it was 'exceeding normal flying parameters' – a polite way of asking if the pilot had lost his mind. Dog struggled through an uncontrolled invert; with the computer's help he leveled off at fifteen thousand feet.

They were beyond the missile batteries.

'You did it, Colonel. They cooked each other. We're past them.'

'We got a way to go yet, Jazz,' said Dog, hunting for the heading to the launch area.

Northern Arabian Sea
0614

Danny landed on a body as bullets flew by. He saw someone rising behind him. Thinking it was Boston, he hesitated for a moment, then saw the silhouette of a pistol in the man's hand. He fired two rounds from his shotgun point-blank at the shadow's head.

Someone grabbed him by the throat. Choking, he pointed the shotgun backward and fired once, twice, three times before the hand finally let go. He jumped up, firing two more times at the prone body.

Boston loomed behind him, waving his hand. They'd subdued everyone aboard the submarine.

Breathing heavily, they began trussing the men with plastic handcuffs and grabbing any guns they could find. Danny's leg screamed with pain. He stumbled over the bodies in the aisle, then found his way to the ladder, clambering topside. He crawled out onto the deck of the submarine and pulled down his mask and breathing gear, hyperventilating in the fresh air.

'Sharkboat dead ahead!' said Boston, coming up behind him.

The low-slung patrol craft was less than fifty yards away. Danny dug in his equipment belt for the flare they were supposed to use to tell them the submarine's crew had been subdued; by the time he found it, three sailors were already aboard.

'Hey, Captain Whiplash!' yelled one of the Navy men, who'd worked with Danny before.

'About time you got here,' said Boston. 'Put your damn gas masks on – place is a mess down there.'

Sattari felt himself being lifted and carried upward. He was going to Paradise, his battle done.

He sailed through a narrow tunnel, flooded with light.

Was his wife waiting for him?

His head slapped hard against the ground. Water splashed over him – he was wet – he was alive.

The submarine had been attacked. There had been gas and explosions, men . . .

Someone shouted nearby. The words were foreign – English.

Americans!

When he tried to move his hands, he found they were bound in front of him.

They would not take him alive. Sattari pushed over the side, diving into the water.

'Hey, one's jumping in the water!'

Danny turned in time to see a pair of legs crashing through the waves. Without thinking, he dove forward off the submarine, stroking for the man. His leg throbbed as he tried to kick; it went limp on him, stunned, as if anesthetized – except it still hurt like hell. He saw the man surfacing a few feet away and lunged for him. He grabbed the man's back, pulling him to the left; the man jerked away and fell back under the waves.

Sattari's lungs screamed for air but he ignored them, pushing himself downward. He would cheat his enemies of this.

The man who'd followed him grabbed him by the left arm. Sattari shoved him aside. He opened his mouth, trying to swallow the sea.

He saw the man's eyes in front of his face, wide and white. Sattari threw his hands forward and found the man's neck.

'You're coming with me,' Sattari told him.

Before Danny could react, the hands tightened around his neck. Dragged down, he tried to kick but couldn't. He began punching the other man, but the man didn't let go. Both of them continued to sink.

I'm going to die here, he thought.

Danny flailed desperately, poking and punching and kicking, forcing his injured leg to move, using every ounce of energy in his body to push off his attacker. His lungs were bursting, his nose and mouth starting to suck seawater.

Suddenly, the hands slipped away. Danny threw himself up toward the surface. He burst above the waves, gulped a breath, half air, half water. Coughing violently, he slipped back down, fought his way back to the air, tried to float. He gasped and coughed at the same time.

'Here, here!' someone shouted nearby.

Danny turned over to paddle but his arms were too

tired now. His body sagged and exhaustion felt very near. He pushed once, then slipped down below the waves, happy to rest finally.

Then he felt himself moving upward. He took a breath and coughed. He coughed until the world around him was red. When he stopped, he found himself in a small rigid-hulled craft from the Sharkboat.

'You OK, Captain?' said a sailor, standing over him.

'That guy . . .'

'Don't see him anywhere.'

Too tired to look himself, Danny collapsed against the gunwale.

Aboard the *Levitow*,
over India
0614

Zen checked his watch. They were three minutes to Point Baker, where the Megafortress would begin its five-minute climb to the launch point.

'Bandits ahead,' warned Stewart. 'ID'd as MiG-21 Fishbeds. Four planes. They don't see us yet.'

Zen saw them on the sitrep as the copilot read off their heading and altitude. They were at eight thousand feet, flying northwest on a course that would bring them to within two miles of the Megafortress, just at the point where Breanna would have to start to climb.

'Jeff, you think we can sneak past these guys?' asked Breanna.

'I was just about to ask you the same question,' Zen told his wife. While it would be foolish to underestimate the fighters, their radars were limited and there was a decent possibility that the EB-52 could get past them without being noticed.

'If we didn't have to climb, I'd say we take the chance,' Breanna told him. 'But if they see us, they'll be on our back at the worst possible time.'

'Roger that, *Levitow*. I have the lead element.'

'Look at our flight path – can you hold off until they've crossed it?'

'That's not a problem,' said Zen.

'We'll use Scorpions on *Bandits Three* and *Four*,' explained Breanna. 'I'll pivot and fire two missiles. If I recover quickly, I'll be back on course in just over a minute and a half.'

'Roger that.'

As Zen took the Flighthawk northwest and began to climb, he worked out the game plan in his head. The MiGs were flying close enough for him to take both planes out in a single pass. He'd loop in from the west, firing on the wingman first; it would take barely a nudge on his stick to get his sights on the lead plane. The MiGs were moving at 320 knots; he'd be able to close on them easily.

It was a great plan, but the Indians didn't cooperate. When they were less than three miles from the Mega-fortress, the planes suddenly accelerated.

'I think they see us,' said Stewart, her voice shrill.

'Yeah, I'm on it,' Zen told her. 'Relax there, *Levitow*.'

'Trying,' said the copilot.

Zen knew better than to bother chasing the lead element; he might catch one of the planes but couldn't hope to take two.

'Bree, let's swap targets. I'll take *Three* and *Four*, you go for *One* and *Two*.'

'Roger that, Flighthawk. Kick butt.'

'You got it, baby.'

Stewart's fingers grew cold as she worked through the screen, redesignating her targets. It was easy, it was simple, she'd done it gadzillion times in the drills – but she could feel her heart pounding harder and harder.

'Ease up, Jan,' said Breanna. 'You're hitting the touch-screen like you're fighting Mike Tyson.'

'I guess I am,' she said. She put her hands together, warming her fingers. She didn't relax, exactly, but she did pull back from hyper mode.

'Bay,' said Breanna. 'Fire when ready.'

If we wait that long, we'll be dead, Stewart thought.

The second element of MiGs altered course, banking into a tight turn to put themselves behind the Megafortress.

The MiG-21 had been designed in the 1950s, and while outdated long ago, the aircraft retained many of its original virtues. Small and maneuverable, it could touch Mach 2 if necessary, and was tough in a close-quarters knife fight. The two Indian jocks who were turning toward the *Levitow*'s tail undoubtedly thought they had the Megafortress right where they wanted her – about five miles ahead and several thousand feet below them. All they had to do was close in; their heat-seekers would do the rest.

The problem with that strategy came in the form of 20mm shells ripping through the nose and canopy of *Bandit Four*. Zen hit the MiG from above, riding his cannon through the humped midsection of the plane. Two or three dozen bullets hit the aircraft in a fraction of a second, shredding the plane's avionics, engine, and most of all its pilot.

Zen pulled his nose up and found *Bandit Three* dead on in his gunsight. The weapons bar went red; he waited a full second then fired. The MiG rolled its wing left, trying to duck away. Zen had too much momentum to follow and still get a kill; instead he banked back in the direction of the Megafortress, losing sight of his opponent.

'Fire Fox One! Fire Fox One!' warned Stewart. Though still excited, her voice wasn't nearly as shrill as it had been.

Two missiles spurted from the bay of the EB-52, AARAAM-pluses heading for *Bandits One* and *Two*.

Zen looked at the sitrep, trying to figure out what had happened to the other MiG. The plane wasn't on the display, but he knew it had to be around somewhere; the radar had difficulty seeing objects very close to the ground behind its wings.

'*Levitow*, I lost *Bandit Three*,' Zen warned.

'Roger that, Flighthawk. Tail Stinger is activated. We're climbing,' added Breanna.

Zen decided that the other MiG had either gotten away south or was running parallel to him somewhere beyond the Megafortress's right wingtip, where it would be difficult for the radar to spot.

He started crossing, then realized there was a possibility he hadn't considered – just below his own tail.

Tracers exploded past his nose. Now the tables were turned, and Zen was the surprised target. He cut back to his left, hoping to throw the MiG out in front of him as he began to weave in the sky. But the Indian pilot didn't bite, and Zen had to duck a fresh stream of bullets.

He wasn't completely successful. Three shells went into the Flighthawk's left wing. The computer tallied the score:

DAMAGE TO CONTROL SURFACE. DEGRADATION FIVE
   PERCENT.

Zen continued to zig up and down, back and forth, depriving the other pilot of an easy shot. If they hadn't been so close to the Megafortress, he would have started a turn; if the MiG followed, he could use the Flighthawk's superior turning radius and maneuverability to reverse their positions. But that wasn't an option here, since it would leave the way clear for the MiG to close on the Megafortress before he could get back.

The launch warning sounded – the MiG had fired two heat-seeking missiles at him. Now he had to get out of the way. Zen tossed flares and tucked toward the ground, then immediately zigged right and hunted for the MiG. Sure enough, the Indian jock was accelerating straight ahead, trying to close on the EB-52's tail.

Zen's quick roll had taken him below the MiG-21. He

turned into the enemy plane and began firing despite the computer's warning that he didn't have a shot. The hail of bullets broke the MiG's attack; he pushed off to the right, jerking hard and pulling at least six g's. No conventional fighter could have stayed with him, but the Flighthawk wasn't a conventional fighter. The MiG's tailpipe grew fat in the middle of his screen. He leaned on the trigger, giving the Indian craft a 20mm enema. The canopy flew off in short order, the pilot hitting the silk.

'Splash *Bandit Three*,' said Zen, looking for the Megafortress.

Stewart stared at the message in her screen: target one destroyed.

She'd got it! The bastard was dead.

But where was the other plane?

Still flying, six miles ahead. The other missile?

She'd missed.

'*Bandit One* is hit,' she told Breanna. '*Bandit Two* is still there. The missile must have missed.'

'All right,' said Breanna.

'Should I fire another?'

'Just stand by.'

Stewart felt a wave of resentment come over her. But then she realized they weren't in a good position to fire. The pilot wasn't criticizing her; she preferred to stay on course and keep her missiles if she could. It made more sense to at least check first with the Flighthawk pilot to see if he could take the plane.

'Standing by,' said Stewart.

'I can just get there if *Bandit Two* stays on his present course and speed,' Zen told Breanna. 'But only just.'

'Try. We're two minutes to launch point.'

'Got it.'

Zen accelerated ahead, climbing to meet the MiG. The other aircraft was three thousand feet above him.

'Fuel warning,' said the computer.

Zen called up the fuel panel. Sure enough, the Flighthawk was into its reserves, well ahead of schedule. The tanks must have been damaged, though the status board claimed that they were OK.

There was nothing he could do about it now – the Indian fighter loomed at the top of his screen. Zen pulled his nose up and took a shot as the plane passed, getting the MiG to break south. Knowing that he hadn't put enough bullets into him to shoot him down, Zen started to follow. Breanna, meanwhile, had pulled the Megafortress farther south and begun to level off, preparing to fire the EEMWBs.

'Fuel emergency,' declared C^3.

Zen glanced at the fuel screen. The tanks were nearly drained – he had under five minutes' worth of juice.

'How did I use fifteen minutes' worth of jet fuel in thirty seconds?' he asked the computer.

'Unknown command,' it replied.

Was the problem simply with the gauge? Zen hoped so.

He pressed his nose down as the targeting bar began to blink yellow. The MiG was starting a turn to his left, banking to get behind the Megafortress.

'Fuel emergency,' repeated the computer.

'Yup.' Zen leaned the Flighthawk onto its left wing,

pushing his enemy into the sweet spot of his target zone. He pressed the trigger; bullets began flying from the nose.

Then the Flighthawk veered down.

'Engine has lost power. Fuel emergency. No fuel. No fuel,' sang the computer.

Zen slapped the computer's audible warning system off.

'*Hawk Three* to *Levitow* – Bree, I'm out of fuel. Something must have hit the Flighthawk and caused a breach in the tanks. Didn't show on the damage panel. That MiG is still out there.'

'Acknowledged,' said Breanna. 'Ninety seconds to launch point.'

**Aboard the *Abner Read*,
in the northern Arabian Sea
0619**

Starship took the Werewolf over the Sharkboat, circling as the last of the submarine's survivors were taken aboard. The Sharkboat was preparing to tow the vessel back to the *Abner Read*, some sixty miles to the west.

Sixty perilous miles between the Chinese and the Indian forces.

Starship headed west, scouting the area. The closest vessel was a Chinese destroyer, fifteen miles away. It had been hit by two Indian missiles, and had a gaping hole at the bow; it was unlikely to come for them. More problematic was the guided missile cruiser rushing to its aid.

'Werewolf to Tac. I have an update on the two Chinese

vessels closest to the Sharkboat,' said Starship. 'Destroyer looks pretty badly damaged. Cruiser's going to help it. I'd say go now while the going is good.'

'Acknowledged. We have a contact for you to check out five miles north of us – we think it's a downed pilot in the water. Can you get there?'

'On my way.'

The Megafortress that dropped the manpod had turned on its surface radar, giving the *Abner Read* and Storm a good picture of the battle. The Indian carrier appeared to be sixty miles southeast of them – in range of his Harpoon missiles.

And the Standards. He'd use a mix; it was the only way to guarantee he could take out the Chinese carrier as well.

And he was *going* to get them.

The two fleets were repositioning themselves after the first wave of attacks. Two Chinese escorts had been severely damaged, and it appeared that one Indian vessel was sunk. The *Deng Xiaoping*'s radar helicopters and two of its fighters had been shot down, but only one of the Indian missiles managed to reach the ship, and it had not done enough damage to impede air operations. The Indian ship *Shiva* had not been hit and was beginning to recover the aircraft involved in the attack.

'Weapons, target the Indian carrier *Shiva*,' Storm said. 'I want a mix of Harpoons and Standards. Use the plan we established earlier.'

'You want me to target the carrier, sir?'

'Am I speaking English? Target the *Shiva* with enough

weapons to sink her.' Storm pounded the side of the holographic display. He looked down at the table. A pool of water disrupted the projection.

Was it water? Or blood?

His head felt as if it was going to lift off from his head.

'Captain,' said Eyes. 'Storm – we can't sink the Indian ship.'

'Like hell I can't. Our orders said that we were allowed to defend ourselves. The Indian ship is regrouping for an attack.'

'The planes on the Chinese carrier – we're already out of position to act as backup against them, and –'

'Don't second-guess me, Eyes. No one's going to attack us and not get a fistful of explosives back in their face. Weapons – use a mix of missiles. Keep enough to sink the Chinese carrier if we have to, but you lock on that damn Indian ship and sink the bastard!'

Aboard the *Wisconsin*,
over India
0619

Chu, the pilot of *Dreamland Fisher*, began speaking as soon as Dog cleared the communication.

'I have two Chinese aircraft on my wingtips telling me to get out of the area or face the consequences, Colonel. They're not specifying what the consequences are.'

'I assume you've told them you're in international air space?'

'I told them in English and in Chinese, Colonel. They weren't impressed.'

'All right, Chu, stand by.' Dog hot-buttoned to the channel reserved for Jed Barclay at the NSC during the operation. 'Jed, are you there?'

'I'm here, Colonel.'

'What's the status on the *Deng Xiaoping*?'

'Tai-shan aircraft have not appeared on the deck. NSA has not yet picked up the command to launch.'

Well, that was something at least, thought Dog. But it might be only a matter of time – the Chinese might not have picked up the Indian launch yet.

'The Chinese are challenging *Dreamland Fisher*, which is supplying radar information to the *Abner Read*. I'm going to have the pilot back off a little bit to avoid provocation.'

'Your call, Colonel.'

'Both of the aircraft with EEMWBs are within ninety seconds of their launch points,' he added. 'Are we cleared to go?'

'Stand by. I have Mr Freeman right here.'

The National Security Advisor's face came into view on the screen. It was gray and deathly.

'Colonel Bastian, I have just spoken with the President of the United States. You're ordered to proceed. God be with you all.'

Never had a blessing sounded so dire.

'Thank you, sir,' said Dog, pressing the button to flip back to Chu.

Aboard the *Levitow*,
over India
0620

Breanna cleared the transmission. Her father's face came on the screen.

'Proceed with End Game,' he said.

'Roger that – I'm sixty seconds from launch. What's the status on the Chinese aircraft carrier?'

'Responding with conventional weapons so far. Launch your three EEMWBs and reserve the last for the carrier as planned. Chu is flying to the west and will back you up with conventional weapons. Give him enough warning to get south before you launch.'

'Will do.'

Breanna checked her position, then told Stewart to get ready to launch the first two missiles.

'Ready,' said Stewart.

'Any fighters nearby?'

'Negative.'

'Crew, we're thirty seconds from weapons launch. First explosion will follow in ten minutes.'

Breanna turned her attention back to the helm of her ship. She was climbing through twenty thousand feet. Somewhere far above her, Indian missiles were arcing on their course toward Pakistan.

'Counting down from ten,' said Stewart. 'Nine, eight, seven . . .'

Breanna stared at the blue sky ahead. At this altitude, the world appeared blissful.

'. . . three, two, one.'

'Fire EEMWB one,' said Breanna. 'Fire two.'

'Firing EEMWB one. Firing EEMWB two.'

Missile one rocketed off its launcher on the right wing, climbing ahead with a furious spurt of energy. Breanna turned to left, looking for the contrail from missile two. But it was nowhere to be seen.

'Stewart, where's missile two?'

'Launched – engine failed to ignite.'

'Retarget missile three and fire.'

'Retargeting. Firing missile three.'

The missile shot up ahead.

'Missile one is on course,' said Stewart. 'Missile two has been lost. Missile three is on course. Time to launch missile four is zero-seven minutes. You have a turn coming up in thirty seconds.'

Breanna acknowledged, then keyed in the Dreamland communications line to tell Colonel Bastian that one of the missiles had malfunctioned.

Aboard the *Wisconsin*,
over India
0622

'What's the status on that SA-2 missile site?' Dog asked Jazz.

'Tracking us.'

'Our EEMWBs?'

'Missile one is on course. Missile two is on course,' Jazz told Dog. 'Sixty seconds to launch point two.'

Dog began a ten-degree turn to the north, positioning himself for the final launch. The first of their missiles would explode approximately two minutes after he fired; he'd be on manual controls after that.

The Dreamland communications line buzzed.

'*Levitow* to *Wisconsin*. One of our missiles failed to ignite. Motor failure. We fired a replacement.'

'Acknowledged.'

'Should I fire the last missile or reserve it for the *Deng*?'

'Fire the missile as planned,' Dog told her. 'Then get back to use your Scorpions against the Tai-shan planes. I'll alert *Dreamland Fisher.*'

'*Levitow*,' said Breanna, acknowledging.

'Thirty seconds to launch point,' broke in Jazz.

'Very good,' said Dog, making sure he was precisely on course.

Aboard the *Abner Read*,
in the northern Arabian Sea
0622

Storm's head hurt so badly he had to sit on the small fold-down jumpseat at the side of the holographic display. He knew he was bleeding – every time he wiped his forehead, his fingers were drenched in fresh blood.

'Weapons, what's our status?'

'Ready to launch on command, Captain.'

'Stand by. Weapons will launch on my command.'

In the days of sailing ships, the order to attack another ship could take hours to carry out, with crew working feverishly just to position the ship, let alone fill and fire the cannons. Now it took only fractions of a second.

'Weapons, fire all missiles.'

'Firing, Captain.'

A pair of missiles flared from the forward deck, followed by two more, then another pair, then another. The ship's bow bent down toward the waves with the fusillade.

'Deal with that, you bastards,' Storm muttered as the missiles leapt away.

Aboard the *Levitow*,
over India
0626

EEMWB four clunked off the launcher, its rocket motor igniting with a burst of red flame. Breanna immediately changed course to the southwest.

'Flight of Su-27s closing in on us from the south,' said Stewart. 'Thirty-five miles away. Four aircraft. They have AA-12s.'

'Target the lead element. Reserve four Scorpions. I want two missiles apiece for the Tai-shan aircraft.'

'Targeting.'

'Bay.'

'Bomb bay open.'

'Fire as soon as you're locked.'

'Bree, I have launch warnings.'

'Fire Scorpions. Crew – stand by for evasive man-euvers.'

'Talk about impotent,' muttered Zen as the Megafortress jerked away from the Indians' antiaircraft missiles. He switched his main view from the sitrep screen to the *Levitow*'s forward video camera, then killed the display altogether and took off his helmet. Flying wasn't a spectator sport, especially when you were under attack.

'They going to hit us?' asked Dork. He sounded scared.

'Nah. Captain Stockard likes to cut things close, but not that close.'

The Megafortress jerked so sharply Zen's restraints cut into his chest.

'We ought to work on getting you a new nickname,' he told the other Flighthawk pilot as the plane straightened out. 'What were you called in high school?'

'Dork, sir.'

A flight of Pakistani aircraft appeared to the north; very possibly the Indians had been looking for them when they found the Megafortress instead. That was of small consolation to Breanna, who was desperately wheeling *Levitow* between the clouds, trying to duck their missiles.

'SA-12 site tracking us,' warned Stewart.

'The more the merrier,' said Breanna.

'I have every ECM –'

'Keep them there,' said Breanna. 'Chaff, flares,

everything you got. We have another sixty seconds until the EEMWBs go off. That's all we need.'

'Scorpion One has scored. Two – uh, near miss.'

'Good.'

'AMRAAMski going off track.'

About time, thought Breanna.

'One more.'

Breanna put her hand on the throttle, even though she knew it was at max power. Then she jerked her stick hard right, trying to turn the Megafortress into a hummingbird and veer out of the way of the missiles.

The computer complained that they were about to exceed eight g's. Breanna kept the pressure on her stick anyway.

'Two more missiles missed,' said the copilot. 'I can't find the last one.'

Breanna sensed where it was and let off on the stick. The Megafortress stumbled, but began to recover.

As it did, the enemy air-to-air missile exploded under her right wing.

Aboard the *Shiva*,
in the northern Arabian Sea
0632

Somewhere below, a pair of close-in weapons began to fire. Fear surged through Memon so strongly that he could not move nor breathe, not even think. Cold air invaded his chest; his heart and lungs turned to ice. He waited, unable to do anything else.

The first explosion seemed incredibly far away; he heard a light rumble but felt nothing. The second, a half second later, was like the peal of thunder when lightning strikes a tree at the edge of a yard.

The third reverberated as if it were under his feet, twisting his chest and head in opposite directions. He flew against a console, thrown so abruptly that he felt as if he hadn't moved at all. He lay on the deck, watching the others scramble to get up.

Only Admiral Skandar managed to stay on his feet. The Defense minister reached calmly for the phone, speaking as the ship rocked with fresh explosions. Memon wanted to get up and join him but could not; he wanted to move but found his body paralyzed. All he could do was stare from the depths of his cowardice and fear.

Aboard the *Levitow*,
over India
0632

The aircraft lurched in the sky, then felt as if it was going to fall out from under her. Breanna pushed against the stick, finally leveling off – the computer began compensating for the damaged control surfaces.

'Engine four – gone,' said Stewart. Her voice was surprisingly calm.

'Compensating,' Breanna told her. 'Where are the other missiles?'

'One more going north. We're clear.'

'Assess the damage.'

'Assessing. Ten seconds to first EEMWB pulse.'

Each individual system on the plane had its own shielding, but *Levitow* also had special deflectors – antennas that could attract the waves and disrupt their pattern – in the wings. As the techies explained it, the deflectors reduced the overall amount of T-Rays washing over the ship, making the components easier to shield.

Or, as the metaphor they used had it, reducing a hurricane surge to high tide.

'If you need help, we're here,' said Bullet, the relief copilot behind her.

'Thanks,' said Breanna. 'Stand by for EEMWB wave.'

'EEMWB One –'

'EEMWB One what?' Breanna asked Stewart.

The copilot didn't answer. The interphone system had been wiped out.

And so had the GPS guidance, and half of the indicators on the systems panel.

Aboard the *Wisconsin*,
over India
0635

Dog checked his watch. 'Sixty seconds to first EEMWB,' he told his crew. 'Jazz?'

'I'm ready, Colonel. Looks like that SA-2 is trying to lock on us to launch.'

'He's beside the point now,' said Dog. 'Let's go to manual control. Emergency manual procedure, authorized Bastian 888.'

The computer accepted the code, and Dog reached to the bottom of the center panel to engage the hydraulic controls. The stick felt almost dead in his hand.

As soon as they calculated that the last EEMWB had exploded, Jazz would remove their backup radio from its shielded case and plug its antenna lead to the auxiliary antenna at the side of cockpit between the copilot's station and the radar operator. Dog and Jazz would be able to talk on the Dreamland communications network via a pair of headsets.

The Dreamland communications panel buzzed.

'Bastian.'

'*Wisconsin*, we've been hit by an air-to-air missile,' said Breanna. 'We've lost some systems because –'

The transmission went blank, and the cockpit went dark. Their first EEMWB had exploded.

X

Tai-shan

Aboard the *Abner Read*,
in the northern Arabian Sea
15 January 1998
0635

'Multiple hits! Multiple hits!'

Storm pulled off the headset. Whatever else happened today, the course of sea warfare had been changed as dramatically as it had at Hampton Roads in 1862, when the *Monitor* met the *Merrimack*, or in June 1942 at Midway, when the U.S. and Japanese fleets fought each other completely by air. A small, relatively inexpensive warship had just crippled, and maybe even sank, a large aircraft carrier, until now considered the mainstay of any great naval power. His name would be written in the history books.

Storm sat on the jumpseat next to the holographic display, staring out the window of the bridge. He wasn't meditating on history; he was trying to will away some of the pain. Finally, after little success, he pulled the headset back on.

'Eyes – where's our Sharkboat?'

'They're under way, but still an hour off.'

'All right.'

'*Dreamland Fisher* reports the Chinese carrier *Deng Xiaoping* is launching a new wave of aircraft,' said Eyes. 'We have an Indian destroyer thirty-five miles south of us. We should not be on his radar, but he is moving in our direction.'

The Chinese – he'd take them out too. All he needed was an excuse.

'Captain?'

'Nothing,' Storm said. 'Keep me informed.'

Starship circled the Werewolf back over the area where the Indian pilot supposedly had gone down. He couldn't see anything, not even debris.

'Tac, how long do you want me to keep at this search?' he asked. 'There's nothing here.'

'Head back to the Sharkboat and escort them toward us.'

'I'd like to refuel first, since I'm nearby and they're quiet for the moment. We may not get a chance later.'

'Roger that. Come on in.'

Aboard the *Levitow*,
over India
0635

Breanna worked through the systems with Stewart, checking for units that had been affected by the electromagnetic pulse weapons or the missile blast. The main flight computer itself seemed fine. She had lost engine four; parts of its shredded housing could be seen from the copilot's station. Engine three's temperature was a few degrees higher than normal, but the oil pressure and power output were steady. Two of the compartmented fuel tanks in the right wing had been damaged; the fire retardant system had prevented a catastrophe, but the indicators showed that fuel was leaking. The last three feet of the wingtip on the right side were gone, and the control surfaces were damaged but intact.

The satellite radio, the internal communications system, and the navigation gear were all offline. The self-diagnostic on the Megafortress's native radar – not the larger, more powerful unit installed above the wings – indicated a number of circuit problems, yet the radar seemed to be working, identifying the Pakistani flight they had seen earlier. The PAF planes were in serious trouble, flying erratically and dropping altitude. They were deep in enemy territory, and their prospects for survival seemed dim.

'Recheck the weapons systems,' Breanna told Stewart. They'd pulled off their helmets so they could hear each other. 'Open the bay. Make sure everything is online.'

'Weapons?'

'Yes.'

Stewart hesitated. 'OK,' she said finally. 'Testing weapons.'

Breanna looked at the fuel panel. The damage to the tanks added one more level of complexity to the problem of keeping the Megafortress balanced – an important consideration under any circumstance, but especially when you were missing an engine and a good chunk of a wing.

The computer was doing a good job directing the flow, however, and Breanna turned her attention to engine three, whose temperature was continuing to sneak higher.

The aircraft shook as the bomb bay doors were opened. The increased drag cost them nearly thirty knots in forward airspeed, a huge hit. But Stewart was able to rotate the missile launcher and confirm that it was operable.

'Weapons system is in the green,' said the copilot.

Breanna had asked Lou and Bullet – the relief pilot and copilot – to run the diagnostics on the environmental and some of the secondary systems from the auxiliary panel on the starboard radar station. Lou came over and told her that aside from some of the lights and the fan in the upper Flighthawk bay, the systems were functioning.

'Coffeemaker's gone, though. Ditto the refrigerator and microwave.'

'Don't tell Zen about the coffeemaker,' said Breanna. 'We have to keep his morale up.'

'There's probably a pattern to the circuits that took the hit,' said the other pilot. 'But I can't quite figure it out.'

'We'll save it for when we get home,' Breanna told him. 'Give the scientists something to do. How's your stomach?'

'Much better. I think some of your twists and turns jerked it back into place.'

The Megafortress contained only six ejection seats. If they had to ditch, two people would have to don parachutes and jump from the Flighthawk bay. Ejecting from the Megafortress in the seats was a harrowing experience – Breanna had done it and been banged around quite a bit in the process. Jumping out without the benefit of the forced ejection was even more dangerous. The slipstream around the big aircraft was like a violent, flooded creek, completely unpredictable. It *might* give you a decent push downward and away from the aircraft. Or it could bang you against the EB-52's long body, smacking you like a rag doll caught under the chassis of a car.

If it came to that, Breanna knew she would make one of the jumps herself. But how to choose the last person?

She pushed the thought from her mind. It wasn't going to come to that.

NSC Situation Room
2038, 14 January 1998
(0638, 15 January, Karachi)

Jed knew the EEMWBs had worked as soon as the feed from one of their satellites died. He immediately turned to the screen that showed data from one of the ELINT 'ferrets,' or radio signal stealers, just outside of the effected area. The screen did not provide raw data, which would have been meaningless to the people in the room; rather, it presented a line graph of the volume of intercepts on frequencies used for missile control. The line had plummeted. Jed stared at it, willing it to stay at the bottom of the screen.

But it didn't. It jerked back up, though only to about a fourth of where it had been.

467

'What's going on?' he asked the operator.

'This is in the northern Arabian Sea. It's too far from the explosions to affect them. But the target area was wiped out totally. Just about over to the coast – better results than expected.'

'Are the nukes down?'

'I don't know for sure. Too soon.'

Jed went to the screens showing the U-2 feeds over the Arabian Sea. The display from the northernmost aircraft shocked him: Seven missiles had just struck the Indian aircraft carrier *Shiva*. The photo captured the exact instant of impact of two of the missiles, and showed two more about to strike.

'That's the *Shiva*?' Jed asked.

'Yes,' said the technician.

'Wow.'

'That'll sink her.'

National Security Advisor Philip Freeman had joined the President and his small entourage at the side of the room. He came and looked over Jed's shoulder.

'The Chinese struck the Indians?' he asked.

'Those missiles came from the *Abner Read*,' said the techie.

'*Our* missiles?' asked the President.

The man nodded.

Freeman glanced at Jed in alarm.

'They came under attack,' said Jed.

'Captain Gale is certainly living up to his name,' said Martindale. 'It's too late now, Philip. We'll deal with Storm later. And Balboa, who probably authorized this.'

468

'I want Balboa's scalp,' said Freeman. 'It's way past due.'

'Mr President, Jed – the NSA just picked up a transmission from China for the carrier,' said Peg Jordan, the NSA liaison. 'Tai-shan. It's a go.'

Aboard the *Wisconsin*, over India 0645

The Megafortress's stick felt surprisingly light in Colonel Bastian's hand, the big aircraft responding readily to his inputs. They were in good shape; while the plane's electronic systems were offline, Dog could talk to Dreamland Control via the shielded backup radio. When they reached the coast, Major Cheshire would be able to track them via one of the U-2s that was surveying the northern Arabian Sea. She would guide them to Chu and *Dreamland Fisher*, or all the way back to Diego Garcia if necessary.

A buzzer sounded in Dog's headset. He said his name and then his clearance code. The system had to process both before the communication was allowed to proceed.

'Colonel Bastian?' said Jed Barclay, coming onto the line.

'Go ahead, Jed.'

'The Chinese have ordered the aircraft carrier to use the nuclear option.'

'All right, Jed. We understand. I'm in contact with the other aircraft and will be right back with you.'

Aboard the *Deng Xiaoping*, in the northern Arabian Sea
0645

Captain Hongwu looked at the cable again, even though it contained only two characters: *Tai-shan*.

Much was left unsaid in the cable, beginning with the target. The captain knew it to be Mumbai, the large port on the coast that housed a major naval facility. The cable also did not say why the order had been given, though he knew it would only have been issued if the Indians had ignored the Chinese ultimatum not to fire their nuclear weapons. The cable was silent, too, on what the consequences of the action would be. These, Captain Hongwu tried to put out of his mind.

'Clear the flightdeck and prepare the Tai-shan aircraft,' said the captain. 'Launch all aircraft.'

The men on the bridge began to respond.

'Captain, Squadron One is reporting multiple missile strikes on the Indian aircraft carrier,' said the air boss. 'The missiles have apparently come from the American vessel.'

'The Americans?'

'It's the only explanation.'

Without their radar helicopters, the carrier had no long-range sensors. While it was an exaggeration to say it was blind, Hongwu and his officers had a very limited picture of the battlefield.

'Investigate. Send two aircraft to find the precise location of the American ship and keep it under surveillance. Make sure they are prepared for surface attack.'

'Are the Americans our allies now, Captain, or our enemies?'

'Perhaps both,' said Hongwu, staring out at the sea.

Aboard the *Levitow*,
over India
0645

The temperature in engine three had moved well into yellow. If she'd had three other good power plants, Breanna would have shut it down, but given their present condition, she decided to push it as far as she could.

Managing 390 knots, the *Levitow* was still about twenty minutes from the coast. They wouldn't be out of danger once she got there either – the effects of the EEMWBs wouldn't quite reach that far, and any aircraft operating on the western coast of Indian and to the south would be a threat.

'We ought to head farther south,' suggested Stewart. 'If we go back to our original course, we can pick up the Flighthawk.'

'It'll take too long to get into position to join *Dreamland Fisher* and watch the Chinese carrier.'

'We're not going to be able to do that.'

'What?' Breanna turned toward her copilot.

'We're not going to be able to do it,' repeated Stewart, her eyes welling.

In all the time since the missile struck the Megafortress, Breanna hadn't even considered the possibility that she would have to scrub her mission. She'd thought of everything else – everything – but that.

'We have to try.'

'If we're down to two engines, it'll take a miracle to position ourselves for a Scorpion shot,' said Stewart.

'You're right,' said Breanna. 'We'll get the Flighthawk. Zen can make the interception. Plot a course.'

Zen folded his arms, leaning back against the stiff seat. He hadn't completely given up the chance to walk, just put it off.

The docs might be pissed, Vasin especially. But they'd get over it.

Was he afraid to walk?

They might accuse him of that. But he knew why he was here.

'Hey, Major, Lieutenant, we're changing course again,' said Bullet, the relief copilot who'd climbed down from the upper deck. 'Bree wanted you to know. We're going to try and pick up the Flighthawk if we can. Have it target the Tai-shan aircraft.'

'Sure,' said Zen. 'How's the engine?'

'Not very good. I'm surprised it's gotten us this far. Breanna's babying it, but unless she can crawl out on the wing, it's a goner.'

'Do me a favor. Don't suggest that to her.'

'Colonel, we may not be able to make it to the carrier in time for the intercept,' Breanna said, speaking over the Dreamland communications network to the

Wisconsin. 'Engine four is gone, and I'm going to have to shut down engine three in a few minutes. We're going to try and rendezvous with our Flighthawk. Once we hook up with it, we'll head that way. I'm sorry, but I can't give any guarantees. We're going too slowly.'

'All right, Breanna. We have Chu and the *Abner Read.* Your priority is your aircraft and crew. Hear?'

Maybe it was because he was her father, but she thought he sounded as if he were telling her to hurry home after a late date.

'Thanks,' said Breanna. She killed the connection.

'Engine three's going critical,' said Stewart.

'All right, let's shut it down. Work with me, Jan. Let's do this together.'

Aboard the *Wisconsin,*
over India
0646

Dog clicked into Chu's channel on the *Fisher.*

'*Wisconsin* to *Dreamland Fisher.* Chu? What's your situation?'

'I have two J-13s shadowing me, Colonel. The Chinese carrier has launched a dozen planes within the last ten minutes. They're headed in the direction of the Indian task group.'

'How close are you to the *Deng*?'

'Sixty west. You wanted me to back off.'

'The Tai-shan order has been given. Set up an intercept on the aircraft after they come off the carrier.'

'*Fisher.*'

Aboard the *Abner Read*,
in the northern Arabian Sea
0647

Storm relented and let the corpsman treat his wound, daubing at the ripped flesh with gauze that felt as if it had been dipped in kerosene. He squeezed his fingers into a fist and ground his back teeth together, trying unsuccessfully to ward off the pain.

'Sir, communication from *Dreamland Wisconsin* for you,' said the commo officer. 'Colonel Bastian.'

Never had Storm been so glad to talk to Bastian. He put up his hand, stopping the corpsman mid-swipe.

'I have to talk.'

'Sir, if it hurts –'

'It doesn't hurt,' snapped Storm, holding the headset up. 'Gale here.'

'The Chinese have issued the Tai-shan order. *Levitow* has been hit and won't be able to help in the attack. *Dreamland Fisher* is moving into position for the intercept.'

Storm struggled to his feet. 'All right. Good. We'll proceed. We have to move farther east.'

'You all right, Storm?'

'Don't worry about me, Bastian.' Storm reached to the

communications controller. 'Eyes – the Chinese have issued the Tai-shan order. Move us east. Get ready to intercept those aircraft. We have roughly twenty minutes.'

'We're not in good position for the intercept, Captain. The action against the *Shiva* took us away.'

'Then get us back into position. We have to back them up.'

'Aye aye.'

Storm leaned against the hologram table, orienting himself. They weren't that far out of position. Granted, taking the aircraft was a long-range shot from here, but they were still within the targeting area.

He was close enough to sink the damn carrier. That's what he should do. Sink the damn thing. His order justified it.

'Captain, *Dreamland Fisher* reports two J-13s coming hot at us,' said Eyes a moment later. 'Dreamland's radar analysis shows they're armed with anti-ship missiles.'

The bastards knew what they were up to! They were going to sink them so they couldn't interfere.

Attack. Attack them now!

'You're sure about this, Eyes?'

'They're just coming into our radar range now. Should I target them?'

He had four Standards left. He wanted to fire two apiece at the Tai-shan planes, guarantee a hit.

Two now? Two later?

If they sent another wave of planes, he'd be defenseless – or he'd fail his mission.

'Target the carrier *Deng Xiaoping*. Same mix we used against the *Shiva*. Have the Sharkboat fire as well.'

'The carrier?'

'They've just launched an attack on us, Eyes. And they're about to drop a nuke. We have to take them down.'

'Agreed,' said Eyes. 'But if we use the same mix, we won't have any missiles left for air defense.'

'We'll use the close-in weapons against these two airplanes. If we sink the carrier, we won't need anything else. Do it. Give it everything we've got.'

'Aye aye, Captain.'

Storm steadied himself against the holographic display. Two aircraft carriers in one day? His name would be linked with Nimitz, with John Paul Jones.

'Captain, you have to let me treat you, sir,' said the corpsman. 'We need to clean the wound.'

'Later.'

Aboard the *Fisher*,
over the northern Arabian Sea
0648

Lieutenant Chu had eight Scorpion AMRAAM-pluses in his bomb bay, but even twenty more would do him no good if he wasn't close enough to use them. The planes would be most vulnerable when they came off the carrier, and to guarantee a hit he wanted to be as close as possible. At the same time, the Chinese were watching him carefully – they'd sent two J-13s to shadow him, and the four planes flying combat patrol above the carrier were prowling the area he wanted to be in. Chu decided that his best approach would be to extend his patrol area as nonchalantly as possible, widening his orbit and flying south before going farther east.

'The J-13s are right on our wings, Tommy,' said his copilot. 'I'm afraid that once we open the bay to fire the Scorpions, they're going to pounce.'

'The Flighthawks will hold them off,' said Chu. 'We'll hang in and fire everything we've got.'

'Everything?'

'Too important to take a chance.'

'What about the patrol near the carrier?'

'We'll go toward the *Abner Read,* get coverage from them. The Flighthawks can hold them off in the meantime.'

Chu told the Flighthawk pilots what they were going to do. Neither man said anything more than 'Understood.' He started his turn, focusing on the heads-up display in his windscreen. A calmness settled over him; his muscles relaxed; he felt almost as if he were watching himself from the comfort of a living room sofa far away.

Aboard the *Abner Read,* in the northern Arabian Sea 0649

The missiles flew from the forward tubes in quick succession, spiraling upward in a glistening arc of white against the brilliant blue of the sky. Storm waited until the last one had gone before turning back to the holographic display where they were being tracked.

The other ships would come for them, he realized. He had to prepare.

'Take us south, Helm,' he said, reaching for his communications controller. 'Eyes – the Sharkboat. Tell them we're going south. We want to put some space between us and the Chinese.'

'Aye aye, Captain.'

Starship touched the Werewolf down on the helipad behind the *Abner Read*'s low-slung superstructure, killing the engines. The two seamen assigned to fuel the robot ran out and began tending to her.

He turned and looked behind him in the Tactical Center. Eyes was standing only a few feet away, a perplexed look on his face as the men around him took turns shouting information in his direction.

Starship waited a few seconds, hoping for a calm patch. When none came, he asked, 'Eyes, do you want me to attack the carrier when I'm topped off?'

'The carrier?'

'The *Deng Xiaoping*. With my Hellfires.'

The Tac commander's mouth squirreled up, his cheeks puffing out. 'Hellfires?'

'It's something. I can get up there in fifteen minutes tops, once I'm reloaded. That should be ten minutes from now.'

'Too late.' Eyes's frown turned into a forlorn smile.

'But thanks for the offer. Get back in the air as soon as you can. We'll need you to show us what's going on.'

Aboard the *Fisher*,
over the northern Arabian Sea
0650

'Multiple missile launches from the *Abner Read*!' shouted the surface radar operator, his voice rattling Tommy Chu's headset. 'Eight missiles – more from the Sharkboat. Targeted – they're going after the carrier!'

'What the hell are they doing?' Chu reached to the communications panel to contact the *Abner Read*. Before he could, the screen indicated an incoming message from the ship. The *Abner Read*'s tactical officer's face appeared in the screen. 'What the hell's going on?' Chu demanded.

'We've launched our attack on the Chinese carrier. We need you to intercept the two fighters.'

'I'm not in position to do that. Why did you launch the attack without telling us?'

'I need you to intercept those planes.'

'I can't. Why did you launch without contacting us first?'

'I don't need your permission to accomplish my mission.'

The screen blanked. Chu angrily smacked at the kill button anyway.

'The *Abner Read* has launched an attack on the

479

Chinese carrier *Deng Xiaoping*,' he told the rest of the crew. 'We'll take down the J-13s before they realize what's going on, then remain on course in case the strike fails.'

Aboard the *Deng Xiaoping*, in the northern Arabian Sea 0651

Twelve missiles had been fired at the *Deng Xiaoping*. Captain Hongwu listened closely as the threats were identified: A total of eight Harpoon missiles had been fired, four from the *Abner Read* and four from the small patrol boat, along with four SR-2 or Standards from the *Abner Read*. The threats had to be prioritized; they no longer had enough missiles to intercept them all.

He turned to the officer in charge of targeting the weapons.

'Target two of the SR-2s with our anticruise missiles. Target all of the Harpoons from the *Abner Read*. Attempt to intercept the missiles from the small patrol craft with our fighters, and turn the close-in weapons on everything else.'

'Yes, Comrade Captain.'

He had known it would come to this. But there was no satisfaction in being proven correct. Hongwu folded his arms, demonstrating to the others that they must be resolute and calm.

'Have the aircraft aloft engage the American warplane. Shoot it down immediately. The two planes observing the *Abner Read* – divert them and have them attack the Megafortress as well. The warship will be easier to deal with once the radar plane is gone.'

Aboard the *Fisher*,
over the northern Arabian Sea
0652

'Ready?' Chu asked the copilot.

'Ready. Flighthawks will go on your signal.'

'Now!' said Chu, and he pushed the stick forward, tucking the Megafortress away.

The air roiled as the two robot planes closed in for the kill. Chu began a sharp turn south, then cut back.

'Missiles in the air!' warned the copilot. 'Heat-seekers!'

'Flares.' Chu pushed the plane onto its wing, unsure exactly who had fired the missiles.

'Russian AA-12 type missile launched,' added the copilot. 'Not a factor. The two planes that were tracking toward the *Abner Read* are turning in our direction.'

'Splash one J-13!' said one of the Flighthawk pilots.

'The other plane is on our tail,' said the copilot.

'Stinger air mines,' said Chu as the air around him began to percolate with tracers.

'Two Standard missiles intercepted. One Harpoon lost.'

Storm stared at the hologram, letting the report sink in. Already, the Chinese had done much better than the Indians, who had managed to shoot down only one of his missiles.

Another of the Harpoons disappeared from the display. That might not mean it had been shot down; the ship's systems occasionally lost track of the missiles as they dipped toward their target.

God, his head hurt worse than he thought possible.

'*Dreamland Fisher* is under attack,' said Eyes.

Storm nodded, as if his tactical commander was standing on the bridge next to him.

'Standard missile three has struck the carrier,' said Weapons. 'Standard missile four has struck the carrier.'

Two out of four. Acceptable against such an accomplished opponent. As an opening volley.

'Harpoon One is on target. Harpoon Three is on target. Harpoon Four is off our screen, possibly intercepted.'

Another two out of four performance?

He should have been closer. He should have reserved more of his missiles. He should have made better use of his people.

'Harpoon Three has struck the *Deng Xiaoping*. Harpoon One – unknown.'

'Unknown?'

'Sorry, sir. We're working on it now. At this range –'

'The Sharkboat?'

'SB Harpoon One is off course. SB Harpoon Two and Three running true. SB Harpoon Four has been intercepted.'

'Where are those planes that were attacking us?' said Storm.

'Turned off – going after the *Fisher*.'

'Can we help them?'

'Too far. We have no more missiles.'

'Very well,' said Storm. 'They'll come out of it. Those Dreamland people always do.'

Aboard the *Fisher*,
over the northern Arabian Sea
0654

Chu tried to shut out everything but the sky in front of him, concentrating on getting the Megafortress away from its pursuer. He knew eventually the Stinger air mines would take the J-13 down; the trick was to survive until then. The plane rocked up and down as he zigged south. He knew one of his engines had been hit, but this wasn't the time to deal with it; a fresh warning indicated four AA-12s had been fired by the planes coming up toward his nose.

He wanted to use all eight of his Scorpions against the Tai-shan aircraft, but it would be at least fifteen minutes before the planes were in the air. He'd never make it that long if he didn't knock down some of the J-13s nearby.

'Target those fighters,' he told his copilot. 'One missile apiece.'

'*Hawk Six* has been shot down,' said the copilot.

'Bay.'

'Bandits are targeted. We have two missiles coming for us.'

'Fire. ECMs. *Hawk Five*, stay with me,' added Chu as the air around him exploded with shells from the Chinese aircraft.

The first Scorpion clunked from the dispenser. Chu kept the plane steady as the next rotated into position and fired. The plane began to shake.

'*Hawk Five*, we're going north,' said Chu. He sank deeper into the sofa, even calmer.

'Following.'

'Missile closing.'

'Chaff, ECMs.'

Chu pushed the Megafortress's stick hard to the left, trying to get away from the missile. The Megafortress shuddered and began dropping. He couldn't hold the plane steady; alarms sounded, warning him that engines one and three had been damaged, warning him that there were holes in the fuel tanks, warning him that he was surrounded and faced certain death.

'Target the carrier with our AMRAAM-pluses,' he told the copilot. 'Fire as soon as you're locked.'

'Engine one is gone.'

'The hell with the damn engine. Fire the missiles!'

The left side of Chu's face imploded. He saw red and then black, and felt himself relaxing again, sinking back on his couch, easing back, enjoying a nice scotch for one last time.

Aboard the *Deng Xiaoping*,
in the northern Arabian Sea
0654

Captain Hongwu nearly lost his balance as the ship absorbed the blows of the Harpoon missiles. The lights blinked off but came back.

There were three more missiles. Hongwu heard the air boss trying to direct the aircraft to intercept them. The Harpoons were subsonic and flew relatively predictable patterns, but shooting them down was exceedingly difficult, and it did not seem that his pilots could accomplish the task.

Still, if only one was intercepted, he felt they could survive.

The close-in weapons were so loud that Hongwu could hear them even here as they aimed at the incoming missiles. He grabbed the nearby table, sensing they would miss. The ship shook with an explosion, this one much closer than the others.

The lights went out. Captain Hongwu found himself on the deck, the emergency lights on. Someone helped him up.

'We've taken two more strikes to the hull below the hangar

deck,' said the damage control officer. 'Compartments 103, 105, 107, are taking water. We have not heard from –'

'Can the Tai-shan aircraft take off?' asked Captain Hongwu.

'We believe so, sir. They are still being prepared.'

'That is of primary importance. Deal with the damage expeditiously, but those aircraft must launch.'

'Air Group One reports that the Indian aircraft carrier has begun to sink at the bow,' said the air boss. 'Should they attack alternative targets?'

'Have them attack the American warship,' Hongwu told him. 'They are our priority now.'

NSC Situation Room,
Washington, D.C.
2101, 14 January 1998
(0701, 15 January, Karachi)

All of the missiles launched from both Pakistan and India had been disabled by the T-Rays. But the attack on the *Deng Xiaoping*, though it left the aircraft carrier on fire, had not stopped preparations to launch the Tai-shan aircraft. A near-real-time photo from the U-2 spy showed a swarm of men prepping the planes, even as a damage control party played a fire hose on a piece of decking a few yards away.

'Bastards are going to go ahead and nuke India anyway,' Freeman said, looking at the image.

'Maybe they don't know we've destroyed the missiles,' said Jed.

'They should by now. They see an advantage and they want to take it.'

'More likely, the Chinese aren't entirely sure what's going on,' said President Martindale. He put his coffee mug down – a Secret Service agent had retrieved some from the cafeteria upstairs. 'Time to talk to them.'

'And say what?' demanded Freeman.

Rather than answering him, the President turned to Jed Barley. 'You ever play poker, young Jed?'

'Um, sure.'

'One of the advantages of stud is that your opponent knows part of your hand. The better the hand looks, the more he has to guess.'

'They'll never trust us,' said Freeman.

'I'm counting on that. Give me the phone.'

Aboard the *Levitow*,
over India
0704

They hadn't spotted the Flighthawk yet, but India's western coastline lay fifty miles ahead. The *Levitow* had made better time than Breanna had hoped.

But their free ride was about to come to an end.

'Two Su-27s coming from the west,' Stewart told her. 'Their radars are working.'

'Do we have the Flighthawk?'

'Not on radar. It may be too low for us to see until we get closer.'

They should have found it by now. But it was just one more problem she didn't have time to worry about.

'Lou, do you think you could operate the Stinger air mines from the auxiliary station? I'll need Jan to help me fly the aircraft if we have to do any sort of maneuvering.'

'Not a problem.'

'Ground radar active,' said Stewart. 'Rajendra – phased array. Fire control for Akash.'

'The missiles have a thirty-kilometer range,' said Bullet. 'About nineteen miles. We should be able to steer away from them.'

'That's what we're going to do,' Breanna said. 'Give me a heading.'

Zen sat at his station, waiting for the Flighthawk to pop onto the tracking scope. While they were not precisely on the flight route the plane was supposed to take, they were close enough. Even if for some reason they couldn't find it on radar, the Flighthawk would periodically send out a signal, in a sense 'calling home.' Its power was limited for tactical reasons, but he knew they should have no problem finding each other at fifty miles.

'I guess this is what girls go through waiting for a guy to call back after a first date, huh, Dork?' Zen asked.

'Must be.'

'You got a girlfriend?' Zen asked the other pilot.

'Kinda.'

'Kinda?'

Before Dork could answer, the Flighthawk's locator beacon lit on the screen.

'All right,' Zen said. The Flighthawk was about fifty-three miles behind them, off the east. He was about to tell Breanna that via the interphone, then remembered that the system was out.

'Run up and tell Captain Stockard our escort is behind us. Present speed and course, it ought to catch up in about ten minutes.'

The course around the Akash missiles also took them out of the path of the Su-27s, which for the moment at least did not appear to have seen them. Her airspeed tacked below 250 knots; no matter what Breanna did, she couldn't get it any faster. She was at 23,000 feet, and had to keep edging lower as her speed crept downward.

'Big base at Puna,' warned Bullet, who was working to psych what might lie ahead. 'MiG-29s. They'll be patrolling near Mumbai.'

Breanna planned to turn back west and make the coast well north of Mumbai, but there was a good possibility that the radars in the area would see them. Nor could she risk getting under the radar coverage – on two engines, she'd never be able to climb out of danger.

'Su-27s are turning in our direction,' said Stewart.

'The Flighthawk is behind us,' shouted Dork, coming onto the flightdeck. 'Pick us up in about ten minutes.'

'Something to shoot for,' said Breanna, starting her turn toward the coast.

Aboard the *Wisconsin*,
passing over the coast of India
0705

The morning sun had painted the northern Arabian Sea a brilliant azure blue. But black clouds dotted the horizon as Colonel Bastian flew his aircraft over the coastline at treetop level; the naval conflict had continued, unaffected by the electromagnetic pulses originating from the east.

Dog pushed the aircraft down closer to the waves. They'd seen four contrails as they approached the coast, but so far no other aircraft. If they'd been targeted by anyone, they had no way of knowing.

'Colonel Bastian?'

Dog recognized Major Catsman's voice on the Dreamland communications channel.

'Bastian.'

'The *Fisher* has been shot down. They were attacked by at least six Chinese fighters when the *Abner Read* launched its attack on the *Deng Xiaoping*.'

'They attacked the *Deng*?'

'Two fighters were headed in their direction. They may have been under attack and saw that as their only chance to strike,' said Catsman. 'The *Deng Xiaoping* has been hit but is still afloat. They're preparing the Tai-shan planes for launch.'

'Do you have a location on where the *Fisher* went down?'

'We have an approximate location, Colonel. The *Abner*

490

Read is too far south to conduct rescue operations at this time.'

'How far am I from them?'

'I can only give you an approximate location. You're northeast about sixty miles.'

He had four Harpoon missiles in the bomb bay, but no way to fire them.

'I need to talk to Storm,' he told Catsman. 'Stand by.'

Aboard the *Levitow*,
nearing the coast of India
0706

A layer of turbulent air rattled the plane. Breanna was forced to edge the *Levitow* still lower, her airspeed dipping precariously.

'The Su-27s are challenging us,' said Stewart. 'What should I tell them?'

Breanna considered saying they were a civilian airliner, but that was unlikely to stop them from coming and having a look; civilian flights had been banned.

'Tell them who we are. Say we were on a reconnaissance flight and are returning home.'

'You think that's going to make a difference?'

'I think they might have to ask their ground controller what to do. Maybe we'll gain a few minutes.'

'We still have the Scorpions,' said Stewart.

'We'd have to turn and get in their faces to fire,' said Breanna. 'We'll hold off for now.'

There were three other reasons not to fire. First of all, opening the bay doors would deprive them of even more momentum, making it more difficult to fly the plane. Second, the fighters would detect the missiles and undoubtedly launch their own. And last – and most important for Breanna – using the missiles would lessen the possibility that she could intercept the Tai-shan planes.

Sixty seconds later one of the Indian pilots told them they were in Indian territory and would have to divert to the air base at Puna 'or face the consequences.'

'What consequences would those be?' asked Breanna.

'Dire,' responded the pilot.

Breanna told Bullet to find out how long it would be before the Flighthawk caught up. Then she went back on the line with the Indian pilot.

'I don't think I can make it to Puna,' she said. 'My intention is to ditch in the sea. One of my engines tore loose from its mount and damaged the wing. We're very low on fuel. I do not want to cause a national catastrophe.'

The pilot told her to stand by.

'Three minutes,' said Bullet, running upstairs.

'Five more to get to the coast from here,' said Stewart. 'Maybe if you make a feint for Puna, you can gain some more time.'

'I'm worried about their missile batteries,' Breanna told her. 'SA-12s. Our best bet is to stay on course.'

Zen spent the time waiting trying to work out exactly how he would take down the two fighters. They were now east of them, not quite aligned with the

Megafortress's tail but headed in that direction. The Flighthawk was approaching from the east as well, though to the south of the Sukhois. Given the Megafortress's condition, he wanted to engage them as far from the mother ship as possible, certainly before they were close enough to fire their infrared missiles. But he had no control over that – even when the Flighthawk got close enough to reestablish its connection, he'd still be more than ten miles behind the enemy fighters. Worse, the loss of the interphone system made it almost impossible to coordinate strategy with Breanna. Sending people back and forth between the decks took too much time.

'Dork, tell Breanna if these guys stay in their present formation, I'll take *Bandit One* to the east.'

'OK,' said Dork. 'Major, you ever play telephone?'

'Huh?'

'You know, where you whisper a message in someone's ear and they pass it on? We could do that here.'

'Isn't the purpose of that to show how mangled a message can be?'

'Well, yeah, but it's better than nothing.'

'All right, it's a good idea, Dork. Set it up. Hey – you just got yourself a new nickname: Telephone.'

'I think I like Dork better.'

'You will proceed as directed. Emergency vehicles are standing by,' the Indian pilot told Breanna.

Ain't that sweet, thought Breanna. Prison cells too, no doubt.

'Can you give me a course heading and a – um, a – uh . . .' Breanna continued to stall. 'Distance. I need a distance.'

The Indian pilot, clearly losing patience, told her to change her heading forty degrees – *now*.

'Zen has control of the Flighthawk!' said Bullet, the last link in the communications chain. 'Needs another two minutes to get behind them.'

'Tell him I'm going to descend a bit,' said Breanna.

'The Indian fighters are right on our back now, Bree,' said Stewart.

'Visual range?'

'Not yet, but very close. Just about within range for an A-10 heat-seeker.'

'Lou, be ready to turn the Stinger radar on as soon as I say.' Breanna pushed the nose of the Megafortress forward, descending. Five minutes on this course – five minutes to the sea.

But so what? The Sukhois could easily follow them there.

'American aircraft – you are ordered to change course or face the consequences.'

'He's activated his gun radar,' said Stewart. 'I think he'll close and try throwing some warning shots across the bow.'

Come on, Zen, Breanna thought. Hurry up with that Flighthawk.

Zen could see the two Indian fighters ahead, flying parallel and very close to the Megafortress's tail.

'Megafortress descending!' said Dork.

'Sixty seconds.' Zen flexed his hand around the joystick.

The Indian pilots, so focused on what they were doing, had not bothered to check six – or maybe they had looked behind their aircraft and missed the diminutive Flighthawk.

'Can you get both planes?' Dork asked.

Maybe. But he couldn't guarantee it.

'No,' said Zen. 'Tell Breanna to take the one to the west with the Stinger air mines. She has west. Confirm.'

The Flighthawk pushed on steadily. He was two miles away – the screen began blinking red.

'Confirmed. She has west.'

'Ready!' yelled Zen as the screen went solid red.

'Ready!' yelled Dork.

'Go!' Zen began firing.

Breanna pushed the Megafortress to her left as hard as she dared, throwing the rear Stinger battery in the face of the Indian fighter. At the same time, the Stinger began firing even though it couldn't possibly have locked on its target yet.

The *Levitow* began to shake. Tracers were popping to its right.

'Going for the coast!' Breanna shouted, her words intended for Zen. 'Stewart – what's our status?'

'*Bandit One* breaking off. *Two* is still behind us.'

Breanna started to push the nose of the Megafortress forward, wanting to increase her speed and give Zen some room to work with as he went for the other fighter. As she did, the Megafortress started to flail to the side, and within seconds she was fighting a yaw.

* * *

495

Zen got two long bursts into *Bandit One,* enough to draw smoke from her tailpipe. He let the fighter go, turning to try and get some shots on the other one. *Bandit Two* rolled away, just as a hail of air mines exploded behind the Megafortress.

As Zen followed the Indian plane downward, he caught a glimpse of the damaged EB–52. It was much worse than he had thought – the right wing had several large cracks running through it, with gaps big enough to see the foam protection for the fuel tanks. The starboard tailplane had been chewed up; less than a quarter of it remained.

Bandit Two, still concentrating on the Megafortress, swung into position to fire his heat-seekers. Tucking his nose down, Zen got the Sukhoi in the middle of his crosshairs and sent a stream of bullets across its wings, across its fuselage, across the burning hulk he turned the plane into.

'Scratch *Bandit Two*,' he told Dork, pulling off. 'I'm going to bird-dog over the coast.'

It was then that he finally noticed that the Megafortress was moving back and forth in the air, each swing a little stronger.

Desperate to control the ship, Breanna had Stewart dial back power to engine one as she tried to rebalance her aircraft. It helped, but it also cost more airspeed. The water, at least, was just ahead, beyond a thick line of factories and boats.

'Radar – Top Plate – there's a patrol boat off shore,' said Stewart. 'Correct that – a frigate. They'll have Geckos.'

'Gecko' was the NATO code word for SA-N-4s. The missiles would be potent under any circumstance, but the Megafortress would be an easy target now.

'Where are they?'

'Ten miles ahead.'

'ECMs.' Breanna had the plane back almost completely under control, the yaw reduced to a wobble. Her altitude was now below fifteen thousand feet. Forget the missiles, she thought, they'd be low enough for the antiaircraft guns by the time they got close to the frigate. 'I'm going to go north,' she said. 'We need to get some distance between us and that ship.'

As she prepared to bank, the Megafortress abruptly dropped thirty feet.

Zen turned the Flighthawk back toward the Megafortress. As he came close, he saw a chunk of the right wing's skin fly off, pried loose by the plane's violent shakes and the wind's ravenous appetite. He couldn't tell for certain, but he thought the cracks he'd noticed before were longer.

They weren't going to make it.

'Tell Breanna to select the view from *Hawk Three*,' he told Dork.

Breanna alternately wrestled and coaxed the airplane, knowing it was a losing battle. The only question was where they were going to crash.

She preferred ditching at sea, where the shot-up plane wouldn't kill any civilians when it crashed. It would also be arguably better to bail there, since they might have a chance of being picked up by a U.S. ship or even the Osprey, rather than the Indian authorities.

'All right, crew, here's what we're going to do – we're

not going to make it much farther. We have six ejection seats and eight people. I'm going to go out with a parachute from the Flighthawk deck. We'll draw straws for the other place.'

'I volunteer,' said Stewart.

'I'm sure everyone will volunteer,' she said. 'That's why we're drawing straws.'

Zen had already decided what he was going to do when Dork passed the word. He turned the Flighthawk over to the computer, then pulled off his helmet.

'Doesn't make any sense for me to use the ejection seat. I have nothing left to protect,' he said. 'I'll take my chances dropping.'

'But Captain Stockard said –'

'I outrank everyone aboard this aircraft, including my wife,' said Zen, pushing himself up out of the seat. 'Besides, I'm a much better swimmer than anyone else here. I can make it to the coast if I have to. You guys won't. Yo, Bullet, this chair's for you. Grab a brain bucket and saddle up.'

Aboard the *Shiva*,
in the northern Arabian Sea
0706

Memon saw Admiral Skandar mouthing the words before he heard them, as if he were watching an out-of-sync motion picture.

'You are ordered to abandon ship,' said the admiral calmly. 'I repeat. Abandon ship.'

The ship's fantail was now well out of the water, and the list to starboard so pronounced that Memon could see only the water outside the ship. He'd managed to get to his feet but gone no farther since the first explosion. He had no idea how much time had passed; it seemed both an eternity and a wink.

Down below, one of the armament stores had caught fire, and weapons cooked off with furious bangs. The explosions seemed fiercer than those caused by the American missiles, more violent and treacherous, as if the ship were being torn up by demons.

The ship's crew began moving in slow motion, following routines established during drills they'd hoped never to perform in real life. One by one the Defense minister bid them farewell.

I am so much a coward, thought Memon, that I cannot even move. I deserve to die a coward's death.

'You must abandon ship too,' Skandar told Memon. 'Go. Save yourself.'

'I will stay,' said Memon. His throat was dry; the words seemed to trip in it.

Was it the coward's way to save himself? He wanted to live, and yet he could not move.

'It is your duty to carry on the battle,' said Skandar. 'I am an old man. It is my turn to die.'

There was no question that Skandar was brave, and Memon knew himself to be a coward. Yet their fates were the same. Here they were, together on the bridge, stripped bare of everything but nerve and fear.

'Admiral. You must live to help us rebuild and fight again.'

Skandar did not answer.

'Admiral?'

The sound of metal twisting and breaking under the pressure of water filled the compartment.

Memon wanted to live. Yet he could not move.

Skandar turned away and looked out through the broken glass at the sea. 'In the next life, I will be a warrior again,' he said.

Before Memon could answer, the deck collapsed below them, and he and Admiral Skandar plunged into the howling bowels of the burning ship.

Aboard the *Abner Read*,
in the northern Arabian Sea
0706

Storm struggled to ward off the pain as the Chinese aircraft began their attack from thirty miles off – too far for their radars to lock on the slippery ship. They were relying on the guidance systems in their missiles to lock as they approached the target.

There were four J-13s, each armed with four cruise missiles. The *Abner Read* was an awesome warship – but she wasn't invincible. In simulated trials the ship had managed to shoot down seven out of eight missiles in a massed attack. More than eight missiles, and the systems and men running them were overwhelmed. His strategy would be to push the odds as close to his favor as possible.

They got one break – rather than firing all of their weapons en masse, the Chinese launched a first wave of only four missiles.

'Helm, hard right rudder,' he said. They turned the ship to lower its radar profile, making it more difficult for the missiles to acquire them on final approach. This also limited the number of Phalanx guns he could put on the missiles, but it was an acceptable trade-off if the Chinese were only firing four weapons at a time.

Two of the Chinese missiles quickly lost their target and exploded in frustration. The final two kept coming in their direction.

'Status!' barked Storm.

'Neither missile has locked, Captain.'

Storm studied the holographic display. The missiles *looked* like they were going too far east. They *looked* like they were going to miss, though not by much.

One did. The other veered toward the ship. Before Storm could even say 'Defensive weapons,' the Phalanx operator had shot down the missile.

Four down. Twelve to go.

Starship stayed south of the *Abner Read* as the close-in weapons system fired; the automated system had mistaken Werewolves for missiles in the past, nearly shooting them down.

Besides his Hellfires and the chain gun, he had two Sidewinder missiles for air defense on the Werewolf's wingtips. The Werewolf couldn't take on the J-13s in anything like standard air combat; it might be fast for a

501

helicopter at 450 knots top speed, but that was far slower than the Chinese jets.

On the other hand, if he could set up the right circumstances, he knew he might be able to take one of the planes. As a fighter jock, he was aware that helicopter pilots were taught to turn and fly toward their attacker, staying as low to the ground, zigging, and making a straight-on shot hard to line up. As the pursuing fighter passed, the chopper should then turn and fire.

Assuming, of course, it was still in one piece.

The J-13s had split into two groups. Two tacked to the east and launched a fresh pair of missiles. A second group of two planes was swinging around to the west, obviously aiming for their own try from that direction.

'Tac, I'm going to the west and take on one of those fighters,' said Starship. 'Probably *Bandit Four*.'

'Werewolf?'

'I'm going to take on one of these fighters. No, belay that,' he said, using a Navy term for the first time in his life. 'I'm going to *nail* one of those fighters.'

'Colonel Bastian for you, Storm.'

Storm clicked into the circuit. 'Gale,' he said.

'The Tai-shan aircraft are almost ready to launch,' said Dog. 'Are you in position to shoot them down?'

'I regret to say . . .' The words stuck in Storm's throat. The close-in guns were firing again. 'I regret to say it's unlikely we will be in position to shoot down the planes. We may be sunk ourselves.'

* * *

The J-13s dropped their speed and altitude as they approached the *Abner Read*. Starship singled out his target. The enemy plane, flying at only a hundred feet, ignored him at first, too focused on his target to notice the tiny bug coming straight at him. For a second Starship thought he might be able to fly *into* the jet, but the J-13 began to climb, either because he'd spotted him or to launch his missiles.

Time to improvise.

Starship leaned on his stick, pushing the Werewolf's nose nearly upright. He fired two Hellfires in the general direction of the Chinese fighter, hoping to distract him rather than shoot him down. Then he slammed the helicopter around and leaned on the throttle, trying to pick up some momentum as the plane passed overhead. He cued the Sidewinder, got a growl – or thought he got a growl – indicating a lock, and fired.

The missile immediately went off to the right, a miss from the get-go. But Starship was still on the fighter's tail. Spooked, the Chinese pilot abandoned his target run and started a turn north to evade him. The Sidewinder growled again; Starship fired.

This time he watched the missile run right up the rear end of the Chinese plane and tear it to pieces.

The Chinese cruise missile hit the *Abner Read* so hard that the ship's bow rose several feet under the water. Storm tried to grab onto something but could not; he was thrown against the helmsman and rebounded against the jumpseat near the holographic display.

'More missiles! Four more missiles!' warned the defensive radar.

'Jam them,' said Storm, even though he knew his crew didn't need his order to do so. 'Jam them – get them. Destroy them.'

He tried to get up to see the holographic display tracking the missiles. But his head was light and his legs were shaky. He found himself back on the deck.

I'll be damned if I'm going to die on my back on the deck of my ship, he thought, struggling to get up.

Aboard the *Wisconsin*,
over the northern Arabian Sea
0708

Dog turned around in his seat. 'Crew, prepare for emergency bailout!' he shouted. 'Dish, tell them downstairs. You're going out in sixty seconds.'

'Sixty seconds?' said Jazz. 'Why are we bailing?'

'Because it's time to get out. That's my order.'

Dog turned his attention back to the plane. They were thirty miles north of the carrier. He could see one of the aircraft on combat patrol in the distance.

'Colonel, why are we bailing?' demanded Mack Smith, appearing behind him.

'I have to stop those planes from taking off,' Dog told him. 'Go prepare to eject.'

'You're going to crash into the carrier?'

'I'll bail out at the last minute.'

'Then I'm going with you,' said Mack.

'No.'

'I'm going too,' said Cantor, appearing behind him.

'I appreciate the sentiment – but get the hell back to your stations.'

'Colonel, Jed Barclay on the Dreamland channel says the U-2 picture shows one of the Tai-shan planes being wheeled into position.'

Dog turned the Megafortress south. 'Tell him we have it under control. And then everyone bail out. Bail out!'

NSC Situation Room,
Washington, D.C.
2110, 14 January 1998
(0710, 15 January, Karachi)

'The point is very simple, Mr Premier.' President Martindale paused to let the interpreter translate his words for the Chinese leader. 'I've just stripped India and Pakistan of their nuclear weapons. I can do the same to China.' He looked over at Jed. 'Not just those in the Arabian Sea, but *all* of your weapons. Under those circumstances, some of my people might strongly advise me to end our China problem once and for all.'

Jed glanced at the display from the U-2 near the *Deng Xiaoping*. The planes were getting ready to take off. Would an order even reach them in time?

They could physically link the phone conversation through the Dreamland communications network through the Situation Room's communications setup, but they could not get it to the ship. The *Wisconsin* could not broadcast on regular radio frequencies.

The *Abner Read* could. Maybe they could retransmit it over the radio frequencies.

'Yes, the hawks are extremely strong in my country,' President Martindale told the Chinese premier. 'A shame. I'm really very powerless against them. Very regrettable.'

Freeman rolled his eyes, and even Martindale winked.

'Can you broadcast that command immediately? I'll stand by.' Martindale cupped his end of the receiver. 'He's agreed to rescind the order.'

'I think we can broadcast it from the *Abner Read* to the carrier,' said Jed. 'If you can get him to say it over the phone.'

'They may think it's a trick,' said Freeman.

'The Premier is using his own network,' said the President. 'When he comes back on, I'll suggest it.'

'Let's have the *Abner Read* broadcast the information in the meantime,' suggested Freeman.

'They've just attacked them,' said the President. 'They won't trust them at all.'

'What if Colonel Bastian tried talking to them?' said Jed. 'He's well known in China because he saved Beijing from the Taiwan renegades and their nuclear weapon. We might be able to have him communicate through the *Abner Read*.'

'See if you can do it,' said the President.

Freeman walked to the NSA screens, looking to see

if the Premier issued the order. 'What do we do if he calls your bluff, Mr President?'

'Let's hope he doesn't,' said Martindale.

Aboard the *Wisconsin*,
over the northern Arabian Sea
0711

Faced with a mini-mutiny, Dog concentrated on his course. The fact that his radar wasn't working was an advantage in a way – it meant there were no aggressive signs from the aircraft. Sooner or later, however, the Chinese would decide he had to be dealt with.

They'd undoubtedly used many of their weapons in the earlier battles. The question was what they had left. If he was just facing cannons, Dog thought he'd make it to the deck – as long as he was there to steer it all the way down.

Dreamland Command told him he was now thirty miles from the carrier – roughly three minutes flying time.

'All right, crew. This is it. One by one we go out. Mack, you're first.'

'Colonel –'

'I can't jump if you guys don't jump. We're two minutes from impact. Time to get out. *Now!*'

Mack cursed, then Dog heard the pop and whish as he pulled the yellow handles next to his seat.

One by one the others jumped. Jazz was the last. 'Colonel, I'll stay until you're ready.'

'Out, Jazz. We're two minutes from target.'

'I know what you're doing. We don't have the computer, so you need to stay with the plane to guarantee it'll go where you want.'

'Go.'

Dog's voice shook the cockpit. The copilot ejected.

A J-13 appeared at his side, making hand signals. Dog waved to him.

'Colonel Bastian?' said Jed Barclay on the Dreamland Command line.

'Bastian.'

'Colonel, the Chinese Premier has ordered the carrier to stand down. We want you to relay the order.'

'How?'

'We're rigging something through the *Abner Read*. Just start talking.'

Dog pushed the stick down, starting into a plunge toward the carrier. He was too far from the ship to see the planes, but Jed could via the U-2 – he wouldn't be asking him to do this if the planes weren't ready to take off.

'Colonel?'

Tracers flew in front of him.

'I'll talk, Jed. But I doubt they're going to listen.'

Aboard the *Deng Xiaoping*, in the northern Arabian Sea
0712

Captain Hongwu was surprised by the voice. It was deep and calm, sure of itself without being haughty, exactly

508

like the voice he had heard on television after Beijing was saved.

'This is Lieutenant Colonel Tecumseh Bastian of the United States Air Force. I'm going to destroy your vessel unless you stand down the Tai-shan aircraft. The nuclear weapons launched by India have been neutralized. Your government has rescinded your order to attack.'

'I am honored to speak to the man who saved Beijing from disaster,' said Hongwu. 'But I must follow my orders.'

'Your government is in the process of issuing the order. You will receive it shortly.'

Hongwu turned to his executive officer. 'Have we received an order on the encrypted fleet frequency?'

He shook his head.

'A nice trick, Colonel. I am afraid my duty requires me to shoot you down. It is with regret. You saved many of my relatives and friends with your bravery over my country.'

'Then you know I am not a liar or someone who uses tricks. And you also know that you will not be able to shoot me down.'

'The American plane is five miles from us!' warned the executive officer. 'He's coming up the stern.'

'Fire the guns when he is range.'

'Only two are left.'

'Two should be enough.'

'A communication!' shouted the radio officer. 'An encrypted communication from Beijing directly!'

Aboard the *Wisconsin*,
approaching the *Deng Xiaoping*
0713

Dog could feel the Megafortress tucking her wings back. He was still too far to see the airplanes on the deck, but he knew about where they would be.

A pair of black clouds rose from the rear of the ship – flak. The bullets rose in an arc and fell away. He thought he could get in between them, though perhaps that was merely an optical illusion.

Tracers danced in front of his windscreen. Then he heard the sick *thump-thump-thump* of slugs slapping into his right wing.

Dog struggled to hold the plane steady. Without the computer to help trim the aircraft, the Megafortress was a stubborn beast. Once she had her momentum going in a certain direction, she insisted on following through.

Which was just as well in this case.

More tracers. Then the J-13 zoomed ahead and banked in front of him.

The ship was starting to get bigger. He'd have a fat target now. He could see the antiaircraft fire. It had been fired too early, too desperately.

The ship moved to his right, turning.

To get away?

He pushed on the stick. He was close enough. They were dead.

For a brief, flickering moment Colonel Tecumseh 'Dog' Bastian thought of his daughter Breanna. He was proud of her, the woman she'd become. His one regret in life was that he'd been too busy to pay much attention to her growing up. He'd done his best to make it up now, but there were shortcomings you never really could excuse.

He had them now. He leaned toward the windscreen.

'They're standing down!' yelled Jed Barclay in his headset. 'They've pulled the Tai-shan aircraft away from the launchers. They're turning out of the wind! Colonel – don't attack them! Don't attack them!'

Dog pulled back, clearing the carrier deck by three feet.

Aboard the *Levitow*,
over the Arabian Sea
0713

The six ejection seats fired almost simultaneously. The long explosion morphed into a howling wind.

Breanna helped her husband cinch the substitute helmet a few feet from the gaping holes in the floor of the Flighthawk deck.

'You ready?' she shouted in his face.

'Hell, no, but let's do it anyway,' said Zen. He pulled her close, squeezing as tight as he could.

The plane rocked violently.

'We have to go out!' she yelled.

'Why were you mad at me?'

'Mad?'

'You were mad at me. I didn't pick it up at first, but then I figured it out.'

'It wasn't important if I was.'

'Yes.' He held her tight, though she tried to pull away.

'I didn't want you to give up.'

'Who gave up?'

'Your dream of walking.'

'You want me to walk?' he said.

'I want you to be happy. I want – I *do* want you to walk,' she said. He could feel her tears on his cheek. 'But I don't want you to give up fighting. I want you to keep fighting. I don't want you to give up for me.'

'I didn't give up,' said Zen.

They looked at each other for an instant, a moment of time but an eternity in every other way.

'We have to go,' said Breanna.

'Well, let's get the hell out of here.'

Breanna stayed next to Zen as he crawled close to the blown-off hatches in the Megafortress.

She'd jump with him, holding on for as long as possible. If the slipstream slammed them against the jet, if it pushed them away to the water – they'd be together.

That was the way it should be. The only way.

'Here we go!' yelled Zen, and with one push they tumbled through the hatchway.

XI

Fates Unknown

NSC Situation Room,
Washington, D.C.
2120, 14 January 1998
(0720, 15 January, Karachi)

Jed had stood on the thinly carpeted cement floor for so long that his legs seemed to vibrate when he collapsed into the chair in front of the console.

'You look tired, young Jed,' said the President.

'A little.'

'You've done yeoman's work.'

'We're not done yet.'

'True,' said the President grimly.

The Indians, Pakistanis, and Chinese seemed to have tacitly accepted a ceasefire, certainly for the moment. All three navies were conducting rescue operations in the Arabian Sea. But the situation remained exceedingly chaotic. Good portions of India and Pakistan, including both capitals, were without electricity and communications. It was anyone's guess how long it would take to rebuild the systems damaged by the EEMWBs. Just as it was anyone's guess whether tempers would eventually calm.

In the meantime, the U.S. had two aircraft down in the northern Arabian Sea and a third facing a several-thousand-mile trek without any electronics. The fate of the men and women who had bailed from the planes remained unknown. The *Abner Read*, herself badly damaged by the attack from the Chinese, was directing the Sharkboat and the Werewolf in rescue operations to recover the downed flight crews. Dreamland's *Whiplash Osprey* would be in the area in two hours to help out.

'Coffee, Jed?' asked Peg Jordan, the NSA liaison.

'Coffee'd be great. Better get a pot. We're going to be here awhile.'

Plan of Attack

Dale Brown

When an almost-forgotten enemy prepares a shock attack on America, only one man can see it coming.

Stuck in a desk job in Air Force Intelligence, maverick pilot Patrick McLanahan uncovers disturbing evidence that the Russians are secretly arming their bomber fleet with nuclear warheads. Worse still, he realizes that despite the lessons of 9/11 the USA is still vulnerable to air attack by a determined enemy.

But his warnings come too late. A flight of Russian bombers penetrate American airspace and launch devastating nuclear attacks on key airbases. As panic grips the country, McLanahan takes matters into his own hands and slips into Russia with the elite Air Battle Force rapid-response team – to strike back at the heart of the Russian bomber fleet.

'When a former pilot turns his hand to thrillers you can take their authenticity for granted. His writing is exceptional . . . far too good to be missed.' *Sunday Mirror*

ISBN-13: 978-0-00-714249-1
ISBN-10: 0-00-714249-8

Air Battle Force

Dale Brown

Maverick pilot Patrick McLanahan takes aerial warfare into unknown territory in an explosive new adventure.

On America's newest combat base McLanahan and his crew are devising the air combat unit of the future – the Air Battle Force. An elite team backed by leading-edge technology, they control an armada of unmanned planes that can reach any spot on the globe within hours, and they will have their first target when an oil dispute turns Turkmenistan into an international battleground. But can a handful of commandos and an unproven force of experimental warplanes fight and win a war in which seemingly everyone – even 'friendly' forces at home – wants them to fail?

'When a former pilot turns his hand to thrillers you can take their authenticity for granted. His writing is exceptional . . . far too good to be missed'   *Sunday Mirror*

0-00-714246-3
£6.99